The Pajama Game

By Eugénie Seifer Olson

THE PAJAMA GAME
BABE IN TOYLAND

The Pajama Game

EUGÉNIE SEIFER OLSON

AVON
TRADE

An Imprint of HarperCollinsPublishers

HarperCollins books may be purchased for education, business, or sales promotional use. For information please write: Special Markets Department, HarperCollins Publishers Inc., 10 East 53rd Street, New York, NY 10022.

FIRST EDITION

Designed by Elizabeth M. Glover

Library of Congress Cataloging-in-Publication Data

Olson, Eugénie Seifer.
    The pajama game / by Eugénie Seifer Olson.—1st ed.
        p. cm.
ISBN 0-06-073209-1 (acid-free paper)
1. Lingerie industry—Fiction. I. Title.

PS3615.L74P35 2005
813'.6—dc22   2004016182

05 06 07 08 09 WBC/RRD 10 9 8 7 6 5 4 3 2 1

Acknowledgments

This book would not have been possible without the unwavering support of my amazing agent, Stacey Glick. My delightful and talented editor, Kelly Harms, was a one-woman cheering section for me and Moxie both, and the fashion-forward Lucia Macro lent a helpful hand when I needed it. I'll be forever indebted to Meredith Obst for her endless enthusiasm about this story, and I offer a grilled cheese of gratitude to the Charlie's Kitchen crowd, who never missed an opportunity to ask how the writing was going.

The good-natured Sue Faulkner provided inspiration for the good-natured Sue Fisher. Brad Kaiser offered sound advice from nine to five. R. Sands kept me from discharging Moxie much too early.

Motivation was regularly and energetically provided via cell phone calls from Kevin Silver. Carolyn Komerska, Reneé Gontarski, Maryjane Carlin, Todd Honeycutt, Ed Mason, David Colp, Debbie Robinson, Amy King, Kerri Bennett, and Neil Bindelglass all get smooches for giving unconditional friendship and support; and I thank Ronald McDonald House friends for providing my weekly Wednesday-afternoon dose of inspiration.

My new family members Paul and Betty Olson, Nancy Olson, and Susan and Scott Allison offered a brand of encouragement that every daughter-in-law or sister-in-law could ever hope for. Ben Seifer gave shout-outs from Jersey, and John and Julie Cargill served up support Southern-style. Extra-special thanks must go to my parents, Les and Amy Seifer, for providing me the kind of moxie a girl needs to write novels. And to my husband, David, who inspires me to write, helps me measure kayaks, and keeps me sane, I offer immeasurable amounts of love and thanks from the bottom of my heart.

Most any poor old fish
can float and
drift along and dream;
But it takes a regular
live one to
swim against the stream.

—MAURINE HATHAWAY

1

Low-Rise Brief in Petal Pink with Rosette Detail

THE SHIPMENT CAME IN TODAY. FIVE HUNDRED PAIRS OF panties packed one hundred shimmery pairs to a box. Lou, the deliveryman, has stacked the five latte-colored cardboard cubes on the hand truck and left it out on the loading dock at the back entrance to the mall, just the way he knows he's not supposed to. Lou claims he has ADD and that's why he has such difficulty following instructions, but I don't buy it. I instead tell him that he suffers from ABP, or Au Bon Pain, syndrome. In other words, he prefers to pick up a danish and coffee and sprawl out at one of the patio tables at the Au Bon Pain in the morning, rather than roll the boxes of satiny booty around to the store's back entrance. I can't say I blame him. I'd take a sticky-sweet treat and the chance to tip my face up to the crisp autumn sky over hauling these undies around any day.

Alas, the panties aren't going to haul themselves, so I sigh, hook my foot under the bar of the hand truck, tip it back ever so slightly, and grasp the handle hard as I feel the weight of all that polyester inching toward me. *This shows how a fulcrum works*, I think to myself, momentarily forgetting that I don't teach middle school science anymore, and that my days are now filled with peignoir sets and push-up bras, not bathroom passes and pop quizzes. *The wheel becomes the fulcrum*, I continue silently as I walk down the dark cement-stone hallway, winding along behind Brookstone, J. Crew, Nine West. *It allows the weight to shift. Similar to a seesaw, but imagine the middle piece pushed closer to one end than the other. Understand, everyone?* I look up with a start as I reach the end of the hallway and shake the early morning basic physics lesson from my head. Talk about fulcrums is all well and good, but there are panties that must be removed from their polybags, counted, and sorted, and all one needs for that is a pocketknife and rudimentary math skills. I've got both of these this morning, and it sounds just about my speed.

XS, S, M, L. This batch, I note, came all the way from Indonesia. I always pay attention to the country of origin, which is both stamped on all sides of the boxes and printed in blocky, sans serif type on the label in each pair of panties, as though their wearer might take pride in something created in near-sweatshop conditions three-quarters of the way around the globe. I like to imagine the seamstresses sitting shoulder to shoulder, hunched over industrial sewing machines, the glimmery fuchsia and emerald green and mango orange fabrics sliding between their worn fingers, as they laugh about the American women who will wear them. "What do they need these for?" I picture them saying, shaking their heads as they pause to grab tiny polyester rosettes to sew onto the waistbands. "Underpants with rhinestones on the backside? With the word 'sexy' embroidered across the front? Or these tiny ones, with the string? What are they thinking?"

I'm joylessly plunging my pocketknife into the packing

tape on top of the fourth box, when Mary Alice sticks her head around the corner into the dank stockroom and recoils in horror. "Be careful, Moxie," she admonishes, frowning at me. "You could cut the panties." She swoops down to grab a light pink, padded, six-way bra that escaped its bra bin during the night and now sits on the floor like a baby octopus marooned on the beach, its many straps, clips, and other elaborate attachments springing in every direction. As she bends to pick it up, I notice how closely she matches the bra. Mary Alice is pink and puffy, with that soft, freckly South Boston face and physique that so many women around here seem to have. Mary Alice takes her duties as assistant co-manager seriously and wishes that I did the same. Sometimes I wish I did the same too. It would make it easier for me to fold each pair of panties into a crisp, tidy square and place it evenly in the scented drawers without wanting to scream my fool head off.

While thinking about screaming my fool head off, I realize that today is Monday, which means that when my shift is over at six o'clock tonight, my walk home will be action packed, with lots of people screaming their fool heads off. I'm excited. Only four hundred and fifty more pairs of panties to count, sort, and fold.

———

I am about to take my lunch break, when I walk by one of the fitting rooms and hear a yelp, an annoyed squeal, and then a *thunk*, as though something is banging hard against the wall. It's not unusual to hear noises drifting out from behind the curtains, but they generally take the form of low groans, when customers realize that they can't fit into the alluring item of their choice. This is something entirely different, and the squealing and banging grow more frenzied with each second, until I hear a "pssst!" from the fitting room. I look around, hoping that this customer is perhaps trying to catch the attention of a friend, but no such luck.

"Yes?" I ask.

"I'm *stuck*," comes the reply from behind the curtain. "I think I need help."

"Oh, that happens sometimes," I say reassuringly. In truth, it happens with alarming regularity—what can be pulled on cannot always easily be pulled off, and I briefly consider giving this a scientific name, such as Brecker's Law of Camisoles, when I hear more banging and some labored grunting.

"No, I'm really stuck in this chemise," she says pitifully. "Can you help me?"

"OK," I sigh, sliding in past the curtain and finding myself eye to eye with a stout, sweet-faced girl in her early twenties, with a wild, wiry nest of curly black hair, and an emerald-green chemise adhered to her body. "It won't come off?" I ask, realizing what a stupid question this is.

"No!" she wails, wriggling this way and that and futilely trying to yank the garment over her pudgy shoulders. The lace trim is swallowed up entirely by her armpits, and the satiny fabric is stretched tight across the small of her back.

"Try lifting your arms over your head," I suggest, and she assumes a diver's position, with her arms pointing to the ceiling and her hands neatly overlapped. I grab the chemise under both armpits and give a yank. It doesn't budge, and all I succeed in doing is nearly knocking both of us off our feet. "All right, that didn't work," I say lamely.

"I'm so *fat*," she hisses at the mirror. "I bet this doesn't happen to anyone else."

"Actually, that's not true," I say in a gentle tone, gesturing for her to lift her arms over her head so we can give it another try. "We had some girl in here the other day who was a professional cheerleader, and she got stuck in a silk nightgown.

So you never know." This makes her brighten a little bit until I give another yank on the chemise, and we both realize that she's been sweating so profusely that now we've got extra friction thrown into the equation. The fabric is one with her damp flesh, tenacious and gripping every curve.

"Just cut me out of it," she moans. "I'll pay, I don't care."

"That's ridiculous, to pay $40 for this and not even wear it," I say. Truthfully, it seems ridiculous to pay $40 for this either way—the color is vile, and the cheap lace is brittle and sloppily sewn. She slumps against the wall and frowns, and I notice little beads of perspiration on her upper lip and around her hairline. The sweat is working against us, I realize suddenly, meaning that wet is getting us nowhere fast. But dry, maybe dry might help. My thoughts float from a block of blue chalk being rubbed on the end of a pool cue, to the subcompact gymnasts from the summer Olympics, big puffs of white powder billowing into the air as they flipped and turned on the uneven parallel bars, to my friend patting cornstarch on the insides of her infant's chubby thighs in the heat of August.

"Wait here," I order her, as though she might be willing or able to do anything else. I walk over to the fragrance and body lotion display and grab a round, pink cardboard container with a garish illustration of freesia depicted on the top. I return to the fitting room and hold up the package triumphantly. "OK, here we go," I say, removing the fluffy powder puff and loading it up with powder. I'm about to begin powdering her shoulders and back, when I think better of it and hand her the powder puff instead. Between the grunting and touching and yanking, it's already starting to feel like a weird, girl-on-girl porno film in here, and she can do it herself. She liberally applies the powder all over her upper body, making both of us sputter as the air becomes heavy with faux freesia. Finally, she holds her head high and assumes the position.

"I'm ready," she announces, looking at the ceiling. I grab the fabric under her armpits, and it starts to slide up ever so slowly. She gives an excited whoop of joy.

"Take it easy," I warn her. "We're not there yet." But after a few more careful minutes of tugging and shimmying, I've pulled the tightest part of the chemise up over her shoulders. Now her face is completely shrouded by the fabric, and her big, white briefs are in plain view, but she is so overcome with relief that she can't help herself.

"Thank you, thank you, thank you!" she gushes, her nose protruding from the satin and her mouth shifting the fabric into odd shapes as she moves her lips behind it. She continues to express her gratitude so sincerely that she sounds as though she is starry-eyed before a superhero. I take my leave before she decides to address me as the Chemise Avenger, and go to lunch.

———

"Don't kill your baby! Don't kill your baby!" the greasy, skinny, fifty-something man with the too-short pants and stained tie shrieks at me as I walk past him at the end of the day. I grin and say nothing, but I always wonder the same thing: Doesn't he recognize me walking by here every day, day after day, week after week, month after month? Doesn't he realize that I have never made use of this Planned Parenthood, even when I knew that they were giving away free condoms, and I needed several dozen to decorate my friend Nancy's bachelorette party outfit?

At first I was terrified, when soon after moving to this neighborhood I realized that I was a mere five doors away from a Planned Parenthood. But then it started to become sort of exhilarating. Your walk home is never boring when these passionate people are hanging around. Maybe you'll get shrieked at, maybe you won't. Maybe one of them will suddenly brandish a pistol and shoot it into the air (as one did a few months ago), and then again, maybe not. Maybe you'll get smacked in the face with a flying string of rosary beads. I figure the odds of this last one happening to me in any other setting are remarkably slim (especially since I'm Jewish), so why not take that chance and saunter down the same side of the street as these folks? It gives the walk home a sense of tingly anticipation, a current of electricity in my limbs.

I never say a thing—don't have to, since they always have plenty to say to me, about sin and Jesus and my unborn angel. The only time I've seen someone effectively shut them up was when my friend Gerard, while on a screaming sugar high after eating an entire oversized container of strawberries purchased at the outdoor produce market, grabbed an enormous cantaloupe from me (which I'd also bought at said market), and hastily stuck it under his shirt. He pushed past their doctored-up, gooey baby posters and yelled at the top of his lungs, "Keep your laws off my body!" The too-short pants man was there that Saturday morning, and he seemed all ready to go with his stock rantings—until his brain actually registered that standing before him was a man, and not only that, but a man with a large piece of overripe summer fruit quickly slipping out from under his T-shirt. He opened his mouth and nothing came out, which I marveled at just long enough to appreciate his stunned silence, but not so long that I allowed Gerard to utter anything more, potentially giving away his sexual orientation and thus whipping too-short pants man into a rage for a whole different reason.

I dig the key to my apartment building out of my purse, put it in the sticky lock, shove open the huge metal door, and immediately trip over three packages, all addressed to Steven Tyler. There are two large, flat manila envelopes on the floor, which I pick up and inspect as my eyes adjust to the dim light of the anemic bare bulb hanging from the ceiling. The return address on one reads Ohio; the other, Wyoming. Both feel like they have a piece of cardboard within, meaning almost for certain that the envelopes contain naked or nearly naked photos of women with their legs sprawled and their dyed-blonde hair styled to stiff perfection.

So says my neighbor Steven Tyler, who lives downstairs and does not sing with Aerosmith or stash cocaine in his bandannas or have enormous lips. Yet because of his name, he gets fabulous offerings from fans all over the country and the entire world, people whose devotion to Steven Tyler is matched only by their refreshing naiveté. The fact that they actually believe that the address of their rock idol would be listed in the Boston phone book is eclipsed only by the insane notion that he would also choose to live in a crappy hovel located at 224 Tremont Street, Apartment 4.

Whenever we happen to arrive home at the same time, Steven Tyler generally opens some of his gifts on the spot and shows them to me, which I always enjoy after a long, challenging day of debating whether to dress the window mannequin in baby blue or peach pajamas. I think my favorite gift to date is a giant floor lamp a California fan lovingly crafted from an old-fashioned gas pump, with the words "Sweet Emotion" spelled out in oversized rhinestones across the top. It took all of our might to haul it up to his second-floor apartment that evening. This little box on the floor next to the manila envelopes can't contain anything too heavy, I decide as I nudge it with my foot. Probably food; they also like to send him food. Cookies and brownies and Rice Krispies treats. Steven Tyler usually eats them—he says at first he was nervous, but then he decided, what the hell. They wouldn't want to poison Aerosmith's lead singer, would they? Not with the tender fan mail that is included with the snacks, he reasons.

When I reach my apartment on the top floor, I'm exhausted and achy. I kick off my sensible pumps (one of the few styles of footwear deemed acceptable at the store), peel down my slimy pantyhose (also required), and walk around on the linoleum in my bare feet. When I signed the lease for this apartment, Gerard was horrified, largely because the floors in every single room of the place are covered in deep green, marbled linoleum. He said it gave it the look of the types of dwellings they show on *COPS*, and that it was only a matter of time before I began living with a guy who wears white, sleeveless T-shirts and falls down drunk on camera while shouting unintelligibly at law-enforcement officials. Although that lifestyle does offer the perk of sounding like there's never a dull moment, it's not why I love the place and its slick floors that cover the expanse of the bedroom, bathroom, living room, and kitchen.

I love it because it's all mine. It's the first apartment I've ever had all to myself, and the only way I could spring for such luxury was to get it cheap. Laughably cheap, in fact. It's exactly the kind of place they show in a movie where a girl goes to the Big City to chase her dreams, and she ends up in a squalid apartment in a noisy part of town. My place isn't squalid—I've got too many throw pillows and candles for that—but it certainly has that hollow wooden doors/dirty drop-ceiling/soot-soaked window sashes quality that makes some visitors anxious. And it's in the Combat Zone—or what's left of Boston's Combat Zone, anyway. There is one strip club left two streets over, a few tiny adult bookstores, and there's Joe's Joke Shop in the building next door, but fake dog doo and fart spray and wind-up hopping penises hardly qualify as the depths of depravity and debauchery these days, I think. Whenever I listen to classic rock radio and hear that old Billy Joel song about his misspent, wild youth and how he survived being "stranded in the Combat Zone," it makes me smile in that indulgent way that parents smile at kids when the kids complain that homework is so much harder today than it was when their parents were young. He couldn't get stranded in the Combat Zone today if he tried. Probably the most combative things that happen in the neighborhood nowadays are in front of the Planned Parenthood.

I flop down on the sofa, put a little green pillow under my feet, and fight to keep my eyes open—even though it's only six-thirty, it may as well be midnight. I'm always surprised by how tiring it is, this business of peddling panties. I'm about to drift off to sleep when the phone rings. I panic a little when I realize it's probably Gerard, who has spent the entire weekend in feverish anticipation of the season premiere of *Boston Public*, which he has unilaterally decided we should watch together this evening. I pull myself off the sofa and answer the phone, hoisting myself up onto the worn, cracked yellow kitchen counter and very nearly sitting on a whisk in the process.

"Are you ready? Are you ready, Moxie?" Gerard asks breathlessly as I fling the whisk into the stainless steel sink.

"Who is this?" I joke. I yank out my ponytail, throw the elastic across the room, and watch it land precisely in the center of a green linoleum square. He sighs loudly.

"You know who it is," he says, exasperated. "Are you ready to watch *Boston Public* tonight?"

"No, I don't really feel like it," I say. "That show is stupid. All those dramatic story lines, they wear me out. It's not an accurate representation of a school at all. Don't they ever just have a school day where there's an assembly about hygiene?"

"Oh *yeah*, I'm sure." I can hear him shelling peanuts in the background, and I just know he's throwing them directly onto the pale blue tile floor of his beautiful kitchen. "Besides, you don't know what happens in high school. You were in a middle school. Maybe it's different."

"It's not that different, trust me. You don't go from standing against the wall at your eighth-grade dance to huffing glue with your high school guidance counselor while wearing only your jockstrap, or whatever it is they do on that show."

"But I bought that stuff that you like," he pleads. "The bean dip. The one that you say looks like Alpo."

I jump down from the counter, reach on top of the refrigerator, and pull down the Boston Yellow Pages. The weight of the book and the slick cover conspire to keep me from getting a good grip, and it slides from my hand and hits the linoleum with a soft *squish*. "I'm just going to get a pizza," I decide aloud, as I pick up the phone book and set it on the counter, rifling through it until I reach PIZZA.

"Awww," Gerard whines. "You've been hitting Pizza Pad so hard lately you're going to start sweating oregano." He pauses at the thought of it, dried green flakes oozing from my pores. "Well, am I at least going to see you for lunch this week?" he says a little more tenderly.

"Of course," I answer, thinking about another work week in the brightly lit, rose-scented store. "You have tomorrow off and I have Wednesday off, so I guess Thursday it is, right? How about one o'clock?"

"OK. I'll try to be on time."

"Yes! On time, Gerard. It's something all adults appreciate. If you're mid-spritz, even if it's some rich old bag, you drop that bottle and come over. See you then."

———

It's the end of a long yet mercifully uneventful shift. I am looking at my watch and realizing that I've only got forty-five minutes to go until my day off, when a woman approaches the counter with an armload of solid-colored, cotton panties from the four-for-$20 table and flings them down with something that can only be described as poorly restrained contempt. Her bob is sprayed into a tight helmet, and her nostrils are flared, the big, black holes of the perpetually pissed-off. I pick up the first ivory pair and begin scanning.

"Your diamond bra," she begins sourly.

"Yes?" I ask, steeling myself for a line of questioning about the jewel-encrusted undergarment made famous by the store's Christmas mail-order catalog, which began shipping this month. Billed as the height of opulence, it is covered with tiny diamonds, rubies, and emeralds, making it what must be not only the costliest but also the heaviest bra on the planet. It is a $1.35 million exercise in scoliosis. We get lots of questions about the one-of-a-kind diamond bra from curious customers, jovial queries that generally center on whether or not the company actually produces this bra (they do); whether or not any customer has ever purchased it (not to my knowledge); and what on earth a bra like this is good for (using your own bosom to cut your way out of a phone booth is my standard answer).

"I'm sure you are aware of the human rights implications of the diamond industry," she says, setting her jaw and fixing me with an icy gaze. "The mining involved with these bras."

"Yes," I say, and then immediately burst into a grin against my will, as I picture the filthy miners emerging into the sunlight from the dark mines, staggering under the weight of dozens of brassieres. They struggle to lift the cups, and their knees buckle from the bejeweled straps and fastenings.

"It's not funny," she snaps.

"No. Of course not," I say as I continue to scan the tags.

"Because of this company's support of the secret world of the diamond cartel, I will no longer be shopping here," she announces, folding her arms across her chest.

I look from her to the pile of panties on the countertop, and take a quick glance at the LED readout on the register. $34.99, and there are still a few pairs left to scan. "But you're shop-ping now," I say pointedly as I finish scanning, bag up her purchases, and pick her cash up off the counter.

She gives me a look of pity and rolls her eyes. "Well, I need new underwear, and this is a *good sale*," she barks, taking the bag from me and haughtily striding out of the store.

———

As I arrive home, I see Joe closing up shop next door. Joe boasts that he has the longest hours of any joke shop in Boston, open until eight o'clock every weeknight and until ten o'clock on Saturday. That may also be because his is the *only* joke shop in Boston. He spies me as he drags down the metal grate in front of the plate-glass windows and says in a low voice, "Moxie, Moxie, sweet and foxy." Normally this kind of talk from a man would make me puke, but when it comes from someone old enough to use Gold Bond Powder regularly and wax poetic about the Sansabelt slacks sale at Fi-lene's Basement, I don't mind.

Moxie, Moxie, sweet and foxy, I repeat in my head as I unlock the door to my apartment. I've had the name Moxie for al-most ten years now, but sometimes I'm still not used to it. My real name is Rebecca, which isn't too bad in itself. But my parents very clearly displayed their sense of humor and love of rhymes when the first name is coupled with my last name, Brecker. Rebecca Brecker has a singsong quality that I hated as a child; it sounded like a little girl straight from a nursery rhyme or jump rope ditty, and kids taunted me mercilessly. It wasn't long before I re-dubbed myself Becky, and this stayed with me all through elementary and middle school. I was a clever student, quick to grasp long division and commit per-fectly to memory the provinces of Canada, and Becky Brecker suited me, the sprightly girl with the long, dark brown braids.

But when I got to high school, I decided that Becky Brecker was *too* sprightly. Too cheery. At fourteen, Becky Brecker sounded like the name of a head cheerleader, a perky-titted, rosy-faced, all-American beauty who wore her boyfriend's jersey on game days and shopped at the mall with her hip mom on weekends. Since I had average boobs, a long messy tangle of hair, a surfeit of blackheads, no boyfriend, and a mom who had no use for the mall stores, there was only one choice: Becky had to go. She was quickly replaced with Bex, which I liked a great deal. The name Bex Brecker had a machine-age, streamlined quality—like Lex Luthor, only not nearly so evil.

When college rolled around, I decided I was sick of Bex and it was time to resurrect Rebecca. I was heading off to a small but well-respected teaching college right in Boston, and I'd decided that whereas the New Jersey dopes couldn't pass up the opportunity to poke fun at my real name, surely the educated New England folk would not even notice. *They* would take it in stride. Rebecca Brecker was just the right kind of name for strolling around the pretty campus while wearing a fuzzy sweater, laughing and kicking crisp Massachusetts leaves with my sophisticated roommate. When I got there, I could bear learning that the campus seemed much smaller than when I'd visited, with very little room to stroll or even amble. I could handle the fact that Boston was in the middle of a scorching early September heat wave, and that a fuzzy sweater would be out of the question for a little while. I even was able to console myself about my roommate, who turned out to be a painfully shy and withdrawn girl with an incipient drinking problem.

But I couldn't believe what they did to my name. Because this school boasted a lot of in-state students, they didn't just bring their love of clam chowder and Cape Cod. They packed up and brought their accents right along with their shower caddies and CD players and hot pots, and they called me Rebecker Breckah. Say it again with me: Rebecker Breckah. Despite hailing from the state where people *tawk* over *cawfee*, nothing could have prepared me for extra consonants that appeared in words at will and then disappeared from others, popping up and then hiding where you least expected them, like a mole in a verbal Whack-a-Mole game. Some students mysteriously were able to work in even *another* "r," this one ahead of the "b," so it sounded like "Rurbecker Breckah." And none of this was done with the slightest hint of malice. This is how they talked, so this is what they called me. By sophomore year, all of these people had successfully exorcised their accents, working hard to avoid asking for a tuner fish sandwich in the cafeteria and straining to get it right when consoling the dean's wife about her husband's recent hat attack.

I couldn't wait that long, though. I needed a new name, and fast. I didn't want to go back to Becky or Bex; and Becca, the only other obvious choice, sounded like a spoiled, snobby girl who drove a Saab and had perfectly tanned arms and legs year-round. In between classes and decorating my dorm room and coaxing my roommate to go to the dining hall, I started to panic. What if I didn't have an identity? Then walking along Newbury Street one day with my new friend Kelly, we stopped into a little shop that sold antiques and ephemera and reeked of mold. Kelly was in heaven, but I soon grew bored and told her I'd wait outside, eager to do some people-watching on Boston's famous, glossy shopping street. When she didn't come out for ten minutes, I became impatient and pressed my face to the dusty glass, and there it was: An old, red tin sign with a simple line drawing of a young baseball player poised with his bat, and printed in white enamel. It read, "Ted Williams says . . . Make Mine Moxie." Next to him, all out of scale, was another drawing, this one of a giant bottle of cola with a red label—and that jaunty Moxie again, this time in bright white with a dark blue outline. Whoever Ted Williams was, he looked so self-assured and happy, and Moxie was just such a cute word, brimming with energy and vim. When Kelly stuck her head out of the store and called for Rebecker, I told her I had a new name and pointed to the sign.

"Ted?" she asked, craning her neck to read the sign from the doorway.

"No," I laughed. "Moxie."

"Like the soder?" she asked.

"Yup. Just like the soder," I answered.

2

Seamless Racerback Bra in Coral

"YOU WANT THE WHALE WATCH OUTING WITH THAT?"

"No," I answer.

"IMAX show? *Into the Deep* in 3D, narrated by Alec Baldwin?"

"No."

"Dolphin extravaganza in our new state of the art—"

"No, thanks," I say firmly, cutting her off before she can finish describing the new dolphin tank. "Just the aquarium ticket is fine."

"Ten dollars." She sighs and pushes the ticket out through the tiny slot at the bottom of the window as I shove in my ten-spot, and she immediately turns away from me to take a long slurp from her paper soda cup. I grab the ticket and make my way toward the gigantic steel doors, open one as wide as I can against the howling Boston Harbor wind, and slip inside. Slowly my eyes begin to adjust to the low light, and my nose twitches from the twin dank odors of mold and mildew, warm and wet and filling my lungs. A teenage boy with a crew cut and a jaunty, cobalt blue polo shirt with the cute little fish-shaped New England Aquarium logo on the breast pocket rips my ticket, hands me a pamphlet about the new jellyfish exhibit, and I'm off.

As I wander toward the Penguin Pond, my pupils widen fully, and I begin to take in everything around me, smiling as broadly as a little blond girl I see kicking up her feet in a stroller a few steps away from me. The aquarium is my favorite place to visit on my days off for reasons that confound most people but make perfect sense to me. It's as though they asked someone to design a place that is the exact *opposite* of where I am normally forced to spend my days. It's very dark, almost pitch black in the eel and octopus areas; no blazing lights trained on merchandise here. It smells murky and musty and sometimes like brine shrimp, never like a sweet sachet of delicately scented flowers. On weekdays—when I always come here—it's usually very quiet. The only soundtrack is provided by the occasional loud flapping, random honking, and water-splashing of the penguins, instead of a banal collection of inoffensive classical songs that play on an indefinite loop beginning when the store opens, and ending when the last customer has left and the doors are locked behind her. In other words, it's my fantasy realized.

I come here so frequently that some of the aquarium staff has begun to recognize me, which sort of frightens me. What kind of adult likes to spend her time with octopi, jellyfish, and turtles? That's the question Gerard posed the one time I allowed him to accompany me here. It was an experiment to see if perhaps it would be fun to visit the aquarium with a friend, someone I could impress with my knowledge of what makes the blue lobster blue (it's genetics, not diet), or why so many of the angelfish have what looks like another eye down by their tails (to confuse a predator, so it doesn't know if they are coming or going). The visit went fine, and Gerard was quite delighted by the starfish and sea horse areas in particular, but then as we left, he declared that he really had a hankering for seafood, maybe sushi. I thought this perverse, and we had a spat about it in front of the seal tank outside, and I haven't asked him back since.

Today I decide to focus on the penguins. I feel as though I don't ever give them enough attention because you have to pass them to get to everything else. I'm often in a big hurry to get to the second floor to see the candy-colored boxfish and lemon-yellow butterfly fish and all their pretty undersea brethren, all swimming placidly in a big tank set into the wall and backlit with a soothing azure glow. So I lean over the slimy wall and watch the penguins in their specially designed Penguin Pond, a giant open area with lots of brackish water to swim in and mossy stones to play and preen on. They are waddling around and taking neat little dives into the water and generally behaving like penguins, which is sort of cute but not what you'd call newsworthy. They all even look pretty much the same, and I wonder for a moment if this is what the penguins say to one another about the visitors to the aquarium, when I notice one penguin with flair. It's a little bigger than the others and has a wild hairdo that sticks up rakishly into the air. Its dives are grander than the other penguins', it chases nearby penguins with crazed intensity, and it shits on the stones and other penguins with reckless abandon. This is a penguin with personality, a penguin that could walk out of this aquarium, hit the streets of Boston, and have tons of friends who hang on his every honk. I impulsively decide to name it Chaka Khan, whisper goodbye to Ms. Khan, and head over to the new jellyfish exhibit, where I hope not to be given the shivers by all those wispy tentacles.

———

This morning I am busy tidying the counter area, putting pens into pen cups that are cleverly dropped down into the surface of the counter, placing pink and white credit card applications neatly in their designated plastic stand, and occasionally checking the register as it spits out the day's directions. Each Thursday, the home office shuffles the store's stock and prices like so many sexy, lacy cards and deals out the mandated discount prices on a slim piece of register tape. Today the thongs are $7 apiece, but next week they will be three for $21. The week after that, they will be $5 each, and then three for $15. It's all very sly and ingenious, this reliance on marketing tactics and pretty, rose-colored SALE and 40% OFF and THIS WEEK ONLY signs that snag the eye and eventually the cash of virtually every person who comes in here. When I once tried to explain to Mary Alice that if you do the math, the customer can't really win; that the switcheroo we play with the numbers and the percentages is just to make them think they are getting a deal, she looked at me as though I had completely lost my mind. My job, her look suggested, is to carefully tear the paper across the serrated metal edge of the register, find the appropriate signs in the back, place them in the store, and move merchandise around if necessary. End of story.

It appears that the little cotton nightgowns are on sale today, and as I am bending to pick out the 20% OFF sign from the messy stockroom drawer that contains all the cardboard signs, I let out a yawn so big it almost dislocates my jaw. You'd think after a day off from this place, I would bounce back and be raring to sell all this sultry stock, but you'd be wrong. I'm still sleepy and looking forward to my lunch with Gerard, where I'll order a bucket-sized coffee along with my sandwich.

I am on my way to the front of the store when I let out a giant sneeze. It reeks in here today, courtesy of some extra spraying by Mary Alice, who opened with me this morning and decided it didn't smell as frilly-fresh as it really should. So she grabbed our regulation in-store scent and held down the nozzle for what seemed like an eternity, waving her arm around and infusing everything in her path with the chemical smell of ersatz rose petals. My sneeze catches the attention of an early-morning shopper, a middle-aged black woman with a mixture of hope and sadness etched on her face. The hope is in her eyes, but the sadness sits hard on her lips.

"Excuse me, miss," she says politely, turning to me. "I'm looking for a pair of pajamas for a friend . . . something soft with buttons down the front. Buttons that are far apart."

"That's an easy one," I say, smiling at her and ignoring the unusual button-spacing request for the moment. "Follow me, please." I walk to the middle section of the store, where we sell the bulk of the pajamas and bathrobes. The front section of the store is the grab-em section, where we fan out thongs into polyester rainbows on little tables and display the chemises with the most eye-catching prints in order to lure in customers. The middle section is the safest section and where I most frequently make use of my hefty employee discount; it's where the natural fibers can be found and the items do what clothing is meant to do. That is to say it covers your secondary sexual characteristics and offers some warmth. The back section of the store is not for the timid or those looking for a simple lingerie solution. This area is where the lace, sequins, sheer fabrics, mesh, and embroidery let loose in an explosion of garter belts, merry widows, baby dolls, and some of the most elaborate bras known to man. They smack of hasty sewing and reek of cheap fabric dyes. I like to think of the sections of the store as something akin to Dante's circles of hell.

"All right, how about this?" I ask, holding up a cute pair of flowered cotton pajamas. The top has pink satin piping and tiny, pink satin-covered buttons, and the bottoms are shorts, with the same pink piping around faux pockets on the backside. This was something I actually considered buying for myself when I unloaded them and hung them on puffy, padded pink hangers a week ago.

She presses her lips together. "No, that won't work," she says firmly.

"OK . . . maybe something with long pajama bottoms, then." That makes sense, since a Boston winter soon will be upon us. "Do you like these?" I hold out a pair of flannel pajamas with a big lavender check.

"Oh, I like them fine. It's just that the buttons are all too close together on these. I need something with the buttons spaced very widely apart."

"Hmmm," I say, thinking for a minute. I remember a pair of pajamas where the buttons were spaced much wider than normal—presumably to be sexy? I reach deep into another rack and pull them out, a cornflower blue pair with a simple snowflake pattern.

"These are great," she exclaims, holding them out and studying the buttons. "You see, my friend is in a coma, and they need a lot of open space to run the tubes in and out. But this blue," she says, grimacing slightly. "She does *not* like blue. Do you have it in another color?"

I'm about to burst out laughing when she says this—blue pajamas, pink pajamas, donkey-vomit brown (Gerard's favorite made-up color that he used to describe my new purse last week) pajamas—who cares? *She's in a coma!* But she catches my look and her hopeful eyes start to match her sad lips, and I suddenly remember a story I heard on the radio about a devoted California cop who was rear-ended in his police car during a chase and was sent into a deep coma. They were using a police scanner as part of his rehabilitation, and whenever they would put out an APB, they would include his car number. When the number was transmitted and the sound filled his chilly room, his blood pressure would rise and his respiration rate would zoom up. His pulse would quicken. Sometimes, depending on the severity of the crime, he would even perspire, those dendrites deep in his brain screaming, racing down the freeway, even as his body lay still. So who was I to argue that a cozy pair of pajamas in an appealing color might not help rouse her friend to full consciousness?

"Let me look in the back," I say kindly.

———

"I win," I say excitedly. "I win, I win, I win, I win!"

"Not so fast," Gerard answers as we take our place in line at the Au Bon Pain. "What's your story?"

"A woman buying pajamas for a friend in a coma," I say proudly, tipping my chin up to him and lacing my fingers together behind my back, as though I'm about to be given a major award.

"You win, Moxie. Mine was only a woman who let her toy poodle barf on the carpet and then walked away," he says, frowning. "That's small-time. What would you like?"

"A shortbread cookie, of course." Gerard and I like to play Adventures in Retail, where we compare outrageous stories about customers, and the winner gets a sweet of his or her choice. Most of the time, the winner boasts a story that involves customer rudeness, a tale so unbelievable that it would be discussed at great length over lunch. But it doesn't have to be rudeness. It can be anything, so long as it makes the seller's jaw drop open in awe, fear, or stunned amusement during the transaction. Gerard hasn't won for a while now, so I almost wish the coma pajama lady came in on another day. Gerard's last win was a big one: a man who hurled a bottle of Michael Kors Men squarely at Gerard's shoulder when the customer was politely told that a two-thirds-empty bottle of cologne couldn't be returned. Still, fair is fair, and I'm happy about my cookie.

We get our food and I find what seems like a good table, right near the window, but Gerard shakes his head when he looks over from the condiments area and sees me seated there.

"Uh-uh," he says as he arrives at the table, jerking his head toward the right and clutching his tray in front of his chest. "No way. You can see right into the perfume bar from here." I turn around and see that he is right; we have an unobstructed view of Neiman Marcus, with its gorgeous marble floors, plush white carpets, and warm, soft lighting that makes people and products alike look irresistible.

"Yeah, so?"

"So I don't want to have to look at where I work when I'm on my break," he says with his eyes wide and his eyebrows raised, as though I'm the worst friend in the world not to have considered this when descending on one of the few available tables.

I roll my eyes and put my sandwich down. "Well, how about over there, then?" I ask impatiently, pointing to a table right in the center, flanked by the salad bar on one side and the cash registers on the other. "That looks pretty good. You're a pain, you know," I complain, plopping my coffee, cookie, napkins, and plastic flatware back onto my tray. "I had everything all set up."

"Well, it serves you right for starting to eat without me," he shouts over his shoulder as he races toward the table. I begin to open my mouth in response but then realize that this is a pretty good point, so I don't say anything back.

We're settled in with our sandwiches and snacks, and I'm watching the cashier ring up lunches with rapid-fire speed when Gerard wipes his mouth on the sleeve of his pale blue oxford shirt and says, "Guess what I'm doing Saturday."

"I have napkins, you know. Look at your sleeve! Where are you going this weekend?"

"My sleeve doesn't matter because I have to put my jacket back on anyway," he says, lifting the limp sleeve of his houndstooth jacket that he's slung over the back of his chair. "I'm going on a date with a guy I met at the Celtics game."

"What were you doing at a Celtics game? You don't like basketball." I don't like it either—generally speaking, and more specifically speaking, I don't like the Celtics. With their gangly, latter-day hero Larry Bird and that kelly-green uniform shade that makes T-shirted fans look sickly and wan, regardless of their race, creed, or color. Yet another reason I believe that Mary Alice regards me, the transplanted Jewish girl from New Jersey who doesn't appreciate her beloved Celts, as something between a curious museum exhibit and a deranged mental patient.

"I was at the Celtics game because my younger brother was visiting, and he likes basketball. And I'm a good older brother, so I got tickets. And this guy—he brings food up to the stands. Nuts. He sells you a little bag of peanuts for $4. He had dirty blond hair, and I thought he might be checking me out. So I asked him out," he finishes nonchalantly, as though asking out a gay Fleet Center food vendor who hurls hot dogs and nuts and ice-cream sandwiches to Celtics fans in between quarters is the most mundane, everyday experience.

I finish my coffee, taking big swallows in an effort to will the caffeine into my bloodstream more quickly. "You know, there's a great joke in here somewhere about this guy's nutsack, but it's too easy."

"*Much* too easy," he concurs. He is now crunching on his straw, gnashing it between his back teeth, his molars making a sick squeaking sound as they crush the soft plastic. "Don't say what you're going to say," he warns, taking the straw from his mouth, turning it around, and putting the pristine, unchewed half in.

"What, about how chewing on things is a sign of sexual

frustration?" I ask, biting into my cookie and savoring the melting shortbread.

He fixes me with a stare. "Yes, *that*. As if Freud knew anything. Which reminds me, don't you see Luttman tonight?"

I sigh and stuff another small bite of shortbread cookie in my mouth. "No, not yet. I only go about once a month now."

"Well, I don't think you need to see him at all. Shrinks are so passé these days. And he doesn't seem to be doing much."

"That's true," I admit, leaning back in my seat and watching an older woman in a Chanel suit try to navigate the salad bar. She is peering into the crouton bucket as though it contains a live grenade. "But I had to fight so much with my HMO just to get these visits, I feel like I really should go. Besides, he's got two degrees from Harvard."

"Big deal. *Someone* has to graduate in the bottom of the class, even at Harvard," he says, squishing his napkins into a ball and jamming them deep into his empty lemonade cup.

"Oh, well, that's encouraging, Gerard."

"Sorry. Who knows, maybe it helps." He stands, puts on his houndstooth jacket, and pulls himself up to his full six-foot, one-inch height. "I have to go now, the new Guerlain line is in. 'A divine potion. A day at the ocean,'" he intones in the languid manner of a haughty fragrance commercial and then laughs. "Actually, I'm looking forward to it. The samples they sent last month really did smell like the beach. Brings back memories, no?" he asks, smiling and rolling his eyes in a conspiratorial way before getting up and slowly shambling toward Neiman Marcus, where he will make up lies about fruity top notes and separate rich people from their money.

Indeed, it brings back memories of days at the ocean, but not all of them divine. Gerard and I met during an ill-fated Labor Day weekend trip to the Cape, right before my second year of grad school. It was sweltering hot, and my roommate's friend Leila had invited a large group of people to spend the holiday weekend at her parents' enormous, beach-front house in Wellfleet. This was the fulfillment of a lifetime dream for Leila. An only child, she grew up wishing the cavernous vacation home were a more boisterous place, with the sounds of people laughing on the deck and enjoying clambakes on the sand. She invited as many people as the house would comfortably sleep and then some—roommates were encouraged to bring friends, friends were told to round up neighbors, girlfriends could accompany boyfriends, brothers could tag along with sisters. We would have fun from sunup till sundown, our biggest worry centering on whether or not there would be enough lobster bibs for everyone.

It was an unmitigated disaster. A friend of a friend of Leila's drunkenly jumped around on the bed and got his hand clipped by the ceiling fan, spraying the crisp, white room with blood before going to the local hospital. A girl from Boston College and a guy from Emerson got into a heated argument about capital punishment, after which the girl overturned the patio table they had been shouting at one another across. A tiny little thing, she must have underestimated her own strength, because she sent it crashing to the driveway below, where the glass top broke into a thousand pieces. A handsome blond who'd arrived with a girlfriend only hours before got high and had noisy sex in one of the bathrooms with the younger sister of someone who'd never moved from in front of the TV the entire weekend. The sump pump backed up, sending foul-smelling sludge into the washing machine during the rinse cycle. Leila seemed to cry hourly, her beach house fantasy fading right before her eyes. It was when she gamely unfolded a Twister mat one evening and a loud chorus of "fuck you" rang out that I knew I needed to step onto the deck and be alone for a minute.

But Gerard, who had snagged his invite from a friend of Leila's brother, had beaten me to it. He looked as miserable as

I felt. One of his sneakers was untied. His face was sun-burned, save one thick, white stripe, where he'd draped a sock across his eyes and proceeded to fall asleep for several hours. He was wearing an oversized T-shirt incorrectly branding him as an Aries; his laundry had been in the washing machine when it filled with sewage, and he'd gone through all the dresser drawers in the house until he found this chic piece of resortwear. A playful drawing of a ram danced across his chest, and in bold letters the T-shirt announced, "I RAM WHAT I AM." We traded defeated looks—we knew we were stuck in this vacation purgatory for the duration, since neither of us had a car, and we'd both gotten a lift out here from Leila. He smiled and took a step toward me.

"I can think of at least three things I'd rather be doing right now," he began thoughtfully, resting his hand dangerously close to a citronella candle on the deck railing. "You can jump in whenever you're ready, but I'll begin." He inhaled and looked up and to the right, and I noticed how sweet his brown eyes were. "Getting screened for cancer of the rectum. Taking a taxidermy class. Seeing any movie with any Wayans brother." He finished and looked at me eagerly, but I didn't respond, and his face soon clouded with the expression of a man who fears he's horribly misread his audience. But he needn't have worried.

"Standing in line at a convenience store while the cashier points to *every single brand* of cigarettes behind the counter until he figures out which kind the customer ahead of me wants. Churning my own butter. And, um," I said, searching the night sky, "walking the Freedom Trail from start to finish on a ten-degree day." These weren't great, I knew, but who knows how long he had been out here crafting his list? It didn't matter. Gerard grinned from ear to ear, then I did too, and for the remainder of the weekend we were inseparable.

When we returned to Boston, I worried that our tentative

friendship might fall apart, since there was that unmistakable lifeboat mentality in Wellfleet that didn't exist in the city. But evidently the bond was strong enough to withstand the trip back from the Cape. Gerard and I began talking on the phone, then meeting up once a week for dinner or drinks, then meeting up twice a week or more. He was so good-natured and funny that I would always find myself remarkably content after spending time together, chuckling as I remembered a silly observation he'd made or reflecting on some helpful advice he'd given me. I experienced such a kinship with him that it nearly felt like the stirrings of love—not romantic love, of course, but a platonic one.

And as with all new love affairs, I started to wonder if I wasn't coming on too strong. Perhaps Gerard didn't appreciate it when I called just to tell him that I saw my least favorite student step in dog shit while wearing her brand-new sandals. Maybe he had better things to do than accompany me to the MIT Swapfast and help me root through piles of battered electronics in search of parts to use in science experiments. This growing feeling of doubt made me anxious and cautious, until one October evening, when Gerard called from a nearby hospital. He was visiting the mother of a childhood friend. The prognosis wasn't good, he'd told me in a whisper over the phone only the night before.

"Moxie," he said in a thin voice, "it's Gerard. I'm at the hospital, and I'm thinking of you." He stopped to sniffle a few times. "Guess why."

"Why?" I asked, biting my lip.

"Because it's Screening Awareness Week for cancer of the rectum," he said, his voice cracking as he burst into tears. "I . . . even . . . got . . . a . . . brochure." Then his weeping gave way to little fits of laughter. "I think we should see one another more, Moxie," he decided. When he said it, I could tell he was smiling through his tears.

3

Shirred Peek-a-boo Baby Doll with Matching High-Cut Panty

"ALL I'M SAYING IS THAT YOU SHOULD USE YOUR DISCOUNT TO buy some prettier things," Mary Alice says, scanning the ticket of my new, fluffy white bathrobe into the cash register and then punching in the code for my employee discount.

"And all *I'm* saying is—shit, Mary Alice, look!" I hiss, pointing to the front of the store. There, standing next to the thong table in all her dirty glory, is Catherine. Well, not really Catherine; that's just the code name we've been taught to use when we suspect that someone is shoplifting. We are supposed to stride confidently up to a co-manager or manager and say in a normal tone of voice (or as normal a tone as is possible when someone is sauntering out of the store with a pair of flannel pajamas on underneath her clothes), "Catherine is here." I'm clear on that procedure, but then what? It's not as though we have a special panic button that immediately summons the mall security guards, or are given lessons in how to wrestle people to the ground and reclaim our brassieres.

Mary Alice demonstrates this lack of protocol in the clumsiest way possible: She rushes to the front of the store, bearing down hard on the pink-and-green floral carpet, and shouting, "How can I help you?" Of course, this sends Catherine flying, the legs of her ratty pink track suit making a *swish-whoosh* noise during her quick getaway, her greasy blonde hair swinging from side to side halfway down her back. Mary Alice runs out of the store and into the mall, but I don't follow. I decided a long time ago that my life is worth a lot more than $5.99 worth of polyester, and if someone was going to steal, then so be it. After a few seconds, she stomps back into the store and takes her place behind the counter. She hitches up and straightens her navy blue skirt, which got turned around in all the action, and grumbles loudly.

I decide that I am not up for the tirade about shoplifters that she's getting ready to deliver, so I offer to stand up front, in case Catherine comes back for another hit. When I reach the front and take my place between the thong table and the racks of the new daisy-print chemises, I notice a man standing in the doorway, right beneath the faux gold scrollwork. He looks like he's in his early thirties and is quite tall, with dark, chocolate-brown hair and just the hint of a smile on his face. Probably out buying something for his wife or girlfriend, I decide as I look him up and down and admire his well-made white shirt, striped silk tie, and neatly pressed chino pants. We get four types of men in this store: The kind who approach lingerie purchases with some modicum of calm and class; the kind who approach lingerie purchases like a retarded, horny teenager; the kind who want their women wearing garments exclusively from the third circle of store hell; and the kind who want to wear the garments themselves. This guy seems very much like the first type.

"You know, that woman just stole a lot of underwear," he says to me in a calm yet slightly amused voice. He points to the thong table, and sure enough, there is a big hole in the polka-dot-patterned section. "She was pretty quick," he adds, trying to find a place in the store to rest his eyes that won't embarrass him or me. This is my favorite quality in a male customer.

"She *is* quick," I agree. "She comes here a lot. Maybe a few times a month, even." I stop for a minute, thinking about what Catherine might be doing with huge handfuls of cheap underwear. "So, can I help you find something?"

He smiles sweetly at this request. "Of course. Are there ever men who come into this place who *don't* need help?"

"Oh, sometimes," I say, remembering the time last month when a guy came in immediately after winning $300 on a scratch ticket purchased from the newsstand in the mall. He quite literally ripped the store apart, buying up gigantic, purple, lace bras and painful-looking merry widows for his "lady," as he called her. He got so excited that he tripped over the carpet, tearing up a small corner and making Mary Alice glower at him during his entire shopping spree. He was a delighted and delightful customer, giddy with joy and unconcerned about whether or not his lady liked her frilly undies in red, pink, white, or black. When he couldn't remember, he just bought them all.

"Well, I suppose I'm looking for something a woman might sleep in. A nightgown, perhaps? But the type that's short and sleeveless." He uses his hand to make a motion like he's sawing the side of his upper thigh, to illustrate the desired length. "I guess I'm not doing a good job of describing this, am I?" he asks, putting his fingers to his lower lip.

"No, you're doing fine," I reassure him. "Do you want something in cotton or polyester? Oops, sorry, I mean poly-*satin*," I add, quickly correcting myself when Mary Alice shoots me a look as she neatens the pantyhose area on my right. He looks mystified.

"What's the difference?" he asks.

"There is none," I whisper, watching her walk back over to the register to ring up a customer. "It's the same thing! It's just that they do something to make the polyester softer. I guess they figure that people wouldn't be jumping up to buy a polyester nightgown," I finish, suppressing a laugh. Normally, I'm never so honest with customers, but this guy and his sweet face and friendly disposition are putting me at ease, making me almost enjoy standing here under the hot lights.

"Well, I appreciate your candor . . ." His voice drifts off as he raises both eyebrows.

"Moxie," I say, immediately sticking my hand out and shaking his. He's got smooth skin and a firm grasp.

"That's quite a name. Do you have moxie?"

"A little. I used to. You know." I shrug and try to keep from blushing.

"Well, my name is Allan. Two 'l's." He holds up the index and middle fingers of his right hand to illustrate two lower-case 'l's, but it ends up looking like he's giving the peace sign, which makes me wonder if Mary Alice will become suspicious that we've got a hippie on the premises. "And I suppose I'd like to see some cotton nightgowns. So show me what you've got, Moxie."

I'm strutting down Tremont Street at the end of my shift, and singing "Bennie and the Jets" at the top of lungs to ward off would-be attackers and freaks. The store closed at nine o'clock, and after vacuuming, picking up stray pins, and counting all the greasy bills in the cash register, it's now nearing ten o'clock. And although the Combat Zone ain't what it used to be, it still isn't completely safe at night. The truth is that Elton John isn't even my favorite, but Gerard and I decided that the staccato, stuttering *b* in "B-B-B-Bennie" lends to the song an inherent looniness that might work extra well at making people afraid of *me*. Some nights I get sick of singing, but the only other choice that sounds at least as effective is peeing myself, which is the other thing they recommend that you do when you find yourself alone in a dangerous neighborhood. Remember that I'm always wearing pantyhose while on this walk, and so that's not a pretty picture. It's bad enough that I have to wear the damn things, but the thought of having pee streaming down my legs inside of them is enough to make me belt it out like I'm Reginald himself.

It's getting cold—only late October, and already my breath hangs in the night air like the little clouds of Honeysuckle Rose powder Mary Alice spread through the store with a powder puff. Every year when the weather turns brisk, I think about the very first time I saw a cardboard container of Dunkin' Donuts Munchkins in Boston. It was sitting on my friend's desk, and I found the illustration on the side cute and charming, if a bit perplexing. It was a winter scene, and the little Munchkins were depicted frolicking in the snow, bouncing around on the ice, building a tiny Munchkin snowman. But here was the thing: they were dressed for the outdoors, and in a big way. They were wearing balaclavas and mittens and ski vests. The powdered one had a long, striped scarf on; the chocolate one was sporting oversized red boots. A fuzzy, coconut-covered one wore fuzzy, coconut earmuffs. But after my first Boston winter, I understood much better. These New England illustrators drew what they knew, and they knew about bitter, unforgiving cold. They knew about wind chill factors and snowstorms which neither man nor donut hole would survive without serious gear.

When I reach my apartment building, I start to open the door but gasp with surprise when it flings outward and nearly hits me in the face. Standing there is Steven Tyler, on his way out for the evening. For a split second we are shocked and speechless, eye to eye. Steven Tyler isn't very tall at all—maybe five feet eight inches on a good day, when he's got his Doc Martens with the sizable heel on. Tonight he is wearing black, peg-leg jeans with a formidable four-inch cuff; a nondescript navy blue sweater; a short, black leather jacket; and a tiny gold stud in his ear. This is more or less his standard cool-weather uniform, a sort of post-punk look that contrasts with his small, wiry frame, bright red, curly hair, dancing green eyes, and light pink freckles that look as though someone stuck the nails of his thumb and forefinger into calamine lotion and went *flick-flick-flick*, distributing little misshapen flecks of pigment all over Steven's face. But his most compelling features by far are a torn earlobe (on the ear that doesn't have the stud) and two crimson scars that run across his neck, starting under the messy earlobe on the right and ending directly above the collarbone on the left. When you combine the wardrobe, earring, scars, and maimed ear with his gee-golly Opie look and his general friendly demeanor, the result is the overall appearance and countenance of a sweet pirate. Like he would rape and pillage but then make sandwiches for everyone and tidy up afterward.

"You're just coming home?" he asks, absently kicking a coffee cup lid that's outside the door to the building. "They work you like a dog!"

"And you're just going out?" I reply, trying to remember what it was like to be able to hit the town at ten o'clock at night. Sure, I've got about five years on Steven Tyler. He's young and fresh faced, and he takes full advantage of the fact that even though our immediate neighborhood is unpleasant—the most exciting local entertainment is *Porgy & Bess* playing down the street at the Majestic Royal Theatre—we are very close to many hip clubs and bars. But availing myself of all these things is beyond my capabilities at this late hour, and all I want to do is slip into my heather gray sleep shirt (only $12.99 with my discount) and watch a rerun of *The Larry Sanders Show*.

"Yup. Were you singing before?" he asks. "I thought I heard singing before when I was coming down the stairs." He checks his watch and decides not to wait for my answer, which is good, because I don't feel like providing it right now. "Well, I have to go. See you around," he finishes, and I breathe a sigh of relief.

———

For the next several days, I keep an eye out for Allan at the store. He doesn't come back to shop, and I am at once bitterly disappointed and somewhat relieved. I am disappointed because he was handsome and kind and has fueled some of my sexual fantasies of late. Also I've been dressing a little nicer, breaking out my new, pink wool cashmere sweater that Gerard bought for me with his Neiman's discount; and putting my hair up with a series of little beaded clips instead of a ponytail held in place with the rubber band that comes wrapped around my *Boston Globe* each morning.

But I am relieved, because I don't want him to ask me again if I have moxie. This question nearly caused me to vomit onto a nearby camisole-and-tap-pant display after he left that afternoon, and is the reason for too much rumination since. When I chose the name Moxie that day on Newbury Street, I had no idea that it actually meant something other than the name of a locally made, funny-tasting cola. At eighteen, I had never heard the word before, didn't know that it meant self-assured and gutsy.

But it turned out to be very apt. Everything went my way in college; I got high marks and was a superstar student teacher, confident and unafraid of students, principals, or parents. When the professors at my school read the rolls, tallied the grades, and realized that Moxie Brecker was right there at the top of the list *and* that teaching science had turned out to be her calling, there was no question about what to do. Moxie Brecker would be strongly encouraged to pursue a graduate teaching degree. And they would even offer her scholarship money, because it is still relatively unusual for a woman to want to teach science, and a lady science teacher would ostensibly set a good example for all the little girls out there. They had so much faith in me that they even let me defer for a year, so I could go home to New Jersey and help nurse my favorite uncle back to health after a bad car accident.

Graduate school was more of the same: I adored every minute and was unstoppable. I connected with all types of kids and learned more about education theory and the best ways to engage different kinds of students. I decided that I liked middle school best, the kids with brand-new cystic acne and squeaky voices. Erikson, my preferred authority on childhood development, said that this is the age when children begin to recognize their place in the world—the family unit grows less important each day, and they begin to redefine themselves through peers and new experiences. I relished the idea of being a daily influence during this period in their lives, and when I graduated, I was immediately hired by the school system in Brookline, a town known in Massachusetts for its exemplary public schools.

The first few months were everything I dreamed of, and I was quickly cemented in seventh-grade lore as the teacher who wasn't afraid to hold her hand on the electricity dome and frizz her hair out for the remaining five periods of the day. But by Christmas vacation, things had gotten bad. For reasons that were a total mystery to me, I became alternately anxious and sad. I was tired all the time, an unremitting sluggishness overtaking my body that made me feel as though I was constantly slogging through a vat of Jell-O. My job became very hard for me, the pressure mounting with each school day. The kids started to get on my nerves, their never-ending confusion about the periodic table making me cross. I worried that I wasn't doing a good job, and this made me feel even worse. I went for a series of general blood tests, to see if there was something swimming in my cells that wasn't right, and the tests showed nothing. The administration at the school was helpful and sympathetic in ways that made me embarrassed. They offered me paid time off, which was patently against the rules for a brand-new teacher, but they would bend them for me. They said the nurse would let me rest in her office on an empty cot during lunch periods. Moxie had become a total misnomer. I had no more moxie, just a constant feeling of drowsiness and profound sadness and shame.

Although no one asked me to, I decided to leave at the end of the school year. I felt like I wasn't the kind of teacher I wanted to be, and even if the kids seemed mostly blind to the situation, I knew in my heart that I wasn't doing a good job. The school principal, a portly man who plastered the walls of his office with Red Sox posters and pennants, gave me a referral to a psychiatrist on the last day of school. I will never forget how I felt as I stood next to the cotton-candy stand at the party on the school lawn, staring at that little scrap of paper in my hand. "Why arentcha coming back next year, Miss Brecker?" asked Lucy, a chubby girl in my fourth-period class who learned the hard way that when I said to be careful around a Bunsen burner, I wasn't kidding. Her pink plastic bracelet still looked like an abstract sixties sculpture, and she fiddled with it as she shifted her weight from foot to foot, waiting patiently for my answer.

I told her I didn't really know, and I still don't. Dr. Luttman says that I grew depressed and anxious because the pressures of teaching were more than I could handle. He decided that I got so used to being told what to do in school that when it came time for me to tell others what to do in school, I found it overwhelming. This accounted for the crummy feelings, both physical and mental, he claimed. Then he scheduled another appointment and presented me with a bill, and these two actions made me suddenly realize that I needed a source of income. Gerard, who majored in sociology but took to retail like a fish to toilet water in Men's Fragrances at Neiman Marcus, immediately began to sell me on trying to get a job in the mall. It's a fancy mall, he reasoned, with Neiman's as the anchor store, a Gucci with quality Spanish leather you can smell four stores away, and even a glittery Tiffany's. You're used to working with immature children, and this puts you in a prime position to work with impetuous customers, he said. And best of all, many people who work in retail are complete boneheads, so you'll be promoted in no time. That's what happened to me, and I have it pretty cushy, he cooed.

So that's how I ended up, at twenty-eight, as assistant co-manager at the store, folding bras, using the industrial steamer to coax wrinkles out of peignoir sets, and pretending to care when Catherine steals thongs. The pay is OK—sadly, almost what I made as a teacher—but I haven't made the career leaps Gerard predicted. That's because even as the economy crumbles and stores all over the mall are laying off employees, we've expanded our staff. People can't seem to get enough of this polysatin stuff, even in this current economic climate. It's as though Alan Greenspan, after delivering his last somber speech about the nation's money woes, hurriedly raced back to the podium and said, "Oh, yeah, but be sure to keep getting it on. It is your duty as an American to seduce your loved one, by any means necessary." So instead of promoting me from lowly salesgirl to co-manager, as the bleached-blond regional manager promised they would do, they created two assistant co-manager positions and moved

Mary Alice over from the Faneuil Hall store. Luttman thinks this a good job for me—lower stress, it will help me get myself back together. I explain frequently that the job is very physical and this ends up making me more tired than before, but he promises that the malaise will dissipate when I become happier. But I *was* happy, I want to say to him. I *liked* teaching. I want my moxie back.

4

Lace-Trim Slip with Empire Waist and Adjustable Straps

"No, NOT OVER THERE, JOE. YOU CAN'T EVEN SEE THE chattering teeth when you put the novelty toilet paper in front of them. See?" I walk outside the store, look at the window, and shake my head disapprovingly.

"Not really. But that's why I asked you here—I knew you'd be able to help out an old man!" he replies joyfully, slowly leaning into the window and groaning as he nudges the toilet paper ("Never tears! Drives your guests crazy! They'll be stuck on the bowl all night!" boasts the package) a few inches to the left. "OK, now what about Weepy the Wee Wee? Where should he go?"

We've been at this for an hour now, and I'm suddenly wondering if this was a bad idea. On the rare occasions that my work schedule blesses me with a free Saturday, I tend to steer clear of all retail establishments. No piped-in music, no SKU numbers, no free gift-with-purchase. I don't want to try on any merchandise, don't want to smell any fragrances, don't want to mess up any garments for other salesgirls to have to refold and tidy while all of their friends are out having fun on a weekend shopping trip. But on my way past the joke shop this morning, Joe came out and asked me if I wouldn't mind helping him with the window display. Business is down, he complained. Maybe he just needed a fresh look, and since I work in retail, perhaps I could lend my expertise. I looked into his hopeful, watery blue eyes and said all right, as long as I don't have to touch the plastic barf. He rubbed his hands together with glee and put me right to work, and I've been periodically climbing down from inside the windows and walking out to the sidewalk to review the display. It's noisy out there today; Saturday mornings are the busiest time of the week at the Planned Parenthood, and too-short pants man is red-faced and shouting like a banshee at girls who bow their heads as they enter and exit the building. I notice that he is accompanied by an old, black nun who is silent and placidly swaying from side to side and a thirty-something woman with a bad perm, who is holding a giant cross aloft.

"Moxie?" Joe sticks his head out the door, his white hair glowing in the cold morning light. "Look at the dribble glass. You like?" He's perched it on top of the oversized, red fuzzy dice.

"Yes," I say, rubbing my upper arms as I try to keep warm. It's very windy outside, but it's too much trouble to keep pulling on and shaking off my navy blue pea coat as I go in and out of the shop. "You know what would look good there? The fake blood. Because the tubes are clear, with the red inside. That would pick up the red of the dice and the clear of the dribble glass."

"That's my girl!" he cries, walking back into the store, reaching in the window, and placing a pile of tubes of fake blood next to the dribble glass. He comes outside and joins me on the sidewalk, hiking his blue knit pants up to his chest.

"You're *good*. That mall store is lucky to have you. Who is making all that noise?" he asks in an annoyed tone, turning his good ear in the direction of the hollering. "All that shouting, it's bad for business."

"It's the people at the Planned Parenthood," I say as we walk back into the store and he hands me a small cardboard box of clear acrylic ice cubes, each with its own tiny fake fly in the center. "The people outside, they stand around and yell."

"I know, I know what they do," he says, sounding slightly injured because I provided him with what is obviously an unnecessary explanation. "Thing is," he continues, "I agree with those people. But you don't see me hopping around like some damn Hare Krishna, do you?"

"No," I say slowly, setting down the box of ice cubes. "But I thought that was a religion."

"Yeah, yeah, I know it's not the same," he says, dismissing my confusion with a quick wave of the hand. "I mean that I'm not forcing my beliefs on anyone, the way they used to jump out at you at Logan Airport with a flower. 'Hey buddy, I'm just on my way to the novelties trade show in Dallas, no offense,'" he jokes in a robust voice, tilting his head and putting his palms in the air in his one-man, one-act show, *Joe Meets the Eager Hare Krishna*. "I'm saying people have to make their own decisions. Oh, look who's here—it's Sam and Evan," he says, gesturing to the two lanky teenage boys who have just entered the store. "I have to go and help them. Can you finish, dear?" he asks, pointing to packages of very realistically molded plastic dog doo in three distinct styles (dark brown and loglike; light brown, swirly, and compact; and something bombshaped and black that could only come from a Great Dane).

"I'm not sure," I answer honestly, feeling a bit sick. "Maybe I'll just sit here for a minute while you help the boys." The boys look about sixteen and are hovering around the magic area in the back of the store, picking up the trick decks of cards and two-headed nickels and magic rope. They are both wearing oversized, flannel shirts and baggy cotton pants, and they push the greasy hair out of their eyes with the exact same motion. I'm momentarily transfixed as I watch them play around with the trick rope, and Joe whispers, "Twins. Fraternal, I think. Good customers, too." He ambles to the back of the store and makes a big show of asking how he can help these two good men this morning. They smile shyly and simultaneously push the hair out of their eyes. Joe opens a deck of cards with a flourish, sets it out on the table, offers basic instructions, and leaves them to it.

"I got a problem with these two," he says quietly when he returns to find me with the still-unopened packages of dog doo. "They always buy a lot, but they're getting too old for this. Eleven-, twelve-, even fourteen-year-old boys, I get loads of them. But I feel like these two should be out trying to make it with girls, not learning magic tricks in the back of this old store. I don't want them to end up thirty-year-old virgins, living in their ma's basement." He looks genuinely worried at this prospect, and his white moustache curls down at the edges as he watches them goof around.

"Oh, Joe, don't worry. They'll be fine." I sneak a peek at them, and one is still engrossed in the card game, but the other is fondling a plaster of Paris torso that is sporting the edible bra-and-panty ensemble that Joe says is so popular these days. "Well, maybe not that one," I say, and we both laugh.

An hour later, I am walking slowly up the steps to Dr. Luttman's office in Kenmore Square and cursing myself for having asked him to move my appointment to Saturday, after I found out that I would have the day off from work. Who but me goes to the shrink on a brisk Saturday afternoon, I wonder, as I watch the groups of cheery Boston University coeds laugh and knock into one another, all swaddled in their cozy Lands' End sweaters and Timberland fleece jackets. One of them suddenly stops short in front of the pizzeria and leans down to tie her sporty suede boot, and this causes three of her friends to tumble down around her, giggling as they hit the pavement and try to avoid the broken shards of glass that litter the sidewalks in this part of town. I used to like dirty Kenmore Square a lot better before I began associating it with Luttman; it's got great musty little record shops, one of the best Indian restaurants in town, with curry dishes that make you want to eat more and cry all at the same time, and a well-stocked Army-Navy store where they used to know me by name when I was in college.

Once inside, I take off my coat and have barely settled in with the current issue of *Spin* when Luttman comes out to greet me. "Moxie, so nice to see you," he says curtly, taking me away from the tantalizing table set with numerous courses of reading material. It's a cruel irony: he's the first doctor I've ever visited who keeps current copies of good magazines (last time I read *Rolling Stone* with REM on the cover!), but he's also the first one who keeps very closely to his appointment schedule, so I've never got time to read them properly. Eight-year-old issues of *Redbook* and *Field & Stream*? Be sure to triple-book, doctors, so your patients can suffer through these painfully outdated periodicals. Fresh, slick copies of *Jane* and *Self*? Stay on task, so no one can really enjoy them. They must learn this in medical school, I think.

"So," he begins, waiting for me to sit down in the plush velvet, sage-green chair before taking a seat opposite me. "How have you been since last we talked?" He crosses his legs and plays absently with his coarse, black beard hair as he awaits my answer. My answer is always the same.

"Umm. OK, I suppose." I look up and study him during

the protracted silence that follows. He's wearing his itchy-looking blue suit, which is what he always wears, unless he is wearing his itchy-looking brown suit or his itchy-looking gray suit. These suits always make me want to start scratching myself all over; they have that sort of sympathetic effect. But I'm careful not to scratch, because then I'd have to explain *why* I'm thinking that way. And I have enough trouble explaining things to Luttman without having to worry about this.

"Well, have you been feeling better? Less sad?" He cocks his head and purses his lips, all the while maintaining a therapist's façade of complete indifference. This is the start of the line of questioning that I go through each visit, and it is an exercise in frustration for us both. I am unable to make him understand that I simply feel tired and generally out of it—that I never once suffered and still don't suffer from a stick-your-head-in-the-oven sorrow, the kind that incapacitates my friend Annie, making her unable to do anything but stay in bed and listen to Joy Division CDs for days at a time. And Luttman remains stymied about my stance on mood-elevating drugs. I don't want them, and this irritates him to no end. I see nothing wrong with them for other people, but they just don't feel right for me. Whenever I visit his office, I'm always clutching a paper cup of coffee, and I'm fully convinced that if I ever left it unattended while I went to the bathroom, I would return to find a Zoloft Latte.

We bat the standard questions and answers back and forth for another half-hour or so. Yes, the job is fine. No, there's nothing to be ashamed about—selling panties is an honest day's work. Yes, I still feel down some of the time. No, I haven't been on any dates lately.

"What about your exercises? Your meditation and breathing exercises?" he asks, crossing his legs and resting his chin in his palm. I look at his pudgy fingers and am reminded of

the sticky hands of a toddler who came into the store yesterday and got grape jelly stains all over the hemlines of the
long silk nightgowns while her oblivious mother tried on
bras in the fitting room for twenty minutes.

"I try to do them. I try to do them at work when I'm feeling
down," I answer semi-truthfully, taking a long slurp from my
coffee.

"And you think of the calming scenes we talked about?
Waves crashing on the beach or a serene meadow, perhaps?"

Or Edward Norton. I like to think about him when I'm on
my fifteen-minute break, crouched in the stockroom, sitting
in a tiny chair sandwiched between the new shipment of
pantyhose and the plastic bin full of hangers. "Sometimes I
think about Edward Norton," I offer, but choose not to dis-
close full details. That's because although I *should* imagine
him shirtless and buff in *American History X*, or black-clad
and sexy in *The Score*, the truth is that I like to picture him in
Fight Club, when he's got a big shiner and is sitting at a meeting, and he opens his mouth and blood and pulp pour from
between his teeth. I'm not a violent person, so I'm not quite
sure why this is what I imagine. But I don't dare tell Luttman
any of it—I'm sure he would determine that this pathology
would merit much, much more intense treatment.

"The actor? How is Edward Norton going to help you,
Moxie? No, no, I think you should stick to the scenes we
talked about," he says, slightly annoyed.

"Well, he certainly can't *hurt*," I retort, eager for this visit
to be over. I'm actually surprised that Luttman even knows
who Norton is. Luttman is easily sixty years old, and not a
hip sixty. Maybe when no one is looking, he reads the *Us* and
People magazines out in the waiting area that he shares with
three other shrinks in this office suite.

"All right," he sighs. We're finished for today, I suppose.
I'll see you in another month, then." We both stand up and

shake hands like an irritated teacher and disappointed parent after a very unsatisfying parent-teacher meeting.

———————

"No way. And to think *he's* the one giving advice! That guy is crazy," Gerard assures me a few days later as we ride the T to the Cuddle 'n' Bubble to do our laundry. "If you want to picture Edward Norton instead of some stupid nature scene from a *Successories* poster, that is your prerogative."

"Thank you," I say, plunking down in a seat that was just vacated by a tiny Chinese woman gripping a blue straw tote bag filled to the brim with cauliflower. I shift my huge bag of laundry awkwardly, and the bottle of Tide falls out of the top and hits the floor of the train. "This is a pain, going all the way to Cambridge. The Cuddle 'n' Bubble made more sense when you were living there. But now?" I ask as the train slows to a halt and we gather our bags and detergent.

"It's got movies. And pizza. And . . . it's fun to watch movies on the giant plasma-screen TV while you do your laundry," he says, smiling as we step off the train. "Hey, hold up, Moxie!" he shouts at me as I walk down the platform, eager to get to the escalators, where I can lean on the railing and not have to propel all this filthy laundry forward with my own power. "Slow down!" he says a bit angrily.

I turn and feel guilty; I certainly know by now that Gerard's limp always slows him down, especially when he's got things to carry. His peculiar gait—languid and uneven, with one leg dragging slightly behind the other in a way that suggests a confident swagger to some but is a source of burning shame to him—is the result of a childhood incident that started with his parents fighting in his Providence home and ended in an outlet store in the wee hours of the morning. His father, a wretched jerk by all accounts, was smacking his mother around and generally scaring her half to death one winter night when Gerard was nine. Fortunately, Gerard didn't hear any of it, as he was sitting in his bedroom with headphones on and daydreaming about his friend Daniel. His mother packed Gerard and his brother Mark in the car at midnight and made a break for her parents' house in Caribou, Maine—an eight-hour drive from Rhode Island. She drove fast and stayed focused, her fear and rage hurtling her through Massachusetts, New Hampshire, and into Maine.

But by three in the morning, mom was exhausted. She was broke. And Caribou was still very far away, so when she saw the exit for Freeport, she did what any good mother would do. She took the boys into L.L. Bean's enormous, 24-hour outlet store, bundled Gerard into a lightweight sleeping bag, and zipped him into a gigantic display tent. As it was the middle of the night, the store was quiet, with just a few shoppers and sales clerks wandering the floor. She swept Mark up in her arms and sat looking into the roaring fake fire three aisles away from Gerard, wondering what her life had become. She was so wrapped up in her thoughts that she didn't notice that the night staff had begun to freshen the displays. She didn't hear them discussing that it was stupid to dismantle the tents—it took so much time, and it was so much easier to use a forklift to move them around. Nor did she hear them paging the guy who works the forklift.

But she certainly heard Gerard screaming as the forklift lifted that tent high in the air, and he swears that having the limp is *almost* worth it when he recalls the look on the face of the hapless forklift operator as he watched Gerard frantically unzip the airborne tent and crash down fifteen feet onto the cold concrete floor, all while his lower half was tucked mummy-like into the red sleeping bag. True to form, L.L. Bean was courteous to a fault, behaving as though boys found slumbering in store displays is an everyday occurrence, and even giving his mother some clothing for the road. Gerard still keeps in touch with Betty, one of the women working on a cash register near the scene of the accident.

We ride the escalator up to the street, drag our laundry bags to the Cuddle 'n' Bubble, and begin sorting. Gerard's laundry is positively overwhelming tonight, and not with the kind of smells you'd imagine would cling to the clothing of a man who works at a perfume counter. It's more like old boat shoes and sweaty locker room, and it nearly makes me gag as he overstuffs the washing machine with underpants and socks that probably should be quarantined. I try not to inhale, but he catches me mouth-breathing and says, "Like your fine, dainty items smell like a bunch of daffodils, Moxie." He pulls a shirt from the bag and looks at the care label with a baffled expression. "What the hell does this mean?" he asks himself as he studies the cryptic international symbol laundering instructions. "Don't put your shirt in a beaker?"

"I never said they smelled like daffodils," I retort. "Do you want a piece of pizza? I'm going to get a brownie." The excellent snack bar at the Cuddle 'n' Bubble makes doing laundry almost bearable.

"Yeah, thanks. No, make mine a brownie also. No nuts." He drops the lid of the washing machine heavily, and the young couple nuzzling on the sofa and watching *Titanic* look up angrily. I head off to the snack bar for two brownies, no nuts, and when I return, Gerard is seated on an adjacent loveseat and looking unhappy.

"What?" I ask, handing him his brownie and breaking off a piece of the corner of mine and plopping it into my mouth. "You don't want to thrill to the soulful crooning of Celine Dion? You know they weren't going to let you watch *Pretty in Pink* again, Gerard. Let's just sit over there and talk," I suggest, pointing to some stylish but uncomfortable-looking plastic chairs. We walk over, settle in, and eat our brownies in silence; they are chewy and fudgy and demand to be enjoyed with an intense, wordless focus.

When I finish my last bite, I say, "Hey, speaking of no nuts, whatever happened to the Fleet Center guy? The nut vendor? You haven't mentioned him lately."

He licks his fingers, wipes them on his pants, and shrugs. "He is young and confused. His only gay sexual experience before he met me was with someone in a local commuter train station restroom."

"And you're looking for someone more sophisticated—with experience in an Amtrak station restroom, perhaps?"

"Can it, Moxie," he says. "We just didn't have that much in common, either. It's no big deal. This just makes me available for James, anyhow."

I know better than to reply to this and instead busy myself studying the vending machine mounted on the wall behind me. Tiny packages of All, Cheer, and Dreft, sized just right for a midget family's laundry. For as long as I have known him, Gerard has been convinced that James Spader is his ideal mate. It doesn't seem to faze him one bit that James Spader is decidedly straight, with a wife and two boys as proof. Gerard is certain that if he could have just one date with James, he could make him see the beauty and joy that comes from loving a man, and more specifically, a man named Gerard Oliver, of Boston, Massachusetts.

Gerard is a man of peculiar goals in general, which, over the years, I've generally chosen to embrace rather than laugh at. His list of things to do also includes someday appearing on *The New Candid Camera*, which airs weekly on a saccharine, family values-oriented cable network and is hosted by the bland Peter Funt, who, regrettably, lacks the quirky, sharp-witted Funt gene that his father possessed. Because Gerard majored in sociology, he fancies himself a bit of an expert in human behavior and delights in trying to predict how people will respond to the set-ups on the show. Although I don't like the show nearly as much as Gerard does, I do enjoy watching it with him because his accuracy is uncanny. "She's a single mother; she won't have time for this nonsense," he'll sniff disdainfully as the young woman pushing a stroller screws up her face in disgust when someone asks her if she'll sign a petition to give away free cotton candy at the DMV. "Oh, look at this guy," he'll crow, clapping his hands as the disembodied voice booms through the drive-through window speaker, asking the hefty motorist in the SUV if he would like the Five Hundred French Fry Special with his order. "He won't be able to resist, I just know it. Not because he's overweight, but because he just has that look in his eye." Invariably, he is correct, and this brings him more pleasure than such a lame hobby should. Another goal of his is, some time over the course of the next year, to work each of the following phrases into contextually appropriate conversations:

1. I don't expect to be talked to this way in my own home.
2. You can't fire me, because I quit.
3. The girl is, was, and will always be, nada. (From *Pretty in Pink*. Guess whose line?)

The thing is, I think, as I move my mass of wet clothing into the dryer and toss in a limp sheet of Bounce, at least Gerard *has* some goals, even if they are not the kind that people talk about in self-help books or on talk shows. I used to let short-term goals shape my entire life. Make lesson plans. Think of science project that doesn't involve explosions or potential for explosions. Grade reports on mammals of the Northern hemisphere. And now I haven't a single one. This plagues me all the way through the drying cycle, all the way back on the T as Gerard yammers about the new Yves Saint Laurent deodorant, and all the way up my dark staircase and into my drafty apartment. As I am folding my laundry and shoving it into my big, antique dresser, I decide that I must have a goal. What it will be, however, eludes me.

5

Signature Cotton Sleepshirt with Three-Quarter Sleeves in Starlight Blue

I AM ON FITTING ROOM DUTY THIS AFTERNOON, WHICH IS NOT only boring, but has the potential to be quite disgusting. When customers take a handful of panties into a fitting room, we not only have to count the panties, but also take note of what they look like. That's because it's not at all unusual for a woman to wriggle out of her dirty skivvies, put on a new pair under her clothes, emerge with a grin, and hand you five pairs of panties back—the four pairs she went in with and one of her old pairs. Before you know it, she's walked out of the store, and you're left holding a stranger's old, ratty underpants, often complete with mystery stains. I've seen period panties and worse. Fitting room duty is a job you really, really don't want to have. But Amy, the salesgirl who is scheduled to work with us on Tuesdays, called in sick, and Mary Alice is up front talking to her friends, so that leaves me to hover around the fitting rooms and pray that nothing sneaky is going on behind the pink and white striped curtains.

My new heels are too high, and my legs feel wobbly today, so when I'm sure that Mary Alice isn't looking, I plunk down on a tiny, spray-painted gold footstool with faux-antique styling, and longingly watch her talk to her friends. I don't envy very many things about Mary Alice. I am satisfied with my long, dark brown hair and light brown eyes, and I never wish for her ashy blond hair color, light blue eyes, and pink-lemonade complexion. I'm glad that I'm fairly compact—just a shade over five feet one inch—and don't have the height and hips and shoulders of Mary Alice, who isn't fat but is broad and solid and manages to lumber like a truck driver even when wearing a neatly tailored Ann Taylor suit. I don't covet her boyfriend, a dopey-looking guy who services cash registers for a living. I don't envy her devotion to her position, her feeling that we sell quality merchandise, or her un-wavering belief that the company knows best.

But I am envious of all of her friends, who come to visit her periodically in the store on days we are not busy. I'm not en-vious of *these* girls specifically; most seem rather dull, blath-ering on about new, themed bars downtown, where people spill out onto the sidewalks and all the men wear identical khakis and polo shirts. I strongly dislike one friend in partic-ular who works as an administrative assistant for an ad agency in the gigantic Hancock Tower across the street. Her name is Shelley, and she is like a five-year-old without the charm or impulse control; she shrieks and rips through the merchandise whenever she visits and leaves the store a wreck, with bras strewn every place like they'd be in a soror-ity house. But even Shelley's behavior doesn't curb my wist-fulness as I watch Mary Alice joke around by the thong table with her pals, because I don't really have any female friends.

Well, I have them, of course, but none are nearby. Certainly not near enough to drop in and spare me from putting S, M, and L stickers on pajama tops for a little while, anyway. After sticking it out in Boston for a few years, my friend Annie decided she couldn't stand one more winter here and headed for Arizona, where she teaches sixth-grade English outside of Tempe. My friend Melinda married and moved to a giant, rambling farmhouse in Vermont, where she promptly gave birth to twins. Hers was the first set of twins born in Vermont in the new millennium, which netted her a free year's worth of cloth diapers from a hippie-run company in Bennington. A dear friend from grad school named Deirdre stayed in Boston but got very involved with The Forum. She repeatedly begged me to attend a meeting, and I finally relented, mainly because I hadn't seen her in so long and was hoping for a chance to catch up. Boy, was I misguided. At the end of the meeting, they all surrounded me and wanted to know when I could come to another one. I stammered that I had left my date book at home (this sage advice came courtesy of Gerard), and several of them insisted that they would drive me back to my apartment so I could run up and grab it. Deirdre was one of the eager ones in the crowd that encircled me, and I promptly severed our relationship.

Of course, my friends and I talk on the phone. But because of my retail schedule, I'm often free when everyone else is working, or vice versa. So there isn't a great deal of female companionship in my life, and I don't think that thrilling to Janeane Garofalo's character sassing back to Larry Sanders during my nightly TV watching counts. Come to think of it, there isn't a great deal of male companionship either—well, naturally, there is Gerard, and Steven Tyler, and Joe of Joe's Joke Shop, but none of these men are the kind who'd inspire me to model something sexy I used my employee discount to buy. Even Chaka Khan is male. I've been back to the aquarium twice since naming her, only to become suspicious that she is really a he. I started to wonder when I began thinking about the size of the penguin (large), the behavior (aggressive), and the X-rated scene I witnessed (some no-nonsense mounting of a more diminutive penguin). It appears I've struck out in more than one species.

When two pre-teen girls come out of the fitting room, I take their merchandise, carry it to the register to ring it up, and gasp aloud when I notice Allan meandering around the front of the store. I see Mary Alice leave her group of three pals, walk over and do a quick check-in with him, and amble back to her friends. She leans on the rack of new silk body-suits with painful-looking snaps in the crotch and babbles away as I watch him. The cheaper looking of the two pre-teen girls says, "Hell-o!" and shoves her credit card in my face, pouting at me because I was momentarily distracted from ringing up her mint green bra-and-panty set. I finish the transaction and hand the credit card back to her, saying thank you but thinking, *You rude thing. If you talked to me that way in my classroom, you'd be dead.*

I stay behind after the girls leave, watching Allan look at and touch a few items with a bewildered expression. I don't want to bolt out from behind the register and fall all over him, so instead I lean back against the counter and play it cool. Under his unbuttoned, black wool coat, he is wearing a deep gray V-neck wool sweater that looks soft and expensive and brown trousers. The picture of natural, understated style stranded in this sea of man-made muck. After a few minutes, he leaves the store, and as I pull out the Employee Binder to see who can fill in for Amy later, I decide that I have a goal. I will get to know Allan. I will keep an eagle eye out for him, flirt with him, and perhaps someday I will have a reason to use my employee discount on something feminine and frilly after all. I have no lesson plans to do anymore, but that doesn't mean I'm no good at planning.

———

"Are you thinking of getting a manicure?" I turn with a start to see Steven Tyler standing next to me, holding two plastic bags from 7-Eleven and smiling.

"No, I'm not really the manicure type," I answer, pulling off my brown mitten and studying my short, stubby fingers and short, stubby fingernails that have been bitten down to the quick. I slide the mitten back on. "I've never even had one, actually. I just like to watch these women while I'm waiting for the light to change," I explain, nodding at the Awesome Nails storefront. This nail salon has been on this street as long as I have, but I never had occasion to take notice of it until about six months ago. While standing in this very spot one afternoon, I looked in past the hideous neon sign in the shape of a manicured hand holding a rose, and I saw something one doesn't usually associate with a walk-in, $10 nail salon. Along with the standard wall-mounted display of hundreds of shiny bottles of nail polish, the dated, '80s-style posters featuring garishly manicured hands clutching fistfuls of hundred-dollar bills and flowered oriental fans, and rows of dark-haired women leaning over the hands and feet of customers, there were several wall-mounted TVs. But these TVs weren't tuned to *Judge Judy* or a rerun of *Cheers* or any other type of show you'd think would be the appropriate mindless visual accompaniment to the manicure experience.

No, each and every TV was showing CNBC. The ticker crawled across the bottom of the screen displaying the NYSE and NASDAQ stock prices in cryptic numerals and decimal points and up-and-down arrows that quickly skidded by. A man with a conservative haircut and a navy blue suit talked about something I couldn't hear, but his unsmiling expression suggested that it was fiscal in nature. The stoplight changed, and I crossed the street, thinking it had to be some kind of mistake. But then I noticed that these TVs were *always* on and *always* tuned to CNBC. And the tiny Vietnamese

girls and women of all ages (I am pretty sure the Awesome
Nails is a Vietnamese-owned business; the door is painted
with "Trang Nguyen, Proprietor" in flaking, gold script, and
I had not one, not two, but three bright-eyed Vietnamese
girls all named Trang Nguyen in my classes) constantly
looked up at the screens. They would pause mid-clip with
the cuticle nippers and squint at the TV, then turn back to
their customers. I've become fascinated by them, wondering
if they all own a staggering amount of stock and are just
waiting to hit it big and hightail it out of this dingy salon. I
like to imagine the eldest one, a woman with a deeply lined
face, messy bun, and ever-present pastel-flowered house-
dress (Trang herself, perhaps?), throwing down her bottle of
base coat forever and retiring to St. Barth's with her new-
found fortune.

"I like to watch them because I wonder why they always
have the TVs tuned to CNBC," I admit. "It's just business
news. Of all the TV stations in Boston, why that one?" I ask,
still staring into the salon. He peers past the neon sign in the
window and twirls the handles of the plastic bags on his fingers absently, then starts to lace his hands together as though
he's about to play a game of Cat's Cradle with the handles.

"You should ask," he suggests, dropping one of the bags
on the ground and scratching between the collar of his
leather jacket and his olive-green scarf, exposing a few inches
of one of his scars.

"No, no thanks," I say, yawning. It's the end of a long
day, and I suddenly don't care about the financial fate of our
manicurist neighbors. "I'm sure their answer won't be nearly
as exciting as the one I've imagined, and I don't want to be
disappointed." He smiles at this and picks the bag up off
the ground. "Heading home?" I ask hopefully, gesturing toward our building. Today was dreadfully dull at the store,
and I'm in the mood to see some homemade guitar picks or

Chocolate-Chocolate Brownies or talent show photographs lovingly packaged up for Steven Tyler.

"No, I'm on my way out," he answers, totally unaware of just what a high point his mail is for me some days. He walks off toward the T station, and I peer in once more to the Awesome Nails, just in time to catch a manicurist with a long, black braid and sky-blue leggings, staring at the TV open-mouthed as she pumices her customer's heel.

"Oh, you poor thing," I whisper, pressing my face to the glass. "You *are* truly misunderstood." The octopus shifts ever so slightly from his corner spot where he's curled into a tight little ball, and I can see into one of his sad eyes. I reread the old, chipped enamel sign that's been bolted to the wall next to the tank. In a dated, lumpy typeface, it explains how octopi have been given a bad reputation in books and movies, and how they are actually very shy and retiring creatures that just happen to look terrifying. Just as I finish reading, he unfurls one of his tentacles into the tank, and I jump back slightly. I smack hard into a woman and immediately begin apologizing, even before turning to face her.

"I'm sorry," I say quickly, assuming it's a young mother with an infant in a stroller, and that the ensuing dirty look she will shoot my way as we continue to pass by one another throughout the aquarium will sully the rest of my visit. But to my surprise, it's an aquarium employee; a woman in a blue New England Aquarium polo shirt, whom I've previously seen around the starfish pond and the shark area. I recognize her instantly because she has what Gerard calls an STLB, or "Short Top Long Bottom." Most people would refer to it as a mullet; it's spiky in the front and short on the sides and cascades to the bottom of her neck in a messy bunch of layers. I'm fascinated by both the cut and the strength of her coiffure convictions. This is someone who chose a look and stuck with it, naysayers be damned.

"No problem," she says, unruffled. "It happens." She looks over at the octopus tank. "Especially with this one here. When he makes sudden moves, people freak." She speaks in a deliberate and businesslike way, as if she's reporting the news. "I've seen you around here a lot," she adds, putting her hands in the pockets of her khakis, which are held up on her stout form with an unnecessary braided leather belt. "I hope you have a membership," she chuckles.

"Actually, I don't," I say quietly. I can't afford it.

"Well, you should," she replies forcefully, leaning in toward me and nodding. I decide immediately that I like Sue (as her plastic, fish-shaped name tag reads), with her no-nonsense conversation style, broad Boston accent, and open, welcoming body language. She sees me glance at her nametag and introduces herself. "Sue," she says, grabbing my hand and pumping it up and down. "Sue Fisher."

"Really?" I ask, astounded. "Your last name is Fisher?" We move a few steps away from the octopus tank as a small group of schoolchildren make their way toward the hapless creature.

"Yeah, what about it?"

"Well, it's got the word 'fish' in it," I explain, trying not to offend. "And you work in an *aquarium*. It's just a funny coincidence, that's all."

"Well, if that doesn't beat all!" she exclaims, shaking her head and looking at an imaginary spot on the damp floor. "You know, I never thought about that? Can you believe it?" I actually can believe it; I had a similar conversation in grad school with a dermatologist whom I had the misfortune of visiting no less than six times after using a trial sample of a so-called "herbal" body wash. My skin was covered in a pink, velvety rash that itched so badly my roommate caught me attacking my back with a fork one evening. When student health services referred me to a Dr. Patrick Hyde, I burst out laughing in between bouts of feverish scratching, and at my first visit, I asked him what it was like to be a skin doctor with a name that sounded the same as "hide." As in, skin. He put down his magnifying mirror and his jaw dropped open.

"I can believe it," I say to Sue. "You have your name your whole life; you don't think about it. My name is Moxie," I add, smiling but thinking, please don't ask me too much about it.

She reads my mind and says, "Like the soder. Very nice. I like it. Well, Moxie, I've got fish to feed and exhibits to check out, so it was nice to meetcha," she finishes briskly.

"Are you a marine biologist?" I ask excitedly, even though it's clear she needs to leave. The idea of someone spending her working hours with fish and assorted sea creatures is enough to make me hysterical with envy.

"Hell, no!" she laughs. "Feeding and general care and maintenance. Fell into it after volunteering here when I was younger. I don't have the head for the science stuff. But they saw that I worked hard and was good at keeping things up, so here I am." She gestures around, scratches her mullet, and then looks at her watch. "Hope to see you around soon, Moxie."

After Sue shuffles off, I head downstairs to check on Chaka Khan. He's still there, cocky as ever, hopping around on the stones and strutting his stuff. Perhaps Sue will let me get close to Chaka Khan someday, I think, as a lost-child announcement blares out over the PA system. Allan first, though, I decide, catching myself. I need to get close to Allan first. Penguins are plucky and cute but I doubt they'd be much fun at the movies. Or in bed.

6

Seamless Sheer Black Hose with Floral-Lace Garter Belt

WE HAVE A MOUSE PROBLEM. IT'S NOT REALLY A SURPRISE; IT'S getting well into November now, and the furry little creatures don't like scampering around windy Copley Square any more than I do. So they've found their way into the mall, undoubtedly the same way that countless ancestors have done before them. I've seen them out of the corner of my eye lately as I sit in the stockroom and lean back to rest my head on the wall with the OSHA regulations poster pinned to it. They flit by, their tails waving, and disappear into an invisible place where the floor and wall meet, behind the panty bins. I'm not bothered enough to try and chase my new, fuzzy co-workers, and even if I were, I doubt I would be fast enough to outrun them.

Mary Alice, however, is evidently quite bothered, as I've heard her on the phone complaining to our home office, her voice getting higher and reedier as she describes the fate that might befall all of our merchandise if the stockroom were overrun with rodents. Judging by the one side of the conversation I can hear, they tell her that this is the mall's problem to fix. So she calls the mall's maintenance office, and they claim that no, this falls under the jurisdiction of each company's individual store. She can't win, and I feel sort of sorry for her.

It's nine-thirty and we're set to open the store in thirty minutes; the cash register is spitting out the day's directives and I'm refolding some cotton pajamas that weren't folded last night when Mary Alice lets out a giant scream. She's in the stockroom, and I'd bet my paycheck that I know what the problem is. Sure enough, when I round the corner, Mary Alice is standing on the fifth step of the rolling ladder that we use to reach the highest boxes of merchandise. And on the floor is a slow-moving bra. It's from our new full-coverage line, with large, lightly lined cups and wide straps covered with embroidered daisies. It's shimmying ever so slowly across the floor, with one cup inching forward and slowly dragging the other one behind it, like a car on a trailer hitch. I start laughing, and she glowers down at me from her high perch.

"I'm sorry, Mary Alice, it just looks funny," I say unapologetically. Now the bra is wiggling this way and that, as the poor mouse flails around in one of the cups, trapped in all that padding and polysatin. I reach down and gently pick up the daisy-enhanced monstrosity by one of the straps, and the bewildered little guy blinks a few times and races to the spot behind the panty bins. Mary Alice waits a few seconds before wobbly descending, and I watch her as she tries to keep an eye simultaneously on the spot that the mouse scurried toward and the narrow steps of the ladder.

"We've got to be more careful with food around here," she says firmly as we walk back out to the store. I'm thinking that she's the only one who frequently snacks in the stockroom, when I see Naomi standing patiently outside the locked glass doors. Thank goodness, I say to myself, as I walk over to unlock the door. When my alarm went off this morning, I was so sleepy that I mistakenly washed my hair with a tube of Thierry Mugler body lotion that Gerard had left in my bathroom as a little surprise. It wasn't until I was just ready to step out of the shower that I realized that my wet hair was hanging in slimy sheets, and I had to lather, rinse, and repeat all over again. I still feel exhausted and am not up to unpacking the new shipment of winter robes today; I loathe having to pierce the thick terry fabric with the two-part plastic sensors that make the detectors chirp if someone tries to make off with something. I hate battling with the pin and the backing, and the infernal *click* of the two pieces connecting makes my hair stand on end. Luckily, Naomi is willing and able to do such tasks; she's a Northeastern University student with a hardy work ethic and a penchant for sexy sleepwear, so she was drawn to the job for the 35% discount and the flexible work hours.

After I get Naomi settled with the robes, I go behind the counter and study the cash register paper. Not too many in-store changes today: Change mannequin to feature signature cotton sleepshirt SKU N-734452 in color of manager's choice. Display cozy slippers SKU C-114397 in window according to in-store availability. Feature new low-rise V-strings, in winter colors, on panty tables. And at the bottom, this weirdly worded directive:

NEW TERRY ROBES:
FACTORY MISMARKED SIZES.
L SHOULD BE M, M SHOULD BE S.
S SHOULD BE XS.
PLEASE INFORM CUSTOMERS.

It takes me a minute to translate this, and then I realize that it essentially means that unless we think of a way to correct this problem, we will very soon have a store full of women in tears because they normally wear a size S and suddenly are being forced to don an M. For a company that preys on how women perceive their bodies, this seems like an enormous oversight. And "informing customers" one at a time doesn't feel like a very efficient way to handle these mismarked garments. I grab rolls of XS, S, and M stickers and an indelible black pen and head back into the stockroom to see Naomi. She is sitting on the floor, wearing a Walkman and tearing the robes from their polybags. The air is thick with the acrid smell of plastic.

"Hey," I say, tapping her on the back. "There's a problem with the sizing on these. Take this," I order, holding out the pen and rolls of stickers, "and these." She slides her headphones around her neck and dutifully takes them from me. "If something is marked 'Small' on the tag, put an 'XS' sticker on the pocket. If it's marked 'Medium,' put an 'S' sticker on it. And if it's marked 'Large,' put an 'M' sticker on it. Then use this pen to ink out the original size on all the tags. OK?"

"But this one says 'Medium,'" she says bemused, holding up a pink terry robe and showing me the tag inside the collar.

"I know. But it's really a small. So we need to pretend it's a small."

"But it's a medium," she repeats.

"Yes, but we need to call each one the size below it. So what's marked medium becomes a small, and so on." She looks confused and silently shows me the 'medium' tag again, and I suddenly realize that this conversation is getting dangerously similar to the one in *This Is Spinal Tap*, in which Christopher Guest's character keeps explaining why the band's amp goes to eleven. "Look," I say in what I hope is a more patient tone, "I know it's a little confusing—it took me a few minutes to figure it out. Why don't you start, and see how it goes." It's only bathrobes, after all.

I walk to the front of the store and focus intensely on a spot in the near distance as I think about how I could have called on my teaching expertise to explain the sizing situation in a better way, when someone appears in front of me. It's Allan, looking adorably pink-cheeked from the wind.

"Hello!" he says warmly. "Are you admiring the view from here?"

"Oh yes, it's quite breathtaking," I deadpan. "Especially at dusk. You should see the sun set over the Watch Hut," I add, nodding to the kiosk in the middle of the mall, over by French Connection. "Sometimes even the people from the Crate and Barrel come down to watch it."

He laughs raucously and steps into the store and does that same thing he does every time, where he chooses a place to look that won't make him seem like a pervert. This time he picks the rack of dowdy-looking rose-patterned gowns, a loss leader that I am convinced was only designed to appease the CEO's mother. I watch him look at the gowns and notice how green his eyes are. Then he turns them on me and says, "I get the feeling you're a little clever to be doing this job. Am I right?"

"Thank God you get that feeling," I say, genuinely grateful. I lean against the thong table and take a furtive look around for Mary Alice. "I think if they could train a robot to do this job, they would," I confide in him.

"Oh, that can't possibly be true," he protests. "A robot can't match colors and things like that." He smiles and arches an eyebrow. He's clearly waiting for some kind of explanation about why I'm stuck in this climate-controlled shopper's paradise, and I'm trying to decide how much to share.

"I used to be a teacher," I say softly as I look around. I'm always afraid that a parent, teacher, or administrator from my old school will see me and think, holy shit, what happened to that girl? "And . . . it didn't work out. So I'm . . . taking some time to figure out what to do next." This isn't entirely true, but it's close enough.

"I understand totally," he says too quickly. "Sometimes you've got to recharge, right?"

"Sure, recharge," I say wearily. If that's what Allan wants to call this, that's fine with me. "So are you shopping today?" I ask, suddenly thinking that this question must make me sound awfully grandiose, as though he might not be shopping, but has come here with the express purpose of visiting me.

"Yes, and I can use your non-android eye," he answers, grinning at his own joke. "To pick out a gift for the cold months ahead."

I sell Allan a new terrycloth robe, fresh from Naomi's pile, and mash it into our biggest gift box available. Despite the special folding technique I learned as part of my training, the plush fabric keeps squishing every which way, and as he helps me force the top onto the box, our fingers touch. His are warm, and I can barely concentrate as I work the register and tear off his receipt. And it isn't until almost an hour later, long after Allan has left the store, long after Naomi has hollered, "Aha!" from the back room when she finally grasps the sizing problem and its solution, as I'm on my way to meet Gerard for lunch and to hear today's Adventures in Retail, that I realize I have a huge crush on a man who is buying lingerie for someone else.

———

"All right. Let's go over this one more time."

"There's nothing more to go over, Gerard. I told you everything I know," I say, holding my palms up in the air and shrugging. I am sitting cross-legged and fully clothed in Gerard's bathtub as I watch him paint his bathroom a glossy, light yellow-green hue, similar to the shiny flesh of a Crenshaw melon. It's a rainy Sunday, and by some miracle, we both have the day off. So we've spent the day in sweatpants, first watching *sex, lies, and videotape* on DVD together (until I couldn't stand to hear Gerard's blissful moaning over James Spader anymore and retreated to the bedroom to thumb through old copies of *GQ* at Gerard's behest, in hopes of finding someone who looked like Allan), then eating pizza, and finally settling in the bathroom with the painting accessories and little can of Benjamin Moore.

I stand up and reach behind the shower curtain to open the window wider, and a chilly breeze enters the tiny bathroom, making Gerard shudder. "You don't need to do that, it's low-odor paint," he says, picking up the can and showing me the label.

"Just because it's low-odor doesn't mean it's not bad for you. You still need ventilation, even though you can't smell it," I reply, settling back into the tub.

Gerard dumps some paint in the paint tray, loads up the roller, and begins painting the long wall, laying down a few slick swaths of color before saying, "So. What do we know? We know that he's got a job where he can visit a mall in the middle of the day. We know that he isn't married."

"I don't *think* he's married. He doesn't wear a ring." I made sure to check during Allan's last visit. It was very easy to surreptitiously do as he paid for his pink terry robe; you tend to absentmindedly watch customers' hands anyway as they fish through their wallets and purses for cash or credit cards, so looking for a telltale band was no problem. "But who knows? Oh, Gerard, please say you're going to remove the switch plate cover. It's so easy," I plead, just as he slides the gooey, paint-filled roller right over it. A split second later the bathroom goes dark; he's now flicked the switch into the off position to paint over the area he couldn't reach before. He carefully flips the switch back up with one finger, wipes his finger on his sweatpants, and looks up to see the expression on my face.

"Moxie, some people are the type to take the cover off before they paint," he explains in an exasperated tone. "And I'm just not that type, OK?" This is a rhetorical question if ever there was one; I know Gerard inside and out, and I am certain beyond a doubt that he is not that type. When he came out shortly after finishing college, his mother and wealthy new stepfather were so intent on supporting his lifestyle decisions that they set him up in a spacious condo, deep in Boston's South End. They bought it for a song—mainly because at that time, the area still bore the deep battle scars of poverty and drugs and failed plans for inner-city rehabilitation. But stepdaddy Hank didn't make millions in real estate by being unobservant, and the light, tentative sprinkling of trendy restaurants and floral shops suggested to him that something much better was on the horizon.

Soon enough, the area flourished, Hank more than quadrupled his investment, and Gerard found himself living smack in the center of Boston's stylish, tidy gay Mecca. An up-to-the-minute clothing boutique on one side of his condo, an art gallery on the other—and in the middle sits Gerard, who stubbornly remains very much the pig he always has been. The exterior of the condo is lovely, of course, but no one would ever confuse the interior with something from *Will & Grace*—it's more Willfully Graceless. He has no use for the coordinated soft furnishings and textiles that fill the storefronts in his neighborhood. No use for the expensive California Closets system that Hank had installed—his clothes just end up in a messy heap next to the bed, until the heap grows so unwieldy that he can't see his clock-radio without sitting up in bed, and it necessitates an emergency visit to the Cuddle 'n' Bubble. And no use for the petty temporary removal of a switch plate cover.

"All right, forget it," I say, closing my eyes. The lids feel heavy, my eyes grainy, even though the most strenuous thing I've done today is pry open the can of paint. "So let's assume he's *not* married, then. So the lingerie is for a girlfriend."

"Could it be for him?" he asks. He sticks his tongue out as he concentrates on twisting the roller just so, in order to keep from getting paint on the mirror over the sink. I'm about to mention something about putting masking tape over the mirror, but then think better of it.

"No way. We get that type in the store, and he's not it. Also, everything he buys is a size small. No, wait—medium," I correct myself, thinking of the robe he bought and then remembering the sizing snafu. "No, no, it's small," I say, correcting myself once more as Gerard rolls his eyes.

"Small, medium, who cares?" he asks impatiently. "The point is that he's in there flirting with you and buying lingerie for someone else. I don't know what to make of that, but I do know that no one would say that it is good and healthy for you to have a crush on someone like this."

"'Good and healthy'—you sound like Luttman. It's bad enough that I need to see him soon. Don't you start analyzing me, too," I retort as we both turn to see YumYum gingerly move to dip her paw into the paint tray. YumYum was a tiny, malnourished stray that Gerard valiantly rescued from near a dumpster behind the mall. Although she is a sentient creature, this cat bears the distinct appearance of something hastily assembled from a children's craft kit: Two googly eyes, unevenly spaced. A white, asymmetrical muzzle that brings to mind soggy pompons glued on without regard to proportion or size. Bristly whiskers at all different lengths, like miniature pipe cleaners snipped unevenly. And a mountain of chunky gray fur, sticking up at peculiar angles like bits of canvas-backed acrylic plush.

"No, YumYum!" we both shout at the same time, as Gerard tries to swoop in and knock the tray away. He is too late; her paw lands squarely in the paint, and all our yelling serves to do is send YumYum from the bathroom flying, leaving tiny yellow paw prints all over the hardwood floors. I sigh as I look at the ones right outside the bathroom, realizing that these prints will remain until Gerard moves from this place someday.

"I think I need to go undercover," Gerard decides, setting down the roller and sitting on the closed toilet lid. "I need to get a look at the two of you in action." His eyes light up, and I know it's at the prospect of hiding stealthily in the store, possibly in disguise.

"No, I'm not ready for that level of research," I say firmly, standing up as I picture him in a fake nose and glasses, teetering on his haunches behind a chemise display. "I'm not even sure he's flirting with me. It can be hard to tell sometimes." This was, hands down, the topic I dispensed the most advice about during my short tenure at Brookline Middle School. When we weren't talking about the properties of boron or seeing what we could culture in a petri dish, many kids would solicit my opinions about all sorts of other topics before class started and in between classes, when the noisy halls were teeming with students, and I would loiter outside my classroom door. Girls were usually more apt to do this, and their questions always sounded eerily similar: "Miss Brecker, Ted said he liked my shoes today. Do you think he likes me?" "Miss Brecker, Javier told Melanie to tell Andrea to tell me that he's going ice-skating this weekend. Does that mean he likes me? Should I go?" "In cooking class, Brandon said my soufflé looked like what his dog threw up last weekend, but he was totally smiling when he said it. Do you think he likes me, Miss Brecker?" I would always say the same thing: It's often hard to know what boys are thinking. And sometimes even *they* don't know what they are thinking. So just try to have fun, and don't think too hard about whether or not they like you. Don't worry, because you'll know in due time.

Allan is easily twenty years older than the pimply objects of these girls' affections. And I'm not far behind. So why does it seem so hard to take my own advice?

———

I wake with a start today, in the midst of a recurring nightmare about angry customers yelling at me and threatening to have me fired. In reality, this has only happened once. A customer was trying to return a very costly peignoir set—a chemise and matching robe, both made from creamy silk and lace. It's one of the better made, more delicate items we sell, and also one of the few items that requires us to be vigilant about attempted returns. It's one thing for a customer to resignedly sigh but still decide to purchase a flowered flannel nightie with a tiny ink stain on the breast pocket or a pair of lounging pants with a few loose threads around a seam. It's quite another for someone to drop a sizable amount of cash on a sexy something for her wedding night, only to find that one of the embroidered roses on the robe's belt is missing.

Or to discover an unseemly stain, which was the ultimate reason for the one-time threat. This woman was attempting to return the $169 set, claiming that yes, she tried it on for her new husband on their honeymoon, but he just didn't like it. When Mary Alice and I took both wrinkled garments from the box and began to examine them, I nearly gagged when I saw a white and murky stain, about the size of a small plum, on the front of the chemise. Near it were some other drips in the same suspicious color. I turned to show it to Mary Alice, but the phone rang just then, and she had gone to answer it, leaving me on my own.

I cleared my throat and calmly told the woman that we couldn't accept this return. I explained to her that we'd be happy to offer her some in-store credit, but that there was no way we could sell this garment to someone else. Her nostrils flared and she thumped her Coach bag on the counter, leaning in over it to try and intimidate me. "What is your name? Why can't I return this?" she asked loudly, sticking her face in mine. The line of customers had grown very long while Mary Alice and I had been first studying the peignoir set; now her booming voice caught everyone's attention, and they shifted around to try and get a better look at what was happening up at the counter. "My name is Moxie," I answered evenly. "Moxie Brecker." The same Moxie Brecker who single-handedly broke up the famous Brookline Middle School Halloween Food Fight, and she isn't going to be bullied by a customer with a stained chemise and an overpriced handbag. "And you can't return this BECAUSE YOUR HUSBAND CAME ON IT." The women in line erupted into laughter and the customer went white with rage. She grabbed the box and raced from the store, swearing and sputtering and promising to have me fired. We never heard from her again.

As I lie in bed, I realize that the shouts from the pissy customers in my nightmares are actually people yelling down the street at the Planned Parenthood. This is unusual; my windows are closed and the ambient street noise of a weekday morning in downtown Boston usually drowns them out. I pull on my hooded sleepshirt and walk to the window, open it, and stick my head out. I turn my ear in the direction of the commotion and hear shouting, shrieking, singing. And finally, what must be a Boston Police cruiser, its siren set in slow, *whooop-whooop*, non-emergency mode.

After showering, watching TV, leafing through the latest copy of *Scientific American*, and pulling on my sweater, skirt, and dreaded pantyhose-and-pumps combination, I'm ready to head to the mall for my two-to-ten shift. After quickly sifting through Steven Tyler's packages (just one today, but all the way from Alaska!), I check my watch and realize that I can fit in a quick trip to Joe's Joke Shop. Since my painting date with Gerard last week, I've been hankering to see him in a fake nose and glasses.

"Hi, Joe," I say a few minutes later, stepping into the store. He is seated behind the counter on a high stool, where he likes to survey his kingdom of stink spray and trick gum and snakes in cans.

"Moxie, Moxie, sweet and foxy!" he says, smiling. "Long time, no see. You working hard? Or hardly working?" He cackles at this joke, which he has used on me no fewer than fifty times. I always laugh, not because the joke is funny, but because he uses it so often and derives such joy from it. But I think he interprets this as encouragement, and so we are endlessly trapped in this cycle.

"I came to shop today, Joe," I announce, putting my hands on my hips and scanning the store. Christmas is just over a month away, and he's obviously begun gearing up, with lumps of coal for $4.99 apiece and a farting Santa. "I need a fake nose and glasses."

"For you, anything. I've got just the thing," he says, slowly climbing down from the stool and walking over to a display rack with disguises. He pulls a bagged item down from one of the long silver pegs and hands it to me for inspection. It's precisely what I have in mind: oversized hooked nose, thick-framed plastic glasses, and bushy Groucho eyebrows.

"This is it! Another satisfied customer. How much?"

He waves my request away and walks back to his stool. "Bah," is all he says in response.

"Thanks, Joe!" I exclaim, pleased. I can't even imagine what type of punitive action would be taken if someone ever *gave away* any merchandise at my store. There's even a name for when merchandise isn't accounted for yet and hasn't been logged as sold: shrink. Shrink is to be avoided at all costs. But Joe is from a time before shrink, before focus groups, before in-store merchandising, before computerized records of every sale, every return, and every exchange zap instantaneously from cash registers to headquarters at the close of every single day. "Hey," I add as I near the door, "what was happening this morning down the street? Did you hear it? At about eleven?"

"Oh yeah," he answers disinterestedly, picking up a stickering gun and opening a box of blister-carded vials of itching powder. "Some man there got inside the circle. Got too close to someone, people started shouting." He sets down the stickering gun to fiercely scratch the back of his neck and casts a suspicious glance at the vials of itching powder. "You know, there's a red circle."

"I know it, yeah," I say. It's a thick, red painted line that arcs around the entrance to the clinic, and it serves to keep protesters at least twelve feet from the entrance. They can stand with their toes right up to that line, but if in a moment of religious or moral fervor, they step over it, they are in trouble. I hate that the line is red; red reminds me of anger and blood, the fury of the people outside the line and the pain of the people within it. I wish it were green or yellow or even orange, my most hated color.

"Well, that's what happened. Some man who is always there flipped his wig, got too close to a girl. So they called the cops, and he got off with a warning." He's talking about too-short pants man, I know it. I sigh and look at the backwards-face novelty clock above Joe's head. It's two minutes of thirty o'clock, and I've got to start my shift soon. On my way out the door, my eye falls on a new item: a pen encased in an enormous plastic piece of dog doo. It's about seven inches long, light brown, highly textured, and at the bottom is a tiny nib. I think there is great potential for this pen, and as I turn it over in my hands, Joe says it's just come in. I should be the first to try it, he adds, and urges me to take it without payment. All I get is another "Bah!" when I attempt to pull out my wallet, and then I'm on my way with my disguise and dog-doo pen.

7

Body Wash Sampler with Matching Loofah and Bath Beads

"HERE, LET ME HELP YOU WITH THAT," DR. LUTTMAN SAYS IN A voice that sounds pained but I think is supposed to sound empathic. I've pulled an unopened box of tissues from off the windowsill and am trying to open them with no success. I've managed to tear away the perforated cardboard top, but piercing the thin, taut plastic beneath is proving impossible with my slippery, tear-soaked fingertips. I hand him the box and wipe my cheek with the back of my hand, watching him do battle with the overstuffed tissue slot and wondering why they make it so hard to open a new box of tissues. Tissues are rarely used for fun, I think as I look out the window and into the bleak clouds. Crying; nose blowing; peanut-butter-and-jelly-face wiping for small children; these are all situations in which you shouldn't be expected to work too hard. I look back from the window to see Luttman holding the box out to me. I take it from him, extract a tissue from its plastic restraints, and blow my nose loudly.

"Sorry," I say quietly, hiccupping and trying to compose myself.

"There's no need to be sorry," he replies, stealing a glance at the clock. We've only got ten minutes left, and my outburst coming so late in the appointment can't be very convenient. I hadn't meant to do it—it took me by surprise just as much as it did him. I began by talking about how listless I still felt, segued into how much I was dreading the upcoming post-Thanksgiving rush with the extended holiday shopping hours and harried customers and twice-daily shipments to unload and sort, and finished when I tasted salt at the corners of my lips and realized I had been crying. I was so good this visit—I was careful to avoid any talk about daydreaming about Edward Norton with his black eye and bloodied face, and I even humored Luttman by solemnly swearing that I would think about going on antidepressants. But when I began putting my frustration about my life into words, everything fell apart, and the next thing I knew, I was gulping and sniffling.

"Moxie, I think you're doing much better. You've gotten used to the stresses of your job. It sounds as though you're having fun with your friend"—he pauses to flip through his notes and looks up triumphantly when he finds his answer—"Gerard. You're doing the meditation and deep breathing exercises. You should be giving yourself a pat on the back."

A pat on the back for deciding that the coral panties and seamless bra looked best on the torso mannequin that sits on the table in the center of the store; yes, that *is* certainly something to be commended for, I want to say to him snidely. Is that truly progress? If it is, then I think I may be even sadder now than I was before I began crying.

This morning is very slow at the store, and to keep myself busy, I've removed several shrink-wrapped bricks of credit card applications from the stockroom and am now refolding each application front-to-back, so the name, address, phone number, and signature fields are the first thing that people see, rather than the last. Presumably, this is to keep them from scrutinizing the annual percentage rate, billing cycle, and late payment fee scale too closely. Mary Alice says that the home office encourages us to fold the applications this way during the Christmas season, because you can sign people up for the credit cards much more efficiently. She also says that you can't sign them up fast enough. It's easy to imagine eager customers, desperate for gifts and short on funds, digging themselves deeper into debt for the chance to lovingly place some satiny britches under the tree. Just last week, a woman opened a charge and proceeded to purchase almost three hundred dollars worth of pajamas and robes and nightshirts, as her infant sat in his stroller sucking on a baby bottle filled with cola. I couldn't help but think that she'd be paying for these items long after they'd disintegrated in the wash, and it depressed me. I'm no monument to money management, but even I know that this card is a bad idea.

That, however, won't keep me from trying out Gerard's stealthy plan, which is why I'm so motivated to get the applications ready. In a flash of brilliance, he suggested that I sign Allan up for a credit card, in order to get his last name, address, phone number, and all sorts of other particulars. Then we can trot right over to the BPL (the Boston Public Library is directly across the street from the mall, creating a funny juxtaposition of conspicuous consumption and stolid bookishness), go online, and learn *ev-er-y-thing*, Gerard said, smacking his lips. I had to admit that this was truly inspired; Allan's habit of always paying with cash is driving me insane, and I haven't been able to devise a way to slip questions like "So, what's your last name, anyway?" or "Say, where do you live?" in between queries like "What size?" and "That doesn't come in pink; how about dusty rose instead?" I smile as I continue to fold the applications back, hoping that Allan comes by today. I look around the store and settle on a very slutty, black, lace-and-tulle babydoll and indulge myself for a moment, imagining Allan ripping it off me. Just as I'm getting to the good part, Mary Alice's voice cuts in.

"No, I'm going from London to Ireland. I have *that* ticket. But I don't have the one from Logan to London. No. That's right. December twenty-sixth." She is twisting the phone cord around her index finger and rolling her eyes heavenward as the poor, faceless airline agent on the other end undoubtedly does the same. From what I could gather from a conversation I heard between Shelley and Mary Alice, a bunch of the girls and their boyfriends are going to Ireland to ring in the New Year. Mary Alice made a mistake when booking her tickets online and only realized when she pulled the tickets from their jacket last week. I feel her pain; the same thing happened to me several years ago when I was en route to the airport and broke into a flop sweat when I realized that my ticket to Los Angeles was actually a ticket to Las Vegas. That was the last time I entrusted my travel agent with anything, the same grown woman who would send me emails that read, "i can get u 2 LA, 4 sure," and "here is a gr8 deal 4 u . . . r u able to do a stopover in providence?" as though she were Prince, penning a sexy new tune about business class and blackout travel days.

"Well, that would be OK, I guess—wait, what? No, I *can't* travel the night of the twenty-fifth, no way. Uh huh. I'll wait." She sighs heavily and turns to me, and I can hear the loud Muzak blaring through the earpiece. "They wanted me to travel on Christmas night. *Christmas night!*" She rolls her eyes again as I excuse myself and walk over to freshen the new push-up bra display. Bras are hateful things to keep looking tidy and crisp; the straps slip and slide around and people never re-hook the backs. They hang at different heights and crooked angles on the hangers, and it makes me think of what the back room at Hef's mansion would look like if every single bunny punched in late one day and was forced to disrobe in a huge hurry.

Of course I know there is no way Mary Alice would travel on Christmas night, I think to myself as I begin to straighten the bras. Mary Alice is a proud Irish Catholic lass, taking her mass and the ever-present Celtic cross around her neck very seriously. Even though I grew up in a predominantly Catholic town, I never met a twenty-something who was nearly as devoted, as churchgoing, as faithful as Mary Alice. I had many schoolmates who went to the obligatory CCD classes and whose front lawns boasted Virgin Marys in bathtubs, but these rituals and symbols always seemed trivial, smaller, less important than the fun trappings of a jolly Santa Claus and the glitter of a decked-out Christmas tree. Many of my friends' parents were quite easygoing and would even let their kids invite me over after the gifts had been opened, so the only little Jewish girl on the block could eat a fat piece of homemade lasagna and sit and play with the huge pile of new toys nestled in the crinkly wads of wrapping paper beneath the tree. More than once, and especially if there was a lot of siblings in the family, I got piled in the car for mass. I didn't mind and even got good at reciting the Lord's Prayer from start to finish. My parents found this a little worrisome but soon came to realize that when I said it, the words fell in a meaningless tumble from my mouth and had nothing to do with religion or Jesus. I committed it to memory the same way I'd committed the jingle for Almond Joy and Mounds bars to memory, so they decided to let it lie. On Earth, as it is in Heaven, Peter Paul Almond Joy's got nuts; Mounds don't.

"Hey, you should see if you can fly Iceland Air," I suggest to Mary Alice after she hangs up the phone. "Gerard flew that airline to London once. He said you can listen to Björk on the in-flight radio station the whole time." Mary Alice gives me a look that suggests she would rather fly in the cargo hold with the drugged pets and pulls the yellow pages out of the low cabinet beneath the cash registers. She reaches for the phone and it rings before she picks it up. She listens for a split second and wordlessly hands me the receiver.

"Moxie? I really need help. Can you take a break?" It's Gerard, sounding panicked.

"Are you all right? What's wrong?"

"Just come to the Au Bon Pain as soon as you can. I prom- ise, I won't keep you away for long. But I need you soon." He seems like he is in pain, and I am frightened.

"Mary Alice, I need to go downstairs for a minute, OK? It's not busy," I add, looking around the store. There is just one customer, a middle-aged obese woman, holding a pale blue chemise against her body and spinning in the mirror. I leave without waiting for her answer.

Three minutes later, I stride into the Au Bon Pain, tired from walking so fast but pumped with adrenaline from worry. When I see Gerard, he is standing awkwardly next to a small table, with one leg crossed in front of the other. He looks . . . fine. Normal. Dressed in brown woolen trousers, a white shirt, and a jacket with a small check. I squint and am still perplexed. I know he had a much-anticipated date last night with a sexy bartender from a trendy, local bar, but surely this can't be the reason for the sudden visit.

"So?" I ask, putting my hands on my hips. "What's going on?"

"Moxie," he says, biting his lip. "I have a problem. I can't work it out by myself." I'm still looking him up and down, trying to assess the emergency.

"If you're going to get sick on me, I will be *really* angry," I warn. This was one benefit of not working in a school anymore. Although pre-teens aren't as likely to puke as elementary aged kids, I still had to deal with my share of vomit now and then, first while student teaching and then as a real teacher. One girl ate too many jellybeans at an Easter party and the resultant lumpy rainbow on my shoes was quite memorable.

"No," he says, turning to the side. Sticking out from inside his pants, right below his waist and above his rear, is a bulky rectangular shape. As though someone has taken a long box of gourmet teabags and shoved them in there. I look at the spot and raise my eyebrows. He inhales deeply through his nose and tries to muster whatever dignity he can.

"It's my Handy Stitch," he says in a loud and clear voice, holding his chin up. Then he is suddenly deflated, dropping his head and slumping. "It said on the commercial that you could stitch clothing while you wear it. I wanted to fix the waistline of these pants. But I couldn't see what I was doing," he continues, frowning. "The next thing I knew, everything was all bound up back there. My underwear is caught in it too, all twisted around. My balls are killing me," he whimpers.

I am unsympathetic. "Gerard, what do we know about ordering from TV?" I cock my head, remembering the ProActiv Solution and the Ronco Chicken Broiler and all the other items Gerard feels he must order when he's up in the middle of the night and consumer bliss seems only a mere phone call away. I'd seen the commercial for the Handy Stitch and knew it was just a matter of time before it was shipped and handled to Gerard's condo. "You know, on that commercial, they show an old lady sewing her *curtains* when they talk about stitching things when they are on you. Curtains, Gerard. Nothing with body parts," I finish, shaking my head.

"I know, I know. But please. I've got to get to work, and I'm in bad shape," he begs. I acquiesce and we head to the employees' bathroom in Neiman's, which we thankfully have all to ourselves. I kneel next to him, lift his shirt, and begin to gently pull the fabric out of the Handy Stitch. It's not as bad as I thought it would be, but it does require a careful, slow hand and is certainly something he couldn't have done alone, with his poor balance on his weak leg. It's very quiet, and the slow drip of the sink is starting to annoy me.

"So how was your date?"

"No good. We went back to his apartment, and he has no books," he says, sharply sucking air in through his teeth as I mistakenly twist the waistband of his underwear the wrong way.

"So what if he has no books? You're too picky. It's not like you're such a reader." This isn't entirely true; Gerard loves to read gay erotica and Archie Comics. He says he strongly identifies with Jughead.

"Also he likes to do puzzles . . ."

"Big deal. It's a boring hobby, but sweet," I say, cutting him off. I throw a long piece of amber thread on the floor. $19.95 for this thing, what a racket.

". . . and then frame the puzzles and hang them on his walls." He looks down at me and smiles.

"OK, enough said," I say, returning the smile. I look down and get back to work. I pull threads and twist fabric in silence for another few minutes until Gerard says, "Moxie, what's wrong with your hair?"

"What do you mean?" I ask, touching the side of my head.

"I mean, I'm looking down at your head, and your hair looks weird. It's like I can see through to your scalp in a few places." He crinkles his nose in distaste and I give a sharp yank on the waistband of his underwear. "Uggggh," he groans, doubling over. "Why'd you do that?"

"Don't talk badly about my hair! My hair is the only body part I am vain about, you know that." It's deep brown, thick, shiny, and free of split ends. I love feeling it cascade down my back when I wear it down, and I relish how it always behaves no matter how I choose to put it up.

"Sorry! I guess I just never studied your head before."

"Well, don't do it again," I warn. Gerard's got a full foot on me; now I'll feel self-conscious whenever we're together, knowing that he can look down at any time and make sweeping pronouncements about my follicles. "My hair is fine. See?" I grab a handful and hold it out from the side of my head. "I think you're all done here," I add tartly, handing him back the Handy Stitch. "Please throw this away. Or, maybe stitch your clothes when you're not wearing them? I've been here too long, and now I'm going to have to apologize to Mary Alice."

"Screw Malice," he spits. This is his bitchy nickname for Mary Alice, which he gave her quite by accident last year when speaking her name too quickly and unwittingly making a contraction of "Mary" and "Alice."

I walk Gerard back to Men's Fragrances and trudge up the steps of the escalator, when who do I see racing down the other side but Catherine. She is wearing a huge, bulky trench coast, and as she sails by, the sides of the coat billow slightly, and I catch sight of dozens of thongs. She's got them in iced mint, platinum, and crimson—all from the Christmas line that arrived earlier in the week. Her cheeks are flushed and her eyes wild, and I am dying to know where she is going with all those stolen panties, but I can't indulge myself. I step off at the top of the escalator and look straight down, where I see her throwing her full weight against the door that's meant solely for handicapped shoppers and racing out of the mall.

"These aren't bad," I say, smiling through the salt that sticks to my chapped lips and sets them stinging and burning. I've just eaten the last of my snack bar French fries, and Sue seems pleased that I'm enjoying my lunch. It's Thursday afternoon, my last day off before we swing into extended holiday shopping hours, and I impetuously decided to spend it at the aquarium. Initially, I went downtown to do some shopping at Faneuil Hall, but the sight of all the holiday shoppers scurrying to and fro with their snowflake-patterned scarves and mittens and little money envelopes made me feel like I was at work, and I turned and fled for the musty security of my favorite hiding place. Sue spotted me as I studied a huge group of fish schooling around the giant ocean tank, and came over to wordlessly watch for a minute or two. Around and around the fish went, their silvery scales flickering in the low light, with every one of their heads and fins moving in perfect unison. We made small talk for a moment and I was about to ask about Chaka Khan when my stomach growled loudly. This prompted Sue to ask me if I wanted to join her for lunch in the aquarium's snack bar, which in turn prompted me to pretend I hadn't heard her, just so she would have to repeat the question and I could hear her say "snack baaah" again.

"Well, this hot dog's pretty rubbery, I'll tell you that much," she says, squeezing the part that's hanging beyond the end of the bun with two fingers. "But for a dollar-fifty, how can I complain, right?" she laughs, shrugging. "It's not like I'm gonna go out for lunch today," she adds, reaching for the plastic bottle of mustard on the table and quickly shooting out a thick stripe of electric yellow on top of the hot dog. "Too damn windy. Shoot, I thought I was going to get blown off the Tobin Bridge today, driving to work in the Corvette."

I stop scrunching up my cardboard French fry container. "A *Corvette*? Is it yours?" I ask politely. I've been sitting stiffly on my red vinyl stool at the snack bar, not exactly sure how to comport myself during this impromptu meal. Sue's invite was so offhand, so relaxed, that it seemed like she invited aquarium guests to dine on salty snack bar treats with her every day of the week. But as I sit opposite a painted mural of a grinning crab with an ice cream cone in one claw and a cheeseburger in the other, I feel strangely formal. I'd only run into Sue once since the time she introduced herself, and our conversation was friendly but brief. Who is this woman, with her lunch invitations to near strangers and her Corvette?

"Oh, yeah, of course it's mine!" she exclaims. "A real beauty. Canary yellow. I got it when my husband left. I *always* wanted one, from when I was young," she breathes, with a faraway look. I instantly imagine her as a teenager, slimmer and wearing a smaller, more stylish mullet, lovingly admiring the car of her dreams in the school parking lot. "So when Dwight hit the road, I said, 'That's it. I'm gonna enjoy every day.'" She takes a swig from her can of Pepsi and nods to another aquarium employee who's taken a seat at a small table in the snack bar, near the corner. He's got sandy hair and what looks like a sloppily repaired hair lip. "Thomas," she says to me, pointing her chin in his direction. He looks up from behind his *Boston Herald* and gives us a cursory nod.

"It sounds like quite a car," I say, not exactly sure how to respond. "I bet a lot of people like getting rides in it?" This seems like a good question, and I am instantly rewarded for my efforts with a huge smile.

"Well, it's only a two-seater. But yeah, of course they do! Except my daughter, Katie. Oh, she squashes right down on the floor of the car on the days I drive her to school. She wishes I drove an SUV like the other moms."

"You have a daughter? How old is she?"

"Thirteen. Thirteen going on twenty-five. She's got a mouth on her these days, too," she says, shaking her head and dropping the last piece of her hot dog in her mouth.

"Oh, I know," I agree, and Sue looks at me askance. "I mean, I know what thirteen-year-olds can be like. I used to be a middle school teacher. So I understand."

Sue crumples up her napkins into a tight little ball and throws it toward the big trash can in the corner, missing by about six inches. She sighs heavily and begins to get up from her stool, but Thomas saves the day by putting down his paper and pitching the ball in the trash. "No kidding?" she asks after she finishes watching Thomas. "You used to be a teacher—why you working in a store?" The last time I talked with Sue, I told her that I sell lingerie in the mall. She loved this and laughed so delightedly at the prospect of helping people pick out panties for a living that I swore the giant turtle looked over at us in anger because she woke him up. Now her blunt question catches me off guard, and my face starts to burn with shame. The way it always does when I look in the mirrors in the fitting rooms and think, You used to be a teacher—why you working in a store?

"Teaching was harder than I thought it would be, I guess," I say quietly, looking intently at the crab on the wall. The artist has blessed the crustacean with very wide eyes and long, curly lashes, giving it a "Who, me?" look, as though it was caught red-clawed while indulging in both an ice cream cone *and* a cheeseburger. "I found it really tired me out. I was sad a lot of the time and felt really cruddy." A ridiculous explanation, of course—but the only one I can give, because it's the only one that's true, even if it's nonsensical. I am waiting for the Luttman look—the expression of disbelief and slight impatience at my problems—but it doesn't come. Instead, she guzzles the last of her soda and says, "Well, what can you do? I can't say I blame you. Some of those girls Katie's age? Total bitches. They make me nuts when they're at my house for three hours. You had 'em all day, five days a week? You should get a *medal*, Moxie."

THE PAJAMA GAME

I hug this kind comment to my chest as I leave the aquarium, and it stays with me fully for the next two days, through a dispute with a customer over whether or not we have stores in London (we don't), through a missing shipment of shortie pajamas that I tracked down at Brookstone, and even through a pile of mouse droppings discovered deep in the panty bin.

8

Low-Rise Hipster in Holiday Plaid (Just Right for Gift-Giving)

THIS THING WEIGHS A TON, I THINK TO MYSELF AS I GRUNT AND adjust the angle of my forearm to get a better grip on the back right-hand corner of the box. When I finish moving my arm, my purse strap slips off my shoulder and slowly slides down the sleeve of my coat until it comes to rest in the crook of my elbow, leaving it dangling annoyingly between my knees. "God damn it!" I hiss loudly.

"Take it easy—it's OK," says Steven Tyler, who has front-end detail and doesn't seem to be faring much better. I can just see the tips of his curly hair over the top of the box and his knees buckling beneath it. "We're almost there," I hear him say reassuringly. When we reach the landing, we unceremoniously let the box drop between us and look at one another. "You're pale. You should sit down," he says, pointing to the step.

"I know; I didn't have time to eat this evening," I complain, sitting and massaging my temples. When it was time for my dinner break, there was such a frenzied crush of customers, that I spent the full thirty minutes on the register inputting SKU numbers and coupon codes and credit card information that I know will haunt me as I fall asleep tonight. The numbers end up etched on the insides of my eyelids, sometimes in a jumble, sometimes falling in linear formation like *The Matrix* screensaver that one of my former students had on his iBook.

"That sucks." He shrugs off his leather jacket and throws it over the banister. "You don't have to help me with these packages, you know," he adds apologetically as he glances down at the label; the return address is Cedar Rapids, Iowa. "Here goes," he says, peeling the packing tape away. I watch his hands as he goes to work; they are dry and chapped, with the cuticles chewed away and big smudges of dark gray on the second knuckle of his ring finger and his pinkie.

"What is it?" I ask excitedly, peering into the box from my seated position on the landing. Packing peanuts are flying everywhere, the static in the dry air sending them momentarily aloft before they cling to his black turtleneck sweater and my pea coat.

"It's . . . it's a *bust*," he says tentatively. "I think it is, anyway." He frees the piece from the last of the Styrofoam and pulls it awkwardly from the box, grimacing. It is an enormous, stone monstrosity, and I think it is meant to be Steven Tyler. If it weren't for the distinctive lips and hair, I'm not certain I would guess correctly. Even with the oversized mouth and stylish locks, it's still not a sure thing. The nose is all wrong, and the eyes are too wide and earnest.

"It *is* a bust," I say, nodding. "In every sense of the word, I think." Steven Tyler laughs aloud at this, sets it on the floor, and scratches his head. We both study the painful piece of sculpture for a long moment.

"What am I going to do with this?" he asks plaintively.

"It's at least eighteen inches high. It's not like I've got a stand all ready for it."

"You know who it really looks like? Carly Simon," I joke, standing up and chuckling at my own wit. "If you want, I can help you carry it in and find a place for it," I say helpfully, nodding toward his apartment door. "I'm feeling better now."

Feeling better and dying to see your apartment so I can glean something about you, I want to add. This is because after sharing an apartment building with Steven Tyler for well over two years, I have no idea what he does all day, and I am consumed with curiosity about it. He seems to come and go as he pleases, never keeping to a set schedule. Often at home during the daylight hours, he freely wanders in and out of the building on the days I have my two-to-ten shift at the store. He doesn't seem to have work clothes of any kind, always preferring his Doc Martens and Converse low-tops and slightly shabby regulation black and navy blue gear.

Gerard and I have probably spent no fewer than a hundred hours pondering it, and he claims that there are only two possibilities: (a) dealing drugs, or (b) trust fund. I rejected the first one outright, despite the menacing scars on his neck and his chewed-up earlobe. Steven Tyler seems too clear eyed and, well, *nice*, to be a drug dealer. More importantly, I've never heard people stumbling in and out of the building at odd hours or scuffling around on the stairs, hallmarks of that sort of business enterprise. When I lived in a dumpy, off-campus apartment during graduate school, two adorable guys on the first floor had a booming business, and were buzzing people into the building at all hours for pickups. Certain customers were so eager to sample their purchases that it wasn't at all unusual for me to spy them getting high in the alley next to the building some evenings. Gerard always enjoyed running into these types of patrons on his way in or out; he would fix them with a withering gaze and say, "Oh, *really*, now."

The second possibility I also rejected, but for reasons that were less concrete and more difficult to put into words. Steven Tyler is what he is, was as close as I could get to a cogent explanation. I never get the sense that he is slumming, taking up residence in this questionable apartment building in a dicey neighborhood just for kicks. Besides, successful slumming really takes a lot of work, and that doesn't seem like his speed, I argued to Gerard. All of the trust-fund people I've ever met usually retain some distinguishing quality that gives them away when you study them hard enough. There was my friend Haley from Greenwich, Connecticut, who looked retro punk in every way, as long as you didn't happen to see her perfectly trimmed and neatly buffed toenails. Although I only caught her in sandals twice, it was quite evident that those feet more likely stepped out of a let's-have-lunch-and-then-go-to-Lilly-Pulitzer world than a Sid-and-Nancy-where's-my-studded-belt world. There was also a kid in my class who *looked* like he was well on his way to the punk lifestyle; he wore torn jeans and sneakers with more holes than canvas, but at age twelve not only knew what a sommelier does, but also how to pronounce "sommelier" flawlessly.

"Oh, gosh, no," Steven Tyler says, hoisting the bust up and groaning. "You did so much just helping me get it up the stairs. I think you need to relax now. Thank you again, Moxie." He smiles and carefully reaches into his pocket, extracts his keys, and opens his front door. I wave and try to peer casually past Steven Tyler and the Steven Tyler bust, but his apartment is dark, and he quickly closes the door behind him. I realize that *The Larry Sanders Show* is probably starting soon, and I bend my arm to look at my watch and become furious when my purse slips down to my elbow again.

———

Where in the hell are those panties? I wonder as I put my hand on my hip and glance around the stockroom for the second time. I thought I'd left them right here on the table, between a box of blister-carded pantyhose and a small shipment of glossy S, M, and L stickers that have yet to be adhered to night-gown and pajama pockets. I slowly and deliberately push up the arms of my sweater, look more closely at the table, and spy an open notebook that wasn't there before. It's our store's official Operations Binder, and its dry chapters cover everything from which way the hangers should face (always with the hook opening toward the right if you are facing the hanger head-on) to how many pieces of tissue paper should be included in a gift box (for small items like bras and panties, one; for larger items like chemises and babydolls, two; and so on). I loathe the Operations Binder, because it saddens me to think that one hundred and fifty pages sandwiched between three rings and two vinyl covers can dictate my entire day, from the minute I turn on the lights to the minute I exhaustedly lock up at night. But this, in fact, is the point of the Operations Binder; it takes not only the guesswork but also any creativity out of the job and our daily tasks. If you aren't sure how many rows of thongs should be fanned out on the thong table in the front of the store, there is neither need nor impetus to do any inno-vative panty placement yourself because it's all in the binder. Mary Alice adores the Operations Binder and even has been known to clutch it tightly to her chest, Marcia Brady-style. (The correct answer to the thong question, by the way, is seven.)

I'm just about to walk back out and break the news to my customer—who will most assuredly be despondent—when a tiny leopard spot catches my eye. Sure enough, the satin, leopard-print panties I'd set aside were hidden under the binder, which Mary Alice must have hastily consulted and then thrown on the table. It is open to Chapter Seven, page Nine: *Returns of Out-of-Stock Merchandise.* I flip the cover closed and grab the panties, the silky polysatin sending a queasy shiver down my spine when it catches on a hangnail on my left hand.

"Vera, today is your lucky day," I announce triumphantly, holding up the panties. They are an XL, one of the few over-size pairs sent in the most recent panty delivery. It's a challenge to lay one's hands on an XL anything in this store; the number of extra-large-size-items included in any shipment is laughably disproportionate to the number of extra-large-size women who hope to surprise their loved ones with a flash of sexy satin and lace but almost always end up leaving the store dejectedly because there is nothing that will fit them. When I unpacked this pair and it unfurled from its polybag, I immediately checked the tag and then stashed it in a small ball on the table for Vera.

Vera is a discerning customer who knows what she likes. She likes long bubble baths and pointy-toed heels, and the fact that I am unflappable in the face of a six-foot, three-inch drag queen shopping for well-fitting lingerie. Whereas Vera makes Mary Alice's spine stiffen, I find her quite relaxing and genuinely enjoy listening to her soft Southern accent as she crows over recent arrivals and thinks aloud as she imagines the outfits she will pair these pieces with. In truth, as far as drag queens go, I prefer The Lady Bunny, who I saw at Wig-stock all four times I attended with Gerard. Although I know in my heart that The Lady Bunny would never shop in a buttoned-down mall in the middle of an even more buttoned-down city, I like to imagine her coming in and choosing items with care, sifting through the merchandise and pulling to-gether something with style and panache. But I am happy to settle for Vera, who may sometimes have a tiny bit of fuzzy stubble on her fingers but is certainly one of our more inter-esting customers.

"Ooh, honey, you know what I like!" she exclaims, holding

them up and studying them with a critical eye. Her manicured nails are neatly painted a deep crimson, and they make
me think of the Awesome Nails, where I spied the girls
watching CNBC this morning as they pushed back their first
cuticles of the day. "Any other patterns?"

"Yeah, but not in this size," I say apologetically. "We
hardly ever get this size; that's why I had to set it aside for
you in the back," I add, nodding toward the stockroom. I see
Kayley and Shondra, two of our new temporary "Christmas
Hires" (as they are called in the Operations Binder), doing
battle with a box of bras, trying to untangle them and place
them on pink, padded hangers.

"Well, I am just so glad you got *these* for me at least," she
says earnestly, fluffing her curly, auburn wig and looking
around the store. "How about large-size bras? That would be
just too much to ask for, I'm sure," she sighs with the resignation of someone who has grown used to not expecting much
from people.

"I'm afraid so. Try the catalog or the Web site; they have
more sizes." If I had a nickel for every time I've dispensed
this advice, I could fly Vera to New York for a shopping spree
in a proper drag store.

"Well, I'm going to take a look around anyway. You never
know what you might find. And don't look now, but one of us
has got a secret admirer," she whispers, jerking her head toward the front of the store, where the new collection of candy
cane-patterned, cotton camisoles and tap pants have been
causing quite a commotion lately. They are quite cute, and I
may even put one aside for myself. We're not supposed to do
this, when merchandise is fresh off the truck, still looking
crisp and sitting full-priced on the sales floor, but I feel em-
boldened by my success in placing Vera's panties aside. "I
hope it's you, because he's not really my type," she adds out
of the corner of her mouth. I turn slowly to see Allan, who is

smiling shyly and looking at the floor. His hair is a bit tousled, and he's got a fluffy, tan scarf bunched around his neck. I look back at Vera, who smiles and silently heads toward the back of the store in what I am sure will be a fruitless search for bras.

"Hi," he says, grinning broadly.

"Hi," I answer as I walk to the front of the store, feeling grateful that I decided to wear this sweater to work today. It's black, a bit tight, and Gerard says it makes my boobs look like two kittens fighting underneath it. This is a compliment, believe it or not.

"I came in to do a little shopping, and you're the best. At helping me, that is," he says, blushing a bit and causing me to lean on the candy cane-patterned tap pant rack because I actually feel a bit lightheaded with this flirtation. "But if you're helping someone else . . ."

"Oh, no; no," I say much too quickly, righting myself and standing firmly next to the rack. "We're all done. What are you interested in?" I ask, pulling my arms taut behind my back and lacing my fingertips together. If the kittens are indeed fighting, Allan should have a ringside seat with a clear view.

"Well, this is pretty nice, right?" he asks, looking at the tap pants and folding his arms in front of his chest. "What do you think?"

"I really like it, actually," I say, smiling and inhaling through my nose. I am inexplicably overcome with the urge to yawn, and my hope is that I can suppress it with some well-timed nasal breathing that won't appear too obvious. "I was thinking about getting it for myself." Now it's my turn to blush, as my mind immediately flashes to the two of us cozy and warm in a big bed . . . where? In a quaint Vermont bed and breakfast, with me in my candy cane ensemble. Yes, that sounds just about right. I practically lick my chops with anticipation.

"That's good enough for me, Moxie. Anything else I should get?" he asks as I find a size small and extricate it from the overstuffed rack.

"Well, you should also get the camisole, I guess, because it's a complete set. Oh, and we have red and white slippers; that would make a good gift."

We stroll over to the cash register, where Mary Alice is furiously punching register keys, ringing up Vera's underwear. Behind Vera is a long line of customers, shifting their weight from hip to hip, impatient to get their polyester gifts home and under the tree. As Vera signs her credit card slip, Mary Alice looks up at me with her eyes flashing; she and I both know that between my drag queen and my crush, I've spent way too much time yammering and shouldn't have left her stranded at the registers. "I have to take a break, Moxie," she says tartly, putting the leopard-print panties into a bag and shoving it at Vera. "You need to ring for a while."

I slip behind the register as she flounces away and heads into the stockroom, mutter something apologetic to the next woman in line, and begin ringing up her black, sequined babydoll. There are about five women behind her, and Allan takes his place all the way at the end of the line. He pulls out a cell phone and begins listening, periodically looking up at the ceiling and pressing his index finger into his other ear when the classical music swells and fills the store with carefully orchestrated string arrangements. I robotically ring up the customers' purchases: a flowered sleepshirt here, a four-for-$21 set of low-rise briefs there; a medium-sized box with extra pink tissue paper here, a small box there. When Allan finally reaches the front of the line, I look up and am overcome with a simple joy when I realize that there is no one in line behind him and Mary Alice is still in the stockroom.

"You know," I begin, gently taking the slippers and garments from him, "you would be a good candidate for our credit card. You would get fifteen percent off today, and all kinds of special offers in the future," I purr, parroting the words I've heard Mary Alice use countless times this holiday season. I slide a specially folded application across the counter at him, and pull a pen from the cup.

"Hmmm. I haven't really got time to read all of this today," he says disappointedly, flipping the application over but not studying it too closely. "What do you think? Do you think it's a good deal?"

Just do it, I say to myself. Tell him it's a great deal, just like Mary Alice told that woman this morning, the one who maxed out two Visa cards already and required more credit to make her family and friends' visions of pajama sets dancing in their heads come true. "Well . . ." I begin, biting my lip and staring at the counter. I glance up from the application to see Allan looking at me expectantly. I clear my throat and realize that I can't do this. "Actually, it's not a very good deal at all. You'd get a better deal from the Mafia, I think," I say ruefully.

Alan bursts out laughing and then quickly clams up when an elderly woman looking at flannel nightgowns shoots him a dirty look as though we're in a library. "The Mafia? Really?"

"Well, I'm not really sure about that. But the APR is really very high, and the late fees are pretty intense," I admit, quickly ringing up his purchases. He absently fingers the application but doesn't look at it and instead seems to be watching me as I remove the hangers, pull off the price tags, and grab two gift boxes. I open up a big shopping bag with a *snap*, put everything neatly inside, and take his crisply folded pile of bills.

"Thanks," he says as I hand the bag to him across the counter. The register is spitting out his receipt, the itemized list of adorable purchases for some woman. I tear it off and he stuffs it in his coat pocket, cocking his head and pausing for a few seconds before speaking again. "And thanks for telling me the truth about the card. See you soon, Moxie."

After I watch him leave the store, I pick up the phone and hurriedly dial Gerard's number. "Neiman Marcus, Men's Fragrances, this is Gerard," he says crisply. "Can you hold?"

"It's me!" I yelp quickly as I hear the click of the hold button, a low buzz of static, and then some up-tempo, brassy jazz. Thirty seconds later the phone clicks again and I hear Gerard's voice. "Well, if you like citrusy top notes, then this one is for you, certainly. Why don't you walk around, smell some other fragrances, and then we'll talk? Sorry for the wait, how can I help you?"

"It's me," I say again. "Is that really true, about the top notes?"

"How the hell should I know?" he whispers. "I just read the marketing info that comes with the stuff."

"I'm just calling to tell you that your friend is a wimp," I sigh. "I almost had Allan signed up for a credit card and I blew it."

"Oh yeah? Well, she isn't such a wimp that she couldn't put a huge piece of *dog shit* in the breast pocket of my coat," he says, a bit more angry than amused.

"What? Oh, that! No, it's a *pen*, Gerard. You can write with it. Don't you like it?"

"Oh yes, I love reaching into my pocket for my T pass and pulling out an enormous turd at rush hour. How long was that in there for?" He doesn't wait for my answer. "All I can say is, just you wait, Moxie," he finishes ominously.

I hang up the phone and studiously avoid meeting Mary Alice's eyes; she's come back from the stockroom and is making a big display of neatening the satin panty display, which is a futile activity if ever there was one. No sooner are satin panties aligned and overlapped at perfect intervals than customers rifle through them and the tabletop becomes a slippery, shimmering mass of fabric. I turn away from her and look in the mirror behind the register, my cheeks freakishly flushed from my flirtation with Allan. I study myself and think about Allan's gratitude for my leveling with him about the credit card. He thanked me for telling him the truth, and I'm starting to wonder if I'm ever going to learn the truth about him.

I can't get up today, and I don't mean that I am sleepy and it is overcast outside and my bed is warm and that all these things are conspiring to keep me home from work. I mean that I actually can't move—every bone, every joint, every muscle in my body has a dull, painful ache. Each time I shift in bed, it feels like a thousand twist-ties around my limbs. Even my hair hurts. But fortunately it is December twenty-fifth, which is just the right time for a Jewish person working a retail job to regroup and spend the day trying to forget the fury of the last few days in the store. Yesterday we sold $47,788.46 worth of merchandise to 1,742 customers, and very few of them behaved in a manner befitting good Christians. I saw two women sparring over the very last tartan plaid flannel gown in size medium, and the loser loudly cursed the winner, involving all of the other shoppers by waving her arms and shouting, "Look, the fucking whore got her nightgown!" I saw a woman pull a glittery, petal-pink thong up over her jeans in the front of the store, spin to look at her butt in the mirror, grimace, then peel it off and throw it back on the table. It was sleeting out yesterday, and all of Boston's downtown streets were covered in a muddy, pulpy slush, which she tracked in on the soles and sides of her boots. Naturally, as she slid the thong on and then off, the fabric grazed the boots and became tinged with a shade of gray-brown that I definitely didn't recognize from the color swatch pages in the Operations Binder.

I spent almost ten minutes in the stockroom looking for a

white, lace bodysuit in an extra small, only to triumphantly return to the sales floor with my Spandex bounty and discover that the woman had grown impatient and left the store. I had an argument with a male customer who strode in and simply handed me an index card with sizes and measurements written on it, fully expecting me to do his Christmas shopping. Judging by the contrast in his age (early sixties) and the measurements listed on the card (size 4; 36–22–34), he was obviously shopping for a mistress or sexy, new trophy wife; and when I curtly informed him that the store does not offer a personal shopping service, he sized me up as though he were seriously thinking about spitting on me.

By two o'clock, there was a towering pile of bras on the floor nearly three feet high, and all seven salesgirls, Mary Alice, and I kept tripping over hangers strewn across the carpet. The panty tables were torn asunder, and we ran out of medium-sized gift boxes. There were screaming children, line-jumpers, and complainers. And shoplifters: when everyone was distracted, Catherine swooped in and took her usual, armfuls of thongs and bikini briefs in every color of the rainbow. Allan was nowhere to be found, and I was relieved. My mascara was smeared, my hair was falling down all over my face, and I was so hot from the combination of the packed store and the running around that I felt atrocious.

My buzzer rings and I slowly lift myself out of bed, walk toward it across the cool linoleum, press the button, and climb back under the covers. A long minute later, there's a knock on the door. "It's open," I croak.

I hear Gerard walk in and then the *thump-thump* of two suitcases being dropped on the ground. He walks into my bedroom, shaking his head. "Look at you. All sick on Christmas. Are you *sure* you can't rally and come to Providence?" he asks, sitting on the bed. He takes off his green gloves with the hole in the right index finger and unbuttons his coat.

"I'm not sick," I retort. It's true; I don't have a fever, sore throat, or stomachache. I'm just inexplicably weak and exhausted, as though I've turned old overnight. "And I don't mind being alone on Christmas, either," I add. I'll talk to my parents at their winter home on Hilton Head Island, watch TV, daydream about Allan, read the book about James Watson that I keep meaning to get to. "Being a Jew on Christmas only seems sad to Christians. It's actually not bad."

He looks at me dubiously. "Well, if you say so," he says. "Although I have to be honest—I am a little jealous, because I'd really love to watch *The New Candid Camera* marathon today. But I've got the TiVo ready, so it'll all be waiting for me when I come back," he finishes happily.

"God deliver us from TiVo," I sigh, putting my hands together in mock prayer and looking heavenward. I finish my plea and play with the ribbon on my yellow, thermal cotton pajamas that I got for $10 with my discount. They were from last season and a major bust; I like them because they are so simple.

"Moxie," he begins apologetically, "I can't stay all that long. I have to get the train at South Station in a little while."

"That's OK. I do have a little 'pre-present' for you, though," I say, pulling open the sticky top drawer of my nightstand. It's a pre-present because when you work retail and your friend works retail, you know that only dopes buy gifts for one another at full price, instead of waiting until the day after Christmas, when everything will be drastically reduced. I hand him the fake nose and glasses mask, and he smiles and immediately gets up from the bed and walks out of the bedroom. He returns two seconds later, holding YumYum's cat carrier in his left hand. It's made of deep teal plastic, has several mysterious-looking stains, and there is a round "Gore/Lieberman 2000" sticker on the top.

"I didn't know that YumYum was so political," I say, peering at the top of the case. The cat begins mewling pathetically at the sound of her name, and Gerard gently slides open the metal latch and opens the squeaky lid. A spindly, gray leg pokes out of the hole as he tears the cardboard header off the plastic bag and pulls out the mask.

"It's true, she does usually like doing things more at the grassroots level," he answers, making me laugh, which causes my ribcage to smart. "Here, I think this will make you feel better," he says, reaching in and freeing YumYum with one hand. He sets her on the bed, where she sits blinking and meowing, and he very gently puts the mask on her. Unlike smarter pets who won't tolerate accessories, YumYum suffers fools gladly and sits placidly with the mask on her face, as we both watch in hysterics.

"Please, please, take it off her," I laugh. "My ribs. Are killing. Me. I can't. Breathe," I gasp in staccato bursts. Gerard removes the mask, drops YumYum back in her cage, and fastens the lid. He buttons his coat and runs his fingers through my hair. "You really look like hell," he says.

"I know. Don't worry. I'll be fine, really. I've been working ten- to fourteen-hour days for almost a week, don't forget."

"I know; I have, too," he says as he slowly gets up from the bed. "Oh yeah, I forgot to tell you. I had a celebrity retail sighting. Rik Ocasek bought some Liz Claiborne junk."

"That's not much of a celebrity," I sniff, unimpressed. "The Cars? I know we can't expect much here in Boston, but you'd think we'd get someone a little more exciting." Although I can't really cast judgment; the closest thing I had to a celebrity retail sighting this season was a brassy, blond local newscaster trying on satin robes, and it wasn't pretty.

"I know . . . maybe someday I'll get to wait on James," he says dreamily, pulling on his gloves. "He's from Massachusetts originally, and his parents still live nearby," he adds, as though he's not told me this at least fifty times already.

"Wouldn't it be great? My favorite man in the world, in a retail setting."

"Don't forget, I've already had a very famous sighting in a retail setting," I say, snuggling down under the covers and resting my head on the pillow. "I saw Billy Corgan in that store at the airport, remember? He was buying a Cookie Monster toothbrush."

"That doesn't count. You weren't *waiting* on him. Someday I'm going to wait on James," he says with finality, as though James Spader were booking his fragrance appointment with fate at this very moment. "Merry Christmas, Moxie," he says, leaning over and kissing me on the forehead. "Don't think about underpants today."

"Don't worry," I promise him as he picks up YumYum's carrier and waves goodbye. Well, I'll probably think about Allan's underpants.

9

Stretch Satin Demi-Cup Bra in Ivory

Pssssssssssht! THE WATER FROM THE PRESSURE HOSE NOISILY hits the rocks in the Penguin Pond, leaving them wet, glossy, and slightly freer of penguin droppings. Virtually all of the penguins are scared of the hose and stay a respectable distance away, peering out from behind the giant center rock area. Except, of course, for Chaka Khan, who is playfully thrashing around near Sue as she awkwardly maneuvers around in hip waders and sprays the rocks. "Get outta here," she growls, squeezing the nozzle on the trigger and aiming the hose about a foot away from Chaka Khan, which causes me to gasp loudly and makes Chaka Khan swim hurriedly away.

"This one's a big pain in the butt, I'm sorry," she says apologetically. "I know you like it—LaToya Jackson, or whatever you call it—but it's really in my face right now."

"I call him Chaka Khan," I say, injured. "LaToya Jackson—that isn't even close to the same."

"Well, point is," she begins, changing the subject, "I think it stinks. And I don't mean all this penguin crap. You *know* what I mean." She waggles the hose at me, and for a split second I wonder if I should hop down off the wide ledge of the Penguin Pond because she's going to spray me. Sue is referring, naturally, to what I told her just before Chaka Khan started harassing her. I happened to mention very casually that the guy I like, the cute one who comes into the store all the time, made my day when he brought back the candycane and slipper ensemble during the first week of January. The gift boxes clearly had been opened, but all of the tags were still on, and in the case of the tap pants, it appeared the tissue paper hadn't been rustled around at all. He'd asked for cash back; store credit wasn't desired or required. I'd skipped the standard line of questioning that we are trained to employ ("Was it the wrong size or color? Did she have something else in mind? Can I help you pick out another item?"), because I didn't care if it was the wrong size or color. I didn't care if the mystery gift recipient had something else in mind, and I certainly didn't want to help pick out another item. I wanted to reach across the counter, grab Allan by the collar of his coat, pull him in close, and ask in a husky voice, "Would you like to see me wearing this candycane ensemble instead?" Alas, I didn't; this question appears nowhere in the Operations Binder and would most certainly get me fired.

"Well, I don't know what to say. I like him. My job is boring, and seeing him is exciting," I rationalize.

"So, like somebody else. Not a guy where you don't know if he's single or with someone or what. You're smarter than that." This hurts a bit, because I know in my heart that she's right, but I still can't help myself. I wish for a second that Chaka Khan had made a bigger splash, done something more outrageous that would have sufficiently distracted Sue and made her forget what we had begun talking about. Still, he tried. I knew I liked that penguin.

"Well, I'll see what I can do. It's not easy when my other favorite male customer is a drag queen." Sue screws up her face at this and points the nozzle at a particularly dirty rock, as a group of middle-school-aged kids walks past us en route to a shark demonstration on the top level of the aquarium. A few boys break away from the group and stand about fifteen feet away from us, peering into the Penguin Pond, jostling one another and laughing loudly. "So how is Katie?" I ask, genuinely curious and valiantly trying to change the subject for good. "Did she have a nice Christmas break?"

"Oh yeah, sure," she says flatly, putting the hose down and using a combination shovel/scraper tool to remove some tenacious penguin crap. "Except for the day she came home from the mall reeking of cigarettes. I said, 'What the hell are you doing, smoking?' And she just yells at me and runs up to her room. And then—" She stops mid-sentence as a penny hits one of the stones a few feet away from her. We look over and the three boys are barely controlling their laughter.

"No coins in the Penguin Pond, guys," she says matter-of-factly, pointing to the sign. It has an illustration of a deeply frowning penguin and reads: COINS IN OUR STOMACHS MAKE US SICK! THANK YOU FOR NOT THROWING THEM! At this, the three boys explode, snickering loudly.

"Well, the bad thing about smoking in a kid this age is that if she really gets into it, she'll probably be a smoker forever," I say, frowning and twirling my ponytail. "The peer pressure is really intense, too; we used to talk about that during the health unit in my class." Whereas other science teachers dreaded the yearly, state-mandated, four-week health unit, I embraced it when student teaching and during my one-year tenure at Brookline Middle School. It was one week of general safety (bikes, skateboards, that sort of thing), one week of substance abuse prevention (smoking, drugs, and alcohol), one week of sex education, and one week of violence prevention (guns, anger management, abusive relationships). General safety and violence prevention were always fairly straightforward. Sex education could get a little squirmy, but I like to think I handled it with aplomb, having decided very early on that I would avoid answering questions in the manner of my own middle-school science teacher. When my shy friend Maryjane asked her what sex was like, Miss Williams got a dreamy look in her eyes and said to a class of twelve-year-olds, "It's like being on a roller coaster." This was her answer in its entirety, and for a few years afterward, I was certain that sex must induce vomiting, the way roller coasters always did in me. I also enjoyed the sex education week of the health unit because it allowed me to dispel a lot of myths, many of them hilarious. ("We're Catholic, so my older brother and his wife use the rhythm method. I heard them talking about it one time," a nerdy, ruddy-cheeked kid once said. "I'm pretty sure that means they listen to music when they're doing it," he finished confidently, leaning back in his chair.)

But where I really had fun was in the anti-smoking part of the show. Initially, I looked to my peers for inspiration and didn't find much. Miss Petersen would trot out an old guy with a tracheotomy and one of those creepy-sounding artificial voice boxes in an attempt to scare the kids. That didn't work; no pre-teen can even conceive of being that old someday, so why would they worry now? Mr. Ramirez brought in a plastic model of a cancer-ridden lung, blackened from "carcinogens." The boys thought it was cool, the girls were too grossed-out to look, and neither sex could make the connection between a faux tumor-filled lung and why they should say no when someone hands them a cigarette.

So I thought about what mattered to my students, and I realized it was stuff. Stuff, and lots of it. Sure, I remember being consumed with jealousy when my eighth-grade study partner Dawn Zebrowski sauntered into school wearing her second new pair of Girbaud jeans in a week. And I always wished I could stroll the halls in between classes listening to my very own Walkman. But by the time I became a teacher and had students of my own, it seemed like middle-schoolers had morphed into voracious consumers. Laptops, high-end video game systems, couture clothing—nothing was off-limits. So I bought dozens of packs of cigarettes and borrowed (or bought and then promptly returned) electronic equipment and luxury items. I shook the cigarettes from their packs, counted them out, and determined their consumer goods or services equivalent. I set it up like a game show and let them see what it would cost if they smoked, say, a pack a day, and what they could buy instead. One pack's worth in a little pile; a matinee-priced movie ticket next to it. Five packs' worth in a bigger pile; 2 CDs. Twenty packs, or just shy of three weeks' worth of cigarettes; a pretty sweet pair of sneakers. It resonated best with the girls when we got to the Tommy Hilfiger jean jacket and matching five-pocket skirt, worth thirty packs of cigarettes. I think for the boys it was the Playstation 2 for thirty-six packs of smokes. And everyone was speechless when we got to the Salomon snowboard, attractively priced at just two months' worth of cigarettes.

"Tell her she can buy a lot more cool things if she doesn't smoke," I suggest from my perch on the ledge, as we both watch another penny land in the water.

"Yeah. But I don't want to be bargaining with her," she says, shooting the boys a look of death. "I just need to discipline her, is all. It's hard, with her being this age." Just then, a penny hits the left leg of Sue's hip waders with a soft *ping* and falls onto her foot. She looks at her foot for a long minute and then grabs the shovel/scraper, which is now completely covered with penguin shit. Two of the boys are doubled over with laughter and howling at her; the third intently begins studying the drawstring on his sweatshirt. She takes a few steps in their direction, smiles, and then lets loose. "Who wants this?" she asks loudly, drawing back the shovel as though it's a baseball bat. "I'm coming over there with all this penguin poo, so you decide which one's gonna get it." She quickens her pace, still pretty slow with the hip waders, but fast enough to give the boys pause. "I said, NO . . . COINS . . . IN . . . THE . . . PENGUIN . . . POND!" she shouts, brandishing the shovel. With this, the boys shriek in a way that is decidedly girly and run up the ramp to join their class-mates. Sue gives me a satisfied look and wades over to where I'm sitting.

"You didn't have any trouble disciplining those guys," I say, impressed. "So what's so hard about talking to Katie?"

"Because they're not my kids. It's harder when it's your own. That's why it's easier to do it when you're a teacher," she says, shooting me a look. "You don't have to sit there, looking at their sour puss at dinner every night. Don't underestimate how hard it is to be a parent."

"I don't, Sue," I say earnestly. I harbor no illusions about this—and when watching the worst behaved of my students walk out the door at the end of class, I frequently found my-self sighing with relief and thinking, thank goodness I don't have to see that kid at night and on weekends. "I'm sure it's very hard." Sue hoists herself over the ledge, swinging one wader-clad leg over and then the other. I stand up next to her and brush off the backside of my dark blue jeans.

"Look at you, skinny," she says approvingly, surveying me in last season's camel-colored turtleneck sweater from Ger-ard. "Did you lose weight?" I did, in fact; five pounds that melted off my frame when I was sick on Christmas and for several days that followed. It was by far the most peculiar flu I've ever had: fatigued and sluggish, I'd wake up sweating and gasping at night. I could barely make it around during the day, walking like an elderly woman as I tried to process after-Christmas returns and exchanges. Intense pain floated from one joint to another in my body, so I'd have a bum knee one day, then achy knuckles on my left hand the next. Then, just as quickly as it came on, it was gone, along with the five pounds. I've always been somewhat slight, and the rigors of retail tend to keep a girl pretty fit, but now I'm positively swimming in my sweater and jeans.

"Just a little bit. I was sick over Christmas, so I didn't eat much."

"*Losing* weight over Christmas. I wouldn't have minded doing that," she laughs, smacking her ample butt. "I think I've got eggnog in my veins. What say I take these off"—she points to her hip waders—"and I try to clear it out with a snack bar hot dog?" This mental image makes me sick to my stomach, but I can't resist the draw of a New England Aquarium snack bar lunch with Sue, so I nod my assent and we go on our way.

———

"You want manicure?" the short, dark-eyed woman with the caramel streaks in her hair asks me abruptly. She's rushed from her spot in the back of the salon to the doorway, after noticing me bent at the waist and looking deep into the window. "Pedicure?"

"No," I say, embarrassed. "Maybe another time," I add. Her face remains impassive as she turns away and lets the glass door slam between us. A second later she's perched next to a row of what look like miniature microwave ovens, holding her chin in her hands and smiling as she watches the financial news of the afternoon. I head to the T—it's much too cold for the walk to work, the sky blustery and puffy with clouds—and am a bit perturbed because my purse seems a little bulkier than usual, though I can't figure out why that would be.

I am almost looking forward to work today; it's been deliciously low-key at the mall since the after-holiday deluge of returns and exchanges, with people simultaneously sated by their new satiny gifts and miserably opening credit card bills. This will keep the store quiet until about two weeks before Valentine's Day, when the shipments of all things lacy, red, and pink will hit the sales floor and the store will be flooded with sweating, gulping male customers who make this pilgrimage but once a year, around February twelfth or so. But for now, a late January lull feels just great; I'm still feeling the after-effects of my flu from hell and am tired and weary. When I arrive at work, even Mary Alice is taking it easy: She's sitting and slumped over the counter, a very unusual pose for one of our region's top Christmas earners.

"Hi, Moxie," she says, sitting up on her stool. "I think it's going to be really slow today. They're predicting a big storm."

"Oh, yeah?" I ask, groaning inwardly at my stupidity for leaving my chunky, wool hat and scarf on the kitchen table this afternoon.

"There wasn't even a shipment today. Not one box." She frowns and looks around the empty store. "Not that there are any customers who would be looking for new things," she adds. She looks so full of despair that I feel sorry for her and wonder what it must be like to take these things so seriously.

"Well, here's something we can do," I suggest gently. "Didn't you say you were going to try and bring in your photos from Ireland?" From the eavesdropping I've done in the last few weeks, it sounds like a rip-roaring time was had by all. And although I'm not that interested in seeing innumerable photos of her pals in pubs interspersed with snapshots of rolling green hills, there isn't much else to do and Mary Alice seems in desperate need of distraction.

"No," she says sharply. "I mean, they're at home today."

"OK, it's no big deal," I say warily. This is what I get for trying to be nice to Mary Alice. I go into the stockroom, shrug off my coat, and take off my mittens. When I come out, Mary Alice is at the front of the store, alternately pacing the floor and staring into space, not stopping even once to straighten a messy bra or pick a pin up off the floor. We spend the next several hours in virtual silence. There are hardly any customers, and the classical music sounds too loud without the thong-buying throngs tearing the store apart, so I turn it down to a more manageable level, and this makes the store seem even more deathly quiet. By six o'clock we've sold just two hundred dollars worth of stuff: two demi-cup bras, a satin slip in lime green with magenta lace, three pairs of striped, seamless panties, and a pair of flowered pajama pants on clearance. I know all this because Mary Alice keeps pressing the special register keys that print out the day's sales totals, tearing the register tape, studying it, and then frowning. I'm watching her ball up the third one she's printed today when I see a mall security guard walking toward me.

"How's it going?" he asks, glancing around the store and blushing. He looks all of nineteen years old, with a buzz cut, wispy moustache, and giant gold crucifix on a ropy chain that sits on top of his uniform. "Look, mall management decided to close the mall. There's a lot of snow out there," he says in a bored tone of voice. "So you should leave, unless your store's management says you can't." He strolls out of the store, pausing for a split second to look at a new charmeuse and lace corset on a mannequin in the window. I turn to Mary Alice and her expression is blank.

"So, *we're* store management, Mary Alice. What do you think?" I really hope she chooses to close the store, although I'm sure she will decide otherwise. It would be delicious to have a few hours at home to relax instead of plopping into bed in an exhausted heap and falling asleep within fifteen

minutes of turning the key in the lock of my scuffed apartment door. I also wouldn't mind sending Heather home
early; she was one of our college-aged Christmas Hires who
begged to stay on past the holidays, and despite the fact that
Heather was terrible with customers, disrespectful of her superiors, and about as deep as a cookie sheet, Mary Alice ac-
quiesced and put her on the schedule for about six hours a
week. I am not very nice to Heather, but fortunately, I don't
care what she thinks of me.

"I think we should go," Mary Alice says firmly, and I'm so
surprised she may need to throw the first aid kit's shock blanket over me. "I have my car today. Do you want a ride?" Mary
Alice has given me rides a few times before, usually in in-
clement weather. The strained conversation during the ride
almost cancels out the convenience and comfort factors, but
when wet snow is swirling around your head and you've got
neither hat nor scarf, talking lamely about how the Patriots
are doing this season suddenly sounds very appealing.

"I would; that would be nice," I say gratefully. "I'll tell
Heather she can get going." Heather is currently reorganiz-
ing and tidying the stockroom, which is a really crummy job,
and I think she knows it. After several solid weeks of employees running in and out of it to frantically search for another size, another color, another style for a customer, the
stockroom is a wreck. It's as though we hired a set dresser to
make it look like horny fraternity boys staged a panty raid in
a seventies teen sex romp. We've got piles of panties, sleepwear strewn everywhere, and even a lavender lace bra hanging from a lamp. I walk into the stockroom and Heather is
turned away from me, bent at the waist and picking up packages of panty hose.

"Heather." She turns and looks at me. "Get out." I motion
toward the door with my thumb.

"What?" she asks sharply.

"We're closing the store because there's a snowstorm. So you can leave," I say a little more kindly and head back out to the store. Mary Alice has begun turning off the lights, and the register is spitting out the day's sales totals for the final time. Heather appears a moment later in her ugly, green coat and matching hat and says to no one in particular, "Is someone going to check me out?" This is the term for walking to the entrance of the store at the end of your shift with at least one other employee, then opening your purses, shopping bags, backpacks, and briefcases, so she can peek in and make sure you haven't stolen any merchandise. Because apparently there are *two* kinds of shrink: external shrink (people like Catherine, who steal) and internal shrink (employees who steal). To me, internal shrink is ipso facto pathetic, because I can't imagine anyone risking her job just so she could make off with a free yet itchy and cheaply sewn lace camisole. Yet internal shrink remains a major issue at all of the chain's stores, and so we must bare the personal contents of our bags to co-workers at the end of each and every shift. And if you happen to catch a co-worker doing something devious, squealing is encouraged and, rumor has it, richly rewarded.

"Yeah, wait for us to get our coats, we can all do it together," I say as I notice that Mary Alice is already all suited up in her fleece, electric blue-and-yellow Helly Hansen ski jacket, which looks hilariously sporty in contrast with her tweed trousers and matte black pumps.

"Actually, um, I was going to go start the car. It might take a while for it to get going." Mary Alice has an old Ford Escort that seems to work well when it's not too warm or too cold out, which in Boston effectively means that it runs smoothly during the months of May and October. "Can one of you check me out?" she asks, holding open her black leather purse with the big tassel on the zipper pull. I take a cursory glance and nod my assent. "I'm right over on Dartmouth Street, across from the train station," she says over her shoulder as she walks away.

I finish closing up the store, get into my coat, and stride to the store entrance, where Heather has been waiting impatiently, tapping her foot. She opens her bag and I look inside for a quick second and then unzip mine. She peers in and pulls back instantly. "Ew," she says, wrinkling her nose.

"What?" I ask, confused, but right away I know. I look in my purse, and there it is in all its brown glory, the dog doo pen. Gerard not only got me back, but turned the stomach of a stranger as well. He will be very proud. "Sorry, this is just an inside joke with a friend," I say, reaching into my bag.

"No, I don't want to *see* it!" she yells, backing away from me and into the mall.

"It's a pen! A pen, Heather!" I shout after her. She disappears down the escalator as I lock the doors, and I make my way out of the mall to meet Mary Alice. The wind in this part of town is wild, whipping against the Prudential Center and the John Hancock Tower and making everyone on the ground in between scurry around with their chins firmly planted to their chests. By the time I reach Mary Alice's car, my lips are stinging from the cold, my coat is covered with a layer of thick, wet flakes, and my nose is running lavishly. Mary Alice is rubbing her windshield and looking profoundly unhappy, and she turns to face me.

"I'm out of wiper fluid," she shouts over the howling wind. "And someone put one of those Chinese restaurant menus on my car, but I didn't see it under the snow. I put the wipers on and now it's a big mess." She's not kidding; the snow and pulp have mixed together and now coat the windshield in a layer of tiny red-and-white flecks, with bigger bits of paper here and there. I even see a snippet with a little illustration of a General Gao's Chicken Special. But there is also something lavender, something casting a bit of a glittery sheen on the glass.

"Well, what's this?" I yell, taking off my mitten and rubbing my index and middle fingers on the glass and holding them up to show her. She looks at me shamefully.

"It's—it's body lotion from the new Garden Sampler line that came in last week. I had it in my car, I thought it might help," she says, looking at the ground. I can't believe it.

"Mary Alice, this is oil-based!" I cry, shaking my head in disbelief. "What a mess. All right; think, Moxie. We need something alcohol-based to get all this stuff off. Something that's *like* wiper fluid, you know? You got any other stuff from that line?" I ask.

"I have some hand sanitizer in my purse," she mutters. "Do you want that?"

"Yes, that's alcohol-based—that will be perfect." She roots around in her bag for a moment and produces a miniature bottle of lavender-colored liquid. As she hands it over to me, she bursts into tears.

"I'm sorry, Mary Alice," I say quickly as I dump the contents of the bottle onto the windshield and begin to rub it with my mitten. "I didn't mean to freak out there," I chuckle awkwardly. I thought I was a little short-tempered, sure, but this takes me aback. And although the hand sanitizer is starting to work, my lame apology isn't doing a bit of good; she's blubbering even harder now. "Look," I say cheerily as I point to the windshield, "it's working! Now we can sell it as a hand sanitizer *and* wiper fluid." Like that old Saturday Night Live bit where Dan Ackroyd sells a dessert topping that doubles as floor wax, I think to myself and smile.

"Yeah," she agrees halfheartedly, blowing her nose into a tissue. "I'm lucky I asked to give you a ride. I didn't know about the alcohol thing. You must know a lot about science, huh?"

"A little bit," I say ruefully as we watch an old man run down the street after his hat. In his haste, he drops his newspaper, and the Living section unfolds and swirls all over the sidewalk. "Look, we've been here awhile, and it's a long drive back to South Boston, right? So how about I just jump on the train right here?" It's not the line I usually ride, and it will take me slightly out of my way, but at this point I've really had it and don't favor sitting in the car with a sniffling Mary Alice. I also have a hunch that she'd rather be on her way too, and she seems to have composed herself, so I don't feel guilty about venturing this idea.

"Well, if you want," she says uncertainly. "But I can still take you home."

"No, that's all right," I say, my heart getting lighter already as I think about riding a near-empty subway car, my head buried deep in my new book about James Watson. "You take care, OK?" I ask as I watch her get into the car and give the windshield a few swipes with the wipers. All of the gunk is now stuck to the curb and my mitten, and the windshield only has a hint of the glitter left.

Thirty minutes later, I am trudging up the stairs to my apartment when I run into Steven Tyler, who has arrived just seconds before me and is unlocking his door. He is covered with snow from head to toe and there is even a tiny bit of it stuck to his eyelashes.

"Hey," he says, stopping mid-turn with his key and disappointing me. "Whew! You look beat."

"Rough day with a weepy co-worker," I explain.

"Weepy co-worker? That sounds bad. I'm glad I don't have those." Which makes me want to ask, which? Weepy co-workers? Or co-workers at all? What's the deal with you, man?

"Yeah, well, at least we got to close up early because of the storm," I shrug. "It's always nice to be at home when it snows in the city—it gets so quiet."

"I hope so. That new neighbor was driving me nuts with that song, over and over. It seems to have stopped now, though." He's referring to a woman who moved in at the beginning of December and brought with her an obsession for that Cher dance tune that was so popular a few years ago, the one where part of the refrain is played backward and gives the effect of Cher's head being held underwater as she's singing. The first time I heard it blaring from the new neighbor's apartment, I thought, well, that's a snappy song, I haven't heard that for a while. The next time, I thought, this must be her "going-out song," the one she plays when she's getting ready for a date or a night on the town with friends. The third and fourth time, I sang along in a slightly annoyed tone of voice, and the fifth time, Gerard was present and demonstrated the silly moves he and a friend invented while dancing to the song at a nearby gay dance club. By the tenth time, I'd had it, not least because she would sometimes play it in the early morning on weekdays, when I was deep in slumber and didn't need to get up until noon if I had the two-to-ten shift.

So one Friday when I was off from work, I designed and rigged up a simple pulley system that worked beautifully, if I do say so myself. Very early the next morning, I lowered down a tiny but very powerful speaker on loan from Gerard, put it into position in front of her window, and blasted "Clowny, Clown, Clown" by Crispin Glover at full volume. It is angry, plodding, and nonsensical; during the course of the song, he laughs maniacally, spits deranged lyrics about a clown, a cigar, and a car, and repeatedly invokes the name of one mysterious Mr. Farr. It is, in short, everything a novelty tune by Crispin Glover should be. And as if by magic, after a few rounds of "Clowny, Clown, Clown," Cher fell silent. She may be a show business sensation with both Grammys and Oscars to her name, but her sizzling dance beat was no match for the insane cackle of my audio ammunition.

"I got her to stop," I say proudly, wondering how come Steven Tyler never heard "Clowny, Clown, Clown." "I'll tell you about it sometime."

"Sounds good," he says, nodding and going into his apartment.

10

Classic Flannel Gown in Antique Lilac

"THIS IS HEAVENLY," GERARD PURRS, SPOONING THE LAST BIT of crème brulee into his mouth with a look of unadulterated joy. He's even a little bit flushed. We are belatedly celebrating his twenty-ninth birthday at *good*, a stylish new restaurant right near the Boston Common. We chose *good* partially due to its ambience—spare and clean and done in warm shades of crimson and charcoal—and partially due to the great reviews we've read about the salmon en croute, but mainly because Gerard's co-worker Steven told him that everything in the restaurant is decorated, printed, or stamped with a pretty, lowercase letter *g*. Naturally, Gerard began fantasizing about owning matchbooks and flatware and hand towels with his initial and started hinting that not only would he like to eat here for his birthday, he would also like me to help him steal from the restaurant. I requested a discreet table when I made the reservation, winking at the host, which surely made him believe that I was going to be here with a hot date. But what I was really thinking was *we're going to rob you blind, little man.* Gerard and I have witnessed enough people doing it on the sales floor that we know it's going to be a snap.

"I'm glad you like it," I say, looking around the restaurant from our cozy corner. "You want a napkin ring, too?"

"Yup," he answers, licking the spoon clean. "Two would be better, but I think mine rolled under the table."

"Yeah, it did. And I'm not climbing around under there. But I'll put this one in my sleeve," I say, tucking the hammered ring of silver into the cuff of my black sweater. I've already got a *g*-stamped fork in the left sleeve and a *g*-stamped butter knife in the right, and I think I'm nearing maximum capacity.

"So, I just finished watching my *New Candid Camera* marathon the other night. It was so great, Moxie. They had one where they were offering to put special scents in customers' cars at a carwash—but really weird ones like curry and spinach and licorice. One guy, I thought he was going to kill Peter Funt! Hilarious!" he chatters, quickly picking up his espresso but then setting it down before taking a drink. "Also, a pizzeria where you pay according to how many slices are in a whole pizza. So, like"—he's wide-eyed now, leaning forward over the tea light that burns in a silver, *g*-shaped candle holder between us—"if they cut it into four slices, it costs less than if you want it cut into eight slices. And there were about three people who said OK to the higher price! Can you believe it?"

"I guess," I answer, my desire to cover my ears and scream at odds with my wish to make Gerard's birthday dinner a happy and peaceful one. "You know," I say, looking around, "these colors really are nice together. This would look good in your bedroom. If you were a real gay man, you would be jumping up to redecorate just like this."

"I *am* a real gay man," he pouts, picking up his espresso. "I'm such a real gay man that I had a second date with Charlie from Better Footwear this week."

"Oh yeah? How did that go?" I ask while yawning.

"We went to the movies. But I'm not sure if he liked my movie-time snack habit," he confesses, gulping his espresso and scanning the table for more small, easily lifted, *g*-themed items.

"Oh. Well, is there anyone who likes that habit?" I ask dryly as I roll my eyes. Gerard's favorite movie treat is a plastic-wrapped log of raw slice-and-bake chocolate-chip cookie dough, which he sneakily wraps in a sweater and buries in the bottom of his messenger bag before heading to the theater. Once the lights dim, he slices off the top with a tiny pocketknife and proceeds to squeeze the thick goo into his mouth for the duration of the film. It is easily one of the most perturbing things I've ever witnessed at the movies, and I've seen *Deuce Bigalow: Male Gigolo*.

"I'm sure when I find someone who likes that habit, I'll know he's the man for me," he says, sounding a bit injured. "And what about the man for you? Whatever happened to Allan?" he asks as the waiter drops the check on the table between us. It sits artfully in a small, square, leather-bound box, complete with a silver-foil *g* stamped at a jaunty angle on the top. Gerard immediately reaches for it, but I get there first.

"No, I'm paying. And no, Gerard, you can't have this box."

"I hoped you were paying for dinner. But why can't I have the box?" he whines.

"Because there's no way he's not going to notice if it's not here," I say, jutting my chin in the direction of the waiter, who is fielding a question about the broccoli rabe from an entitled-looking patron in a glittery evening dress. "I think we've got enough stuff for tonight. And I don't know what happened to

Allan. I haven't seen him since he came back to return the things he bought for Christmas," I finish sadly. Why didn't I force that credit card on him? I keep asking myself when I'm in the store and someone with his hair color or his tall frame catches my eye. At least I'd know his last name, where to find him, where he works. I pay the bill and very carefully slip into my coat, all the while tightly clutching the ends of my sleeves to prevent errant flatware from falling on the floor. We make it out of *good* without incident, and once we're on the street, Gerard starts laughing hysterically.

"Is this the rush that people get when they shoplift? I feel so lightheaded," he shrieks giddily as he reaches over to hug me.

"I think that might be the crème brulee and espresso talking," I answer, reaching up to wrap my arms around his neck. It's a long way up, though, and before I realize what's happening, the knife and fork are sliding down the sleeves of my sweater. The knife wedges in my right armpit, and the fork does the same thing on the left. "I can't put my arms down!" I shriek, pulling away from Gerard and lurching around on the sidewalk like Frankenstein. Gerard is laughing his head off, but I'm in pain, especially on the fork side. I'm suddenly very relieved neither of us had beef, as a steak knife in this position would almost certainly require a trip to the ER.

"OK, OK," he gasps, gently grabbing my arms and lifting them straight and high above my head. I feel the cool metal as the flatware dislodges from my pits, and then hear a *clink* as the fork hits the sidewalk.

"You're going to have to wait on the knife," I warn. "It's stuck somewhere between my sweater and bra."

We start walking toward my apartment, and after about three blocks, I am suddenly so tired that I stop right at the steps of a run-down church and sit down. "I just need to sit here a minute," I say. "I'm feeling so out of it. What the hell is wrong with me, Gerard?"

THE PAJAMA GAME

"Moxie, maybe you should just take the pills," he says evenly, rubbing his gloved hands together in the cold.

"What?"

"The ones Luttman wants you to take. For depression, or whatever. You haven't been yourself lately—even tonight, you seemed a little bit pissy at the restaurant." He stops talking as a young couple walks by with their golden retriever, who plants his nose firmly in the butt of an unsuspecting terrier when they reach the corner.

"Is this about me joking that you're not a real gay man? What's going on?" I'm confused, and I suddenly need to suppress the urge to weep.

"No. Well, maybe a little. But you just seem worse lately. Maybe the guy isn't totally off base. Everyone takes them, you know."

I know everyone takes them. This is what Luttman says all the time, and one of the multitude of reasons I cancelled my appointment with him this month. "I know everyone takes them. But I'm not depressed. I just feel weird. Or something."

Gerard sits down next to me on the step and sighs. "I'm sorry, I don't want to ruin our evening. I just worry about you." He says this while staring straight ahead into the darkness.

I worry about me too, I want to say, before we get up, walk back to my apartment, and I cry myself to sleep.

———

Yellow speckles flash in front of my eyes, little fireflies that flit and change direction each time I blink. When the last one has burned out, I finally am able to squint at the screen.

"It's fine, OK," I say quickly, even though the picture is a bit blurry, and the monitor has something sticky on it, as though a Registry of Motor Vehicles employee swiped his hand across it after setting down a Boston cream donut.

"Step to the window on the right, and your license will be ready in a moment," the sixty-something clerk with the frosted hair says sleepily. Then, putting on her purple-framed glasses and twisting around to look at the giant Today's Date Is calendar posted on the wall, says, "Valentine's Day! Well, that'll be an easy way to remember when it's time to renew."

"Yeah," I say feebly as I tuck my book under my arm and walk over to await my license. I don't know which part of this morning's experience is more disheartening: the fact that I don't have a car and am here only because I need a license to prove to dubious liquor-store clerks that I'm not an underclassman aiming to drink myself to death and bring a lawsuit their way, or that I'm in this hellish, downtown government building on Valentine's Day. After waiting at the window for fifteen minutes, it's my turn and another clerk, this one with a big, open bag of Fritos next to him, hands me the license in exchange for my $60 check. "Enjoy," he says, flashing me a toothy, Frito-speckled smile.

I walk outside and start to put on my mittens, but stop when I realize that I don't really need them—it's unseasonably warm today, and people are walking with their thick, winter coats open and their hats and scarves mashed into briefcases and backpacks. I shove my mittens into my pockets and start to walk in the direction of the mall, but a small storefront stops me. It's only about five doors away from the Fleet Center, the replacement for the old Boston Garden, which was torn down in 1998 to make way for a giant, soulless, sterile sports and event arena. Although I'm not a fan of the Celtics, the Bruins, the circus, or any event staged by giant, plush-covered characters on ice, and had never once been inside, I understood the collective sorrow of the city when the Garden was demolished. There seemed to be true history there, and the story of the discovery of a desiccated monkey skeleton under the floorboards, thought to be that of a Ringling Brothers simian escapee in the sixties, only sweetened the deal.

I look more closely at the storefront; the interior is under construction, and the heady smell of warm sawdust wafts through the open door as strapping guys in hard hats heft huge pieces of lumber. There is a small paper sign taped inside the window, next to the building permit, and in a hasty, smeared, blue ballpoint scrawl, it reads:

COMING SOON
COFFEE AND MORE

Beneath that, there is another piece of paper, this one a half-sheet torn from a yellow legal pad. The top, left, and right edges are neat and tidy as a Beacon Hill lawyer, and the bottom edge is wild and uneven. It's taped up at a crooked angle, and in red ink, in the same handwriting, a punctuation-free sentence implores:

NAME THE STORE WIN A PRIZE

I check my watch and realize I've got to hurry, but I'm so overjoyed that this isn't going to be another Starbucks that my curiosity gets the best of me. I tentatively stick my head inside and a burly guy in a red down vest and jeans slowly ambles over. He's holding an open thermos in his right hand, and the steam swirls into the air between us.

"Can I help you?" he asks, looking me up and down.

"Oh, no. I was just curious about this place," I admit. A look of pride crosses his face, and he chuckles a bit.

"Well, this is going to be a coffee shop." He gestures around and takes a sip from his thermos. "Maybe muffins, things like that," he adds gruffly, puffing his chest out on the word "muffins," ostensibly to take the sting out of saying such a word in the presence of all these laborers. "There's nothing like it in this neighborhood, and so I got this idea to be the first one. To be this close to the Fleet Center and get all that business."

"Uh huh," I say, conjuring up a series of images, each more jarring than the last: Bruins fans, drunk and angry, hurling freshly baked muffins around; Celtics fans, drunk and angry, hauling off and slugging an innocent employee when the coffee is too hot; wee circus fans, exhausted and overstimulated, screaming and wailing when they spill their hot chocolate on themselves. Yes, this business venture had all the makings of a success. *Forbes*, here we come. "Well, what about the name?" I say as I point to the flimsy piece of paper in the window.

"It needs a name. I don't know what the prize is yet," he says. "Why, you want to enter? You'd be our first entry, actually."

"Sure," I reply, even though I don't have any idea what to suggest. Then as he's rooting around in his pockets for a pen, it comes to me. There really is only *one* name for this place. He gives me a ballpoint pen, tears a tiny strip of legal paper off the sign in the window, and hands it to me without fanfare. I write my entry along with my name and phone number in small block print, fold it over, and hand it back to him. He slides it into the front pocket of his vest without opening it, and pats the pocket.

———

Ninety minutes later, I am sitting cross-legged on the flowered carpet, my head deep in a bra drawer as I look for an elusive underwire, stretch lace bra in a size 32AA. Despite the fact that each cream-colored, Victorian-styled drawer (complete with ornate, faux brass handle) is only supposed to be home to one bra size, I am finding 36s, 34s, As, Bs, and Cs in there. This must be the work of Heather; Mary Alice normally patrols the bra drawers with the ferocity of an ATF drug-sniffing dog, rooting out incorrect sizes and plucking them from the drawers with speed and accuracy.

"I haven't got it in that size," I say apologetically as I stand up and face the dumpy, middle-aged guy with a bad hairpiece and a plastic sack from the Marshalls down the street.

"But it's Valentine's Day," he replies, crestfallen. "What about the sign?" he asks, pointing to the rose-colored cardboard sign propped on an easel in the center of the store. In pink, girly script so feminine and sweet that it would make a Miss America contestant's eyes bleed, it reads: LAST-MINUTE VALENTINE'S DAY WISHES COME TRUE. Beneath it is our store's logo, encircled with plump red and pink hearts. All that's missing are smiley faces over the *I*s.

"I know," I say, trying to look sympathetic but actually thinking of the yellowing sign that Joe has posted behind the register at the joke shop, which says something to the effect of a screw-up on your part does not constitute an emergency on my part. "A lot of things are sold out, and that's not a size that we tend to get a lot of anyway," I continue as I suddenly start feeling sorry for the guy. A Valentine's Day with no gift, and a teensy-breasted wife or girlfriend to boot. This isn't shaping up well. "You know what I recommend? Maybe a teddy. Those are romantic, and they're cut small, so we have a lot of them." He perks up slightly at this suggestion, and I lead him over to the rack that's exploding with mesh and lace. Once there, I realize that I need to pee so badly that I race to the stockroom and into the bathroom, where I hurriedly pull down my pantyhose and underwear.

I sit down and sigh with relief, but it's short-lived, because a split second later I think, how the *hell* did my sneakers from Target get in here? I bought them last summer with Gerard; they were red, fake suede, adorably perky on my size six feet, and cost four dollars. But that ALL MAN-MADE MATERI-ALS stamped in gold on the underside of each vinyl tongue never could have prepared me for the smell that began emanating from these sneakers after a few wearings. It was as though they were infused with poison, and it probably didn't help that I was wearing them without socks in ninety-degree temperatures. It got to the point where Gerard swore he could smell my feet even when inside the sneakers. "Hippo urine," he would say, holding his nose and grimacing. I personally found the odor to have more of a sickly sweet than acrid quality—to me, it smelled more like rotten fruit or dead flower water or boozy vomit. Either way, the sneakers quickly met their demise at the end of the summer, when Gerard hurled them out the window of my apartment and into the wide-open maw of a passing garbage truck. His aim was impeccable, and he claimed that he had never done anything quite so athletic in his life. He must have been unknowingly saving himself for that very heroic act.

When my brain snaps to full attention and I realize that my Target sneakers aren't the source of this hideous smell, I decide I don't feel like contemplating what it could be and finish up in a hurry. I'm walking back out to the sales floor and quickly drying my hands on the sides of my skirt when I see him. It's Allan, standing in the middle of the store, right next to the sign. Valentine's Day Wishes Come True, indeed.

"Happy Valentine's Day," I say and immediately wish the floral carpet would suck me down into the floor and deposit me far below us. Sure, I'd end up in the Disney Store's loading dock directly beneath, trapped under a pile of Pocahontas snow globes with a Pluto baseball cap askew on my head. But it would be a small price to pay to escape my gaffe. "I mean," I stammer, blushing furiously, "I was sort of reading that sign as I was coming out. So that's why I said it." I am sure I sound like an ass, and my fears are confirmed when the last-minute

32AA shopper and a young mother with a toddler in tow look over at me quizzically.

"Happy Valentine's Day to you, too," he replies quietly, in a voice so sweet and sincere it makes my heart skip a beat, then race with excitement. He smiles shyly and unbuttons his coat. He is very stylishly dressed today, in a sleek, navy pin-striped suit and deep purple tie with wide, white stripes. His hair looks freshly trimmed, and he has a bit of a glow to him.

"So you look fancy today," I say slowly, trying to regain my composure. Breathe in, Moxie; breathe out. The only way his Valentine's Day greeting could be improved upon would be if it came with a defibrillator.

"I just had a meeting," he answers, nodding. I realize that this is my cue to jump in with both feet and start asking some questions. Damn the credit card application—I'm better off doing it myself anyhow.

"So what do you do, then?" I ask this while absentmind-edly straightening some robes on a nearby rack, so I can look busy should Mary Alice catch me ignoring the numerous last-minute shoppers.

"Biotech industry. Gene research? You know what that is, I'm sure?" *Know what it is? I'm reading a book about the guy who discovered DNA right now!* I want to shout over the Beethoven symphony pouring from the speaker directly over our heads.

"I know what it is," I say calmly. "Are you a scientist?" I ask, salivating with anticipation.

"Oh, no! Just sales. Getting venture capital for research that will someday lead to new drugs." He must see the poorly concealed disappointment on my face because he adds, "But I do need to know about some diseases, and how the drugs function, and some basic science."

"That's interesting," I say, smiling and looking right into his eyes. "So do you—" I begin, but I am unable to finish, be-cause Mary Alice is running toward the stockroom and shouting, "Moxie! Take the register!" I groan and roll my eyes. "I'm sorry, Allan. I can help you find something in a minute or two," I offer apologetically as I walk toward the counter.

"That's OK, I'm not looking," he says warmly, giving me a little goodbye wave and walking out of the store.

The rest of the day goes by in a blur, thanks to the rush of men with desperation in their eyes as they search for the perfect Valentine's Day gift. Unlike Christmas, which evokes feelings of yuletide and snuggly warmth with the family, and thus tends to steer male customers in the direction of more modest merchandise, Valentine's Day evokes images of wild sex and steamy nights just for two, which means that they buy the sleaziest items they can find. We're clean out of leopard-print anything by four o'clock, and the thong table is a disaster. And Mary Alice keeps running to the stockroom over and over, which is annoying. When I get ready to leave at six, I head back to get into my coat and there is that pukey, Target sneaker smell again, wafting from the open bathroom door. I gag a little as I slam the bathroom door shut, put on my coat, and I don't even pause on my way out of the store when a customer who'd seen me earlier implores me to help him look for a purple, satin-and-lace gown in a size medium.

When I get back to my apartment building, I am vexed to see that there is absolutely no mail for Steven Tyler, and as I sigh resignedly and unlock my mailbox, he appears on the stairs with a small, black suitcase in tow.

"Going somewhere for Valentine's Day?" I ask.

He looks at the ceiling. "Oh yeah, it *is* Valentine's Day, isn't it? I'm going to Miami for a week to see a guy. I mean, not for Valentine's Day. Just to visit a friend I knew from college."

"That's fun," I say. "Especially now, with the weather so crummy and all. Do you need someone to take in your mail?

Water your plants or something?" I ask sweetly, trying to conceal my ulterior motive.

"No, thanks, I stopped my mail yesterday. There's just so much stuff that comes, it wouldn't be right to ask someone to do it. Some of it's heavy. As you know," he says. "How's your co-worker?

"What?" I ask absently, sifting through my pile of bills and mail-order catalogs.

"You know, the one who was weepy," he says.

"Oh, now it's even better. She must have the flu, because she's all pukey as well."

He grimaces and readjusts his black messenger bag on his narrow hip. "Yeesh. Sounds like a blast. Well, I've got to get the train, so . . ." He drifts off and makes his way down the stairs and opens the door. He throws his suitcase out onto the sidewalk as I begin walking up the dark staircase, and just before the door slams shut behind him, I jokingly shout, "Don't forget to write!"

I continue walking up the stairs, but my feet and legs feel so achy by the first landing that I decide to unbutton my coat and sit down. After a minute, something occurs to me, something that Allan said back in the store. I didn't have time to think about it earlier because I was busy processing an irate customer's return. (The underwire popped out of her bra. We see this a lot more than you'd think.) When I offered to help him find something, he said he wasn't looking. Which meant two things: he wasn't shopping for some other woman, and maybe, just maybe, he came in with the express purpose of seeing lil' ole' Moxie herself on Valentine's Day. The thought excites me from the top of my head to the tips of my toes and some specific spots in between. It fills me with such joy that I leap from the step and begin walking up to my apartment so I can call Gerard.

But then I reach the next landing and another thought

strikes me, leaving me frozen in place. Mary Alice. First weepy, now pukey. I stand for a long moment and consider it. I've spied the unmistakable plastic birth control pill package in her bag countless times as we've checked each other out at the end of our shifts. No, it can't be, I decide.

11

Lace Garterbelt in Peppermint

"FOR THE THIRD TIME, MOXIE, I'M NOT A DERMATOLOGIST," Dr. Luttman says, crossing his arms in front of his chest and huffing exasperatedly. Today he is more casual than usual, in a dated, Cosby-era sweater woven in puffy, alternating rows of black and tan.

"I know, I know," I reply too quickly. "I just think it's a little strange that my hair is falling out. I find it everywhere," I say sadly as I look at the floor, half-expecting to find some dark brown strands on the austere, cool gray carpet. Lately I've been noticing it on my pillow and in the shower drain, as though I've been cast in a hair-restorative product infomercial without my knowledge; on my clothes and my scarf; and even in my food. It's one thing to settle for the crummy clam chowder at the Au Bon Pain because it's the only soup left, but it's quite another to look down and see your own hair gently resting atop its congealed surface. And having to admit to Gerard that he was probably on to something when he remarked on the state of my scalp the day I freed his genitals from the grip of the Handy Stitch, well, that made me actually *want* to pull my hair out.

"Look, it's not uncommon for long-term stress to have an effect on the body, including a person's hair. It's probably nothing. You could see a dermatologist, but as I said, it's probably related to how you've been feeling lately."

"All right," I say, suddenly sick of arguing with Luttman. He always has an answer for everything. I look at the floor for a long minute and un-focus my eyes, trying to recall a time when I didn't feel so tired and unhappy. When I realize that I can't actually remember, and that I've grown so used to this being the norm, it makes me slump further into the couch. "I will try to see a dermatologist if it doesn't get better soon."

"Well, you'll let me know what happens with that. And speaking of how you look, you seem a little thin. It's important to eat right, even if you're down. Remember that," he says, bending his right leg and resting his foot on his left knee. He wiggles his foot back and forth, as though trying to break in new shoe leather.

"OK," I nod, taking a glance at my watch. Only a few minutes left. "Do you mind if I leave a little early today?" I ask as sweetly as I can manage. "I have to meet a friend." A bold-faced lie if ever there was one. But according to Luttman, social support is a key component to curing my depression, and I know this will be met with approval.

"Sure," he answers, smiling as he switches legs and begins wiggling his left foot. Then, throwing me for a loop, "Who is it?"

"Uh," I gulp, nod deeply, and click my top and bottom teeth together, Elaine Benes-style. "Allan. Yeah. Allan. A guy I met where I work."

"Well, you tell this Allan to be there for you. You need him much more than he probably knows," he says earnestly as I snort with stifled laughter and take another furtive look at my wrist. February sixteenth, 3:35 P.M.: the first time ever that Luttman and I see something the same way.

Moxie,

Miami is great. My vacation has been pretty uneventful— aside from when I got arrested on Tuesday. But my lawyer said I can't say much more about it at this time. See you soon.

Steven

Gerard flips the postcard over in his hands for the twentieth time—stereotypical swaying palms on a sun-soaked beach on one side, Steven Tyler's tidy block printing and an inky postmark over a Wright Brothers stamp on the other.

"Moxie. How many times do I need to tell you? *Drugs.* Duh-*rugs.* He's in Miami, buying drugs, and he got arrested. What else could it be?"

"No one who got arrested for drugs would tell a casual acquaintance, all right? Not to mention, on a postcard? Where anyone can see it? Come on." What's weirder still, and what I don't even mention, is that I got a postcard from Steven Tyler at all. I would have thought for sure that he could tell I was joking when I cavalierly told him to write to me, but perhaps he couldn't see my face in the dark foyer.

I sit down on the couch next to Gerard and take a bite of my pancake. He's come over on this drizzly day for an impromptu, early Saturday-morning brunch after spending the night at Charlie's apartment in Beacon Hill. On the up side, he whispered into his cell phone as he crouched in the tub in Charlie's enormous bathroom earlier this morning, this guy has a refrigerator full of things that aren't covered in fuzzy mold, and he's got smooth, golden hair like James Spader. On the down side, he likes to relax by listening to those so-called soothing recordings of crickets and tree frogs and mountain goats. When I pointed out that a mountain goat couldn't possibly be on the same track as crickets and tree frogs, he snickered and then suggested we get together before starting our two-to-ten shifts.

"Mmmm. I like Bisquick, I don't care what anyone says about it," he says emphatically, setting the postcard on the table and shoveling a forkful of pancake supersaturated with syrup in his mouth. He picks up the postcard with sticky hands and scans it again. "Either way, this calls for some sort of follow-up. Maybe he wants you to go into business with him. You know, you're both home at odd hours. I hear these people that make crystal meth, some of them have PhDs in chemistry. So maybe he wants to tap into your science smarts."

I start to ask why he would know anything about people who produce crystal meth, but decide I'd rather not know. "Steven Tyler doesn't know that I used to teach science. He just thinks I'm a dopey salesgirl."

"Hmmm." He looks thoughtful for a minute, and I fully expect him to try and make me feel better about my fate as a dopey salesgirl, but he says, "Some orange juice would really hit the spot right now, Moxie. Can we go get some at the 7-Eleven?"

"OK," I sigh, standing up, pulling my hair back, and slipping a ponytail holder around it. I've stepped up to smooth, fabric-covered elastics instead of gummy rubber bands in an effort to be kinder to my sensitive locks. We get into our coats, lock my door, and in the time it takes us to pause in front of Steven Tyler's door while Gerard studies it with the furrowed brow of a private detective, the rain has given way to a full-fledged downpour.

"Oh, shit! Go back up and get your umbrella, Moxie!" Gerard cries as we step outside.

"No way, I'm too tired. If you want it, take the keys and get it yourself. Besides, you won't melt. You're not made of marzipan."

"That's what you think," he yells down the center of the stairwell as he lumbers up the stairs. I listen to him wiggle the key in the lock for a minute and finally coax it in at the correct angle. "Hi, honey, I'm home!" he shouts into my empty apartment, as I decide to step outside for some air. He appears a minute later and hurriedly opens the oversized WGBH-TV umbrella that came with my membership two years ago.

"Feel safe now?" I ask, squinting into the white-gray sky.

"It's not me I'm worried about. It's the jacket. It's Charlie's. He loaned it to me this morning," he says bashfully as we be-gin walking down the street.

"Ohhhhh, I get it now," I say, nodding. "I didn't take you for a camel-colored suede guy," I add, surveying the boxy-cut, velvety smooth jacket. "Too much potential for food spills and ink stains."

"You bet," he agrees, turning and smiling at me but then quickly jerking his head away and grimacing. "That . . . is *gross*," he says with a hint of queasiness as he points to an enormous, graphically bloody cardboard sign attached to the back of a pickup truck that's parked in front of the Planned Parenthood. It's at least six feet long and two feet wide and is held firmly in place with sturdy twine.

"Oh yeah, that's right, it's Saturday morning," I say calmly as we enter the 7-Eleven. "That's when all those giant posters come out. I don't think *any* of those pictures are real, Gerard," I say reassuringly as a huge yell goes up across the street. There are loads of people there today, including some small children anxiously gripping the hands of their screaming parents.

"No?" he asks uncertainly as he pays for the orange juice. "Just Photoshop, maybe?"

"Yeah, just some talented designer," I say confidently, looking into his hopeful eyes. "How'd you like to see *that* ad in the paper?" I ask as we head outside and Gerard quickly deploys the umbrella while still under the green and white awning. " 'Wanted: Photoshop artist. Must be creative self-starter with a strong stomach.' "

Gerard smiles and finishes the rest of the imaginary ad as we begin walking, raising his voice so I can hear him clearly over the hissing crowd and pouring rain. "Anti-abortion stance required. Hatred of homosexuals a plus. Salary commensurate with experience. Ha!" He throws his head back dramatically, but then nearly gives himself whiplash when he realizes that in laughing this way, he's put the coat in peril. Chastened, he hurriedly ducks under the umbrella.

" 'The wages of sin are death,' " I read aloud from one sign that's been painted to look like dripping blood. It's shoddily done and a bit hard to read. Poor jerk, I think to myself as I study the cross, pasty-faced woman clutching the sign. You're just doors away from Joe's Joke Shop, and he's got a fake blood marker that would have made that a snap. We're almost directly across the street from the clinic by now, and the sea of faces is getting angrier and choppier by the minute. I count one, two, three gigantic crucifixes, five posters with gory photos, and decide to look at the ground instead.

"Moxie," Gerard says breathlessly as he grabs my arm, "it's Malice."

"I know," I reply, keeping my eyes on the sidewalk and twirling my ponytail. "There is a lot of malice on this block on Saturday mornings, but we'll be back soon and eating Bisquick; try not to worry, OK?"

"No," he says forcefully, stopping on the wet sidewalk and looking at me. "Over there." He nods his head in the direction of the clinic and I look, past an impatient-looking, chubby Boston Police officer keeping an eye on the crowd, past a woman in the ski vest singing hymns at the top of her lungs, past two old men brandishing swinging strands of rosary beads. There are so many people bobbing and ranting that I can't get a clear view, and for a split second I think that Gerard may be on crystal meth himself.

But then I do. I see. It's Mary Alice, in her blue-and-yellow Helly Hansen jacket and pale pink sweatpants, hunched over in the rain, leaving the clinic with her hand to her face and her eyes on the ground. The hand on her face is tightly clutching a balled-up tissue, and Shelley leads her by the other hand, leaning in and trying to protect Mary Alice as they slowly begin to walk the gauntlet.

"Jesus Christ," I say slowly, unable to take my eyes off her.

"I see him, too," Gerard says, pointing to a crucifix in the air. "At least three of them, I think."

"Knock it off—this isn't funny," I snap. Now the too-short-pants man has leaped to the front of the crowd and has gotten as close as the twelve-foot red line will let him, and he is seething and cackling, hurling taunts and insults at Mary Alice. I know it's him because I have a clear view of his feet, and there are easily five inches of navy blue sock showing from beneath the hem of those polyester trousers.

"Sorry," Gerard says quickly. "I'm uncomfortable. I really want to leave." He anxiously clutches the rain-soaked carton of Tropicana to his chest, Charlie's suede be damned.

"We need to leave," I agree as I watch Mary Alice heaving and sobbing. This only elicits more excitement from the crowd, and Shelley surprises me with some mettle when she bares her teeth at several of them. The cop intervenes, and the crowd parts slightly to give me a clearer view; Mary Alice's face is a sodden mess of mucus and tears slipping around on top of shame and distress. Her lower lip trembles as she and Shelley slowly make their way to the street. Once she reaches the curb, where she is safe from the judgmental strangers whom she will never see again, she slowly looks up, and her eyes come to rest on the sole person she knows in this neighborhood.

———

Vera is getting into dangerous territory—of this I am sure. Two boob jobs in one year cannot be healthy, I decide as I look for a DD, wine-colored, lace demi-bra with wide-set straps. I want to scream as I paw my way through the disorganized bins of bras and panties; Heather is the only one who can follow her unique organizational system for the stockroom, which means it takes the rest of us twice as long to find anything as it did before.

"We don't have it in that size," I tell Vera as she gives a little *tsk* and stamps her stiletto heel in the center of a rose printed on the carpet. "You should have asked me before you got another operation. I would have told you that we don't get very many DDs! You don't need all that . . ."—I gesture toward the center of her chest—". . . business. You looked fine before."

She arches one overplucked eyebrow at me incredulously. "'Fine?' I don't want to look 'fine.' I want to look better than 'fine.' Isn't that what all us girls want?"

"I suppose," I sigh, thinking of my sloppy hair and bare face. After a horrible night, in which Mary Alice haunted my dreams and hovered in the forefront of my mind during long wakeful stretches, I overslept and was barely able to pull myself from my bed. I am wearing the wrong color blue-black tights with my brown-black skirt, my hair is framing my face in greasy waves, and I skipped my modest mascara-blush-lip-gloss regimen. "In any case, I'll have to put the DD bras aside for you in the future," I say in a low voice, mindful of the friendly yet strict regional manager standing about three feet away and meticulously arranging the new signature satin pajama area.

Vera winks and turns on her high heel to leave, and I smile when I stare down and notice deep little dents in the carpet, pockmarks on the petals. I look up to see Cindy planted behind the counter, reviewing the last few months' tally sheets and absentmindedly chewing the cuticles on her left hand. "Moxie?" she asks, pulling her hand from her mouth. "It's nice that Mary Alice had the chance to get away this weekend, isn't it?"

"Yup," I say quietly, closing my eyes and rocking back and forth on my heels.

"Where did she say she was going again? I can't remember."

"The Berkshires," I answer. Her boyfriend was going to take her away for the weekend, she'd said last week when she begged Cindy for the whole weekend off. It was sort of a last-minute thing, she claimed; she was off on Saturday anyway, so could someone cover for her on Sunday?

"Well, between you and me, I wasn't sure if I wanted to work today. But she's a nice kid, you know? Plus, she earned so good during Christmas and Valentine's Day." Earned so *well*, I think to myself. So *well*, I would admonish the more grammatically challenged of my students. They would grouse and complain that since this was science class and not English class, they should be able to talk however they wanted.

"I'm sure she appreciated the time off," I say in as even a voice as I can muster, thinking of her cowed and crying as she made her way to the street. The Berkshires never have held a tremendous amount of interest for me, but I'm sure what they have to offer would be infinitely more pleasant than whatever discomforts and indignities Mary Alice is suffering as we speak.

"Yeah, although when she gets back, we'll all need to have a talk about this store's thong shrink, I guess," she warns, taking an ugly, teal, velour sleepshirt from a young customer and ringing it up without paying attention to a single one of her movements. She expertly rips off the price tag while searching for a gift box and doesn't even glance in the direction of the register while keying in the discount coupon the college-age girl has handed her. It's both impressive and depressing, these retail motions learned by rote.

"Thong shrink?" I ask, confused for a moment as I imagine a tiny thong, shrunk in the wash and creeping deep into a wide-bottomed customer's ass. Then I realize what she means. "Oh, right. Shrink. Stolen merchandise."

"Thongs in *particular*," she says to me a bit too dramatically. She hands the pink and white striped shopping bag across the counter with a toothy smile and waits until the girl has taken a few steps away to continue. "I gather that this store has a repeat offender, and it often seems to happen when Mary Alice is here. You all need to pull together to catch this shoplifter. Especially Mary Alice—if she's serious about her career, she should make that a top priority. Shrink of this kind just isn't acceptable," she pronounces, taking a lusty bite of the cuticle on her left thumb.

Don't say anything, I think to myself. *Not your problem. Besides, would Mary Alice ever stick up for you? Fat chance.* I chew my lip. I look at the floor. I straighten some credit card applications on the countertop and finally ignore my own advice. "Well, try to go easy on her," I suggest, attempting to sound casual. "I think, you know, she's having a hard time lately."

"Really? How so?"

"Oh, nothing she's said. She just seems, ah . . . not totally like herself. That's all." I return to tidying the already perfectly aligned stack of credit card applications, breathing deeply, and nearly rushing to unlock a fitting-room door for a customer with an armload of polysatin chemises, just so I can avoid talking about Mary Alice with Cindy.

"Ack! I'm fat!" Sue exclaims sadly as she turns and studies her blocky profile in the mirror. The beige, velour sweat suit is baggy where it should be tight and hugs her body in all the wrong places. It makes even her calves seem flabby somehow. But such is the chance you take when you shop at Filene's Basement, where the garments are piled high in bins and the harsh fluorescent lighting flatters not even the most svelte shopper. If you want neatly arranged clothing spaced evenly on hangers and soft carpet on which to pad around while barefoot in the fitting rooms, then you are welcome to head up to Filene's six upper floors, which are brimming with first-run merchandise in carefully crafted settings. But if you're ripe for a bargain and unafraid of conquering lots of unknown, loosely organized territory in exchange for discovering that perfect item, then the Basement is the place for you. With a bare tile floor, garments piled on every surface, and a hodgepodge of every other product imaginable (from gold jewelry to a glittery bridal shop, last season's men's suits to discounted china), the Basement resembles the set of *Sanford & Son* fused with a traditional department store. (Elizabeth, I'm coming to join you, and I'm bringing you some shoes at seventy-five percent off.) Apparently, Sue decided early on today that Filene's Basement would be the place for the two of us during her lunch hour; when I showed up this morning to see the new sea horses from New Zealand, she yanked me from the tiny, illuminated glass cases and suggested we go together. I'm not feeling very peppy today and nearly said no to her request, preferring to study the delicate sea horses instead, but she seemed so excited that I couldn't reject her.

"You're not fat," I say, leaning against an upright floor sign that reads "WOMEN'S BRAS—$4.99 and UP. MAIDEN-FORM, OLGA, OTHER BRAND NAMES" in large, messy red type that is meant to look like it was quickly written by hand but is in fact printed on the paper. I read it, snort aloud, and then back away; I can't even stay away from bras on my day off, it seems. "Honestly, it's just not flattering, Sue. I don't think it would look good on very many people."

"Yeah, but it just came down. Who knows how long it will stay here?" she asks plaintively, referring to the process of merchandise making its way from the main store to the Basement, as though the sweat suit were a beige, velvet serpent snaking through a complex maze. This is what sets the store apart from outlets (and don't dare make the mistake of calling it an outlet; I believe this is illegal in Massachusetts and is punishable by icy stares from even casual visitors to the store, as I discovered when I moved here), because the items actually come right down from the upper levels of the store. When something is deemed too last-season or otherwise unfit for sale in Filene's, it travels down to the Basement, where its tag is slapped with a colored, dot-shaped sticker. As time progresses, the color changes along with the value of the discount, and the item becomes more and more shopworn. The red dot on the tag dangling from the droopy sleeve of Sue's sweat suit means that it's just crossed the border into the Basement.

"It's not a good bargain if you're not going to wear it," I offer, invoking a line I quietly and frequently deploy at the store but would probably be shot for using if any of my superiors ever heard me dispensing such advice to customers. "Seriously. You're not fat, but you have a body shape that isn't suited for this," I say diplomatically.

She looks at me in the mirror for a second and shakes her head. "You're right. This thing is pretty ugly. I almost want to get it just to embarrass my daughter, though," she laughs, turning her attention to a bin full of pastel-colored sweaters on her left. "She almost makes it too easy, I swear. Hey, I'm going to take this thing off and then use the ladies' room. You need to go?"

THE PAJAMA GAME

"No, thanks," I say. Although I've made some select purchases here in my day (one umbrella which promptly broke in a rainstorm three days later, a flowered silk scarf for my Secret Santa at Brookline Middle School, and a designer pair of brown, buttery soft, suede pants for $16.99, which finally helped me fully understand the gospel of the Basement), I won't use the bathroom. This is in large part because Gerard says the men's room is exceptionally dirty, and if *Gerard* thinks something is dirty, well, it's probably ready for fumigation. And since ladies' rooms are often dirtier than men's rooms, it doesn't take much motivation for me to cross my legs and hold it for the duration of the shopping trip. Incidentally, Gerard also claims that the men's room in the Basement is a hopping gay pickup spot, where all manner of naughty things transpire. But when I once suggested he go there in search of some action, he rolled his eyes and turned up his nose at the sheer stupidity of this idea. "If I want to get off in a filthy bathroom, I can stay home, Moxie," is what I think he said.

Sue returns from the ladies' room seemingly unscathed, and we head up the stairs to the exit. She seems anxious to return to work, and I am relieved—the Basement never fails to give me a headache, with its claustrophobia-inducing, casino-like layout, which turns you around so many times that you can't determine which way is out. Outside on the street, I breathe in the crisp March air. It's still quite cold, but there's that tiny hint of things to come, that sense that winter's bitter edge is slowly wearing off and that soon your mascara won't make those runny gray stripes from the outer edges of your eyes back to your ears as you blink in the biting wind. Sue thanks me profusely for accompanying her as we stand huddled next to a cart selling roasted chestnuts. Warm steam wafts into the air, enveloping us and momentarily preventing me from seeing across the narrow, cobblestone street. As we've been talking, I've been focusing on a girl with dyed-black hair who is quickly arranging a display in Sam Goody. She looks so energetic there in the window, springing back and forth between Christina Aguilera and The Strokes, and for a second I wish that I could approach my window displays with such unbridled zest.

When the steam clears, the girl is standing on the tiptoes of her Converse, holding a staple gun at an awkward angle over her head as she plunges a staple into Christina's forehead. And in front of Sam Goody, standing on the sidewalk, are Allan and a woman. A sweet, petite blond with a pointy nose and a camel-hair coat. My mouth falls open as I watch her pull back her cuff with one leather-gloved hand to check the time. And, in a motion that I hope is subtle, I take one large step to the right so I am nearly hidden behind the chestnut cart.

"So I'm going to go, OK?" Sue asks in a voice that suddenly seems loud to me but which I'm sure is actually imperceptible, swallowed up in the downtown noise of shoppers and traffic.

"Sure, no problem," I say distractedly, still staring across the street. Allan and the mystery woman are talking, and although he's smiling, he looks tentative. He's gripping a Macy's shopping bag in one hand, and he's nearly ripped the little die-cut hand hole in two. "I think I'm going to, um, head home." But I don't move an inch.

"You all right?" she asks, furrowing her brow.

"I think I'm hungry or something," I lie. "Maybe I'll get a sandwich on my way home," I say, backing a few short steps away from her but still staying behind the cart. "I think there's a deli over that way," I say, nodding behind me.

"Well, thanks for coming. See you later, Moxie," she shouts as she walks up Winter Street, causing me to wince and then shut my eyes hard for a few seconds. Surely Allan must have heard someone holler "Moxie." But when I open my eyes and peer past the cart, he is still there and oblivious, and Sue's been enveloped by the lunchtime crowd. I continue watching with my mouth open; now the blond is looking at her shoes and frowning deeply. Allan lowers his head and puts his face close to hers in a way that makes my stomach drop; it's clearly an intimate gesture and thus dashes my futile hope that this fair-haired girl is a pal or sister. He puts his hand on her arm and she looks up slowly; they study one another for a few seconds, and she glances away quickly when the Sam Goody girl loses her balance and lands on her behind in the window. She gets up, brushes off her knees, and grins at Allan and the blond, who don't smile back. I'm holding my breath now, my face dripping with sweat from the steam swirling around my head. Finally Allan clutches her hands in his and leans in for a kiss on the cheek, but she pulls back. She tosses her hair over one ear instead and takes a small step away from him, leaving Allan to square his shoulders and try to regain his composure. She gives a rueful smile and a little wave, and then it's all over. They walk in opposite directions, and I turn my head from right to left until they are both out of sight, drinking in as many details as I can.

"Hey lady, you gonna buy some chestnuts or not?" The chestnut vendor interrupts my sleuthing with a gruff voice; he's been standing near me the whole time but hasn't said a word. He is a testament to layering: two sweatshirts underneath a flannel shirt underneath a ski vest, a Red Sox cap poking out from beneath a drawstring hood attached to one of the sweatshirts, and a pair of fingerless gloves worn over the traditional, fully fingered type. His nose is running a bit from the cold, and his lips are cracked. "You done watching your friends over there, right?" he asks a little more kindly.

"Sorry. Yeah, I'm done. And I'll buy some chestnuts," I say, even though I hate the things. "Two bags," I say guiltily, hoping they aren't more than a few dollars apiece. He hands me the warm paper bags, and I suddenly realize that his choosing not to harass me until after Allan had gone is one of the nicer things a stranger has done for me in quite some time. I hand him $5 for the two $2 bags and wave off the change. "Hey, do you have a wife or a girlfriend?" I ask, clutching the chestnuts.

He looks at me warily. "Yeah, why?"

"Because I work in the lingerie store in the mall," I say. "I can give you a discount on something sometime, if you want." Very, very clearly against company policy, but I don't care. We are even forbidden to use our employee discount on family or friends, so random nut vendors are surely out of the question. "In Copley, on the first floor. I'm there most days." I give him a wave and begin walking toward my apartment, very satisfied with myself for my generosity and grace under pressure. It isn't until I open the bags and fling the nuts all over the Boston Common for the squirrels that I start to think about the blonde.

12

Midnight Blue Snowflake
Pajama Set on Clearance

I'VE LET MYSELF INTO GERARD'S APARTMENT AND AM TIPTOE-ing toward the kitchen when YumYum skids by me, nearly knocking me off my feet. "Goddammit, YumYum!" I hiss at her, as Gerard groans from the sofa in the living room.

"Moxie?" he asks, his voice thick and sleepy from too many doses of NyQuil. "Is that you?" His nose is so stuffed that it sounds like he says, "Boxie, idd dat you?"

"Yes, dat is me," I say, throwing my purse on the floor and dropping into an overstuffed, periwinkle armchair next to the sofa. "I got your cough drops," I add, gesturing toward my purse. Gerard doesn't move and instead stares at the ceiling for a moment. A few deliberate blinks and a juicy sneeze later, he is propped up and ready to listen.

"I'm sick of seeing people," I say matter-of-factly. "First I see Mary Alice after she has an abortion, and then I see Allan kissing some woman near Filene's. Why did I ever decide to live downtown?"

He blows his nose before responding and tucks the tissue into the sleeve of the hideous Pierre Cardin robe that currently serves as a gift-with-purchase at the perfume counter. So few shoppers actually want the tawny-colored robe that Gerard took two home—one for himself, and one as a velvety little bed for YumYum. He left it loosely folded in the deep, oversized gift box, and simply removed the plastic lid to make a cozy snoozing spot for the cat, which I thought was quite clever. "Number one, you don't know that she had an abortion. Number two, you told me the other day that Allan didn't actually kiss the woman. He *tried* to kiss her. Big difference."

"Look, women don't come out of that clinic looking that way for any other reason. No one cries like that after getting fitted for a diaphragm, all right?" My head is suddenly pounding, and I close my eyes and wonder if I'm catching Gerard's late winter cold. "And yes, I guess you're right, Allan and blondie didn't kiss. But still. I don't want to be seeing these things, regardless."

"Moxie, we've talked about this—Boston is a small city! People always run into one another. If you want anonymity, move to New York," he says blithely and takes a sip of water from a crusty-edged mug sitting on the floor next to the sofa. No sooner does he set it down than he bolts straight up on the sofa. "Don't move to New York!" he cries urgently. "If you move to New York, I'll just die!" he pleads with the desperation of a man who has watched too many friends leave Boston for hipper climes.

I roll my eyes. "I'm not moving anywhere. Why would I move? So I could sell panties in some other city?" I ask bitterly. "Not likely." I glance out the bay window and see two cheery men sauntering down the sidewalk, swinging their shopping bags and smiling broadly. "Here's a happy couple," I say as Gerard slowly stands up, teeters awkwardly on the sofa cushions, and peers out the window.

"Oh, I know those guys," he says, coughing violently, losing his balance, and plopping back onto the sofa. "One owns that restaurant with the bathroom stalls that you like. Can I get my cough drops?"

I'm still standing at the window, watching the couple wander down the street and into a clothing store that features overpriced British menswear. "Yeah, no problem," I answer, pressing my forehead to the glass.

"Those guys aren't *that* exciting, my friend," I hear him say as he forces out a phlegmy chuckle and dumps the contents of my purse onto the floor. "Hey, did you fart or something?"

I whip around and put my hand my hip. "What? No!" I snicker. "I'm sure that smell is coming from poor YumYum's litter box," I add accusingly, pointing to the squat, plastic container in the corner.

He smiles and holds up my open wallet, which I'd neglected to snap shut before flinging it into my purse during the purchase of the cough drops. "No, I mean, did you fart when they took this driver's license picture? Look at you—you're blushing. You're absolutely scarlet."

"I am?" I ask, taking it from him and pulling the license out from behind the clear plastic insert. I had been in such a hurry the day I got the license that I hadn't looked at it too closely and hadn't had occasion to use it even once or study it since. "I am," I agree. My cheeks are red, and the upper part of my nose is rosy pink, as though I'd just come off the slopes and not the T platform. "Must have been the wind that morning," I shrug, even though I'm pretty sure it was warm that day; I distinctly remember yanking off my sweaty mittens. I hand him the wallet and sit back down. "I don't look like that now, do I?" I try to study my reflection in the window, but the cool, early afternoon sun drains all the color from the glass.

"No," he says, looking from the photo to me, and back again. "Not so much."

"I gotta go," I sigh. I shimmy into my coat and put my hands in the pockets, then suddenly remember that I've come here with one other goal. "Can I go to the bathroom?" I ask. Gerard, nearly back to sleep already, nods his assent. I go into the bathroom, kill a few seconds by sitting on the edge of the tub reading the dog-eared magazines from the back of the toilet, flush, and then emerge and silently tiptoe into Gerard's bedroom. As if by miracle, his olive-green, twill messenger bag is on the floor, right in the doorway. I open the front flap slowly, coughing during the *rrrrrrrip* of the Velcro just to be safe, and carefully place the dog-doo pen at the very bottom, beneath two *Betty and Veronicas*, a single glove, and a rumpled bus schedule.

———

Everything is on clearance now, and when I say everything, I mean every item sewn from tartan flannel, pastel-dyed terrycloth, and waffle-weave thermal cotton; every sugary, lacy bra, panty, and chemise that went unsold through Valentine's Day; every pajama gift set in a matching drawstring bag; and every single shimmery piece of hosiery, which has been discontinued altogether. Putting things on clearance is awful. It requires something akin to deep-sea diving in the drawer of in-store signage to find the only floppy piece of pink cardboard that reads "BUY TWO GET TWO FREE." It necessitates the use of a stepladder and special telescoping hook in order to remove the highest of the displays so something fresh and springy can take their place. It calls for yards of register tape cascading onto the floor each morning with the new, slashed prices for each item. Most importantly, putting things on clearance requires a boundless energy, a sort of life force that I can't even contemplate having one-tenth of right now. When I woke up yesterday feeling draggy and dog-tired, I figured I'd caught Gerard's cold and bought some cough drops of my own so I'd be prepared when the sniffles came. But they never did. Instead, I feel the same way I did at Christmas—so exhausted I can barely hold my eyes open, achy, and fatigued, as though someone is hammering away at my body with a thousand tiny mallets.

"Heather, hold on a minute," I bark across the store as I study the register tape, lean heavily on the counter, and cradle the phone receiver under my chin. I've been on hold with my HMO for ten minutes and don't know how much longer I can wait. Working retail and attempting to place phone calls to large institutions with voice-mail jails is a disastrous combination. This is the third time I've tried to schedule an appointment with a dermatologist about my hair (an alarming amount of which lay limply in the bowl of my bathroom sink after I brushed it this morning), but customers don't seem to care about that when there are thongs to be tried on and purchases to be made. After enduring a few more bars of a Muzak version of an already syrupy U2 song, I hang up angrily, tear off the register tape, and walk over to Heather. She's frowning, running her hands through her frizzy red hair as she leans over a box of hooded, cotton pajamas and plastic hangers.

"What's the problem?" I ask wearily. All I want to do is sit down in the stockroom and think of Edward Norton, but my break isn't for another ninety minutes.

"The problem is that there isn't enough *room* for all of these," she whines, pointing to the pile. "Mary Alice said to put them all out on the sales floor, and that they're marked down to $12.99. They can't all fit here on these racks. Maybe you should ask her what she thinks," she says as she sees me scanning the register tape for the garments in question.

"Oh no, that's all right. I can figure it out," I say quickly. But no sooner do I finish my sentence than Heather hollers for Mary Alice, who casually walks up front from the bra clearance area to help her, only to spot me there as well. Her spine stiffens and her expression hardens. I want to say, it's OK, Mary Alice. These last few weeks have been unfathomably awkward for me too. I sure do wish we hadn't seen each other as you were leaving the Planned Parenthood, but we did. Instead, I say, "Any idea how to fit all these pajamas on just two racks?"

"Put as many as you can on hangers, fold the rest according to the Operations Binder guidelines, and stack them on the floor behind the racks," she says gruffly. Since that rainy Saturday morning, Mary Alice says everything gruffly when addressing me. It's getting better one day at a time; her first day back from her "trip" to the Berkshires, she barely spoke to me and wouldn't meet my eyes when she did. I tried to act nonchalant, but she and I both knew that this situation would be as uncomfortable as the raw seams inside last season's bargain bras.

"Oh, yeah, sorry I didn't think of that," I say, nodding. I look at a small stain on the carpet and think, I'm sorry. But you'll feel better soon. It will get better. It has to. When I look up, Mary Alice is standing preternaturally still and gritting her teeth.

"It's Catherine," she says quietly, clenching her fists. I take a deep breath and slide my eyes to the left, where our number-one shoplifter is quickly stuffing thongs into the waistband of her navy-blue track pants, under cover of a large shopping bag she's holding strategically in front of her midsection. "It's Catherine," she repeats robotically and a little more loudly.

At this, Heather whirls her head around and yells, "What?" at the top of her lungs, giving Catherine the cue to bail with her comparatively small stash of booty. She runs out of the store and into the mall, taking a zigzag path through the jewelry and cellular phone accessory kiosks, which clog the walkways with shoppers.

"For Christ's sake, Heather!" I cry as Mary Alice puts her head in her hands defeatedly. I watch Mary Alice as she slumps her shoulders and shuffles back to the bra clearance area and feel profoundly sad for her. Her baby. Her thong shrink. Her stupid employee. It must be getting to be too much.

I am desperate to crawl into bed after a long day of clearance-related activities, but on the spur of the moment, I decide to stop in and see Joe. With the exception of two quick visits over the last few months (one to regale him with the success story of the dog-doo pen and one to comment on the new blister-carded fake gold tooth in the window—"Snap it on for that pimp look!" the package boasts), I haven't been calling on Joe very much. When it's cold and dark and I've gotten to the last stanza of "You're My Best Friend" (this new song enthusiastically handpicked by Gerard, despite my protests that a Queen song following right on the heels of an Elton John song makes my repertoire much too classic-rock format), I'm generally ready to call it a day. Joe claims he doesn't mind, but I still feel compelled to check in, nonetheless.

"Hi Joe," I call out as the tinkly bell on the back of the door rings loudly. His back is to me, and he is hunched over a box that reads "TRICK GUM 250 PCS/CARTON." He turns and smiles broadly and gestures for me to come in.

"Moxie, Moxie, sweet and foxy. You've been hard at work, or hardly working?"

"Both, I guess," I say, taking a seat on a squat wooden stool, uninvited. "I'm really tired, actually."

"Well, a little hard work never hurt anyone," he replies, pulling a piece of paper out of the trick gum box and squinting at the tiny type. "What does this say? I don't feel like getting my glasses."

I take the paper from him and study it. "It says that your payment to these people is past due," I read aloud, surprised. "FunTime Novelty Company of Bay Head, New Jersey."

He sighs. "Well, it happens. I'm a small-business owner, these things sometimes get overdue."

"Hey," I say suddenly, "that's right. You *are* a business owner. Have you ever had shoplifters?"

"Sure," he chuckles, closing up the trick gum carton and shaking his head at the memories. "Trick nickels, worm lollipops—anything small, kids try to pocket. Though one brave kid tried to make off with a . . . what was it? Oh yes, it was a mask from . . . that movie about a mask. *The Mask*?"

"That was a movie, yeah," I say encouragingly. "So what did you do?"

"Oh, you know, tell them I'm going to call their parents, bend their arm behind their back a little bit until they cry uncle and fess up, the normal stuff." He picks up a giant novelty eraser and starts absently bending it back and forth. "I'd do that more with the boys, I guess," he continues thoughtfully. "The arm-bending, I mean. It wouldn't be right to do that to a little girl."

"No, that's true," I say, wondering how these punishments might work with Catherine. Although I have never cared one way or the other about her shoplifting (still don't!), it would sure help ease Mary Alice's mind if Catherine kept her sticky fingers off our polysatin. But I don't even want to imagine Catherine's parents, and bending her arm behind her back seems highly unlikely, and not just because it would be difficult to get a firm grip on the slippery fabric of her track suits. "OK. What would you do if it wasn't your store, so you didn't really *care* if the stuff was stolen, but the fact that it was being stolen was making someone else look bad?"

"I don't know," he shrugs. "I can't imagine not caring if things are stolen, because it's always mattered to me in this place," he says, grandly gesturing around the cluttered shop and beaming. "But I'll think about it. In the meantime, you get home and get some sleep, young lady. You do look very tired, very drained," he says bluntly, holding out his hand to me. I take it and slowly pull myself up off the stool, my knees feeling full of shards of glass. "You're not taking drugs, are you? Every time I open my *Time* magazine, there's some new, crazy drug you kids are taking."

I chuckle as I make my way to the door. "No, I'm not on drugs, Joe." Not the kind featured in scary exposés in *Time* magazine, not the kind that are advertised in bold, block letters on Luttman's pens and clipboards and tissue boxes. I walk next door and nearly laugh aloud as I open the door to my apartment building. Drugs! The idea was preposterous— on a retail salary, I can barely afford pharmacological substances like cough drops. And then I stop, look at the mailboxes, and think, *drugs*. I never found out what happened to Steven Tyler in Florida, even though he's been back for a few weeks now and has been meandering in and out of the building at odd hours in his devil-may-care swagger. Unfortunately, I'm too tired to get to the bottom of the mystery postcard right now, and I head right to my apartment, where I drop into bed before even brushing my teeth or pulling out my ponytail.

Today I am feeling better, although last night I woke up about ten times, foggy and groggy and hallucinating vividly about the new spring line of daisy-print chemises, bras, and panties that will be arriving on the truck any day now. Mary Alice disinterestedly plopped the print materials from the home office on the counter the other day, saying that I should look them over and come up with any mannequin ideas if I wanted to. I didn't want to, and neither did she, it seemed. So we stood together in silence and pretended to study the new pricing sheet that came stapled to the front of the manila envelope. She closed her eyes and exhaled deeply through her nose, and it looked so appealing that I let my lids slide shut for a few seconds. It was only when a thirty-something guy with an armload of crisp shopping bags from other stores in the mall and a pink, silk robe in his free hand cleared his throat dramatically that we snapped to. He seemed more amused than angry to find two near-comatose managers behind the counter, and I was relieved.

I pull on my long, black rayon skirt, tight maroon top with the low, round neckline, and in a moment of defiance, decide to forego hose of any kind and stick my bare feet into my black, square-toed shoes. True, it's still very much winter, so the few inches of bare ankle between the hem of the skirt and my shoes might get pretty frosty. But I don't care. I'm locking the front door to my apartment when I hear the door to the building slam shut, followed by the sound of a squeaky mailbox door opening, and the rustling of thick paper. I fling my bag over my shoulder so fast that it nearly makes a full rotation and hits me in the head and start walking down the stairs as quickly as my tired legs will take me. My timing is impeccable; I run into Steven Tyler on the second-floor landing as he's digging out his keys.

"Welcome back," I say coolly, taking in his deeply sunburned skin. His face is raw and peeling, and his freckles have turned the color of brown sugar. Even his lips look painful; swollen, pink, and rubbery, they remind me of bits of Trident Bubble Gum that my students used to stick on the tops of their desks for safekeeping when we did the Saltine experiment to learn about simple sugars. And, worst of all, his two scars are highlighted in the worst way possible—thick and ropy against his lobster-red neck, they practically seem to pulsate. "That's some tan," I add, my eyes wide.

"Yeah, I overdid it," he admits, grinning at his own stupidity. "Cookie?" he asks, holding out a shoebox lined with tin foil and brimming with slightly burned chocolate-chip cookies. He puts one in his mouth and chews quickly, crumbs falling onto the collar of his jacket. "They just came today. They're not bad."

"No, thanks," I say, shaking my head, envious of Steven Tyler's trusting nature. I don't think I could ever eat random baked goods sent via FedEx from a total stranger, even one who was baking while cheerily humming a few bars of "Mama Kin." He finally pulls out his keys with his free hand and turns toward his apartment door. "Um," I say awkwardly.

"Yes?"

"I got your postcard," I reply haltingly. "What, um . . ."

"Did you like it?" he asks, a slow smile spreading across his face.

"Well, I guess," I say, completely baffled. "I mean, did you get into trouble down there?"

"Heck, no!" he laughs. "That's something my friends and I always do—send postcards with stupid, made-up stories written on them, you know, for a laugh. So when you asked for a postcard, I thought you'd appreciate that kind of thing." He worriedly studies my face for a few seconds. "It's a joke. See?"

"Oh! OK," I say, blinking. "I didn't know what to think. But I get it now," I add in a tone that I hope is convincing. It isn't that it's not a good joke, of course—it's easily as loopy as the dog-doo pen charade and a lot more clever. It requires some thought, advance planning, and evocative storytelling skills. I'm just not sure what I've done to warrant it.

13

High-Cut Brief with Heart Appliqué and Bow

THE NEW SPRING LINE IS ALL ABOUT BOWS: BOWS TYING THE sides of filmy, mesh panties together, bows that nestle in the cleavage of babydolls, bows nipping at the hems of chemises, and bows at the back of g-strings, which seem like they would slide into your crack at the slightest provocation. The bows come in both ribbon and lace, but more often ribbon; slippery, skinny, pastel-colored strips of satin that slide from my fingers, no matter how tightly I try to get a hold on them. I've been tying bows all morning, because Mary Alice says it makes for a nicer looking display if the ribbons are all tied neatly, as opposed to dragging on the ground.

I can't say I disagree with her, but I'm not in the mood. Although I am feeling much less peaked today—yet another one of my short-lived mystery flus behind me—and my knees seemed strong as they carried me swiftly past the too-short pants man this morning, seeing him put me in such a bad humor that I still feel sour almost three hours later. He was yelling so forcefully at two young Hispanic women that he was actually spitting. One looked terrified as she raced toward the door of the clinic, and the other one became temporarily paralyzed, standing with her eyes wide and her arms held stiffly at her sides, as though he were a feral cat or rabid wolf that somehow found its way to downtown Boston. Her friend shouted something to her in Spanish and she quickly snapped out of her stupor, yelling, "I'M ONLY HERE FOR BIRTH CONTROL PILLS, ASSHOLE!" I wanted to cheer for her then, but of course, he immediately got the upper hand, spouting about the twin sins of birth control and sex for purposes other than procreation. Man, you can't win with this guy, I thought, turning away and walking glumly up the street, where I waited for the light to change while watching the ladies at the Awesome Nails idly chat, apply top coat, and watch today's business news.

I'm putting the finishing touches on a lace camisole that has not one, not two, but *three* bows, when I have the feeling I'm being watched. And because I can't decide whether or not I actually want to be watched by the person whom I suspect, I take great pains to make sure all three ribbons are neat and even, with bows that flop neither up nor down but sit straight at attention. When I figure I can't possibly fondle this camisole any longer without seeming obsessive-compulsive or creepy, I turn and see Allan standing a few feet away. I breathe deeply, trying to compose myself.

"Hello," I say a little coolly. I slowly start to walk toward the front of the store, wondering if he'll follow. He does.

"I haven't been in for a while," he says, unbuttoning his coat. "I wanted to say hi. I . . . I was in this part of town, and I was thinking of you," he finishes, grinning at me.

"You were?" I ask immediately and too excitedly. *Shit*, I think to myself. You're supposed to be playing it cool, Moxie. It is not OK for him to try to kiss some woman near Filene's and then swoop in here, looking adorable, and flatter you in amongst all the pastel bows. What would Sue say? She'd be as disappointed in me as she is in her disobedient daughter. "Well, that's nice," I say flippantly, in a weak attempt to sound nonchalant. "Can I help you find something?"

"No," he answers, shaking his head. "I'm not . . . shopping for . . . anyone anymore," he continues deliberately, looking at the ceiling as he chooses his words. There are two customers at the register and another at my elbow who all need assistance, but I'm riveted to this spot next to the silk baby-dolls with satin bows at the hem, waiting for him to go on. But he doesn't, so I'm left with my mouth open and my eyes wide.

"Oh," I finally utter, the corners of my mouth turning up against my will. "Oh," I repeat, feeling as awkward and goofy as the kids at dances I used to chaperone at Christmas and the end of the school year. All we need is for him to suddenly spring a hard-on and for me to begin chewing the ends of my hair, and we could pass for seventh graders. "Well, that's nice. I mean . . ."

"It's all right. I know what you mean," he smiles, flashing his eyes at me and leaning on one of the thong tables, his hand resting on a purple elastic waistband.

"Well, I guess I should probably do some work," I say, looking around the crowded store and feeling a touch guilty. "Will you come back sometime?" I ask in a voice that I instantly want to kick myself for using. It's too demure, too passive, too feminine. Not enough moxie.

"I will," he promises warmly. "Soon."

———

Gerard's phone rings four times, and just as I'm ready to hang up, he picks up. "Can't-talk-Seinfeld-rerun-with-James-the-one-where-Jason-Hanky-won't-apologize-to-George-about-the-neckhole-comment-call-you-back-at-seven-thirty," he says in one long breath and then slams the phone down. At precisely seven-thirty, the phone rings, and I wait a good long time before answering.

"You're demented," I say in place of a greeting. "What on earth is the point of having TiVo if you're just going to be beholden to the TV schedule like the rest of us? Can't you program it to tape stuff like that?" I ask while absentmindedly stirring some instant potatoes on the stove.

"Yeah, I can. And I usually do. But sometimes I just get in the mood to see something when it's on. Today was awful— so much to unpack and put on the shelves, and Charlie was acting like a bastard at lunch."

"Oh?" I ask hopefully. Since Gerard has been spending more time with Charlie, I often find myself without a lunch partner. No Adventures in Retail, no illicit giggling at mall patrons, no fun.

"Yeah. I don't think this one's a keeper, Moxie," he says wistfully. "He's got too many weird habits. I ended up stealing that stupid CD with all the cricket sounds, by the way—it drives me nuts every time I stay over there," he admits. "Now he can't find it anywhere and complains, and I don't want to have him come across it here."

"Well, give it to me, then. I'll keep it safe. I could use some relaxation; maybe I'll like it." In addition to relaxation, it probably wouldn't hurt me to try and reconnect with nature a little bit. I've been growing more and more fearful lately that I'm starting to lose touch with my former science-loving self; I feel as though bills of lading, return slips, and register tape are muscling their way into my head, barreling down and shoving all my knowledge of earthquakes and ions and the properties of manganese down into an ever-smaller section of my brain. "And if *you* think he has weird habits, he must really have some weird habits, my friend," I add.

"So what about Allan?" he asks over the sound of dry food pouring into YumYum's dish. As soon as Allan left the store, I'd called Gerard to tell him the news, but he was too busy learning about the new Hugo Boss line and couldn't stay on the phone.

"Well, I think he . . . I think he likes me," I say uncertainly. "He's not shopping for anyone else these days; he told me so."

"Yeah, that's what you said," he says, sounding bored. "So is the guy going to ask you out, or just hang around and make googly eyes at you next to the underpants all day long?" He laughs at his own joke as I stir in the garlicky flavor packet for my potatoes.

"I don't know. I'm not in a big hurry. I've been patient this long, right? Look, my dinner is ready so I need to go," I say, suddenly irritated.

"That's my girl, that's my girl!" I hear him saying in a high register to YumYum. Then turning back to the phone, he asks, "What are you having?"

"Just mashed potatoes."

"That's not much of a dinner," he says critically. "You hardly eat anything anymore. Are you sure you haven't fallen in with your junkie neighbor?"

"He's not a junkie; I told you, that postcard was a *joke*. That's what he told me, and I believe him," I say defensively, spooning some potatoes out onto a tiny blue plate.

"Well, if that really is true, then he is the oddest man ever," he decides. "Oh, my God! Look at this! My TiVo *did* tape that episode! Because it looks for everything with James Spader." And the man who just seconds ago deemed Steven Tyler the oddest man ever, in spectacular pot-calling-the-kettle-black fashion, says, "I'm going to watch this episode over again, right this very minute!"

———

"I need to leave this job," I say dully, my hands over my eyes. "I'm forgetting what I used to like about myself. It's a rotten feeling."

"How do you mean?" Dr. Luttman asks.

I snort in annoyance. "I mean that I don't like how I'm starting to forget what it's like to be in a classroom, to be using my intellect, that sort of thing," I explain impatiently. "I'm getting used to selling panties."

He takes a few seconds to formulate a reply. "Moxie, I understand your frustration, I do. I remember the summer before I began medical school, I worked in a Mister Softee truck."

I pull my hands from my eyes. "What?"

"Mister Softee. It's like Good Humor," he says, smiling. "Driving around and selling ice cream."

"Yes, I figured that out," I say icily, then sigh deeply. It's not Luttman's fault that I couldn't cut it in the classroom. "I'm sorry, Dr. Luttman. It's just that the analogy isn't exactly right. You had med school to look forward to. I don't have that luxury." I momentarily focus on the narrow shafts of late-day light piercing the half-closed blinds and making milky patches on the carpet. "My job has also been stressful lately because of that situation with my co-worker," I add, folding my arms across my chest and pulling off a long strand of hair that's hanging from my elbow.

"Oh yes, the one who had the . . . procedure," he says carefully, making me wonder why he can't bring himself to use the word *abortion*. You'd think after all those years of medical school he would become inured to words like these and the cumbersome images they conjure. "Perhaps you should focus some energy on her and helping her feel better. Sometimes when we deflect attention from ourselves, it actually helps us feel better along the way."

I start to open my mouth in shock, but then close it just as quickly. Surely he can't be suggesting that I'm wallowing in self-pity and this is why I'm stranded in my polysatin pit of hell, can he? I breathe in deeply through my nose and decide not to take the bait. "I don't think I am spending too much time thinking about my own problems," I say in a measured tone, my left eyebrow arched. "But maybe I will have a chance to help her." I can't ever imagine how, since we've never talked about seeing one another after her "procedure," and it's not exactly the kind of thing you can casually slip into conversation while you're unpacking bras together. I glance at the clock; it's two minutes past six. I quickly stand and put on my pea coat, grateful that it's time to go. He watches me as I untangle a snarl of cord running from my portable CD player to my headphones and asks brightly, "Listening to anything good?"

"Bill Hicks. He's a comic I really like," I say simply. A sharp-witted, political-minded, foul-mouthed comic whose most stellar performances were recently culled into the CD sitting in the CD player. Gerard bought it for me the day it came out, and although I very rarely wear headphones, I've been enjoying listening to his raucous tirades as I walk and cackling aloud at his acerbic observations while riding the T.

"Well, maybe if he comes to town, that would be something fun for you to do," he suggests hopefully.

"Oh, he's long dead," I reply cheerily. "So I don't think so," I say, slinging my bag over my shoulder and walking out of the office.

———

I am busily ringing up the last of the line's customers and counting down the minutes until my shift is over, when someone unceremoniously plunks down a rose-colored chemise on the counter in front of me. I snatch it without looking up and begin tearing the tags, pausing to wipe the perspiration from my upper lip because Heather is steaming today's shipment of silk peignoir sets and decided to plug the steamer into the outlet closest to the cash registers. The steamer is hissing and bubbling, and she is standing a foot away from me, energetically rubbing the steamer attachment up and down the front of the garments like an eager but clumsy virgin groom on his wedding night.

"My discount," the customer says gruffly, clearing his throat. "My discount?"

"OK," I say, still not looking up as I run the tag under the red beam that reads the price and zaps it into the register, the inventory system, the warehouse, the books. "If you have a coupon, I can put in the code at the end, don't worry."

"No, ma'am . . . uh . . . I was supposed to get a discount of some kind," he says a bit more forcefully.

I sigh and look up, all the while suppressing the urge to roll my eyes, and see a man in a flannel shirt and Red Sox cap. His hands are dirty and he's gnawing his lower lip, his eyes darting to and fro. He looks familiar, but I can't place him, so I smile expectantly and raise my eyebrows.

"I sold you the chestnuts downtown," he says, after which the steamer suddenly lets out a giant hot belch of air, making Heather squeak and jump back slightly. "Remember?"

"I do. I do!" I say, thinking back. "I'm glad you could come by," I continue warmly. "Do you need a gift box?" He nods and I carefully package up the chemise, put it into a large shopping bag with twill handles (which, according to the Operations Binder, is only meant for customers making multiple purchases), and key in my thirty-five percent discount code. With the discount, the chemise comes in at a manageable $20, which he plunks down on the counter in the form of greasy and lightly chestnut-scented bills.

Today is Saturday, and I am out of it once again. Every time I think I am starting to feel happier and more energetic, that thick, icky feeling returns, and all I want to do is sit down for a good long time. Fortunately, I don't have to work today; unfortunately, I woke up this morning and realized I had absolutely no food in the house. So I slipped into my tomato-red, cotton sweatpants and matching hooded sweatshirt (on clearance, and with my discount, only $7 for the set) and pea coat and am now headed to the 7-Eleven. It's only after I get outside that I realize how badly I've miscalculated my outfit: now that it's mid-April, my pea coat is too heavy; plus the sun is finally shining—quite brightly, in fact—and I need sunglasses. Too lazy to go back up and change, I begin walking, sweating and squinting all the way.

It's a frenetic scene at the Planned Parenthood this morning, and I nearly cross the street and walk on the other side, away from the deranged fray, but ultimately decide not to. I can't take my eyes from the too-short-pants man, who is braying at a girl who can't be more than fourteen years old. He has twisted his face into a hideous mask of hatred and is yelling at her, helpfully informing her that she is most certainly destined for hell. And as the sides of her mouth pull back when she starts to cry, the bright sun hits her teeth, and I see the unmistakable glint of braces. He is screaming at a girl with orthodontia. My heart drops in my chest, and before I know it, I am nearly crying too, thinking of Mary Alice and all the poor women who have had to cross this bully's path. And before I even realize what I'm doing, I'm standing just a few feet from the entrance, safely inside the thick, red line painted on the sidewalk, and screaming at him.

"FUCK YOU, ASSHOLE!" I yell, all my anger at him, intense frustration with my own life, and pity for these women pouring profanely from my mouth at top volume. "Why don't you just leave people the fuck alone?"

A huge noise goes up from the crowd, and the Boston Police officer stationed near the door turns to keep an eye on me but doesn't move. My nemesis with the ill-fitting pants steps all the way to the red line, his face quickly turning the same color. "It's a child, not a choice!" he hollers, turning and basking in the limelight as the crowd begins cheering.

"SHUT THE FUCK UP!" I shriek, momentarily trying to remember the last time I dropped the f-bomb this often. When I was a teacher, I successfully exorcised all curse words from my vocabulary, because I found it was too difficult to deploy them freely when talking with friends and then have to remember not to use them in the classroom. Three times in less than a minute has to be some sort of record for me. I step all the way up to the red line so he and I are practically face to face. I notice that he's got a lazy right eye and dry skin on his sallow left cheek, I'm that close. The police officer is now striding toward us, and I know I need to leave, but I still have more to say. I lick my lips and form the words carefully, savoring them like Gerard's birthday crème brulee. "*You* are going to hell," I say slowly, pointing at him. His mouth shuts tightly and his eyes narrow, and I am barely breathing as I start to watch his face grow calmer, his eyes duller. And then he hauls off and punches me square in the face.

For a split second, there is no pain at all; it's almost a light and beautiful feeling, the kind you have when there is something weighing heavily on your mind, but when you first wake in the morning there are those delicious few seconds when you don't remember that you're upset. I'm not a depressed, low-energy panty salesgirl; I'm a science teacher again, with vim and verve and a full head of hair. But before I even hit the sidewalk, the spell is broken. The pain is intense and unrelenting, the crowd is screaming and running amok, and the police officer is radioing for help as he tries to wrestle my enemy to the ground. I put my hand to my face, and it feels cold and wet; when I put it back on the sidewalk, my fingertips leave little whorls of bright red blood. I woozily stand up and blindly run down the street, to the one person who I know has seen it all.

"Hi, Joe," I call out weakly as I enter the joke shop. He is in the back, putting little cellophane bags onto pegged displays in the magic area.

"Moxie, Moxie, sweet and . . . aaaaahhh!" he yells as he begins walking toward me. He picks up his pace and nearly runs to the front of the store. "What the heck happened?" he pants, pushing me down onto a low stool beneath a wind-up flying pig that hangs jauntily from the ceiling. He holds my chin in his right hand and surveys my face for a minute. "Quite a puffy eye you got there. Did that fruit you hang around with do this to you?" he asks suspiciously.

"Did that—what?" I start to ask. I try to roll my eyes in annoyance but it smarts too much on the left side. "His name is *Gerard*, and no, he didn't do this," I say in a tart tone, irritated but unsurprised. "It was one of the people at the Planned Parenthood. I guess I provoked him, so it's my own fault."

"Well, provoke him or not, that's quite a beating you took," he says, going behind the counter and poking around. He throws a container of silly string, a remote-control farting machine, and three cans of peanuts (snakes) onto the countertop and finally drags out a first-aid kit. It is metal, covered with a dull coat of white enamel, and the hinges are caked with orange rust. "Hmmm," he says, opening it and shaking his head. "I need to get a new one of these. There isn't much in here."

"It's all right, Joe," I say wearily, a sob catching in my throat. The pain is getting worse, and my eyelid is growing more swollen by the minute. "I'll take care of this at home."

"No, no, absolutely not," he says quickly. "I'll figure something out." He pulls a brown bottle of hydrogen peroxide from the first-aid kit, unscrews the lid, and looks around the store for a long minute. Finally, his eyes alight on something on the wall behind me, and he walks over and pulls down a bag containing a pair of giant novelty underpants. Tearing them from their cellophane wrapper ("For the big ass in your life!" the cardboard header reads), he douses them with hydrogen peroxide. "These are all cotton," he says proudly, sounding like Mary Alice when she's enumerating a pair of panties' selling points to a customer. "Like gauze, only bigger and better." He holds the underwear to my eye, and I take it from him and gently begin rubbing away the blood on my face. After a few minutes, the store suddenly becomes busy with three suburban moms and their children crowding the magic area, looking for easy tricks to perform at an upcoming birthday party. Joe continues to sit with me, but I know he's got sales to make, so I wad up the giant panties in the pocket of my pea coat, thank him, and slowly walk home.

———

I'm sitting quietly on my sofa and studying my grotesque face in a hand mirror when there are three sharp raps on the door. When I open it up, two police officers fill the doorframe. One looks as though he's been sent from central casting to fill a role for a hard-boiled Boston policeman: beefy, red skin, watery blue eyes, salt and pepper hair, and a brass name tag that reads Mullaney. The other is much younger and very attractive, with a fit physique, sharp features, dark brown eyes, and black, curly hair. He looks a lot like an actor I would probably have no trouble remembering the name of if I hadn't suffered some minor head trauma forty-five minutes ago.

"Can we come in, Miss . . ." Mullaney asks.

"Brecker," I say warily, opening the door wider. "How did you know where I live?"

"A witness at the scene said they saw you go to that novelty store. We talked to the guy, and he said you lived here on the top floor. Someone was coming out of the building as we were walking in," he finishes, looking a bit bored. "Can we come in?"

"Sure," I say, gulping and getting nervous. I've never had the police in my house in my entire life—and, just as Gerard predicted, they look right at home here in the linoleum-floored apartment, as though we're all getting ready to start rolling film for a new episode of *COPS*. Cute Officer Panucci takes a seat on my sofa and pulls out some papers, while Officer Mullaney strolls around the apartment as though he's thinking about renting it, peering into my bedroom and bathroom. They've left the front door open, which I find unnerving, and something on Mullaney's belt is blaring, his thick waist emitting messages every few seconds. There's an altercation between two homeless men over at the corner of Charles and Boylston Streets, and a window was just smashed in a Chinatown storefront.

"So here's the deal," Panucci says as I sit down next to him. "I need you to tell me everything that happened. Where you were, what you did."

"There isn't much to tell," I say distractedly as I watch Mullaney furrowing his eyebrows at my "I'd Rather Be Salient" bumper sticker on my refrigerator before wandering out into the hallway. "Is he going to keep walking around like that? It's sort of nerve-wracking," I whisper.

"Yeah, try not to worry about it," he answers, while trying to suppress a smile. "So?" he asks, his pen poised over a clipboard.

"Well, I yelled at this guy that I hate at the Planned Parenthood about an hour ago, and he punched me in the face," I say. "I ran to Joe's Joke Shop, then I came home, and here we are."

"Tell me more," he says while taking it all down. He has big, blocky print, and he presses down hard on the triplicate form as he writes. "Do you remember where you were in relation to the red line?"

"I think I was behind it. I'm almost sure," I say, my face throbbing. All I want to do is get some aspirin, but now Mullaney is leaning against the kitchen sink, his rear end bulging above the stainless steel ledge, and the aspirin bottle is in the cabinet right over his head. "I know about the red line rule, so I'm almost positive I stayed behind it the whole time," I add.

"Yeah," he says, continuing to write. "That's the critical part here. We need to confirm with a few more witnesses that you were behind your side of the line, because no one outside the red line is allowed to touch anyone inside of it. I think," he says as he glances up and looks at my face, "this qualifies as touching."

"I should have just stayed away," I lament as Mullaney drops heavily into a kitchen chair and shoots me a look, one that suggests he agrees with me one thousand percent.

"Well, what's done is done," Panucci says, absentmindedly playing with the spring-hinge clip on the clipboard and straightening the forms with his other hand. "The important thing is that this person has received several warnings about this kind of behavior already. This assault may mean that he is barred from protesting outside any clinic in Massachusetts in the future."

I sit straight up on the sofa. "What?"

"He has a record already for not following all the rules," Mullaney says slowly, finally deigning to talk. "So you come down to the station, you fill out a report, they ask you some more questions, now the guy needs to go to New Hampshire to punch girls inna face," he finishes, resting his chin in his hand. I turn to Panucci for confirmation.

"Don't know for sure, but it's certainly looking that way,"

he says, nodding and starting to hand me his card. Just as I take it from him, I hear the sound of approaching footsteps. Now it's Steven Tyler in the door, taking up much less space than the cops did. He looks in and sees me sitting with my new friends from the force, and his eyes go wide.

"What's going on?" he asks, sheer panic in his voice. "I heard noise as I was coming in, and then looked up here and saw your door was open."

"I'm fine," I say, despite the fact that I can barely see him out of my left eye. "I got punched at the Planned Parenthood."

"Well, who was the—" he starts to ask, but Mullaney cuts him off.

"We got everything under control, pint-size," he says, laughing a bit at his own joke and smoothing the back of his buzz-cut. At this, Steven Tyler bristles, inhales deeply, and pulls himself up to his full height, clenching his jaw and look-ing at Mullaney as though he'd like to grace him with a black eye. Instead, he wordlessly turns away and walks slowly down the stairs. A strange silence falls over the room, which Officer Panucci awkwardly breaks by circling the address on the card before setting it down and encouraging me once more to come down to the station as soon as possible.

———

Chirp. Chirp chirp. Chirp chirp click click chirp. "This isn't half bad," I say from my prone position on the sofa, my head propped up on two pillows. We are listening to Charlie's na-ture CD, which Gerard tossed in his bag and brought over as soon as he heard about my injury. "It's sort of nice. You should go easier on this guy."

Gerard rolls his eyes and walks over with a tall glass of root beer, which he very gingerly puts in my hand. "OK?" he asks.

"Gerard, I was hit in the face, not the hand. You don't need to be so delicate with me. I just wanted some company, not a nursemaid."

"Well, I'm staying over tonight, just the same. I'm going to wake you up every few hours. I think your pupils are dilated," he says, leaning over me and pursing his lips.

"My pupils are dilated because you're in the light," I laugh, trying to push him out of the way, but secretly very happy he's going to stay over. "If you move, they'll be fine."

"I still don't get where the blood came from," he says as he moves my slippered feet out of the way and plunks down at the far end of the sofa. "Was he wearing a ring?" He thinks for a moment. "Or maybe brass knuckles," he adds thoughtfully.

"I'm sure it was a ring and not brass knuckles, although who can tell, when someone's fist is traveling at your face at top speed?" I ask while picking up the hand mirror again and looking at my face. My eye is an angry purple slit, surrounded by puffy skin the color of the borscht my grandfather used to eat when I was little. The numerous tiny cuts that produced all that blood are starting to scab ever so slightly at their edges. It's not a pretty picture by any means, and I immediately decide that I'm calling in sick tomorrow. "I'm not going to go to work tomorrow. No one needs to see this, and I'm *so* sick of trying to help Heather lately," I say forcefully. Our last adventure revolved around her inability to make change when the registers went down and we were required to do transactions by hand for an interminable twenty minutes. The store was mobbed, we couldn't find the calculator, and I became thoroughly convinced that whoever was responsible for Heather's math education should be drawn and quartered.

"Don't worry about her," Gerard says. "The girl is, was, and will always be, *nada*," he brays in his best Steff from *Pretty in Pink* cadence. "So what do you want to do?" he asks, looking around the room. He picks up the remote control and begins flipping channels. *"True Lies* is on, but they always put in so many commercials on Saturday night," he complains.

"Ugh, it's Saturday night, that's right," I remember sadly. "I'm dateless and at home with a big black eye."

"It's all relative," he says, shrugging. "Hey, I was supposed to be out tonight with a big, black guy. But I think this is better," he adds, causing me to grin from ear to ear, which makes my eye hurt like hell.

14

Red Merry Widow with Contrast Embroidery

I AM OFFICIALLY WORKING THE SYSTEM, AND I'M SURPRISED AT how easy it is to do. Although it does seem to be taking quite a bit of time; I've been sitting here in the exam room with a limp copy of *Family Circle* magazine looking at the jars of cotton balls and tongue depressors for almost twenty minutes now. Gerard and I hatched this idea on Sunday morning, when I was complaining about my hair and feeling intermittently crappy and what a pain it is to get anyone at my HMO to really listen to me. He said that I should call up and tell them in my pixie voice that I was hit in the face and that I needed to be checked out. But bring your copy of the police report, he urged, because they are going to ask you ten thousand questions about the boyfriend who did this to you. So I called up first thing this morning, and *abracadabra*. An eight-forty-five appointment with a health care provider.

There is a quick knock at the door, and it jolts open suddenly, so suddenly that I drop the *Family Circle* on my lap and it slides to the floor. The doctor, a fiftyish man with black hair, copious dandruff, and round, wire-rimmed glasses, takes one look at me and assumes a serious expression.

"I'm Dr. Cooper," he says, taking a longer glance at my face, sitting on a small stool on castors, and then rolling in front of me. "Let's talk about what happened, and then I'll take a closer look at your eye."

I sigh. "I provoked a guy who stands out in front of the Planned Parenthood, and he punched me in the face." He doesn't say anything for a long time, so I close my mouth and go back to studying the tongue depressors.

"It wasn't someone you know?" he asks soberly.

"No. Well, I mean, I know him, but not by name."

He twists his lips from side to side, trying to decide how to rephrase the question. "So you're sure that someone in your life didn't do this to you?"

Work the system, work the system, I think to myself. Time is money in this place, and you've only got so much time to get to the important stuff. "Look, I think I have the police report in my purse, if that helps," I say tentatively, despite the fact that I am completely certain that it's in my purse. He nods and hands me my bag, which is sitting on the Formica counter behind him. I pretend to hunt through the bag for a minute, fish out the ochre form, and hand it to him without fanfare.

"Well, I can't say I've ever seen an injury related to this before," he says tersely as he scans the sheet and I notice bits of dandruff in his bushy eyebrows. "You should be careful around people like that," he admonishes, standing up and touching gently around my eye. "Any vision problems?"

"No," I say. "But—"

"Swelling going down a bit each day?"

"Well, I guess."

"Did you put any antibiotic ointment on the cuts?"

"No," I admit.

"You should put that on the cuts, to help prevent infection. Buy the store brand; you don't need anything fancy," he finishes, standing up and writing in a chart that's sitting on the counter.

"OK, but . . . as long as I'm here, can you tell me why I'm tired so much of the time? I feel like I get the flu or something, but then it goes away. I don't know what it is. Also, my hair is . . ." I say, my words coming out in a rush.

He cuts me off, looking from the chart to me, and back again. "Try to get more rest, and take vitamins. B12. A lot of people in Boston are worn out at the end of winter—it's tiring. And," he says, rifling through the chart until he reaches a pink page, the page I hate, the page I want to light ablaze and hurl into the Charles River, "it says here you're under a psychiatrist's care. A Dr. Luttman?"

I nod silently and look at the floor.

"Well, being tired is probably related to stress or depression. Apart from your eye, you appear healthy to me," he says, not looking at me. "Try to get more rest and see how you feel in a few weeks. We'll do some bloodwork in the future, if you don't improve." At which point he closes the chart, snaps open the door, and leaves the exam room.

———

Fifteen minutes later, I am walking through the mall and thoroughly enjoying the stares I am getting from the security guards, the cleaning people, and the mall employees who are rushing to open their stores. My black eye has made me formidable, and I slow down to let the rail-thin girls at French Connection gape at me and watch in stunned silence as I sashay by. I am Ed Norton in *Fight Club*, showing up to work with oozing facial cuts and an eye sealed shut from soft tissue damage. I enter the store, where Mary Alice is dressed in what looks like a new spring suit, a pale pink rayon number with matching trim on the jacket and skirt. She is frowning and bent over a brown clipboard, and I realize at exactly this moment that I never came up with a good lie to tell her about why I look like Ed Norton.

"Moxie, the first of the summer items are coming in, if you can believe it," she says without looking up. "It's not even May, and the shortie pajamas are on their way." I don't respond, but she continues. "We need to do some major—holy shit!" she exclaims, her mouth falling open when she finally looks at me. She moves the clipboard away from her chest and the pen slowly slides out from under the metal hinge and falls silently on the carpet. She bends over to pick it up. "How did that happen to you?" she asks somberly.

I look at the thong table for a minute and decide it's now or never. "There is a place in my neighborhood—on my street, actually," I say slowly while looking somewhere between her waist and calves, "where this guy yells at women." At this, Mary Alice inhales sharply and steadies herself on the very last rack of clearance items. "Um . . . so I got sick of hearing him, and I yelled back on Saturday. And I got this," I finish evenly, looking up and pointing to my eye. Mary Alice remains as still as the window mannequins, despite the fact that it's nearly time to open the store, the music hasn't yet been switched on, and the register hasn't spit out the day's directives. "The good news," I say, "I mean, if there is good news in this, is that it looks like he won't be able to do that anymore in Massachusetts."

"Do what?" she asks, her voice low, her face reddening.

"Harass women. Yell at people outside of . . . places like that." I breathe deeply; I realize I've been taking tiny, shallow breaths since this conversation began, and I feel on the verge of hyperventilating. "I need to go to the police station this week to tell them what happened again, but it sounds as though he's *screwed*," I finish a bit triumphantly.

"Oh," is all she says, before biting on her bottom lip and walking stiffly to the cash registers. And as I go to the stockroom to unleash today's torrent of classical music on the store, I think, holy crap, Luttman would be so happy. I did something to make Mary Alice feel better. I think.

———

It's been so long since I've seen Chaka Khan that I've started to become a bit worried about him, and as I scan the Penguin Pond with the outstretched neck and knit brow of a parent who's lost her child at the amusement park, I hear a little *whoo!* from about twenty feet away, over by the aquatic animal infirmary. A few seconds later, Sue is at my right side, smacking me on the back.

"Long time, no see!" she says jubilantly, leaning over the ledge and grinning. "I have something exciting to tell you."

"Oh yeah?" I ask, turning to face her.

"What the hell happened to you?" she gasps, taking a half-step back. She is wearing one of the discount cardigans that she was fingering that day in Filene's Basement, I'm sure of it. It's lavender, shaker-knit style, and eminently unflattering. "Moxie?"

"Oh, right, this," I nod, touching my eye. I've grown so used to my gruesome face over the last several days that I've almost forgotten about it, until someone on the T or street gives me a pained or pitiful look. Here in the aquarium, the lights are so dim that Sue is the first to react to the now green-brown bruises that grace my left eye socket. "I yelled at some guy at the Planned Parenthood in my neighborhood, and he punched me in the face," I say casually.

"No way," she says, shaking her head in disbelief. "Does he work there or something?"

"No, he demonstrates outside. I never liked him, but then he was really awful to someone I know, so I kind of lost it, I guess," I explain, shrugging. "I'll be fine; it's healing all right. So did you go back and buy this sweater?"

"Yeah! Wow, you've got a good memory," she exclaims, tossing her overgrown mullet over one shoulder. "I went back a few days later, and it was still there. I want to show you something," she adds excitedly, unfolding a white piece of paper and shoving it under my nose. "It just became available, and I know it's perfect for you. They won't make it open to the public for a little while."

I take the sheet from her; it's a page that's been printed from what looks like the internal Web site of the aquarium. I have to squint a little in the low light to make it out, because the type is so small. " 'Job 00308: In-house Educator, Fins & Claws Program. Part-time, 20 hours per week,' " I read aloud. Sue is nodding eagerly, so I clear my throat and continue. " 'Duties include leading school tours through New England Aquarium; developing educational curricula for students (i.e., hands-on activities, resource room materials); assisting with school outreach programs, etc. College degree in education required; experience in science education preferred. Knowledge of aquatic and marine life is helpful, but not a must. The right candidate for this position will know how to engage children and make learning about fish fun.' " I finish and look at the salary range printed beneath the description and laugh mirthlessly. It's low, ridiculously so. It's less per hour than what we pay our Christmas Hires. I think the 7-Eleven has a glossy Now Hiring sign that boasts wages higher than this. "Sue, this does sound great, but I couldn't live on this," I say ruefully.

"I was concerned about that," she admits. "It's only part-time, and the salaries here suck anyway," she says bitterly, stepping out of the way as a toddler races to the ledge of the Penguin Pond. "But, you know—science! Children! All the things you used to do," she pleads. "Plus we'd get to work together."

"I can't," I sigh, folding up the paper and stuffing it into my purse. My chest feels tight all of a sudden, as I think about the prospect of actually getting up in front of a group of kids and teaching. The idea that I was ever able to do such a thing seems positively unbelievable. But I used to do it, and do it well. I know it; I was there. "The sea lions have been moved outside, right?" I ask as brightly as I can, ignoring the nagging anxiety in my heart. "Want to go watch them for a minute?"

Sue follows me outside to the glassed-in sea lion area, where the giant, blubbery creatures loll on the rocks and swim languidly through the water, seemingly oblivious to the crowd of people with their faces pressed against the glass. The wind is blowing briskly off the harbor, but it's a slightly warm wind, and it feels good on my face. Sue turns away from the sea lions and squints into the sun, shielding her eyes with her hand. "Well, keep it in mind, Moxie. I know the guy who is interviewing, so if you change your mind, you let me know."

"I can't believe it," Allan says, pushing a little stack of napkins my way and folding his hands together on the tabletop.

I can't believe it either, I want to say. Not that I can't believe I was hit in the face; I can't believe I'm on an impromptu date. Perhaps not a *date* exactly, but an activity wherein Allan and I are in the same place at the same time, and it's not a place where we are surrounded by bra hooks and satin piping and cotton crotches. It's the Au Bon Pain, which, admittedly, isn't a romantic Boston spot that sets my heart aflutter, but I'll gladly take it. I was just sitting down for a tiny cup of soup with this month's *Scientific American* when a man's belt buckle appeared at eye level; it was burnished silver and I knew exactly to whom it belonged. I looked up and grinned, forgetting once again that I'm still in the final, ghoulish stages of a black eye, and Allan put his hand to his mouth before asking if he could sit with me for a few minutes while he drank his coffee.

"It's no big deal," I say, trying to sound tough and crossing my legs, pumping my left foot up and down. "I shouldn't have provoked the guy." I pick up my spoon but then set it down; the soup is still very hot, and I don't want to burn my tongue and look stupid as I futilely wave my hand in front of my open mouth.

"Well, you must be a hero to women everywhere, doing something like that. I mean, that really takes some conviction," he says, smiling broadly and taking a sip of his coffee.

"Yeah, I guess," I agree uncertainly, embarrassed at being dubbed a hero by Allan. "The funny part is that I do understand both sides of the argument, and I can honestly see what the guy is saying. You know, even despite my blind devotion to science," I say, finally daring to slurp a little spoonful of soup. "But I don't agree with screaming at people. That was really my motivation—the yelling at the girls, not the actual issue. Does that make sense?" I ask, suddenly filled with that sinking feeling that settles over you when you're on a first date and have inadvertently shared too much too soon. When I used to teach, I subscribed to all the teen magazines, so I could get a window into the things that were happening in my students' lives. The advice columns were always packed with tips on how to avoid common dating pitfalls, including telling your life story too soon and scaring the guy away. I have a pretty strong feeling that discussing the politics of abortion while on a first date would be strictly verboten.

"Oh, it does," he says emphatically as he grabs two sugar packets, bends down, and deftly places them under a wobbly table leg. He sits back up, holds the sides of the table and gives it a shake; it's solid. "I'm sorry—I hate when the table is moving around like that," he adds apologetically. "Anyway, I do understand. I support the First Amendment, but not when it means a guy like that can terrorize people." He rests his elbow on the table and puts his chin in his hand, and I'm suddenly and irrepressibly elated. I'm discussing First Amendment rights! And politics! Me, Moxie, the girl who customers talk down to when I can't find the bikini brief in the right size, the girl who feels as though her meals are served with a side of condescension each time she shows her store ID to the manager of the seafood restaurant at the other end of the mall so she can get her ten percent discount. *I want to French kiss you*, I think to myself. But instead I lean back in my chair and say, "So how's business?"

"Oh, it's OK," he answers, scratching the left side of his neck and calling attention to the fiery razor burn there. I make a mental note to ask Gerard if there are any good products for that, to quiet the hundreds of little red bumps hovering a few inches above the collar of his blue-striped dress shirt. "I was in meetings all morning; my partner and I are trying to get some seed money for research on a new arthritis drug. With all the baby boomers getting older, it's a pretty ripe market." He licks his lips and looks up and to the right, thinking for a moment. "We didn't count on the people we were meeting with to be quite so young, so I'm not sure if they understood our pitch. But I guess we did the best we could," he finishes, sighing a bit and peering into the bottom of his empty paper coffee cup as though there might be a retooled pitch in there. Then he shifts his weight and a long second passes before I realize that something is very gently grazing my ankle. It's his foot, and I nearly pull back out of instinct, before our eyes meet and I realize that it isn't an accident.

"Well, I'm sure your pitch was *great*," I say reassuringly before leaning into the table a little bit and slowly sliding my left leg forward, so the inside of my ankle is now touching the spot between his shoe and pant leg. I doubt Gold Toe dress socks have ever inspired such breathless excitement. "What's the name of the company you work for, by the way?" I ask, trying to sound casual.

"TechGen, over in Cambridge. It's a small one, but hopefully up-and-coming. Want to see my ugly business card?" he asks cheerfully, to which I give a muted reply, despite the fact that I actually want to yelp with joy. He pulls out a stark white card with a red, embossed logo that looks a little like abstract geese flying headlong into a DNA helix, and I scan all the tiny text as quickly as I can. Allan Donoghue! Telephone number: (617) 555-9499, ext. 12! Fax number (617) 555-51 . . . Mobile (617) . . . email Allan_Dono . . . it's all becoming an eight-point, Helvetica blur in front of my eyes. I can't read fast enough and don't want to appear too intent, so I settle for making a comment about the logo.

"Is that a flock of geese flying into some DNA strands?" I ask in a sassy tone, pushing my hair behind my ear and praying that no strands fall out and land between us on the tabletop.

"No, I think it's actually supposed to represent progress, or something like that. It's awful," he agrees, flipping the card back around and looking at it again. "Here, you can have it," he says, sliding it across the tabletop so it lands at the corner of the paper napkin pile. I pick it up and smile, relieved that I don't have to speed read all those letters and digits and email addresses anymore. "I think I need to go," he says, genuinely sounding a bit sad. "But . . . um . . . maybe we'll see one another again soon," he adds in a voice that is two parts giddy, one part slightly anxious. He gets up from the table and quickly pushes his chair back in, a nod to good manners that makes me want to sing. "I hope your eye gets better," he says earnestly.

"Oh, it will, Allan," I say reassuringly as he walks away.

Allan. It's the first time I've used his name when addressing him, and it sounds nice coming from my mouth. Allan. I look forward to saying it more. I sit for a few minutes after he leaves, studying the business card. As I'm tucking it into the zippered compartment of my purse for safekeeping, I come across a tiny mirror that Gerard gave me (it came free with some Calvin Klein eau de toilette), and decide to take a peek at my eye. And when I do, I notice that once again my face is scarlet across my cheeks and nose, just as it was in my driver's license photo, just as it gets at random times lately before disappearing for a while. Just two weeks ago I caught a glimpse of myself in one of the fitting room mirrors and decided I was totally color-matched to the new fuchsia satin gowns. I only hope Allan didn't think I was blushing furiously. "Talk about uncool," the teen magazines would surely say.

15

All-Cotton, Daisy-Print
Shortie Pajama Set

Moxie,

*I am having a party this Friday night and just wanted to let
you know. If we get too loud then please come down and tell
me, no problem. I hope that your eye is better.*

Steven Tyler

"Motherfucker!" Gerard seethes through gritted teeth as
the third motorist in a five-second period angrily honks at
him. "They make these walk lights so short, Secretariat
couldn't make it across the street in the time they give you,"
he complains bitterly, limping through the intersection as
quickly as possible and frowning. "Over here," he says,
pointing to the imposing iron gates at the edge of Harvard
University's campus. "He lives in through here." We slowly
make our way through Harvard Square, past the teeming

crowd made up of people who chose a decade and resolutely
stuck to it: aging hippies of both sexes with their Birken-
stocks and frizzy halos of hair (sixties), splendidly geeky en-
gineering types wearing pants so polyester-laden they
positively give a sheen in the May sunlight (seventies), punk-
rock kids with heavy black footwear and spiky jewelry (eight-
ies), and flannel-wearing Harvard students with mussed hair
and blank looks of total ennui on their faces (nineties and beyond). I like this walk because nowhere else on the planet can
you feel as though you're traveling through a style space-time
continuum.

"Here we go," Gerard says as we walk on the narrow paths
through the perfectly manicured, leafy quad. "This is his
dorm, over here. Let's sit," he decrees, plopping down on the
grass before waiting for me to agree.

"Now what?" I ask as I drop down heavily next to him
while yawning. I "stretched" yesterday, which is the term for
pulling a double-shift, and after a nearly fourteen-hour day
of stocking new merchandise, dressing mannequins in their
summer garb, and anxiously peering around for Allan every
five seconds, I feel as though someone has beaten my body to
a pulp.

"Now we wait," he says expectantly as he sits up taller to
watch someone emerge from the tidy, red brick building.
"Not him," he says disappointedly.

"How will I know which one is him?" I ask.

"Duh!" he exclaims, letting his mouth fall open in mock
shock. "He looks like James Spader, Moxie. His name is
Robert, and he's a graduate student at the Divinity School.
Oh, and he likes Armani fragrance."

"That's rather fancy taste for a student. And a divinity student, at that!" I say as Gerard takes a black Sharpie from his
messenger bag. "You'd think he'd like something a little
more simple."

THE PAJAMA GAME

"What, he's supposed to wear Old Spice, like that will get him closer to God?" he snorts, turning away from me and facing the post of the emergency phone kiosk that's been hastily erected in an effort to stem campus violence. Someone has written "FREE TIBET" in neat capital letters on the glossy, gray enamel, and Gerard uncaps his marker and writes "WITH PURCHASE OF LARGER TIBET" beneath it in messy ones. He turns and grins, proud in equal parts of his wordplay and vandalism.

"You're going to get into trouble," I warn, shuddering as I think back to my own tenth grade history class. Someone had sketched a small but distinct swastika on my desktop in blue ink, and as I systematically connected the lines to create a less inflammatory shape and began filling it in, my teacher appeared over me, glowering at my impudence. When I explained that I was simply correcting some vandalism that was originally much more offensive, she said that she didn't care; she hadn't caught whoever did the original artwork but she caught me, and I was to pay with one day's detention. I spent the rest of the year imagining the heavy, overhead world map springing from its rollers above the chalkboard and hitting her on the head, at which point the class would gleefully dance around her unconscious body.

"Nah," he says, catching me as I try to surreptitiously peer into his bag. It's been an unusually long time since the plastic dog doo has made an appearance, and I'm starting to wonder when I'll see it next. We sit in silence for a few moments, watching as a bespectacled girl with blond dreadlocks emerges from the dorm followed by two hung-over-looking guys, each carrying a stack of books and looking very unhappy at the prospect of spending a spring day at the library, and a tiny, red-haired girl who doesn't seem a day over sixteen. But no James Spader lookalike.

"Any new *Candid Cameras?*" I ask, leaning back and resting on my fingertips. The grass is a bit damp, and I'm sure I will be picking at my soggy underpants after we move from this spot and head to our next destination.

"Oh yes, they have a new feature where they have a celebrity doing something crazy, and a random person catches them in the act. I saw one with Mariah Carey, and another with Joan Rivers. It was *insane*," he gushes, his eyes glittering.

"I should call up and see if we can book James Spader for one of those with you. That would be the fusion of all the things you love." I laugh giddily at the thought of it and so does Gerard, but we both know that in reality he would require emergency sedation if this scenario ever came to pass.

"I don't think we're going to see him today," he sighs. "So much for my harebrained scheme. Shall we move on to yours now?" He stands and pulls me off the ground, grabbing hard onto my right wrist. We walk over to the T station, and as I search in my purse for the tokens that I know are jingling around in the bottom, I come across the folded note from Steven Tyler and frown.

"Look at this," I say, handing Gerard the piece of paper as we walk toward the train platform. "He left it under my door the other day." He unfolds it just as the train squeals into the station and then reads it in a voice loud enough for the entire car to hear once we board.

" 'Moxie, I am having a party this Friday night and just wanted to let you know. If we get too loud then please come down and tell me, no problem. I hope that your eye is better. *Steven Tyler.*' " He throws a smug glance in the direction of two teenage boys who are clearly (and misguidedly) awestruck that I've received word of an Aerosmith wingding, and refolds the note. "So he's having a party—so what?"

"So why didn't he invite me, is what I'm saying," I shout as the train screeches to a halt at the MIT stop, and I smack into a lumpy guy wearing a black *Lord of the Rings* T-shirt.

The shirt looks as though it's been through an overheated dormitory dryer one too many times, and the screenprinted images are starting to crack and peel, giving Frodo and Sam what looks like a scorching case of psoriasis. Gerard and I get off the train and onto the escalator, where I continue. "I kind of thought we were friends—you know, like apartment-building friends. Maybe I could meet some people at this party."

"You don't want to be at a party with the kind of people he's going to have over, trust me," he says soberly as he pulls his sunglasses down from their perch on top of his head. They are black, angular, and bear an ostentatious, gold Gucci "G" on each temple. "These came free with the shower gel and soap-on-a-rope," he explains impatiently as I study the sunglasses with a look of bemused disgust. "I mean to marker over the Gs, but I keep forgetting, OK?"

"OK, whatever," I say as we leave the station and stand in the bright sunlight, trying to get our bearings in this stark, industrial section of Cambridge. No Harvard sprawl here, and thus no healthy, green ivy; no quaint brick buildings, no ornate latticework on entrance gates. No tweed and elbow patches need apply. "It says '212 Cambridge Street,'" I read aloud, holding out the crisp, white business card. "That's not too far away," I add, looking left and right for some sort of building number but finding none. "Let's just start walking and see what happens."

We walk for a few blocks, past two vacant lots, an energetic group of students with overstuffed backpacks, and what looks like an abandoned factory, complete with the requisite smashed windows. And then Gerard lifts his ridiculous sunglasses off his face, peers at a large, low-slung brick building across the street, and says with finality, "That's it."

"Are you sure? There's no number," I reason.

"Look at the sculpture in front," he says, pointing. I look, and soaring majestically into a hammered silver DNA helix is what looks like a gaggle of red steel geese. "What the hell is that supposed to be?" he asks, banging the walk button and watching the stoplight go from green to yellow to red almost immediately. "See? MIT tax dollars at work," he exclaims, stepping off the sidewalk as the bright white WALK sign becomes illuminated. "You hit these in most other neighborhoods, you wait forever."

"Yeah, I guess," I say, distracted. We cross the street and Gerard walks right up to the sculpture while I hang back on the sidewalk, nervous that we'll run into Allan.

"What's the matter? We're here, let's check the place out a little bit," he says, beckoning me over. "You're not going to see him, Moxie," he adds dryly, reading my mind.

"It's Tuesday at two in the afternoon; I think there's a good chance he's in there," I argue, tentatively stepping off the sidewalk as though my steps will trigger a blaring alarm over Allan's desk.

"No, he's out with vendors or clients or whatever he does downtown. I bet he's probably at the store right at this very minute, pretending to be interested in some vile pajamas but wondering if you're in the stockroom and waiting for you to come out."

"Really?" I ask, smiling broadly as I picture it. He runs his fingertips along one of the DNA strands and pulls back immediately, grimacing. "This thing is hot!" he shouts, shaking his hand violently.

"Yeah, I think I've heard that metal can get hot in the sun," I say sarcastically, tilting my head and studying the building. I'd love to get a tour of the place from him. See what the researchers are doing. Talk science. Talk DNA. Go back to Allan's office and shut the door.

"Get that look off your face, missy," Gerard admonishes, walking away from the sculpture and standing next to me.

THE PAJAMA GAME

"It's positively smutty." He looks at the sculpture one last time and clucks, shaking his head. "Have you seen enough? Or do you want to walk around a bit more?"

"I've seen enough," I say. Gerard excitedly pumps the walk light button on this side of the street, the light changes, and we walk arm in arm across the street.

Things have gotten just a bit better between Mary Alice and me, but when I say just a bit, I do mean just a bit. If taking a blow to the eye from a total maniac only garners me a small, strained smile and some short conversation now and then from Mary Alice, I don't know what organs I'd have to sacrifice for her to be outright friendly. Gerard helpfully pointed out that she never was all that friendly to me in the first place, so I shouldn't expect such a major change in her behavior.

Today, however, she is not smiling at all, and neither am I. The reason for this scowlfest is that the store is actually closed for inventory, and we have been slogging around all day on our hands and knees, pulling old bras from low drawers and bins in the back, yanking panties from the panty tables, and groping the mannequins as we search for hidden bar codes that can be scanned into the computer system. Inventory is such a complicated process that it isn't even covered in the Operations Binder. There is another binder devoted solely to this mind-numbing exercise, this one a spiral-bound affair with a cover the color of Cream of Wheat, and Mary Alice has it splayed open on a panty table so we can check it periodically for instructions. As far as I can tell, its only key themes are to provide some sort of game plan for moving throughout the store (start with the chemises, move to the gowns, etc.), and to stress the importance of taking inventory very seriously. It strenuously suggests, for example, that the person holding the special scanner be "shadowed" by another employee, so she can be sure she has scanned each item and hasn't scanned the same item twice.

I am supremely annoyed about inventory for three reasons: One, it means the store is closed up tight for the entire day, and Allan can't visit. Two, I have to zap each and every one of these polysatin dainties before I can even think of leaving tonight, and I want so badly to go home that I can hardly stand it. And three, I forgot that today was inventory day, and I dressed up extra-sexy in an effort to excite Allan, should he decide to come to the store. I'm wearing a tight, black micro-mini that shows off my skinny but shapely legs, and a snug, deep V-necked, sleeveless, aqua sweater. My hair is styled and falls around my face in large waves, and my lips are stained a deep strawberry red, courtesy of a special lip stain I bought at the drugstore but had no idea how to use. I put on too little, then way too much, then decided to stop before I made it any worse. My feet are shod in high-heeled slingback sandals, and I even brought a different purse that matches the outfit, in case he was so overwhelmed with desire that he needed to take me out to dinner, right then and there. Not the best ensemble for climbing all over the store, in other words. Mary Alice, in contrast, has dressed appropriately, in a navy blue Red Sox T-shirt, baggy gray sweatpants, and white Tretorn sneakers with holes in the toes.

After logging in the seventy-fifth pajama set in size small, I stand up and feel a little dizzy. The armpit seams of my sweater are damp, and I can feel my thick mascara starting to clump. "How much more, Mary Alice?" I ask with unmasked dread in my voice. We've been at it for ten hours now, and I don't know how much more I can take.

"Not much more, Moxie," she answers evenly, poking her head out from behind an enormous, quivering pile of terry robes. "Just these robes, then the summer camisole sets.

Then . . . well, I'm leaving the worst for last," she finishes glumly.

Oh, no, I think. The worst? What could be worse than this? Do we need to scan in the rolls of register tape, the stacks of tissue paper, each and every credit card application? "What is that?" I ask warily, sitting next to her on the floor and starting to scan the bathrobes.

"The thongs. That stupid woman who shoplifts, she's going to get me fired. I know there's way too much shrink in that area. Cindy told me," she pouts.

"Oh. Yeah," I reply, stalling for time as I think of something to say. Inventory is when the managers who successfully fight shrink are separated from those who don't. Too many items unaccounted for, and everything starts to come into question. "Well, maybe it will be better than you think," I suggest lamely, before we finish scanning the remainder of the robes and summer camisole sets. When we get to the thongs, Mary Alice wears a pinched expression while she scans them, as though she's just seen a sad movie with someone she doesn't know very well and is trying not to cry. We log the final number in: 443 thongs in stock in Store 0212, Copley Mall, Boston, Massachusetts. But like Goldilocks in a rose-scented, lace- and spandex-strewn Three Bears' house, I have no idea if this number is too high, too low, or just right.

———

Precisely half an hour later, I am on the corner of my street, feeling grateful that my apartment building is in sight. As I pass the Awesome Nails salon, I see the old woman pulling down the metal grate in front of the plate-glass window, speaking boisterously in Vietnamese to a few of the younger girls. Perhaps the markets closed up today, and it was a good day for the S&P.

I let myself into the building and am immediately struck by two things that are unusual: light. And noise. Someone has put a high-wattage bulb in the normally empty fixture on the second-floor landing, and there are people up there, milling about on the landing, sitting on the steps. Music is blaring, and people are talking and shouting, braying loudly in bursts of alcohol-infused laughter. And then I remember. Steven Tyler's party is tonight. Well, if I'm not invited, that's fine. I'm tired anyway, and I can't wait to get out of this micromini, which feels as though it's ridden up during the walk home and is barely covering my behind.

I walk slowly up the stairs and first notice the number of men—there must be six of them on the landing alone, and there are a few standing in the open door to Steven Tyler's apartment. What's noteworthy is their collective geekiness, and I squint at a few of them as I make my way up to the landing to make sure I'm not imagining things. A couple look decidedly like young Bill Gateses, complete with the smooth swoop of greasy hair in front and ill-fitting, unfashionable clothes. A few are heavy, sloppy-looking guys in oversized T-shirts and low-slung jeans, and a handful look like Steven Tyler: that is to say they possess some remote sense of style. If pressed, I'd have to say there's not a junkie in the bunch, but by the same token, I also wouldn't be able to give a good answer as to what exactly *is* going on here. As I'm studying this motley crowd, I hear two women start yelling, and a giant *woooooooo!* comes from inside the apartment. And then I suddenly realize why I wasn't granted an invitation to this event. It's a bachelor party. I smile as I reach this conclusion, and a few of the guys turn to look at me just as Steven Tyler walks out of the apartment.

"Who's getting married?" I ask, leaning heavily on the banister and trying to avoid the stares that the greasier members of the group are giving me.

"Chris. My good friend Chris," Steven Tyler replies, grinning. "Next month. So we decided to, you know . . . have some fun." As he finishes, out of the corner of my eye I see a black bra fly into the air in the apartment and a topless woman with a shock of long red hair dances by, to the delight of the group. "It's kind of gross, I guess," he says sheepishly, slurring the s's in "gross" and "guess" in a way that suggests he's quite tipsy.

"Eh, whatever," I say, waving off his pseudo-shame. I've never been one to be offended by this kind of thing, and my blasé attitude elicits a few smiles from the guests. Just as I'm turning to go, a dark-haired guy in a pair of Dockers and a too-small, teal, knit polo shirt comes out of the apartment, takes one look at me, and smiles so broadly I can see his upper gums.

"Heyyyyyy, it's the girl of the hour!" he says excitedly, looking me up and down, his skinny neck swimming in the neatly pressed collar of the shirt. I glance quickly at my midsection and in one horrific second realize exactly what he's thinking.

"I am *not* an exotic dancer!" I say loudly, primly putting my hand to my chest. "No offense, of course," I shout into the apartment.

"None taken, hon," is the reply that comes back from a shapely girl with a blond bobbed haircut who doesn't stop gyrating for a moment as she absolves me of my guilt.

"Yeah, just shut the hell up, OK, Chuck?" Steven Tyler asks, annoyed. "Look, everybody inside," he barks, gesturing to the few guys who are left standing around. They file into the apartment, leaving him listing next to me on the landing, looking as though he might fall down any second. And I realize that now is my chance.

"Steven, I have to ask you something," I begin.

"If I can ask you something," he says, closing his eyes for a few seconds and then opening them quickly.

EUGÉNIE SEIFER OLSON

I slowly nod my assent and take a deep breath, readying myself. "Why does it seem like you don't work, yet you have money to live here and go out and things like that?"

"Why do you sing classic rock songs from the seventies at the top of your lungs when you walk down the street?" he retorts.

"Touché," I say, surprised and embarrassed. "I sing them when I'm alone at night and I want to keep people away from me." I stop there, firmly close my mouth, and wait for his answer.

"I'll tell you my answer next time I see you," he says, rubbing his eyes. "It's a long story."

"Oh, come *on*," I complain, exasperated. And annoyed that Gerard is probably right; it's got to be something icky and nefarious.

"I will tell you, it's just not the right time. People are probably breaking shit in my apartment—I have to go," he says, just as we hear the unmistakable sound of a glass shattering on the floor. "Next time I see you," he repeats, turning and heading into his apartment and leaving me in stunned silence on the landing.

———

"Moxie! Moxie, over here!" shouts a man's voice from the tiny, dark alley that runs next to Joe's Joke Shop. I squint and can only make out two trash dumpsters and some other shadowy shapes, but a second later, Joe walks out into the brilliant sunlight, grinning broadly. He is ushering in the warm weather with a lighter-weight blue polyester trouser and a short-sleeved dress shirt with an oversized, orange enamel pin on the pocket that reads, "I'm not out on a day pass, I act this way all the time!" He rests his hands on his hips and proudly surveys the sky, as though he special-

ordered this gorgeous day from the FunTime Novelty Company himself. "It's finally spring," he says, nodding slowly.
"Sixty-four years in this damn state, and at the end of every
winter, I say, 'I can't take one more day like this. I'm moving.'
Then a few weeks later, we get one of these," he clucks,
grandly gesturing with both arms outstretched.

"Yeah, it sure is a nice day," I agree, depressed that I'll be
spending it in a climate-controlled mall, surrounded by the
new summer line of skivvies. They are heavy on the man-
made materials and eye-popping hues and light on the sub-
tlety, and we've been selling out of them already. Yesterday a
woman left the store to return a purchase she'd made at the
Crate and Barrel, so she could come back and buy the filmy
undies in each of the seven colors available. It may, in fact,
have been my display that pushed her to such retail reckless-
ness: I set them up in a Roy G. Biv pattern on the table, creating a lovely panty prism. Mary Alice complimented me on
my "visual merchandising" after the customer left, but I
couldn't help but wonder what she'd returned at Crate and
Barrel and how underwear could possibly have taken its
place. Can a pair of bikini briefs possibly double as a
potholder? A dishtowel?

"Well, listen, I thought about that problem you have, and I
may have a solution," Joe says as he shields his eyes with his
hand and squints down the street.

"OK," I say uncertainly, unsure what problem he is referring to. There are so many right now.

"The problem you have with the shoplifter," he says, noticing the ill-concealed confusion on my face. "You told me
about it a while ago. I'm slow," he says apologetically.

"You're not slow," I laugh. "I'm flattered that you've been
thinking about it, Joe."

"I *am* slow," he insists, stepping under the store's awning.

"Always have been. But back when I was a kid, they didn't have all these fancy names and medicines for when you were slow. They just stuck you in the back of the classroom."

"I'm sorry," I say, frowning as I picture a young Joe unhappily facing the wall with his back to his classmates. "You know, sometimes those fancy names and medicines don't even work," I offer, thinking of just one of my many over-medicated students from my student teaching days, a kid who decided to see what would happen if he cut through the cord on the iron while it was plugged in and turned on. We had been using it to iron leaves to better see their veins, and as he grabbed the giant metal shears, I screamed from across the classroom and begged him to stop. It was the rubber on his sneakers and not the Ritalin in his blood that saved the day and my hide, and I still can't think about that afternoon without shivering.

"Meh. It's in the past," he says with finality. "Anyway. You don't care if this person steals, but you don't want her to make someone there look bad, correct?" I nod as I fold my arms tightly across my chest; it's spring but still brisk breeze territory. "Well, you just need to get that message to her, somehow. Tell her what you told me: that it's OK, but only during certain times. Pretty good, no?"

Well, not exactly. "Um, well, how would I do that?" I ask in a puzzled voice, trying to picture how I would get Catherine still and alone for ten seconds, much less have a discourse with her on the finer points of successful shoplifting.

"Hey, what do I look like here, Einstein?" he jokes. "You're smart, you'll come up with something. Oh, and hey, Moxie?" he asks, pulling open the door to the store and setting the little bells jingling. "Seems you took care of that guy, huh?" He nods his head in the direction of the Planned Parenthood.

"I guess so," I say, smiling. I suppose sometimes there really is justice, although it can move along at a pretty poky pace. After quickly logging my complaint at the police station per the officers' instructions, I fully expected the too-short pants man to be immediately banished from the clinic, preferably by a crowd of people swinging bats and bricks. But nothing happened, and he was still there, still crazy after all these Saturdays. I called Officer Panucci, who reassuringly told me these things take time, and I hung up angrily. But then—much like the healing of a wound, the kind where it's less irritated each morning and then one evening you realize it didn't bother you at all that day—I suddenly came to realize that he wasn't there anymore. His shrill voice and witless rallying cries had disappeared without fanfare or excitement. The crowd he left behind still shows up, still rants, still holds signs aloft. But none of them possesses that meanness of spirit, that unabashed cruelty toward other people. "I'm not sure where he is now, but it's not here," I add.

"Who'da thunkit?" Joe asks proudly. "My Moxie."

16

Scented Body Glitter with
Bonus Zippered Makeup Pouch

I HAVE DECIDED THAT I AM GOING TO PUT A GREAT DEAL OF effort into selling each and every one of these stupid, ribbon-bedecked items in the store, no matter how hard it is. The reason for this sudden burst of motivation is that not only do I loathe tying the ribbons over and over, all day long; but for some reason, I am also having a hard time tying them lately. It's as though my fingers won't bend the way I need them to—they are stiff and swollen and unyielding, and twice this morning, pink, quilted hangers slid from my hands as though someone commanded me to drop them via remote control. It's very peculiar and very annoying. I let out a *grrrrrrrr* from between clenched teeth as a peach-colored ribbon slips through my fingers and decide to close my eyes for a few seconds and collect myself. When I open them, Allan is standing in front of me, smiling.

"Did I wake you?" he asks as he steps out of the way to let a couple of women slide by with armfuls of chemises. I slowly raise my index finger to give him the one-minute sign, walk to the back of the store, and unlock two fitting rooms. I walk back, looking directly into his eyes the whole time.

"No," I reply flirtatiously. "I was taking a break from tying these ribbons. My fingers are acting very weird," I say zanily, drawing out the word in a mad-scientist way, so it sounds like *weeeeeeird*. "I can't get a grip—and I mean that literally."

He laughs at this and unexpectedly reaches out and grabs my hands, causing me to nearly faint with excitement. He studies my fingers for a few seconds and frowns. "You poor thing. They're all puffy. Hey, did you incite any violence in your neighborhood again and punch someone in the face?" he jokes. As he finishes the question, I wince and look around; fortunately, Mary Alice is busy in the front of the store, helping a clueless teenage boy pick out something for his girlfriend to wear to their after-prom party.

"No, sometimes I wake up in the morning and this just happens lately," I shrug, then clam up as I start to listen to myself and realize that I sound positively geriatric.

"That's too bad," he says with concern in his voice, then backs away one step. "So I'm going out of town for a little bit, and I just wanted to stop in and say hello before I go."

"Oh," I say, crestfallen. "Well . . . maybe we could go to the Au Bon Pain again sometime," I suggest, trying to look demure.

"Yeah," he says distractedly, watching as Mary Alice leads the bug-eyed boy to the register with his polysatin camisole set. "I'll be back in soon," he adds, taking another long look at me before turning to go.

———

I've stopped making my bed. There's really no point anymore; I'm so incredibly tired by the time I get home nowadays that I usually just drop into it without books, TV, phone calls, or snacks. The nice thing about leaving the sheets and blanket mussed is that it gives me a few extra minutes during the day to spend however I choose. Today I choose to have Steven Tyler make good on his offer, and for the first time in my life, I knock on his door. I hear strains of music and then the sound of footsteps approaching. He swings the door open, holding a pencil in his right hand and looking bewildered. He is wearing a ratty, black T-shirt, his black, pegleg jeans, and no shoes. His feet have freckles.

"Moxie! What's up?" he asks, leaning in the doorway and scratching his scalp with the pointed end of the pencil.

"What's up is that I wanted to know the answer to my question. From a few weeks back. You know, your party?" I ask, raising my eyebrows.

He looks at me blankly for a few seconds and then remembers. "Oh, right. That. Well, I paint," he says simply, as if this explains everything.

"Paint what?" I ask suspiciously.

"Paintings," he says slowly. "What else do people paint?" he jokes, throwing the pencil in the air and bending down to catch it before it hits the floor.

"But . . . do you sell them?"

"Some of them, yeah. I actually have a few people who buy them overseas, in Germany and Belgium. I put them on eBay. It's going slowly, but people are starting to become interested," he continues before looking right at me and smiling. "But you want to know what I really *do*, right? That's what you said the night of the party."

"Well . . . yeah, I guess," I say, suddenly embarrassed.

"I'm able to do this because of these," he says bluntly, pointing to the two ropy scars on his neck. "When I was in middle school, I had a paper route, and I was attacked by an insane dog. You know that expression, 'to go for the jugular'?" he asks rhetorically, not pausing for my answer. "Well, this dog nearly killed me. My parents won a big settlement out of court, and the money was put away until I turned twenty-one." He inhales sharply, and I realize I'm staring at his neck, so I quickly look at the floor, wishing I had never decided to get to the bottom of this. "So anyway, when I graduated college a few years ago, I suddenly realized I didn't care about computer programming. There are too many people out there already who do. Like the guys at the party," he chuckles.

"Oh," I say softly, remembering back to the party and the high nerd quotient. College buddies. C++ and Linux pals, all gathered on the landing.

"So after thinking about it for a long time, I decided to live on the money for a few years and try to make it as a painter. You know, like maybe I could make more of a valuable contribution to the world as an artist than as a programmer. And that's the whole story," he finishes, shrugging.

"But . . . how come I never see you with canvases or anything like that?" I ask stubbornly. My image of a painter is inexorably tied to enormous, gleaming white canvases.

"Because my paintings are very small. The biggest are maybe six by nine inches," he answers, using his hands to demonstrate the size, as though he's cupping a large guinea pig.

"Well, how come I never see paint on *you*?" I press, realizing at exactly that moment that there's a tiny purple swath of color on his left thumb, and that I have, in fact, seen smudges of gray on his hands before.

"Because I'm neat," he says a bit crossly. "Also, the paintings are small, so it's hard to make a mess. Look, I'm sorry if this isn't as exciting as you imagined," he adds, giving me a wry smile.

"It is," I say apologetically, biting my lip. "Can I . . . can I see the paintings?" I ask hopefully, peering past him into the apartment. He pulls himself up out of the doorway, standing straight and effectively blocking my view.

THE PAJAMA GAME

"Let me get some together that you would like," he says, grabbing hold of the doorknob in a way that suggests this conversation is soon to be over. "I'll tell you when I'm ready."

―――――――

Normal. All normal, the nurse practitioner states when I call up and ask for the results of my bloodwork. I had been meaning to have it done for some time now, and what finally pushed me to the brink was anxiously watching the dog-doo pen slide from my fingers in slow motion and fall onto the floor of the T last week, skipping and rolling as the T shook and shimmied. I pulled it out of the breast pocket of my black linen jacket—mistakenly thinking that it was my new sunglasses case—and before I could stuff it back in, the joints in my hands disobeyed me, sending the pen springing away. I yelped and silently prayed for the lights to flicker out for just a moment or two. Naturally, they didn't, and I was forced to bend down and grope under the seat of a dour businessman, grab the dog-doo pen, and place it in my bag, as though a woman putting an enormous piece of shit in her purse was the most commonplace public transportation occurrence. As I stepped off at the next stop with my dog-doo pen shoved safely down into my bag and my face blazing in embarrassment, I had two thoughts: One, Gerard is really going to pay for this—I don't know how, but I will get him back with such a vengeance he won't know what hit him; and two, something has really got to be wrong with me.

But no. According to the blood tests and the doctor to whom I complained about my intermittent aches and problems when I was examined before the blood tests, everything is normal. I actually didn't feel too bad at all on the day she examined me, and when I tried to explain that my body feels like a car that breaks down on the road but then behaves perfectly when it's in the shop, frustrating the auto mechanics who dismiss the owner's complaints, it didn't help my case. She looked out the window during my analogy, wrote a few things in the chart with a leaky pen, and that was that.

———————

"My daughter was caught cutting school the other day with her friend Tiffany," Sue begins matter-of-factly as I unfold my special pop-up educational booklet that accompanies the newborn sea turtle exhibit. Thanks to Sue, I was able to skip the $4.95 fee for the booklet; she'd stuck an extra one in her locker for me on Monday when the exhibit began, and for this I am grateful.

"Oh?" I ask, trying not to sound a touch impressed. As a child, I always took school much too seriously to even entertain the idea of skipping and was jealous of kids who would dare to go to the mall while the rest of us saps were sitting quietly and learning when to use *tú* and when to use *usted*.

"They were on a class trip to the Institute of Contemporary Art. Some kind of photography exhibit," she says, frowning as she bends to fold up the cuffs on her white, cotton shorts. They have been pressed with a firm crease down the front and graze her kneecaps, even after she's turned up the cuffs. "One of the adult chaperones noticed they were missing and went off in search of them. Of course, she found them in about three minutes, around the corner at Tower Records." She inhales and exhales deeply through her nose, a sniff of anger followed by a snort of resignation. "I mean, how dumb can my daughter be? Where *else* in that neighborhood would you look first for two thirteen-year-olds?" she quips.

"What section?" I ask distractedly as I watch one tiny turtle with interest. One of its flippers is much smaller than the others, which requires the poor thing to work double-time to keep from swimming in circles and going nowhere. I can relate to it.

"What?"

"I mean, what part of the store did they find them in?" Now I am vicariously living out my school-cutting fantasy and wondering where they spent their final moments of freedom before the executioner arrived in the form of an angry chaperone. "Were they looking at DVDs? Magazines? CDs?"

"I don't know," she replies slowly, with a look that suggests this is a very stupid question indeed. "But they sent her to this 'Scared Straight' program later in the week. They took her to a women's prison, and—"

"To a prison?" I cry, nearly dropping my booklet. "I don't really think the punishment fits the crime, Sue," I add sympathetically.

"Also, they were high," she sighs.

"Ah."

"So they go to this program, and the women in prison take turns talking about how they got there and what they did wrong in their lives, blah, blah, blah. I don't think Katie got very much out of it," she shrugs. "Although there was one woman who talked about how they can't wear makeup, and another who said that they have to buy their panties from a woman who runs an underground panty ring. Steals them from the stores and goes and sells them in bulk to some inmate there, so they can have nice underpants. So I think those things might have meaning for my daughter. If not, I'm sure the three-month grounding I gave her will," she finishes emphatically.

I turn and face her and furrow my brow. "Wait a minute, Sue. *What* was that second thing? About the underpants?"

We have a new perfume line debuting at the store this week, and Heather has taken it upon herself to set up the in-store displays, which contain everything a girl needs to stink up a storm: eau de parfum, shimmer lotion, body wash, scented body glitter, dusting powder, body mist, sloughing crème, deodorant, and room spray. They've also designed ornate keepsake boxes, zippered makeup pouches, and bejeweled evening bags around the visual theme of the line—which, as far as I can tell, employs a candy pink and red color scheme with ribbon and mesh and a bit of fluffy, pink faux feather boa material thrown in for some extra schmaltz. Heather is whistling a zippy tune as she opens a keepsake box, sets it on the new, white enamel table, and begins to arrange products artfully inside of it.

"Heather, you can stop working on that when you come back from your break," I say from behind a small cardboard box of racerback bras. I've got the box on the counter and am slashing the prices on the tickets right in plain view of customers, which is a clear violation of the rules, but I don't care.

"Why?" she asks argumentatively, rearranging her headband around her wild curls. "I'm doing a good job."

"Because Mary Alice is coming in very soon, and she needs to do it a certain way," I reply, not looking at her. Only part of this sentence is actually true—I know Mary Alice *wants* to do it, but it doesn't *need* to be done in a certain way. Earlier this week, when we received a special missive via the cash register tape that announced the arrival of the fragrance line ("SWEET KISSES SHIPPING TO STORES 0212, 0237, 0416, 0978, 0515, 0663, 0782, 0114. FULL PRODUCT LINE, MARKETING COLLATERAL, WHITE TABLE, IN-STORE TESTER DISPLAY TO SHIP THIS WEEK," it blared in blocky, black print), Mary Alice squealed with unfettered delight. "I love setting up displays for brand-new products," she gushed so earnestly that I almost got excited for her then, picturing her lying in bed, unable to sleep because she kept thinking about the best ways to display the new booty—much the way I used to do at the start of the school year, my mind looping on which science projects I should lead off with. My motivation to keep Heather from finishing the display isn't totally altruistic, however; I hope to keep Mary Alice happy today for selfish reasons as well.

"Just leave the rest for her, Heather," I say bluntly, pushing the box of bras out of the way to take a sheer, lime green babydoll set and store credit card from a customer. Heather defiantly places a pink powder puff inside the keepsake box and flounces to the stockroom. I roll my eyes at no one and finish ringing up the purchase just as Mary Alice sails into the store, nearly thirty minutes early for her shift. Such is the power of Sweet Kisses.

"What are these . . ." she starts to ask, letting her bag fall to the floor and looking at the boxes of powder and lotion and perfume with a crestfallen expression. "What are these doing out here?"

"Heather started working on it," I explain, tearing the customer's receipt from the register and flinging it into the shopping bag. "But she didn't get too far."

"Oh," she says a bit more happily, peering into the boxes and unfurling the glossy posters, which read EVERYONE LOVES SWEET KISSES, set in a typeface better suited to a Victorian calling card. The poster is so overburdened with loops and swirls that it looks like it says ERERYONE LORES SWEEL KISSES, and I'm wondering how many times I'll have to tell customers what these monstrosities actually say. "Well, I'm going to put my bag in back, and I'll get started right away. We don't want these ugly, brown boxes all over the place," she says with conviction, despite the fact that my ugly, brown bra box is on the counter; there are two ugly, brown boxes of teddies awaiting electronic sensors at the far end of the store, and there is an enormous, ugly, brown box of defective lace nighties on the floor outside the stockroom door, awaiting their fate.

I wait until Mary Alice is safely ensconced in the boxes, sitting cross-legged on the floor and humming excitedly with the shimmer lotion to her left and the body wash to her right before approaching her. "Mary Alice?" I ask sweetly.

"Yes, Moxie?" she says, pulling herself up to a kneeling position in front of the white table and setting a tall tube of body wash down next to a stout, shiny pink tub of scented body glitter. "What is it?"

"Um, well, when Heather is done with her coffee break, I'm going to take mine, and I was wondering if I could take a few extra minutes. Like, ten or fifteen minutes?" I ask hopefully, despite the fact that this would be increasing my break time by nearly one hundred percent.

"Sure," she says slowly, staring straight ahead as she unzips a makeup pouch and places a stick of deodorant and a can of room spray in it—both odd choices for a makeup pouch, in my opinion. But I'm not about to argue about Sweet Kisses, because my fervent hope is that sometime in those extra ten or fifteen minutes, I might get some of my own.

"So what you're saying is, the end justifies the means? Because I'm not sure that I agree," Allan says thirty minutes later, a bit of challenge in his voice. We are strolling along sunny Newbury Street, past the bustling, couture-clad shoppers and noisy outdoor cafés, and I am in a seriously blissed-out state. I've got a cone of Ben and Jerry's Double Chocolate Brownie in one hand and the other keeps grazing Allan's right hand as we amble down the narrow sidewalk. Best of all is that sticking out of my purse are three cellophane-wrapped, candy-colored gerbera daisies, which he shyly handed me when we met on the corner. I spied the little bursts of bright petals from a distance when I was walking toward him from the mall and thought, *No way. This is just too good.*

"How can that be?" I ask giddily. "Of course they do. She is stealing from the store to help women less fortunate, to bring

THE PAJAMA GAME

some beauty and happiness into their lives. Even if it is in the form of polyester crap," I explain, pausing to take what I hope is a seductive lick of my ice-cream cone. I end up with a small swipe of gooey ice cream on my left cheek anyway and quickly wipe it off with a scratchy paper napkin. "She's like Robin Hood, and the mall is like her forest. Catherine takes from The Man, and gives to those who are in need," I finish, trying to ignore the weakness in my legs.

Allan uses his plastic spoon to dig around in his paper cup of Cherry Garcia for a moment as he thinks aloud. "Yes, but you could argue that these women don't really deserve fancy underwear. They are in prison for a reason, so maybe they should just wear whatever the Massachusetts penal system picks out for them." He throws his head back, groans aloud, and accidentally knocks into a blond, lanky college student feeding the parking meter next to her Range Rover. She sneers at him and flips her head around in disgust, thwacking him with her braid. "I hate that word, *penal*. Isn't it horrible? Why did I just use it?" he asks, blushing a little bit.

"I don't know," I reply, grinning and shrugging. "When I was a teacher, I always used to hate it when the kids would learn that word for the first time in history class. You would hear it a thousand times those first few days. Then the novelty would wear off."

"Speaking of which, do you think you'll ever teach again? I'd bet you were very good," Allan says sweetly as we reach the corner of Dartmouth Street and he squints into the bright sun.

I immediately look from him to the sidewalk as I think about his question and how relieved I was that Sue didn't bring up the aquarium position the last time I saw her. Even if the job paid better, I know in my heart there is no way I could handle it, and this admission fills me with revulsion. "Um, I probably need to be heading back now," I say evenly, pointing in the direction of the mall. "Mary Alice gave me a lot of extra time on my break so I could meet you, and I don't want to take advantage."

"I'm sorry, did I say something wrong?" he asks, puzzled.

"Oh, no; I just don't like to talk about my teaching, that's all." I force a smile on my face. "No harm done."

"Well, let's walk back that way together, all right? I'm parked in the garage at the Marriot," he says cautiously, throwing his paper cup and spoon in the garbage can on the corner.

We walk in silence for a few minutes, and after we cross busy Boylston Street, I need to sit down. Immediately. It's as though my limbs can't handle this flirtation for another second, and they've gone as soft as pudding. "Hey, do you mind if I stop for a minute and sit on this bench?" I ask, pointing to a beat-up wooden bench on the perimeter of a large, grassy area in Copley Square. There are about six or eight teenagers skateboarding dangerously close to it, leaping off adjacent benches and crashing down heavily onto the sidewalk, but I don't care.

"Sure, no problem," he says, taking my elbow and leading me to it. "Are you OK?" he asks nervously as we sit down.

"I'm fine," I reply in what I hope sounds like a reassuring voice. "Sometimes this happens to me—I get tired and just need to cool out for a little while," I explain. We sit for a long minute. "I should probably get back now; I feel OK," I say, even though it's not really true.

We walk toward the mall and the whole time I am thinking *sweet kisses, sweet kisses*. Perhaps today is the day. We reach the giant revolving door at the mall's entrance, and, it is! But, alas, it also isn't. Allan slowly leans in and my heart starts to race as I pucker up, but then at the last second, he kisses someplace to the right of my lips, beneath my cheek. I smile awkwardly and say goodbye, quickly pushing the revolving door, so the mall can swallow me up. The place I fear I truly belong after all.

17

Cotton and Eyelet Chemise in Raspberry Print

GERARD IS HUMMING AN ATONAL MELODY AS HE PULLS HIS laundry from the oversized, gray duffel bag and shoves it, unfolded and unironed, into an already stuffed chest of drawers in his bedroom. Each time he tries to close a drawer, its bottom surface catches on the contents sticking up from the drawer beneath it, and this results in much groaning and cursing and rearranging of items. After said items have been rearranged, the same thing happens all over again with the drawer beneath that one. I am sitting cross-legged on his bed watching the show—too late to accompany him to the Cuddle 'n' Bubble, I settled for coming to Gerard's apartment instead, post-laundry.

YumYum bats around a piece of Bounce and begins eating it with gusto, and as Gerard gently takes it from her, he says sympathetically, "Maybe he's got bad depth perception, Moxie. You saw him try to kiss that girl downtown last winter, and he missed with her, too."

"No, she pulled away from *him*," I snap, much more sharply than I'd intended. Gerard reels back and begins to stuff handfuls of unmatched socks into a small drawer, his hunched shoulders to me. "Sorry, that sounded worse than I meant it to," I apologize, as YumYum leaps onto the bed after spotting another scrap of Bounce. I grab it and shove it in my shorts pocket before she can begin her second course of dryer sheet delicacy. "What I mean is, it wasn't a problem with his aim when he was with her. She was the one who didn't want to kiss. *I* wanted to kiss, but he kissed the wrong spot," I pout. "And I'm sure I know why," I add challengingly.

"Why?" he asks as a purple and green argyle sock falls on the floor in front of the dresser. He sighs before picking it up and tosses it in the drawer with resignation. "And this had better not have to do with your chicken pox scar," he warns, referring to a perfectly round, pitted pockmark beneath my lip that I've always hated.

"No, it's not that. It's that I'm a loser, and he realized it right then. I work in a mall, selling underwear. I didn't want to talk to him about my teaching. I got so tired that I had to stop and sit on a bench while we were on a thirty-minute date. Who wants to kiss that?" I ask pitifully as I realize that I've been tearing up a bit. "I am a loser."

"Hey, hey, hey!" Gerard yells, alarmed. He comes over and sits next to me on the bed, taking my hand. "No one calls my Moxie a loser! I don't hang out with losers," he says as YumYum jumps down from the bed and into a pile of shirts, where she unearths another dryer sheet and begins to chow down. "Except you," he says flatly to the cat, getting up and pulling the forbidden item from her mouth once more. "There must be a reason, OK? And you being a loser isn't it. I'm sure of it."

"Yeah?" I ask, sniffling.

"Yeah. I actually think it's a bit sweet. It's sort of chaste. I think it will fuel a new fantasy of my and James's first kiss, I like it so much," he decides. "I am sure that Allan likes you. That was just a weird thing that you two will laugh about later." He walks back to the dresser and looks at the pile of laundry, annoyed. "Listen, I've been thinking that I need to get away. And you seem like you could use a mini-vacation yourself. Do you think you can get two weekdays off in a row?"

"Probably," I say, nodding as I try to exorcise the image of Gerard and James Spader kissing (or nearly kissing) from my mind. "If I volunteer to work two weekend days, I'm sure I can. Why?"

"Because I've decided that we should go to Naragansett," he proclaims, trying in vain to shove the sock drawer shut. "We can stay at my mom and Hank's new summer place for a couple of days. It's really beautiful, Moxie," he says eagerly.

"You don't need to ask me twice," I say, finally smiling. "Will they be there?"

"Oh, no. They're at their other house on the Cape all summer. This is just a place they rent out," he explains. "I told my mom that we might want to use it for a few weekdays, and she said fine. It's even got a semi-private beach—isn't that cool?" he asks, using his shoulder to push the sock drawer so hard that the entire dresser shakes a bit. "Forty-eight hours of sun and fun and R&R," he sighs.

"It sounds great," I agree. "You realize, of course, that this doesn't let you off the hook for me having to scramble around on the T after a piece of dog shit, right?" I ask, my eyes narrowed.

"We're going to have such a good time, you won't even remember that incident by the time we come back to Boston," he says airily, trying to suppress a laugh. "Don't worry about dog shit, or Allan, or underwear. You just find your bathing suit and leave the rest to me."

Luttman is annoyed. In atypical fashion, he is exhibiting human emotion this afternoon, his face reddening and his shoulders tensing as he takes me and my session-skipping ways to task. "Moxie, you cancelled your last appointment—again—but then you come here and complain that you don't feel well. If you can't make a commitment to becoming healthy, then I'm not sure I can help you," he barks.

I grab onto the tissue box and spin it in my hands; it's blue on two sides and green on the other two and bears the name of a new drug in thick, white, italicized letters. "I'm sorry," I say unconvincingly. "I want to get better. I just don't know if this is the right place to do it. I just feel like something is wrong, but I can't put my finger on it." Not least of which because I can't use my fingers all that well these days, I add silently.

He sighs loudly. "You told me that the bloodwork was fine. No one can find a reason for your other assorted aches and pains and feelings of malaise, right?" he asks in a slightly more cordial tone. "And they come and go, with no rhyme or reason, correct?"

"That's right," I admit.

"I don't know what to say then," he says quietly.

"Well, isn't there anything else that can be done?" I ask, exasperated. "Another test or something?"

He shakes his head. "I think you need to make a decision. If you want to get back on track, you need to decide that you're the one responsible for your own health. By that, I mean mental and physical. There's no shame in being depressed. I've told you that before."

"I never said there was," I say defiantly, crossing my arms in front of my chest.

"You could try to get more tests, Moxie, but they are all going to say the same thing," he continues, squinting out the window. The sun is blazing today, and they are predicting a scorching heat wave later in the week. I lean back in my chair and feel deflated, like a helium-filled balloon long after the party's over, pathetic-looking and grazing the ground. When this happens, you either pop the balloon to put it out of its misery or let it slowly become smaller and thinner by the day, until it finally takes up residence in a corner and you find it weeks later, motionless and dusty, its latex skin thick and rippled and ugly. I wonder briefly which fate would be better for a balloon and decide that something's got to give.

———————

The mall is absolutely packed this afternoon, which would be very unusual for a Sunday in July, except that it's pouring rain outside. The summer storm rolled in somewhat unex- pectedly this weekend, sending the weathermen scurrying to retract their assurances that the heat wave was coming just in time for a sunny Sunday at the shore. Now the scorcher's been pushed back to Monday and Tuesday, which works out quite well for me, since I'll be in Naragansett with Gerard, sunning myself on a semi-private beach. In the meantime, however, I must suffer throngs of crabby shoppers, who are bitterly disappointed they're not on Cape Cod but not so bit- terly disappointed that they can't muster the energy to try on numerous V-strings and fling them to the floor of the fitting rooms in a twisted-up mass of shiny fabric.

I emerge from the fitting room with my pile of panties and compulsively check around for Allan. It's been well over a week since our ice cream date, and I am starting to lose hope. For better or worse, I don't have too much time to fret about it right now; the line at the register seems to have doubled since I began cleaning out the fitting rooms, and Mary Alice is des- perately gesturing for me to come over.

"Sorry," I mutter, taking my place at the register next to hers. We haven't even bothered to open this second register since we got here this morning because we weren't so sure there would be enough customers to warrant it. If you open both registers, you must key all the pertinent information into both registers, count and recount each and every bill, coin, credit card transaction, traveler's check, and gift certificate from both registers, and cash out of and lock up both registers at the end of the night. In the interest of making things easier, I convinced Mary Alice that we could make do with one, and as I scan the line of impatient shoppers, I now clearly see the folly of my ways.

I punch in the store code, my employee code, and another special code that gives me access to certain types of transactions (returns and exchanges, mostly), turn my key in the register drawer, and watch it hum to life, the green LED letters welcoming customers to the store. "I'm open over here, for whoever is next," I say loudly and then bend down behind the counter and pretend to pick something up off the floor. This is because whenever you split one long line into two, there are invariably a few women who try to rush from the back of the old line to the front of the new one and madness ensues. And because whomever is unfortunate enough to be working the newly opened register is often called upon by angry customers to referee, I learned long ago to take refuge down here by the stacks of shopping bags and boxes of plastic sensors.

"Hey, I was next!" I hear a woman say disappointedly, as another yells in a thick South Shore accent, "Who do you think you are? That's not fair!" I stay crouched on the floral carpet, carefully pulling at the carpet fibers like a paleontologist combing soil for trilobites. When it sounds relatively peaceful, I stand up, unceremoniously drop a small pile of carpet fuzz and straight pins onto the back counter, and turn around to face a smug customer who pushed her way to the front. Then I ring, and ring, and ring. String bikinis, pajama shorts, garters, satin robes, padded bras, plunge bras, baby dolls, body lotions. Tissue paper flies everywhere as Mary Alice and I reach for a few sheets at the same time. Two gift certificates here, three credit card applications there. After forty-five minutes, it's all over and I'm sweating, but at least the line has finally dwindled down to nothing, and the store is quiet. Mary Alice lets out a huge sigh of relief. "I'm going to take my break now," she says, rearranging the bow on her sailor blouse, which got flipped around in all the retail excitement. "Heather is in back; I'll send her out."

She quickly makes her way to the stockroom, and a moment later, the door swings open and Heather walks out, kicking a large box of camisoles in front of her. "You can work on these here by the registers and I'll go up front," I tell her. She shrugs nonchalantly and begins putting electronic sensors on the camisoles. I walk to the front of the store where I spot Vera, who is holding a sheer, robin's-egg-blue chemise up to her ample chest and grimacing.

"Hey, where have you been?" I ask, tilting my head and putting my hands on my hips.

"New York," she says simply, choosing not to provide any additional explanation. "But I'm back now—for the summer, at least." She runs one of her thick hands through her heavily highlighted blond wig and smiles. "So what's new, honey?"

"Oh, um . . ." I say, looking around the store in desperation. "Not very many things that will suit you, I'm afraid," I admit. "Although we did get some lace, tanga-style underwear that could be good," I remember aloud. When I unpacked them, I recall thinking that the cut of the underwear seemed a little roomier than most, and the lace panel in the crotch had a lot of give, which could provide adequate ball room for Vera. "You want me to show you a pair?"

"No, I meant what's new with *you*, Moxie," she says, shaking her head.

"Oh, nothing, really. Same old, same old," I reply, ignoring the twinge in my heart when I realize that this clichéd answer is actually true. Then I remember something casual-conversation worthy and say triumphantly, "Oh, no, that's not the case! I am going on vacation tomorrow for a couple of days. To Naragansett."

"Ooh, classy place," she purrs, holding up the chemise again. "Not my color," she says sadly.

"Or size," I add. "You can get an extra-large online, I'm sure. Or I can—"

"What's wrong?" Vera asks, looking slightly alarmed and widening her eyes, which have been artfully enhanced with silver and gray eye shadows and eggplant-colored mascara. I've stopped speaking and am standing perfectly still, because right in my line of sight is Catherine. Catherine leaning over the thong table and scooping the new line of ultra low-rise thongs right into her Macy's shopping bag. I study her for a few seconds longer, look behind me ever so slowly to see Heather engrossed in her camisoles over by the registers, and turn back to strong, strapping Vera.

"Can you help me with something, Vera?" I ask quietly. She silently nods and her eyes begin glittering behind the mascara; she knows something is afoot. "I need you to grab that woman over there," I say, sliding my eyes in Catherine's direction.

"The one with the sweatpants?" she whispers, scrunching her nose in distaste.

"The very one. I need you to grab her, and if you can, put your hand over her mouth, too," I whisper back.

"Sounds freaky," she hisses excitedly. "I'll do it." And without further ado, she strides across the carpet and bear-hugs Catherine from behind, who lets out only one frightened squeal before Vera firmly clamps a gigantic hand over her mouth. I walk briskly over and look Catherine right in the eye. From this distance, I feel very sorry for her; she is in desperate need of quality orthodontia, some acne cream, and antibiotics for an oozing, red, right eye. I silently pray that Vera doesn't pick up Catherine's pinkeye. Then I get down to business.

"Don't make any noise," I say quickly to her, my voice low and steady. "And stop squirming. I'm *not* going to turn you in for stealing. Got it?" At this, Catherine's arms go limp, and Vera loosens her grip, but only slightly. "I don't give a shit what you take from this place. But don't take it when you see that big, blond girl working here, OK?" Catherine doesn't reply, doesn't make a sound, just breathes heavily and looks at me wide-eyed and uncomprehending. "Look, I think that you take these to a prison, and if that's true, that's a good thing," I continue even faster, knowing that I need to wrap this up, since a new customer just entered the store and was, as one might expect, suitably alarmed to see a store employee talking to a dirty-looking woman in the taut embrace of a giant drag queen. "You can take as many as you want on the days I'm managing here alone or when there's another manager here, but you don't do it on the days you see the blond woman. All right?"

"OK," she answers gruffly, her voice low and gravelly, as though she smoked a whole carton of cigarettes this morning alone. "All right."

"And just to show you I'm good for it, here's my gift to you," I say pleasantly, opening her shopping bag and quickly hurling in a few thongs. "Free with no purchase."

"Moxie," Vera begins anxiously.

"You can let her go now," I say happily, my back to the rest of the store as I grab a few different sizes from the table and toss them into the bag.

"*Moxie*," she says again, this time ominously. I look up, and standing in the center of the store, their mouths open and arms akimbo, are Mary Alice and Heather. Damn this thick carpet that masks mall dirt and footsteps alike, I think to myself. Then I think, *fuck*. Vera suddenly lets go of Catherine, who is as bewildered as I've seen a person look in quite a long time. She turns tail with her Macy's shopping bag, Vera mumbles something about considering the lace, tanga-style panties and sprints from the store, and I am left next to the picked-over thong table, barely breathing. Mary Alice studies me with dark eyes, and I begin counting the minutes until I am in Naragansett, when who shows up at my right elbow but Allan.

"Hi," he says, a tight smile on his face. "How's it going?"

"It's been better," I reply distractedly as I watch Heather creep back to her box of camisoles and Mary Alice walk stiffly behind the counter. She is frowning and still watching me, and I can't decide if I want to burst into tears and fall into Allan's arms, or just throw up and pass out. The first seems more romantic but inappropriately needy; the second, inexcusably revolting. So I opt for turning my back to Mary Alice and putting on the happiest face possible, which I'm sure isn't very convincing, since my forehead is now dripping with flop sweat. Fortunately, Allan doesn't notice because he's wearing an expression of pure angst himself.

"Yeah, for me too," he says, vigorously rubbing his forehead as though he's auditioning for an Excedrin commercial. "Look, I think you and I should go out this week. Maybe to dinner?" he asks quickly, in a near-businesslike tone.

"OK," I say, my head swimming. "Sure, yeah. I'm away Monday and Tuesday, but maybe on Wednesday?" If I still work here on Wednesday, that is, I think to myself. "I can get an hour for dinner if I skip my two short breaks earlier in the day, but that's all," I say apologetically. "From six to seven."

"That's all right," he says, looking into my eyes. "That's . . . that's fine," he adds almost dismissively. "We can go someplace here in the mall or over in one of the hotels. Where should we meet?"

"How about by the entrance to the Neiman Marcus, down there by the benches?" I ask, knowing exactly where Gerard will be at six o'clock on Wednesday: standing behind a large, fake plant, or perhaps seated on a nearby bench and hiding behind a newspaper with a tiny hole cut in it.

"Great. See you then, Moxie," he says, giving me that same tight-lipped smile before he leaves. I look around the store and realize that Mary Alice has gone into the stockroom—to call home office to put in an official request to have me pistol-whipped, no doubt. I force myself to take a few deep breaths, study my pink face in the mirror for a few seconds, and go back to counting the minutes until Naragansett.

––––––––

Gerard is late—no big surprise there—but it's hot and incredibly sunny, even at ten in the morning, and I can't stand out on this smoldering sidewalk for another second for fear that my rubber flip-flop will actually start to melt into it. I step back into my dark apartment building for a moment and study the postmarks on Steven Tyler's packages once more: a small, squat one from Troy, New York and a puffy, padded envelope from Granby, Connecticut. I give a little harrumph when I realize that despite seeing Steven Tyler and saying our standard neighborly hellos for weeks now, he's never made good on his offer to show me his paintings. Paintings, my ass, I'm thinking to myself, when I hear a loud, peppy honk from outside the door. I pull the twill handles of my canvas beach bag back onto my shoulder and go onto the sidewalk to see Gerard in a gleaming, silver convertible. He is wearing green and yellow striped shorts and a short-sleeve, gray T-shirt and is grinning idiotically.

"Look at this!" I exclaim as I try to open the car door. It's locked, and as he reaches over to pull up the lock, I can see he's sweated through at least one of the armpits of the shirt already.

"It's a Saab!" he crows. "Perry lent it to me to thank me for helping him with his sofa," he says, referring to the time his neighbor and the neighbor's boyfriend tried to move a sofa into Perry's apartment and got stuck on the stairs. But not just stuck in the conventional sense, where they needed some help moving it up or down. No, they pushed and pulled, so certain in their conviction that sheer force would be their ally, that the sofa was literally wedged in the landing and could not be moved one millimeter in either direction. It couldn't go forward, backward, up, or down—and neither could Perry nor his boyfriend, as they both were pinned beneath it. As luck would have it, Gerard emerged to take out the trash and happened upon the miserable scene. He rushed to the local hardware store, politely asked to rent a giant saw, and valiantly freed the men from the shackles of sofa oppression. He took about an inch off one of the sofa legs, and the boyfriend was later able to sand down the other three, thus preserving the sofa and the relationship, and securing Perry's offer to do Gerard any favor he ever wanted.

"It's Swedish," Gerard continues excitedly. "It's the only Swedish thing I've ever had in my possession that didn't come from Ikea."

"Nice," I say, putting on my seatbelt and sunglasses. I stretch and yawn; I didn't sleep a wink last night, my mind working through yesterday's events, churning the images past my closed eyelids over and over, like items in a front-loading washing machine. First my getting caught helping Catherine steal, then Allan asking me out in a most disconcerting manner, then back to Catherine again, until it was time for the spin cycle, and it started over from the beginning. I haven't yet told Gerard about any of it, and I decide to let it wait. We've got two full days together, and I need desperately to rest. "I think I might take a little snooze while we drive, if that's OK," I say, tossing my bag over my shoulder and into the tiny back seat, which surprises me by responding with an annoyed meow. "What?" I exclaim, astounded. "Is YumYum coming with us?" I ask as I turn around and see her plastic carry case in the rear footwell of the driver's side of the car.

"Take it easy, she doesn't eat much," he laughs. "She's never been to the beach, and I thought she might like it," he says, stepping on the gas and speeding to the corner, where we hit a red light and he screeches to a stop. I settle deeper into my seat, enjoying the bizarre combination of warm sun on my skin and cool air blowing on my face, and see a young Awesome Nails employee standing outside the salon, scowling and squinting in the bright sunlight. The door is propped open with a large, cement frog, which suggests to me that no matter how awesome its nail care may be, Awesome Nails isn't air-conditioned. I feel sorry for the undoubtedly sweaty employees and make a quick wish that their stocks soar as high as the temperature today so they can spring for some central air. Then I promptly pass out before we even reach Storrow Drive.

———

Gerard and Vera were both correct in their assessment of Naragansett: This place is classy. And beautiful. His mom and Hank's house is right on the beach and boasts that often elusive combination of looking pristine while offering total comfort. The sofa in the living room is a giant, soft, denim affair, surrounded by a bright white carpet with blue trim. The upstairs rooms have been meticulously decorated with sea themes—the master bedroom is the seashell room, the smaller bedrooms are the sailboat and lighthouse rooms, and the bathroom is the fish room. Normally this sort of interior design would make me gag, but here, with the smell of salt air and the warm breeze floating through the house, it feels just right. The deck furniture is neat and arranged just so, with tiny glass-topped tables flanking cozy chaise lounges that are positively beckoning me to them. I can't lie down yet, though, since Gerard needs help bringing his many items in from the car.

"How much stuff did you bring?" I ask sleepily, shading my eyes with my hand and reaching into the trunk of the car. The sun is blazing, just as the weathermen promised it would be. I pull out a white shopping bag filled with videotapes and immediately drop it to the ground because it's so heavy. I bend down and root around in the bag for a minute, reading aloud. "*White Palace, Less Than Zero, Crash, sex, lies, and* . . . aw, cripes, Gerard. We're not going to sit around watching these, are we?" I moan.

"No," he replies curtly as he reaches into the backseat and picks up YumYum's carrier. "I just thought in case it rains, or if we're hanging around or whatever. I've got *Candid Cameras* to catch up on, too," he adds.

"Well, it doesn't look like rain now," I say gratefully as we head back into the house and bring our bags up to the two small bedrooms.

"You should take the lighthouse room," Gerard yells from across the narrow hallway as I change into my bathing suit in the sailboat room. "It's more classic, I think."

"It's all right, I like this one," I say honestly, admiring the way the gauzy curtains billow over the bed when the wind blows. I step into the hallway at the same time as Gerard, who takes one look at me and grimaces.

"Yecch!" he says, looking me up and down. "You are way too thin, Moxie. I can see your hipbones," he adds, crossing his arms in front of his chest and studying me with distaste.

"Hey, screw you, OK?" I snarl, despite the fact that I actually thought the same thing myself when I looked at my body in the rope-trimmed mirror on the back of the door. "What the hell do you know about how a woman should look?" I challenge.

He gasps. "I don't expect to be talked to this way in my own home!" he exclaims in a haughty voice, accidentally dropping his bottle of sunscreen in all the drama. I sigh and decide to call a truce, which I usher in by picking up the bottle and handing it back to him.

"Well, luckily, you're not in your own home," I say slowly and pointedly. "You're in your mom and Hank's home. And I'm sorry; I'm just a little self-conscious about how I look lately." We go downstairs and Gerard pours two large, clear plastic tumblers of lemonade, pulls two plush beach towels from a narrow closet, and slowly opens the glass sliding doors and YumYum's carrier. YumYum takes a few tentative sniffs of the briny air and darts out to the deck, then leaps down onto the sand, which she immediately treats as the world's largest litter box that it is.

"Well, that didn't go as I planned," Gerard says in a strained voice, and we both start laughing. Nothing like a little cat shit to smooth things over between friends. We take our places on the lounge chairs, I refuse Gerard's offer of sunscreen (I want to look tan for my date with Allan), he snaps open a crisp copy of *Archie*, and I immediately fall asleep in the sun. I sleep all day long, from noon until seven, until Gerard shakes me awake for dinner. We make enormous lobster-salad sandwiches, and in between bites, I tell Gerard about my whirlwind Sunday at the mall, and he makes the appropriate sympathetic noises through his seafood at all the right moments. At eight o'clock we relax on the denim sofa, and I fall into a deliciously heavy sleep once more, until Gerard wakes me and tells me it's time for bed. I look at the anchor-themed clock with puffy eyes and can't believe it's midnight already.

The next day we get up at nine o'clock and decide to do it all over again, as only a beach getaway should be done. Only I'm so tired by now that I can hardly get down the stairs, and when I finally do, I feel as though I'm going to pass out. I sit on a high stool in the breakfast nook until I can pull myself together, and then wobbily walk out to the deck.

"Moxie, are you all right?" Gerard asks from his lounge chair, using the corner of his beach towel to rub extra sunscreen off the palms of his hands. "You look . . ." he begins, but then stops, thinking better of it. "This stuff is so slimy," he complains, holding up one of his greasy palms for me to see. "And they wonder why people don't like to wear it."

"I'm OK," I say, my voice shaky. "I think now that I'm on vacation, my body's just really letting itself relax," I add uncertainly, since I'm afraid that if I were any more relaxed, I'd be in a coma. "I'm going to work on my back today," I decide, lying facedown on my lounge chair, closing my eyes, and entering a dreamless sleep that lasts until it's time to leave Naragansett. I think at one point Gerard tried to get me up for lunch, and then again for dinner, but it's a little too hazy to remember.

18

Convertible Bandeau Bra in Nylon Mesh

I AM IN A QUANDARY THIS MORNING, WONDERING JUST HOW risky it would be to go on my dinner date with unbrushed teeth. This is not because I ran out of toothpaste or left my toothbrush in the ceramic, fish-shaped toothbrush holder in the bathroom of the Naragansett beach house; rather, it is because I can't bend my fingers well enough to get a grip on my toothbrush, and it keeps falling out of my hand, smearing seafoam-green Crest all over the bowl of the sink each and every time. My hands feel like swollen claws, gnarled and painful and thwarting me from honoring those time-honored dating requirements of a shiny smile and minty-fresh breath.

And, to be honest, my filmy mouth is the least of my worries. After sleeping the entire way back to Boston, I still had only just enough energy to slowly walk up to my apartment, read a few pieces of mail, put some lotion on my red, sunburned skin, and crawl into bed. Even though the heat wave is still in full swing, I was freezing all night long, my teeth chattering as sweat poured from by brow and delirium-driven dreams interrupted my sleep. My eyes are tired and puffy, my face is hot, tight, and florid with fever and sunburn, and I ache from head to toe. Each of my bones feels as though it may splinter in two every time I move, and when I do move, all I can accomplish is a slow slog from place to place. And this is only within the confines of my apartment, where going from the bathroom to the kitchen seems to require the stamina of a Boston Marathon runner. None of this augurs very well for a two-to-ten shift and dinner date.

When I called my HMO this morning to ask for a doctor's appointment, the nurse sighed audibly after I read my member number and she pulled my name up on the computer; I told her I had a fever but couldn't elaborate on how high it is, since I don't remember where my thermometer is, and I'm too tired to search for it. In a flat, bored voice, she informed me that she could give me a three-thirty appointment today, which I nearly took before remembering that if I went to a doctor's appointment, I'd have to use some time from my short breaks or my dinner break. And my short breaks and dinner break are already spoken for, since I'm going out with Allan this evening. I made an appointment for eleven forty-five tomorrow morning instead, which happens to be just shy of twenty-four hours from now. Twenty-four hours; I can handle that.

I finish getting ready and decide to sit down at the kitchen table, where I spend a few minutes staring into space and sipping from a glass of water. When it's time to go, I stand slowly, bracing myself on the table and noting the faint buzzing in my head and the shaky feeling in my legs, as though they are conspiring to land me flat on my face. I carefully trudge about halfway down the stairs when I run into Steven Tyler entering his apartment. In spite of the sweltering heat, he is wearing a black T-shirt with a white Newbury Comics logo on it, black denim cutoff shorts that hit him at the knee and make him look even shorter than he actually is, and olive-green Converse low-tops. He is sucking on a Blow Pop, which, judging by the unearthly green hue on his lips, must be green apple flavored.

"Hi," I croak, the word reverberating in my aching head.

"Are you all right?" he asks, pulling the lollipop from his mouth and slurping up a little bit of leftover lolly drool.

"I went to the beach for a few days, and I think I got too much sun," I say slowly, thinking, *Please stop talking to me. I don't have enough energy for conversation. Leave me alone.*

"OK," he says, looking me over critically and twirling the lollipop. "You do look pretty red," he concedes. "But you also look kinda out of it," he adds indelicately. "Be careful, all right?"

"All right," I say wearily, thinking, *Shut up, you!* "I will."

———

It's four o'clock, so that means two hours of my shift down, only two more hours until my date with Allan, then only three more hours of work after that; then only twelve, no that's *thirteen* hours until . . . when I realize that my mind feels too murky to be doing even simple arithmetic, I give up. I can barely stand upright and pretend to neaten the bra drawers, much less calculate how many hours until my doctor's appointment. I haven't been offering to help customers, haven't been cleaning out the fitting rooms, haven't done anything that requires more than standing still and silently aching. No one has said anything to me about Sunday's antics with Catherine and Vera, and fortunately, I am too ill to care even if anyone had. I'm still swaying like a sickly, spindly palm tree after a hurricane, when I realize that it's five forty-five and time to get ready for my date. I head back into the stockroom, and as I put my hand on the bathroom door handle, Mary Alice appears at my side.

"Moxie," she says stiffly, "Cindy is coming tonight at the end of your shift. She needs to have a discussion with you. With us," she finishes, her face impassive.

"Cindy?" I ask slowly, unable to resist the lure of a cardboard box of robes sitting to the left of the bathroom. I lower myself onto it, relieved to be sitting for the first time since getting off the T earlier this afternoon. "Oh, yes, the regional manager," I remember aloud. The same woman whom I urged to go easy on Mary Alice, back in the winter when she complained to me about her thong shrink problem. I close my eyes and lean my head against the wall, unable to muster the energy to even care about what fate is going to befall me. In my dazed state, I wonder how many times I've sat on one of these cardboard boxes in the stockroom thinking about a world in which I'm not selling underpants, daydreaming about Edward Norton. "All right," I whisper as I pull myself up from the box. "So we'll do that later, then," I shrug, not meeting Mary Alice's eyes. I go into the bathroom, take one look at myself, and want to cry. But since this can only make things worse, I instead choose to splash some cool water on my face, swish some mouthwash around, and leave to meet Allan.

Five minutes later, I'm downstairs in front of the Neiman Marcus, sitting with my head between my knees as Gerard gently touches my back. It's a few minutes shy of six o'clock, and I'm at once anxious for him to take his place on a bench ten feet away, but still enjoying the feel of his hand on my skin. "You'd better go now," I say, lifting my head and looking at him. "He'll be here soon."

"You can still cancel, you know," he implores, pulling a *Bay Windows* newspaper out of his messenger bag. This is Boston's premiere gay and lesbian paper, and he has cut a peephole in the front of this week's issue, resulting in the decapitation of two men pictured at a fundraising gala. "You can tell him when he comes here that you're not feeling well enough to go out." He studies me with pursed lips for a few seconds. "Moxie, you're *not* well enough to go out."

"I know," I whimper as he stands up and begins folding the paper into prime spying position. "I know. I'm not even hungry. But I have a weird feeling about this dinner, and I just want to get it over with," I finish sadly.

Gerard pulls me up to my feet, then quickly fixes my hair and squeezes my clammy hands. "I am sure you misread him when he came to the store," he says slowly, trying to reach my brain through the fever. "You had just had the thing with Catherine, and I'm sure Allan is *very excited* to take you on a date. A dinner date, Moxie!" he exclaims. "I'm going to be right over there," he coos, pointing to a bench on the opposite side of the planter, as though I'm his toddler, and he's taking me to preschool for the first time and will be standing with the other anxious parents in a far corner of the room.

He ambles over to his bench, snaps open his newspaper, and we wait. And wait. It's six-ten, then six-fifteen, and then six-twenty. I sit on the bench, alternately between staring at the revolving doors to the mall and closing my fiery eyelids, when a panicky feeling starts to rise in my chest. Now it's six-thirty, and Gerard drops his newspaper long enough to fix me with a quizzical look and a befuddled shrug. He starts to come over, but I wave him away, trying to ignore my pounding heart and short, staccato breaths. At six forty-five, I stand and walk over to Gerard, who pulls his *Bay Windows* away from his face to reveal a crestfallen expression.

"He's not here," I say, a lump developing in my throat. "I'm not on *The New Candid Camera*, am I, Gerard? You're not going to bring out Peter Funt, and then we all have a laugh about this, are you?" I ask dubiously, my voice reedy and thin as the tears start to flow.

"No," he says sadly. "This isn't *The New Candid Camera*,

Moxie. I wish it was." He puts his elbows on his knees and rests his chin in his hands, shaking his head. "I'm really sorry."

"That's OK," I lie as I burst into tears in earnest, heaving and sniffling in front of a tony couple leaving Neiman Marcus, laden with their new purchases. "I gotta go," I sniff, slumping my back and shuffling toward the escalator.

"No, Moxie, wait!" shouts Gerard as he begins walking toward me. I get on the escalator and begin walking up quickly—too quickly, in fact, as I soon get very dizzy. But I don't want to talk to Gerard about it. Don't want to talk to anyone about anything. Just want to get back to the store, so I can spend the last five minutes of my break sitting alone on the cardboard box. A large group of teenagers gets on the escalator and begins shouting and jostling one another, and this propels me up the steps, leaving Gerard standing at the base of the escalator with his limp newspaper in his left hand, looking worried and bewildered.

I walk as fast as my weak legs will carry me to the store, ignoring the thundering pain in my body. I just need to sit down, just relax, just for a minute. I push past a customer at the store's entrance, stride past the cash registers, and just as I hit the rack of merry widows, something happens. The mass of red satin and black elastic suddenly looks very fuzzy; but I press on, opening the door to the stockroom, even though my feet and legs feel like they're slipping into quicksand. I see a big, tall shape with lots of yellow on top, and in Mary Alice's voice, it asks me, "Moxie? Are you all right?"

"I just need to . . ." I whisper, finishing the rest of the sentence in my head, *sit down. Sit here and relax. Just for a minute. I just need to sit. I'll be OK.* And then everything goes black.

There is a mall security guard standing over me first; then, I presume, the mall security guard's boss. I can hear one of them asking Mary Alice inappropriately personal questions about me that I'm sure she wouldn't know how to answer anyway—Does she have diabetes, ma'am? Could she be pregnant?—but no matter how much I think I can answer the questions myself, my brain won't let me do it. I valiantly attempt to form the words, but my mouth won't cooperate; or, if I think I can force my lips and tongue to fall in line, the guards go fuzzy once again as blackness creeps in around the edges of my vision. The next thing I know, there are two more men in uniforms; these have the same polyester content as the guards' but carry a little more clout with sewn-on EMT badges.

"She's tiny," I hear one say as he takes my pulse. "I can probably get her onto the stretcher myself, Don." He puts his lips to my ear and says in a too-loud voice, "Everything's going to be all right." The last thing I remember before closing my eyes and giving myself over fully to this exhaustion is hearing the classical music as they carry me out of the store and a woman's voice saying, "See? That's what happens when you wear a too-tight bustier, missy!"

———

Fluorescent lighting sure is strange, I think to myself sleepily as I look up at the flickering bulbs on the ceiling. It's so ugly to look at, and the strange glow it casts on everything is even worse. Why would someone design a light like that? That's just crazy, I decide, when a doctor appears. Is he the first one? No, no; he's the second one, or maybe the third. I can't remember. Yeah, he's the second one. I've been admitted, I know that much, after much concern about my fever and the results of my blood and urine tests. What the hell was it? Something with kidneys; yes, that's it. Lots of nervous talk about kidneys. My grandparents had a kidney-shaped pool, and the memory of swimming in it when I was young and wearing my favorite striped bikini floats through my brain and interrupts the loop of thoughts about fluorescent lighting.

"Hello, Rebecca." I turn my teary eyes toward the voice and see an ID that says EDWARD L BUCHMAN M.D., RHEUMATOLOGY. What the hell does that word mean? *Rheuma.* That's a Greek root word for something, I know it. But what? Above the ID is a bald head wearing oversized, black-framed glasses that give the doctor a strong resemblance to my favorite Muppet Show character from childhood, Dr. Bunsen Honeydew. This nearly makes me laugh aloud in my delirium. He looks about fifty years old, with tired eyes and a few stubbly spots he missed shaving on his neck.

"Moxie," I whisper, my head pounding. "My name is Moxie," I say weakly.

"All right," he says, writing something in a chart. "Tell me what you told the first doctor you saw when you came in here."

"I don't remember," I say quietly. "Um, I've been depressed and really tired," I begin, fully expecting him to throw up his hands in disgust and summarily admit me to the psychiatric unit. Only he doesn't do either of these things; he just raises his eyebrows behind his Muppet glasses, so I go on. "I get . . . fevers," I say deliberately, "but they always go away eventually. I can't bend my fingers, either," I whisper, my lips so dry they momentarily stick together on the *b* in *bend*. "My hair is falling out. My face gets red. But never all at the same time. You know, like a car, where sometimes it has a problem and sometimes not? I know that's a stupid analogy. I went to my friend's beach house, and I was in the sun the whole time. Then we came back—"

And this is where he does not permit me to finish, and I'm thinking, stop using that car analogy, Moxie; he thinks you're nuts, just like everyone else. I clamp my mouth shut and am screaming to him inside my head, *You asshole!*, when he grabs a young, blond girl in scrubs sailing by. She is wearing a high ponytail that was probably neat and tight at the beginning of her shift but now looks withered and tired; one lock of hair has sprung partially free from the elastic and creates a big loop of hair on the side of her head. He glances amusedly at the loop for a half-second and tells her my name, my age, and the list of tests that I need to have. Not one of them sounds remotely like anything I've ever heard of before. My mind drifts back to the *rheuma* root word that I still can't recall as he turns to me and says, "I need to go now, but I'll see you later. We're going to figure out what's happening. Don't worry." And for the first time in as long as I can remember, I don't.

19

Cotton Hospital Gown in Pale Blue

"WELL, THIS ALL SOUNDS ABOUT AS MUCH FUN AS WHEN I GOT diarrhea on that blind date," Gerard says mildly, dropping the book in his lap and chewing his lip as he looks out the tiny window. Gerard, my hero, the man who had the sense to follow me up the escalator at the mall and demand that I be taken to Brigham and Women's Hospital. Gerard, who waited patiently here all night, and, immediately after I was diagnosed yesterday, walked as quickly as his crummy gait could carry him to the local bookstore to find as much information as he could on the illness I can finally put a name to. He picks up the book, clears his throat, and begins reading aloud.

"'Lupus is a chronic inflammatory disease that can involve various parts of the body, including the skin, joints, blood, kidneys, and brain.'" He looks up expectantly and I wearily extend my index finger to the side and roll my wrist, the universal sign for *get on with it*. "'Normally, the immune system makes antibodies to protect the body against viruses, bacteria, and other foreign materials. But with lupus, the immune system can't tell the difference between foreign materials and its own tissues, so it makes antibodies to fight against itself.'" He raises his eyebrows and blinks a few times, as though a camera just flashed in his face. "'This causes buildup in the body's tissues and can cause inflammation, injury to tissues, fever, fatigue, and pain.' Want me to go on?" he asks tentatively, reaching over and fixing the pillow beneath my head.

"No thanks, I've heard enough," I reply sourly. "Dr. Buchman filled me in. Plus, I have that," I add, pointing to the table next to the bed where there is a crappily designed, two-color brochure that reads "Lupus: Fast Facts" above a photograph of a droopy flower. Inside, it describes the disease, using one panel to explain how the illness develops, another panel to talk about who gets it and why, and another panel to discuss treatments, from steroids to surgery. It's all quite tidy and neat and perfunctory, and it belies all of my suffering of late.

But my favorite panel by far, the one I kept perversely looking at until I committed nearly every word to memory, is the back one, which lists the main symptoms of lupus. Despite the stiffly worded, two-line disclaimer explaining that each person with lupus is different and diagnosis can be difficult because the symptoms can vary from person to person and day to day, I couldn't help crying when I read through the list. Achy, swollen joints. Fever. Hair loss. Prolonged and/or extreme fatigue. Skin rash across the cheeks and nose. In some cases, brain involvement, such as possible depression or other psychological problems. Sensitivity to sun. But not necessarily all at the same time, and often with a propensity to wax and wane. In closing, the back panel of the brochure soberly refers to a lab test that, if there are enough symptoms present, is a lock for lupus if it's positive. Not surprisingly, mine was positive.

"OK, well, here's something a little more uplifting," Gerard says brightly. " 'For most people, lupus is a mild disease that affects only a few organs, often the kidneys.' " He stops suddenly and shuts his mouth, so I start rotating my wrist again. He clears his throat and continues in a low voice. " 'For other people it can cause serious or life-threatening problems. More than 16,000 Americans develop lupus each year.' "

"I think that's enough for now," I say as a handsome, dark-haired nurse enters the room with medication. Lots of steroids and other pills, all unceremoniously presented in a tiny, white paper cup. He puts a blood pressure cuff on my arm and smiles at Gerard, who begins chattering nonsensically about a game show that's currently airing on the nearby wall-mounted TV. After he finishes and leaves the room, I turn to Gerard.

"I'm going to rest for a little bit, OK?" I feel as though I need to carefully preserve whatever minute amount of strength I have left. My parents are flying back from Australia as we speak and should be here later (in true Murphy's Law fashion, they took a rare foreign vacation this week and were just starting to relax and enjoy themselves as I crashed to the floor in the stockroom); I'm supposed to be visited by Dr. Buchman later, and I have lots of questions, and, oh yes, there is this pesky diagnosis to deal with.

"Sure thing, Moxie. Is there anything I can get you?"

"No, I'm fine," I say, even though we now both know for certain that I'm lying.

————

When I wake up several hours later, I realize that the blue curtain that bisects the room is drawn, which can only mean that I now have a roommate, and that can't be good. Then I notice there are people outside my door. I strain to hear the noise over the TV, and I think I can make out the sound of Dr. Buchman's voice, but I can't be sure. A minute later, in walks the doctor, smiling broadly.

"Hello, Moxie," he says, picking up my chart and studying it for a moment. "How are you today?" he asks. My neighbor begins coughing and sputtering from behind the blue curtain, making me grimace.

"I'm all right," I say sullenly.

"I know, this place is no fun," he says, glancing at the blue curtain. "I wouldn't come here myself if I didn't have to," he jokes, and this makes me smile slightly. "We need to get you into better shape, but I don't think that will be *too* hard. I want to make sure things are under control with your kidneys and try to quiet things down—we'll have to see how it goes. We'll take it day by day. All right?" he says, turning to go.

"Wait!" I cry, making him jump slightly. "Sorry," I mutter, embarrassed at the inadvertent histrionics. "I have a question." That's actually a lie; I have three, and each has a subset of questions. But he seems in a hurry, so I stick to my most burning one. "How come no one could figure out what was wrong with me if I had so many symptoms?"

He chuckles and this makes me bristle a little bit until I realize that it's not me he's laughing at; rather, it's the type of chuckle that suggests he's asked this question every day. "It can be easy to miss. Most doctors don't know what to look for. Rheumatologists are trained to catch the things that fall through the holes, things that no one else can find," he says, sounding a bit self-satisfied. "Plus, if the symptoms come and go, as yours did until very recently, and you see many different doctors, no one's getting the full picture."

"Yeah, but . . ." I retort, stalling for time as I decide how to work in another question. "But what if I was seeing someone continuously and that person downplayed my problems?" Like a psychiatrist who made me feel like a dope, for example.

"Well, it's hard to say. It mimics a lot of other illnesses, so it's a mistake that is commonly made, unfortunately," he says, raising his voice to make himself heard over the two noisy children who have come to visit my neighbor. One of them has sent a plastic water jug clattering to the floor, and two seconds later, rivulets of water seep under the curtain onto my side of the room. "Hindsight is 20/20," he adds as he looks down at his beeper while sidestepping some rapidly advancing water. "And I have to go, but I'll see you again soon."

————

"I don't have it in petunia pink in a size small," I mutter wearily at the blurry shape at the end of the bed. "Let me check for . . ." I say, drifting in and out of sleep. I've been plagued by these dreams ever since I got to the hospital; frenetic, disjointed REM cycles that always begin with my running around the store in a panic and end with my being unable to stand any longer and falling head-first into a panty table. Only this is the first time I've crossed into the world of the conscious, as I could swear there is someone in front of my sleepy eyes who I recognize from my retail days. I hear an anxious little laugh as I force myself awake and nearly throw up into a nearby basin when I realize that it's Allan.

"Hi," he says nervously, rocking back and forth on his heels. His eyes look tired but also a bit wild, and he puts his hand to his chin and considers me for a moment. "Should I come back?"

"I don't know," I say honestly as I sit up and reach for my cup of water. A loud page announcing a code blue suddenly reverberates through the hallway outside, making me flinch and bang my wrist on the table. "Ouch," I whimper in a pathetic little mewl. I take a slow drink as I mentally play back the events of the last several days and then look him square in the eye.

"You never met me for dinner," I say quietly, then gesture around the room and decide to try for a weak attempt at a joke. "And now look." He immediately looks at the floor and shifts from one foot to the other; clearly I'm not as funny as I think I am. "I'm kidding, Allan," I sigh. "Being stood up doesn't generally land people in the hospital."

"Can I sit?" he asks, loosening his tie a bit. It's stuffy and overheated in here, and he is obviously very uncomfortable. I nod and he sits down stiffly in the beat-up, vinyl-upholstered chair beneath the window. "It's nice to see you," he begins, and a thought suddenly strikes me.

"How did you know I was here?" I ask suspiciously as I try to rearrange my alluring hospital gown.

"I went to see you at the store yesterday," he replies. I cut him off.

"What day was that?" I ask curiously. Even though my window offers a clear view of the outside sky, it's been hard to remain cognizant of whether it's day, night, six in the morning, two in the afternoon, Monday, or Friday. It's all just becoming a blur of steroids and blood tests and sleep and lime Jell-o.

"Yesterday was Sunday," he says patiently. "I went to the store and the blond woman—"

"Mary Alice," I interject.

"Mary Alice," he repeats, a bit fazed by my constant inter-ruptions. "She told me that you were sick and that you were taken here."

"Uh huh," I say quickly and nod, almost starting to enjoy throwing him off his game. Judging by his awkward posture, rapidly spreading sweat stains on the armpits of his crisp, white shirt, and the pained look in his dark eyes, he's got one or more important things to say. I'd bet the exorbitant cost of all my medications that at least one of those things has to do with why I was left sitting alone on a bench last Wednesday night, and I'm not ready to hear it, or anything else. "Maybe you should come back, Allan," I suggest.

"I—Moxie, I really need to tell you this. OK?" he asks, giving me a pleading look that I can't refuse. "Look, I *like* you, all right? But I . . . I can't . . . I didn't . . . I didn't come to meet you the other night, because I've been trying to work things out with someone else," he says, the words tumbling from his mouth.

"A petite, blond girlfriend?" I ask defeatedly. Yes, this summer is shaping up just the way I hoped it would. Being stood up for a blonde, then being told I have a potentially life-threatening, chronic illness. Yay!

"A petite, blond ex-wife, actually," he says slowly and suspiciously.

"I saw you two together downtown a long time ago," I explain, trying to conceal the strained sound that a lump in the throat always makes. An ex-wife—this just keeps getting better.

"Oh," he replies, reaching down and unclipping his cell phone, studying it for a few seconds and punching a button, then putting it back on his belt.

"You need to turn that off in here," I snap at him, the lump dissipating as I start to get annoyed. "Didn't you see any of the signs around the hospital?"

"Sorry," he says meekly as he unclips it once again and hits another button. He tosses it on the window sill behind him, folds his arms hard in front of his chest, and hunches over, as though he's about to make use of the basin himself. "Look, I think you're great, and I always liked talking to you, and I didn't know what was going on with Denise," he explains with his head down, staring intently at an invisible spot on the floor. Denise! The same name as my archenemy from sixth grade, the girl who convinced my friend and me to eat Gaines Burgers, by telling us that they were cheese and meat brownies, and weeping real tears when she explained that her mom would be sad and offended if we didn't at least try them. I hate this new Denise already.

"So why ask me to dinner? Or *anywhere* for that matter, Allan?" I ask hoarsely.

"Well, that's the other thing. I made up my mind to tell you, but then I started sort of worrying about you," he says, leaning back in the chair and looking at me.

"Really?" I ask, touched in spite of myself. "Wait. What? Why?"

"Well, you know what I *do*," he says, looking pointedly at a crushed-up, leftover paper medication cup on the table.

"You make cups?" I say, mystified.

"I work for a biotech company that has a hand in developing drugs," he says flatly. "Do you remember what kind of drug I was working on selling?"

"Allan," I say through clenched teeth, "my patience is running thin here. If you can't tell, I'm pretty under the weather right now. Why don't you just put all your cards on the table, and tell me what the hell is going on?"

"Moxie, I was worried about you because I thought you might have something wrong with you," he says urgently and then exhales deeply, as though this pent-up admission had been causing him unremitting chest pain. "You were always exhausted and yawning and you complained that your hands hurt so badly—I was working on an arthritis drug, remember?" he sputters.

"*All* the cards, Allan," I say angrily, playing with the paper cup. "Come on."

"So I know a little bit about, you know, the diseases that can cause bad arthritis in a young person." He unbuttons the top button on his shirt and slowly closes his eyes; I'm sure I would find it unbelievably erotic if I didn't want to wring his neck right now. "And I would see you and then go home and sit there and think about you and your hands," he says gently, making me think I must be the only woman in the world who ever got a suitor to sit alone and imagine her gnarly, swollen joints. Not her boobs or her ass or her legs or any other luscious part that would get a man into the kind of funny business that involves hand lotion and tissues. "And I thought maybe . . . maybe you had some kind of autoimmune disease," he finishes tentatively as he opens his eyes and studies a new spot on the floor, this one between his loafer-clad feet. "Rheumatoid arthritis or lupus or something."

"It's the second one," I say quietly. "In between the rheumatoid arthritis and the something." I start to cry for what feels like the tenth time since I've gotten here.

"Come on. Come on, Moxie," Allan says soothingly. He reaches over and tries to touch my arm, but I pull it back.

"Why the hell didn't you tell me, you jackass?" I choke angrily, wiping my tears away with my left hand. "You think I have some horrible disease, so you don't tell me, *and* you lead me on when you have a wife?" I ask loudly enough to disturb my roommate, who wakes with a startled snort.

"She's my ex-wife," he says in a muted volume, suggesting he hopes I'll follow suit and lower my voice. "We'd been starting to see one another again, trying to work it out, and . . . and I didn't know what was going to happen with her when I met you, OK?" He doesn't wait for me to answer before continuing. "And how on earth could I tell you that I thought you were sick? First of all, I wasn't sure—I'm not a doctor, so who am I to say?" he asks, his face reddening from the stultifying air and the emotion. "I made my mind up to tell you after we had ice cream and you had to stop and sit down," he says a bit more calmly. "Tell you my concerns and tell you about Denise."

EUGÉNIE SEIFER OLSON

"Ugh, I knew sitting on that bench was a bad move," I mutter under my breath as I shake my head.

"I was going to tell you at dinner—you know, a quiet place where we could talk, and I could explain everything."

"Yeah, and?"

"Yeah, and I couldn't do it, all right?" he says angrily and more than a bit guiltily. He looks from the rail of the hospital bed to my little plastic bracelet to my eyes. "I'm sorry. I'm so sorry. I'm sorry, Moxie," he says more gently, wearily pulling himself to his feet and starting to speak again. I watch him open his mouth to form the "I" in what I'm sure will turn out to be another "I'm sorry," and decide I can't hear it anymore.

"That's enough," I say, exhausted, holding my hand in the air. "Enough. Please, Allan. Just leave me alone."

———

"I need to take your temperature, honey," says one LaVerne Bennett, RN, as she touches my arm. I open my red eyes and dry mouth, and once the thermometer is safely inside, go back to frowning. I watch with crossed eyes as she pulls the thermometer out and studies it for a second before noting it in my chart. After she finishes writing, she takes a glance at the front page and exclaims, "Lupus! A little white girl like you?"

"Who knew?" I say dully, shrugging. After Allan left and I covered my face with a layer of fresh tears, I decided to take a look at one of the books Gerard purchased for me, where I learned that lupus is much more prevalent in African Americans and Latinos than in whites. I also learned it's many times more common in women than it is in men, which got me thinking about just how little money must be funneled into helping these women of color. Which got me thinking about drug research. Needless to say, this got me thinking about Allan once more, and I'm sure I have the swollen eyelids and tear-stained face to prove it.

"Well, I'll be back to check on you later on," she says, putting her hand on one of her ample hips and looking me over. An exquisitely loud, hyena-like laugh blasts out from behind the blue curtain, and LaVerne yanks it partially to the side, the ball bearings clanking against the metal rod. "You in there," she says accusingly, in a tone of voice I recognize from my teaching days, "I told you before about keeping quiet, huh? People are trying to rest, including your own boyfriend." She pulls the curtain back, rolls her eyes and gives me a wry smile, and leaves the room on silent, white, molded plastic clogs. Faced with the prospect of either thinking more about Allan or reading my lupus book, I decide to go to sleep instead, taking advantage of the guilty (yet assuredly temporary) hush in the room.

When I wake up, it's evening, and my mind drifts back to Allan. Brilliant Allan, who, without so much as basic information about arthritis drugs and the diseases whose symptoms they can quiet, figured out that I had some sort of illness. Spineless Allan, who didn't have the balls to tell me about it *or* his ex-wife. And the more I ruminate about my situation, the angrier I get, until I'm nearly hysterical. The TV on the wall is tuned to a rerun of *The Drew Carey Show*, and I valiantly attempt to focus on some problem that Kate and Lewis seem to be having, but I can't do it. Instead, I grab my pen and pad of paper from the table, and after tearing off the sheet with my questions for Dr. Buchman, start writing a letter. A letter that rants and raves and accuses and questions, and then rants and raves some more. I don't even stop to reread or check my spelling; I just keep going, writing and writing until my knuckles are screaming in pain.

I finish and realize that my face hurts as well; I've been clenching my jaw in anger the entire time. I grab my purse from a chair next to my bed, pull out my wallet and begin rifling through it. *Where is that freaking business card, goddamnit?*

I'm screaming inside my head, when my fingers finally land on it. I pull it out along with a book of stamps, and am nearly panting with excitement when I look at the items scattered on the bed. But I'm crestfallen when I realize I don't have an envelope. I sigh deeply; this wasn't meant to be.

"Hi, honey," says LaVerne, making me jump slightly. "I'm going off-duty soon and just wanted to check and make sure everything is all right," she says, nodding her head in the direction of the drawn curtain. She looks over at the mess on my bed and arches her right eyebrow from behind her outsized, purple-framed glasses. "Purse explode?" she asks uncertainly.

"Sort of," I reply meekly, the heat draining from my face as I come back down from my letter-writing mania.

"You need anything?" she asks. "You OK in there?"

"I need an envelope," I say tentatively. "Is that weird?"

"Yes. But for you, I might be able to do that," she replies, turning and leaving once again in her stealthy footwear.

20

Oversized Casual Sleepshirt with Matching Boxer Shorts

THE TAXI HAS JUST HONKED FOR THE THIRD TIME, AND FOR THE third time, my mom drops her two navy blue suitcases from her hands, as though they are possessed by some sort of Samsonite demon. "I can't go," she says nervously as the bags hit the linoleum floor with a dull thud. "I shouldn't. You've only been home a week. What if something happens?"

"Nothing is going to happen," I reassure her. "You've taken very good care of me, so nothing is going to go wrong. I have Dr. Buchman's phone number. Gerard is always around and can help me. I have all my medicines and stuff right here," I say, pointing to the orange bottles on the tabletop; there are so many of them that the collection of containers is roughly the circumference of a small, personal-size pizza.

"That's true," Gerard says, emerging from the bathroom. He turns his eyes on my mother, putting on his most responsible expression. "I'm going to stick around, and get Moxie whatever she needs. Honestly. You can go," he intones soberly, putting his hands on my mom's shoulders. The taxi honks once more, in that impatient way that suggests that this is the last time, and my mother resignedly sighs and picks up her bags again.

"Tsk, give me those," Gerard admonishes, wresting them from her and starting down the stairs.

"You're sure you're going to be all right?"

"Yes, mom. I *promise* I will tell you if I need you to come back," I say earnestly as I hug and kiss her. I stand out on the landing and wave goodbye, then walk back into my apartment and wave out the window as I watch Gerard nearly get hit in the face by the trunk of the cab, which pops open wildly and unexpectedly. A moment after the cab pulls away, Gerard appears in my doorway, sweating profusely.

"What does your mom keep in those things, railroad spikes?" he asks, helping himself to a glass of water and drinking quickly.

"I don't know," I answer a bit wearily from my spot on the couch.

"You look like you want to be alone," he decides, folding his arms in front of his chest. "Have you been alone for even one minute in the last two and a half weeks?" he asks, cocking his head.

"No," I say, suddenly realizing he's completely right. For ten days in the hospital (where I learned that it's not only possible but probable that you can be lonely even when you're never really alone) it was always a doctor, a resident, a nurse, or my roommate, making their presence known. After I was released, my mother stayed on in Boston for a week helping me settle back into my apartment and keeping my spirits up. But the heat and the tight quarters conspired to make both of us feel claustrophobic, and now I am eager to spend some time sitting silently on the sofa. Plus, there is a huge pile of mail that needs tending to, and two very curious answering machine messages that I want to play back and listen to more carefully. The messages were left by a deep-voiced guy who referred to himself as "Dave of the Boston Bruins," and each identified me by first and last name. The calls were placed on a cell phone, all clicks and static beneath the garbled words, and at the end of each one, Dave informed me that he would try phoning again soon.

"If you want me to go, then I will," Gerard says. "But if you want me to stay, I can do that, too."

I smile and look at him clutching the water glass, his mouth open as he waits for my answer, and decide that he more than deserves a few shifts off. "What would I do without you, Gerard?" I ask honestly. "No, you can go. I'll be fine," I say, waving him off. "You're never alone when you've got—" I pause, picking up one of my new books— "*The Women's Guide to Lupus* to enjoy, right?"

He frowns. "You shouldn't read that book when you're alone. Parts of it are depressing. I'll go only if you promise not to read that book today," he says, setting the water down on the table and folding his arms in front of his chest.

"OK, all right," I acquiesce, throwing it onto the floor. Gerard leans in to kiss me on the forehead and lets himself out through the front door. I pick the book up off the floor and begin leafing through it, stopping briefly on the compellingly titled "Chapter Nine: Sex and Lupus," when I swear I can hear him talking in a low voice to someone out in the hall. A few seconds later, I make out his signature clomping down the stairs, and there's a small knock on the door. "Come in," I say, confused, and in walks Steven Tyler.

"Hi," he says quietly, ducking a little bit in the doorway, even though he is in no danger of banging his head on anything. He peers around the room and looks at me nervously. "I was just talking to your friend, um ...."

"Gerard," I interrupt, tucking my feet under my sleepshirt and pressing the book to my chest. I'm not wearing a bra, I'm hot and sweaty, and I'm going to kill Gerard for not telling him to go away.

"Yeah. I told him that the last time I saw you, you looked sorta bad. He said you were in the hospital, and I just wanted to tell you that if you need anything, I can help you out." He pauses and looks at the refrigerator and cupboards, perhaps for inspiration. "You know, bring you food or, I don't know, do errands." He squints at my chest and screws up his face a little bit, as though he's eaten something bitter. "Oh, and he said you're not allowed to read any books that say the word 'lupus' on the cover. So I guess you need to put that down," he says, not very convincingly, adding, "I don't even know what that is." I snort aloud and put the book down, and he continues, looking at his low-tops. "So, maybe I'll come back tomorrow and see if you need anything."

"OK," I say uncertainly as I look at the clock on the TV and realize I need to take one of my medicines. "I guess I'll see you then," I shrug.

"Mind if I sit?" Steven Tyler asks, pausing in front of one of my kitchen chairs. As promised, he has returned today to find out if I need anything. What he didn't mention yesterday is that he would actually be stopping and *visiting*, and that I might be required to converse and be witty and interesting while I'm stuffing my face with pints of Ben and Jerry's ice cream. The steroids have made me positively ravenous: the worst kind of ravenous, the kind in which only foods that are fatty and sweet and creamy are satisfying to the palate. Fortunately, I lost so much weight while sick that, for now, the ice cream doesn't look too bad on me.

"Nope, go ahead," I reply from behind my spoonful of Double Chocolate Brownie.

"How are you feeling?" he asks, playing with an electric bill on the table, spinning it on its corner.

"I'm all right. It's hard to tell," I say truthfully. "I think—" I begin again, unable to finish because the phone rings, the electronic warble filling the quiet apartment. I reach over and pick it up, wiping my mouth just in time to prevent ice cream from getting all over the receiver. "Hello?"

"Is this Moxie Brecker?" a man's voice asks.

"Yes?"

"This is Dave with the Boston Br—" he starts to say, but I cut him off.

"Look, Dave, I'm sorry I wasn't here to take your calls; I was in the hospital," I say, annoyed.

"Oh, I'm awful sorry to hear that, Miss Brecker," he says. "But I was calling to . . ."

"Well, listen. I don't like hockey, and I'm sure that whatever the Boston Bruins have to offer me is great, but I'm going to have to pass," I bark, getting ready to hang up. "So please don't call me anymore."

He laughs at me and I want to spit into the phone. He actually says the word "ha!" aloud. "No, I'm calling from Boston Brewin'. Boston *Brewin'*, Moxie. B-R-E-W-I-N. You named my coffee shop, way back in February. I wanted to call you for months. It's a funny story, really. My kid, he's such a numb-skull, he took my ski vest to college, and it had your phone number in the pocket. So one day I says to him, I says, 'Kevin, what'd you do with my—"

"What?" I ask, furrowing my eyebrows. I glance over at Steven Tyler, who is grinning and looking mystified.

"You entered a contest to name my shop. In the winter," Dave says, a bit exasperated. "You wrote the name 'Boston Brewin'— you know, like Boston Bruin, right?"

"Yeah, I know why I chose that name," I say dryly.

"Well, I guess you haven't been back to this part of town, because that's what I named it," he says excitedly. No, I think to myself; I was busy with this delightful illness, stupid Allan, and underpants, and didn't have time. "Oh, and I have your prize here," he adds. "For winning the contest. It's a real beauty. You want to pick it up?"

"I'm not really in a position to do that right now," I say stiffly. "So it might have to wait. Is that all right?"

"You bet. You tell them when you come down that you named the place; they'll give you a free coffee or something, too. Oh, and you might want to come with a friend. The prize is kind of big," he shouts into the phone; the connection is breaking up. "I'm about to go into the Ted Williams Tunnel, so I'm gonna lose you. Congratulations and I hope you like your prize!"

I hang up the phone and stare straight ahead for a few seconds, unsure of what just happened. "I entered a contest to name a coffee shop and I won," I say simply.

"Oh, yeah?" asks Steven, leaning forward in the chair. "What did you name it?"

"It's near the Fleet Center, so I named it Boston Brewin'," I say, picking up my ice cream spoon and starting to dig around in the container.

A slow smile spreads across his face. "That's really clever, Moxie!" he exclaims.

"Yeah, I guess it is," I say, my voice a mixture of confusion and pride. "Also, I won a prize, but I told him I can't pick it up right now." As soon as the words are out of my mouth, Steven Tyler practically leaps up from the chair.

"I'll get it," he offers. "I said I could do errands for you, and this seems like as good an errand as any."

"He said it might take two people to carry it," I say uncertainly, trying hard not to look at his small frame.

"Forget that! Don't you want to see your prize?" he asks emphatically, opening his eyes wide.

"Well, I guess I do," I admit.

One hour later, I am dozing on the couch with the TV on, when I am awakened by frightening noises in the stairwell. It sounds as though something large and blunt is lumbering up the stairs and hitting the walls with dull thuds, like a drunk moose, or perhaps a person in a protracted battle with a washing machine. The noise gets closer and closer, and before I can get off the couch, the door opens and in staggers Steven Tyler with my prize. He drops it on the living room floor, then puts his hands on his hips and bends at the waist, breathing hard and sweating to beat the band. After a few seconds, he rights himself and we both look at it.

"I won a kayak?" I ask incredulously.

"A two-man kayak," he corrects me in between labored panting. "The paddles are downstairs; I'll get them in a minute. Can I get a glass of water?" he gasps, stepping over the kayak, walking over to the sink, and pulling a glass out of the dish drainer. He leans forward on the sink and runs his hands under the cold water before filling the glass; the back of his heather gray T-shirt is soaked with sweat and clinging to his shoulder blades.

"What am I going to do with a kayak?" I ask, walking around it and studying it from as many angles as possible. "What a weird prize," I decide aloud, stupefied.

"Well, gift horses, right?" he shrugs. "The guy probably has a friend in the sporting goods business or something. I don't know too much about kayaks, but this seems like a nice one," he says hopefully, scratching his head vigorously and making sweaty locks of his red hair stand on end.

"No, I don't mean to sound like an ingrate, I'm sure . . .

well, I'm sure I'll think of someplace to use it," I say uncertainly as he gulps down another glass of water. I take in the size and breadth of the thing once more and a thought strikes me. "Steven, how the hell did you get this here and up the stairs?"

"Eh, I have my ways. It wasn't too bad," he answers nonchalantly, flopping into a chair.

"But, um—I mean, it's so big!" I exclaim, gesturing with my arms, holding my hands as far apart as my sleepshirt will let me.

"Moxie, I'm short; I'm not *weak*," he retorts, sniffing a bit.

"I'm sorry," I say contritely. "Thank you very much for getting it for me. I don't know how I've been getting by without one in the city all these years," I joke, hoping he'll laugh. He does, and we both relax a little bit. "I need to think of a place to try it out," I add.

"Well, you should try it out now," he suggests, then without delay, comes over and climbs into the black plastic and rubber seat closest to the front of the kayak. "It's nice," he says enthusiastically, as though he's just slid into a heated pool at a posh resort. I stand by the kitchen table, trying to stall for time. Does he want me to get into the kayak with him? I figure I have nothing to lose, so I awkwardly lower myself into the second seat.

"Yeah, I guess it is all right," I agree uncertainly, looking around the apartment. From this YumYum's-eye-view, I can see all sorts of things on the floor that I've never noticed before, including the nature CD that Gerard stole from Charlie's apartment, which we last played the night I got punched in the face. It and a book of matches have migrated to a dusty spot under a short bookcase near the TV, and I can see the silver edge of the CD glinting in the sun. "I have an idea," I say, groaning as I wiggle my way out of the kayak. I reach under the bookcase, pull out the CD, and put it into my portable CD player that sits on top of the refrigerator next to the phone book. The apartment fills with the sounds of rushing water, little chirps, and tree frog noises.

"*Niiiiiiice*," Steven Tyler says approvingly. "This is much more realistic. And the water is so green here," he deadpans, peering at the linoleum floor.

"Well, this has been fun," I laugh, "but I think I should try and rest some now. You know?" I ask, hoping he'll get the message. He nods once, pulls himself up and out of the kayak, and promises to come back later on with the paddles.

"You know what? You look better," says Dr. Buchman, nodding. I'm here for my first in-office visit and am more than a bit nervous.

"I do?" I ask excitedly.

"Not *all* better," he replies, dashing my hopes. "I just mean that your eyes have a little more life in them." He silently feels the joints in my hands. "Tell me how you feel since I discharged you. Do you feel any more energetic? Any more like yourself?"

I think for a moment, and remember how getting into and out of the kayak the other day was pretty painless and didn't completely exhaust me. "Yeah, you know, I think I do have more energy," I decide. "I was getting in and out of a kayak, and it wasn't too tiring."

He arches one eyebrow behind his Dr. Bunsen Honeydew glasses. "So you've had enough energy to go kayaking."

"Oh, no," I say, embarrassed, then make it worse by adding, "This was in my apartment." Dr. Buchman screws up his face and decides to turn to my chart. "The nurse weighed you, and it looks like you've put some weight on. Just be careful; those steroids can make people eat everything that isn't nailed down."

"I'm finding that out," I say, taking a glance at myself in the small mirror above the coat hooks on the wall opposite the exam table. In addition to packing on some pounds, I've developed the classic face of a person on prednisone, with puffy, round cheeks that wouldn't seem out of place on a sweet, young cherub.

"I'm happy with your progress," he decides, handing me a slip of paper with four blue stickers affixed to it. "Please go to the lab on the fourth floor on the way out for blood and urine tests, and make an appointment to see me in one week. Oh, and you should go back to work whenever you're ready, and see how you feel as it goes."

I groan. "I'm dreading going back to work, because I'm going to be fired," I admit. When I called Mary Alice from the hospital to tell her that I'd be out for a little while, her voice was flat and distant, as though she was distracted by the disappointment of having to wait an indeterminate amount of time to have my ass canned.

"They're not allowed to do that," he says firmly, his hand on the door handle. "Ask my nurse to write you a note, and if you have any problems explaining your absence, you tell them to call my office."

"Oh, no; they're not going to fire me because I missed work. They're going to fire me because I did something idiotic," I say, shaking my head at the memory of feverishly stuffing Catherine's shopping bag with contraband thongs.

"I find that hard to believe," he says, walking out the door and leaving me to change back into my clothes.

———

The rain has arrived. It has been coming down non-stop for two days now, and the street is flooded, the ancient Boston sewer drains overwhelmed and spitting swirling water back out into the gutter with remarkable force. Although I am relieved that it is no longer so warm that the floor seemed to be sweating, I am disappointed that I am stuck in my apartment. I've been feeling better each day and was anxious to take a little walk around with my chubby thighs and fortified kidneys. For better or worse, I'm not alone here this afternoon; Steven Tyler has decided to pay yet another visit, and I am working out my frustration by razzing him.

"I don't think you paint at all," I say challengingly as he pulls one of my Oreos from the cellophane sleeve and carefully unscrews the top. "Why should I believe that you paint?"

He rolls his eyes, chews the top cookie slowly, swallows, and holds up his right palm to display a smudge of bright teal paint under the second knuckle of his middle finger. "I was painting last night. What do you call that?" he asks, putting the rest of the Oreo in his mouth with the other hand.

"Oh, that could be anything," I say dismissively, putting an elastic in my hair and noting with pleasure that only two strands fall on my T-shirt in the process. "Why aren't you painting today? Why aren't you painting right now?"

"Because I'm here now," he says simply, eyeing the remaining seven Oreos in the sleeve and deciding against it.

I turn away from him to face the window behind the sofa and jump when a huge clap of thunder shakes the foundation of our building. I peer out the window and through the driving rain, and I can just make out the slight shape of one of the Awesome Nails girls running from the 7-Eleven toward the salon. She is hunched under an absurd lavender parasol, and her flip-flop-clad feet submerge in the rushing water each time she takes a step. "The poor thing," I say.

"Who's that?" he asks.

"One of the girls from the nail salon on the corner," I answer, turning back to face him. "I'm fascinated with that place because they always watch CNBC in there. Business news, all day long, every day. Why?" I ask.

Steven Tyler shrugs. "I think you told me this once before. Why don't you ask them?"

I shake my head ruefully. "I might have in the past, when I was more nervy. But not now."

"Well, I'll ask them, then," he decides, standing up and opening the door.

"What? No; no, Steven, please. It's not important, and it's really raining hard out there," I implore him. But the last portion of my plea falls on deaf ears, since he's already out the door and heading down the stairs. I go back to the window and see him dart, umbrella- and rain gear-free, across the street, and I watch him until he's out of sight. Then I flop onto the couch with the uninspiringly titled and highly clinical *The Lupus Book,* and read about genes gone wrong and chromosomes that don't cooperate. Ten minutes later, he is back at my door, dripping wet and runny-nosed. He steps into the apartment, unsure of how to begin.

"They have stocks," he announces in a bewildered voice.

"What?" I practically scream, leaping off the couch.

"They have lots of stocks, all kinds of stocks. Some domestic, and some overseas, from what I gather. It's a little hard to understand them," he says apologetically.

I can't believe it. "Are you sure?" I ask suspiciously.

"Yes! Yes. I told them about you and about how you always wonder why they are watching that TV station, and that's what they said." He pauses. "They said they know who you are. They always see you looking in the window, and they call you the 'small, sad one.'"

"They know who I am?" I ask, a sickening feeling in my chest. "I didn't think I was that obvious. How embarrassing." I pause for a second and think about the second part of the sentence. "They think I look sad?"

"I suppose you must. But here's the good news: I told them you were sick—well, that's not the good news, you know what I mean—and they said you can come in for a free manicure when you're feeling better. They gave me this," he says, pulling a damp, crumpled sheet of yellow paper from his pocket, unfolding it, and reading aloud. "I guess it's like a list of services? 'Manicure, pedicure, silk wrap . . . ' " he says, reading more and more slowly as he wades deeper into unfamiliar territory. " 'Tips . . . airbrushing . . . acrylics . . . nail jewelry'? Well, it's all here, and they want to give you some of it on the house," he finishes, putting the sheet on the table. "They're nice in there. I feel kind of bad for the old woman, though. When she was living in Da Nang, she was a teacher."

"What?" I ask, not surprised that Trang had gone from a life of pedagogy to one of pedicures when she came to the United States, but surprised that he learned this during a quick visit to Awesome Nails. "How did you find that out?"

"Oh, well, when she said she was the owner, I asked how long she had been doing this, and she told me a little bit about herself," he says offhandedly, as though he engages in sparkling conversation with elderly Vietnamese women every day of his life.

"Huh," I say, shaking my head. "You know, I used to be a teacher, too," I say in a small voice.

"Oh, yeah? Tell me about it," he says, undeterred by his soaking-wet shorts as he sits in his familiar spot at the kitchen table.

21

Tight-Fitting Ribbed Racer-Back Tank in Lemon Yellow

"MY SCHEDULE SEVERELY SUCKS LATELY," COMPLAINS GERARD as he sits next to me on the sofa and slurps a bottle of Dr Pepper through a long, striped straw. "I wish I could spend more time with you here, but they've got me working every single day. I think they were mad that I took so much time off unexpectedly when you were in the hospital," he explains, looking out the darkened window at the pouring rain.

"Well, you'll have to apologize to your manager and tell him I'll try to get sick at a more convenient time next time," I say sarcastically as I cross my legs underneath me and notice that my toenails need trimming.

"Moxie, that's not what I meant," he says, tilting his head and studying me. "I'm just sorry that I can't be here with you more. What kind of caretaker is Steven Tyler turning out to be?" he asks curiously.

"The crazy kind," I decide. "He really is nuts, Gerard. He's very impulsive—he jumped up and ran right off when he heard that this thing needed picking up," I say, gesturing to the eleven-foot polypropylene monster on the floor. "Then he did the same thing when I was talking about the nail salon on the corner. He races out of here before I can even stop him."

"Maybe he has gas," Gerard offers thoughtfully. "Maybe he's just looking for a reason to get out in a hurry. My mom had a boyfriend like that once—always the first one to offer to get something in another room, but it was just so he could fart far away from everyone. Or maybe he's just helpful." He drains the soda bottle and puts it on the floor, where it promptly falls over on its side, dribbling Dr Pepper on the linoleum.

"Well, it's not so bad," I reason. "I've sort of gotten used to having him around; he's little and not very intrusive, like a . . ." I think for a minute and look around the apartment for inspiration, and my eye lands on an old *Scientific American* that features a cover photo of a white lab mouse. "He's like when you have a baby mouse in your apartment," I say, nodding as I decide that this is the perfect analogy. "Yeah. It's like, you don't really mind seeing it come and go, and you sort of know it's around, but it doesn't bother you and it can help you from feeling alone."

"Nice," he laughs, rolling his eyes. "Don't tell him he reminds you of a rodent if you need any more errands done." He picks up *The Women's Guide to Lupus* off the sofa and flips to a page near the front of the book. "I was looking at this section when you were in the shower earlier," he says. " 'Diagnosis,' that's what this chapter is called," he continues. " 'Although receiving a diagnosis of lupus is bound to cause feelings of anxiety and/or depression in most women, some women say that they are so relieved to finally know what is wrong with them that they feel less anxious or depressed than before. That is, not knowing what is wrong can be at least as stressful, if not more so, than knowing what *is* wrong.' "

I consider this for a minute, staring into space as I run the concept through my mind. "I think . . . I think I agree!" I say, a bit incredulously. "No, I definitely agree. I mean, don't get me wrong, I feel pretty wigged out sometimes, but knowing what it is makes it feel a lot less scary."

He reads on, licking his finger and flipping the page. "'As the realities of the disease start to sink in, however, it is important that women with lupus get the emotional and social support they need.' Of course, this only serves to make *me* feel worse about not being here with you every day," he laments, closing the book and turning to face me, his eyes traveling from my face to my waist and back again. "And speaking of needing support, Moxie, I have to tell you, your chest has gotten *huge*," he says emphatically, pointing to my boobs, which are positively bursting out of my tank top.

"Everything on me is starting to get huge," I moan. "I need to have more self-control, I guess. The steroids make me so hungry, and not for healthy things," I admit, glancing at the empty box of Entenmann's donuts, which I combed for every last crumb.

"It's all right," he says soothingly as he tries to surreptitiously check his watch. "I'm with Bunsen Honeydew—you look better to me. More like the old Moxie, you know? Does it really matter if you pack on a few pounds right now, in the scheme of things?"

"No, I guess not," I say happily.

"I have to go pick up YumYum's medicine at the pharmacy before it closes; she's got another one of those ear infections that smells like an old loafer," he says, a sour look on his face. "But watch out with those," he says with concern, pointing at my chest. "If I were a straight little mouse, I don't know if I'd be able to resist."

————

I'm pacing the floor in my apartment this morning, my stomach in knots as I realize that I only have a few more days of freedom before I must return to my fate at the store. When I called Mary Alice to inform her I'd be back in on Thursday, she greeted me with that same impassive voice and hung up briskly, citing a long line at the register as her excuse. I sigh heavily and pick up one of the bottles of SPF 45 sunscreen that I bought at the drugstore earlier in the week. Because lupus is made worse by the sun, I'm supposed to cover up as much as possible, like some sort of modern-day vampire girl, and then slather any exposed body parts in sunscreen, all year round. Since it's finally stopped raining, I've decided to take a walk in the sun-dappled Boston Common, and as I flip open the plastic cap on the bottle and squish the first viscous blob of sunscreen into my palm, there's a little knock at the door.

"Come in," I say as I try to rub some sunscreen into my forearm. It's bright, opaque white, and no matter how much I rub, the skin remains a ghoulish hue.

The door opens a little bit and in pops Steven Tyler's head. "I'm going to the 7-Eleven, and I wanted to know if you needed anything," he says.

"No, thanks; I'm fine," I reply, frowning at the stubborn white swirls that dot my arm. "I've been out and about a bit the last few days, so I've picked up some things."

"Oh. OK, then," he shrugs. "Let me know if you change your mind," he adds before closing the door and starting down the stairs. About twenty seconds later, he returns with another little knock on the door.

"You don't have to knock, I figured it was you," I say, opening the door. His face is much redder than usual, presumably from running all the way down and then back again.

"Well, I realized I forgot to tell you something," he says, putting one of his hands in the front pocket of his cutoff mustard-yellow shorts and resting the other one on the doorknob. "Chuck told me to tell you that he hopes you feel better."

I think for a minute and come up blank. "Who is Chuck?"

"Oh, he's one of my oldest friends. He was at the party I had that time, remember? You thought that he thought you were an exotic dancer," he finishes, smiling at the memory of it.

"He *did* think I was an exotic dancer," I retort, my hand getting sweaty from the slimy sunscreen melting in my palm. "He said, 'It's the lady of the moment,' or 'The chick of the hour,' or something like that."

"I don't remember what he said, but he didn't say it because he thought you were hired entertainment. He said it . . . he said it because I'd told him who you were before that," he says shyly. "So, anyway, I was talking to him last night, and he hopes you feel better," he adds so quickly that he stumbles over his words. And with that, he is out the door, and I lunge for the phone with my clean hand. I speed-dial the Men's Fragrance counter at Neiman Marcus, bark to the girl who answers the phone that I'm calling for Gerard and that it's urgent. Two seconds later, before the on-hold music even has a chance to kick in, he is on the line.

"Moxie?" he asks breathlessly over the sound of a ringing register. "What's the problem? Are you all right?"

"I think Steven Tyler likes me," I say in a measured voice.

"What?" he asks, exhaling and saying to someone, "Believe me, this isn't your father's Aramis—it's an all-new scent. I'll put some samples in your bag."

"I said, I think Steven Tyler likes me," I repeat.

"So what?" he says, bored. "Everyone who knows you likes you, Moxie."

"No, I mean, he *likes* me," I say, realizing at that exact moment how much I sound like my former students. All I need now is to be passing Steven a note that says, "Do you like me?

Check 'yes' or 'no.' " I take a deep breath. "You know what I mean, Gerard."

"Hey, I warned you about those breasts of yours just the other day," he admonishes loudly. "No, not yours, ma'am," he says contritely, covering the mouthpiece. "I'm talking to a friend; I'm deeply sorry."

"It has nothing to do with my chest," I say, walking into the bathroom, turning sideways, and sizing myself up in the mirror. "Well, maybe a little, now. But he was telling me just now that he told a close friend of his about me a *long* time ago. It's crazy," I decide.

"Why?" he asks. "Are you tired of your little mouse?"

"Well, no," I say uncertainly. "I mean, he has turned out to be awfully nice and helpful. A little weird, but very kind, I guess. But I'm not sure I really think of him that way, you know?"

"Well, I think it's sweet, even if we do still have our doubts about his livelihood," Gerard coos as I hear the familiar sound of a paper shopping bag snapping open. "Will that be cash or Neiman's charge? Sorry, Moxie. Anyway, it's nice. It's like Florence Henderson syndrome," he says dreamily. I am about to reply when I suddenly realize that I don't know what he means, and it takes me so long to decipher it that the entire credit card transaction is complete before I speak again.

"First of all, you mean Florence Nightingale syndrome. Florence Henderson is from *The Brady Bunch*, doofus. And I think that in Florence Nightingale syndrome, the patient falls for the nurse, not the other way around," I laugh.

"Well, whatever," he says airily. "Either way, it's nice to be liked, right?" he asks, and I'm about to answer when I hear a knock at the door. I gasp aloud and quickly stand up from where I've been perched on the edge of the bathtub.

"Gerard, I think he's back! What do I do?"

"How should I know? Now, this shave cream you're buying has eucalyptus, did you know that?" he asks someone brightly, and I know I've lost him. I hang up the phone, walk to the door, and sure enough, it's Steven Tyler. He's holding a long, cardboard tube in one hand, and a small stack of mail in the other.

"Hi," I say, attempting to be casual. "What's that?" I ask, pointing to the tube.

"Something for Steven Tyler," he replies, turning it sideways and looking at the address label. "It's from Texas. They usually send good things. Want to see what it is?" I nod and he pries a white, plastic cover off one end and shakes out an enormous piece of thick, cream-colored paper. It's wound into a tight scroll, so he takes hold of one end and I begin unrolling until the entire thing is stretched out between us. Looking up at us is a very large and detailed drawing of Steven Tyler singing into a microphone with what the artist probably thought was fevered passion but actually looks more like crippling constipation.

"Hey, this one's not so bad," he says approvingly, peering down at the image. "Noses are hard to draw, and this nose is pretty good." I gently let go of my end and he carefully rolls it back up and places it in the tube. "Oh, also, I wanted to tell you that I signed for a piece of this mail. I hope it's all right. The mailman was downstairs, and I told him I'd get it to you," he explains, placing the tube down and picking up the stack of mail, flipping through it until he reaches the piece in question, an oversized cardboard envelope with a registered mail label on the front. "So this is you?" he asks incredulously, looking at it and grinning. "Rebecca Brecker? Your real name is *Rebecca Brecker*?"

"Yes," I say testily. "That is my real name, and I would appreciate it if you wouldn't make fun of it. Most people can't really understand what it's like," I say, pouting. Steven Tyler bursts out laughing, throwing his head back so far that I can see several of his fillings.

"You think *I* don't understand what it's like? I don't understand what it's like to have a name that gets unwanted attention?" he cries, chortling hysterically. I bust out laughing right along with him; of course Steven Tyler feels my pain like so few others would.

But my euphoria is short lived, because I realize that very, very few pieces of mail are ever addressed to Rebecca, which could also explain why Steven has never seen my proper name before. Generally, mail that is addressed to Rebecca comes from the places that go by abbreviations: HMO, IRS, RMV. And this instantly gets me worried, because whatever this is, it must be serious. I gesture for him to hand it to me, and I slowly tear back the cardboard pull-tab of the outer envelope to reveal a crisp, white envelope within. In the upper left-hand corner, it reads "FINKEL, FINKEL, AND SHAPIRO, ATTORNEYS-AT-LAW" in large, blocky type.

"What the hell?" I ask, baffled. I open the envelope and scan the first line of the letter, which begins, "In reference to your letter from Brigham and Women's Hospital dated . . ." and I need to sit down immediately. "Oh my God. Holy shit. Holy shit. Holy shit," I say, sounding like a broken record, holding the letter up and reading further. I drop the letter and put my hands to my face. "Holy shit." Steven Tyler stands frozen next to the kitchen table, unsure what to do or say, apprehensive as he looks from me to the letter on the tabletop.

"Moxie?" he asks quietly. "What is it?"

"I . . . I wrote a letter when I was in the hospital," I say, remembering my frenzied search for Dr. Luttman's business card in my wallet, the emotionally charged missive that followed, and LaVerne's generous offer to procure an envelope. There's only one problem: I don't remember exactly what I wrote—enraged, exhausted, and emotional, the letter was one long, unchecked freak-out, unencumbered by the normal editing and rewriting that I would subject any other business letter to. "I wrote a letter to my old psychiatrist, basically calling him a total idiot and a quack for not taking me seriously when I said I was sick. I think I said that he should be ashamed and not allowed to practice, and a lot of other really bad things." I look up at him, my face pinched. "And these Finkel and Shapiro people want me to come and talk to them as soon as possible." *Why didn't I make a photocopy of the letter?* I think to myself as I rub my eyes. Surrounded by billions of dollars of medical equipment in that hospital, and I didn't think to avail myself of a lowly Xerox machine. "What the hell is wrong with me?" I moan.

"Take it easy," Steven Tyler says, sitting down opposite me and looking into my eyes. "Whatever it is, we'll work it out."

———

It's time for my first, and probably last, day back at the store, and I'm nearly ready, walking quickly from my bedroom to my bathroom and back again, when I realize with a small smile that I don't feel as though I need to sit down and rest. Every day I feel a tiny bit stronger than the one before it, and I'm always pleasantly surprised when I've completed an activity and have energy left over. I give myself a final once-over in the bathroom mirror, find my purse, and am walking toward the door when I see a large piece of paper on the green linoleum. In Steven Tyler's blocky handwriting, it says:

USE CAUTION WHEN OPENING DOOR

Intrigued, I dutifully follow the directions and slowly open the door, which reveals a raggedy piece of brown craft paper, sitting about a foot away from the entrance to my apartment. Judging by the way the paper is hovering about an inch off the floor, it's clear that it's resting atop something, and as I bend down to lift it off, I quickly stop as I notice another note from him, this one printed in charcoal pencil on the brown paper:

Moxie,

You have been very patient about this, and here is a reward. Good luck today, and I know whatever you end up doing, it'll be the right decision.

Steven

I crouch on the floor, then change my mind when I realize I'd rather be in a more comfortable position for this, and sit down with my legs tucked behind me. I gingerly lift off the brown paper, and resting there on the beat-up floor are three small paintings, each identical in size and no larger than an oversized index card. They are abstract and arresting, with stippled swirls of neutral and bright colors forming flowing, organic shapes that twist and turn and wind their way across the triptych. The paintings have a depth that belies their small size, a sober quality that peeks out from behind the tiny strokes of cheery pink and tangerine paint. I gently pick up the paintings and bring them back into my apartment, fold the brown craft paper into a small square, and smile as I drop it into my purse.

Forty-five minutes later, I am decidedly out of the world of the abstract and well into the realm of the real, as I sit at a scratched, metal table in the stockroom of the store, my hands folded neatly in my lap as we wait for Cindy. Mary Alice is seated across from me, and other than a semi-friendly "hello" upon my arrival, and the instruction to stand and wait for her by the robes, we haven't exchanged a word.

Cindy enters the stockroom, all bluster and business until she trips over a hot pink demi-cup bra on the floor and nearly breaks her neck. She regains her composure and sits in the empty chair at the table, pushing her blond hair off her forehead before beginning.

"Moxie, how are you feeling?" she asks disinterestedly while rifling through a pile of papers in a blue notebook. I know these papers, which ask questions about recent employers, former retail experience, Social Security Numbers. We use them for hiring. And firing.

"Better, thank you," I say crisply. I sneak a peek at Mary Alice, who has jutted out her lower lip and is looking up at the ceiling.

"Well, I may as well get right to it," Cindy says, setting the notebook on the table. "We had a report from one of our employees that you were seen giving merchandise to a shoplifter. This is a very serious offense, Moxie, and not one that our store can take lightly," she says haughtily, as though she owns the chain and all the stock options and isn't just some lowly regional manager. "I was willing to turn a blind eye when this same employee reported that you used your employee discount last winter on someone other than yourself, someone who seemed, by all accounts, a virtual stranger." She continues on, talking about the ethics and morals of business, and how some people think the rules don't apply to them, but I've tuned her out, because I'm wracking my brain trying to recollect whom I let use my employee discount.

And then I do. The chestnut vendor, the one who gave me a break when I was spying on Allan downtown. I attempt to remember who was on the schedule that day and realize that I don't have to work that hard. It had to be Heather. Heather, who I've never liked; Heather, who evidently understood the value of ratting out co-workers. Heather, who was also there that day with Mary Alice, watching me and standing aghast as I helped Catherine make off with so-called valuable merchandise.

"Heather," I slowly say aloud, and Mary Alice stops looking at the ceiling and begins studying her hands.

"Yes, well all I can tell you is that it was an employee of this store who reported your transgressions against the company," Cindy intones in such a lawyerly voice that I think she may have been preparing for this dramatic conversation her whole retail career and was just waiting for someone like me to fuck up on such a grand scale that she could justify trotting out these hackneyed expressions. "And according to the employee," she says, looking darkly at Mary Alice, "*Mary Alice* was with her at the time you were seen assisting the shoplifter, but *Mary Alice* claims not to have seen anything." She leans forward and fixes Mary Alice with a cold stare, which makes her squirm uncomfortably in her chair. I don't say a word.

"I *told* you," Mary Alice says through clenched teeth. "Cindy, I told you I was in the stockroom, and I didn't see what Moxie was doing. I got there long after Heather did," she lies, crossing her arms in front of her chest defiantly. "I can't talk about what I didn't see, all right?" she snaps.

Cindy sniffs. "Well, I can't *prove* whether or not you're telling the truth, Mary Alice. But as for you, Moxie, these sort of things just cannot stand. And so I'm afraid to tell you that you're—"

I hold up my hand, smile, and then look down and whisper in the quietest voice I can, "I'm sorry, Gerard," because I am seconds away from completing his trifecta. I look up and around, studying for the last time the boxes of thongs, the shimmery piles of chemises, the Operations Binder, the oversized bags containing the peignoir sets. I take a deep breath, turn to face Cindy, and say proudly, "You can't fire me, because I quit."

A few seconds pass and Cindy blinks rapidly as though she's about to have some kind of fit, and she stiffly orders Mary Alice to walk me to the front of the store, where I am to wait for my Termination Papers. Once we are standing under the scrollwork of the doorway, I turn to Mary Alice and lean in close to her.

"Hey, thanks for sticking up for me in there," I whisper in her ear.

"Thanks for getting rid of that awful guy at the clinic," she replies, barely audibly.

"No problem," I say, grinning and leaning away from her. A customer comes toward us with a camisole and tap pant set, and Mary Alice turns her back on her.

"Moxie, that guy came in again the other day, the tall one with the dark brown hair. He looked around for you and left. I just thought I'd tell you," she says, leaning on the thong table.

"Yeah, things didn't exactly work out with that guy. He had good intentions in some areas, but not in others," I snort, shaking my head. "But I think I may have another one lined up," I add, thinking of the note in my purse and the pretty paintings on my kitchen table.

"Well, good luck with everything," she says as we both watch Cindy emerge from the stockroom. "Come in and see me sometime, if you want," she adds as the camisole-and-tappant customer collars Cindy for help. Mary Alice's expression and body language are at odds: her feet and legs are saying walk away, but her face is saying stay and say one more thing. The face wins. "You know, Moxie, I'm not as stupid as you think I am," she says quietly and a bit sadly.

I let out a little gasp and say honestly, "Mary Alice, I never thought you were stupid." I lower my voice, because Cindy is near. "I thought . . . I thought you were just totally and completely devoted to this place. I guess it came off as something different."

"Well, now you can see that's not really true," she says, narrowing her eyes and smiling as she slowly walks back into the store.

22

Knit Polo Shirt in Royal Blue with Fish Detail

"SO, EVERYONE KNOWS THAT HUMANS HAVE TWO SETS OF TEETH, right?" I ask pulling my top lip back and tapping on one of my front teeth. "You have the set that came in when you were a little baby, and you're getting all your adult teeth now. But does anyone know how many sets of teeth a shark has?" I ask, looking at the curious crowd gathered around the shark tank.

"Three?" guesses a girl with thick glasses and a long, messy braid, as two boys shove one other behind her.

"That's right, they have three sets. Very good! And as for you two back there, be careful. If you fall in, those sharks will eat you just like a Fenway Frank." This really isn't true, of course; we keep the sharks well fed around here. But it elicits a little *ooooh* from the crowd, and I figure it can't hurt to discourage them from horsing around. "All right. Now we're going to go down to the starfish pond. Has anyone ever held a starfish?" Nos all around, except for one kid, a lit-

EUGÉNIE SEIFER OLSON

tle boy in too-small shorts who is picking his nose with gusto and not paying attention. "Who wants to?" I ask. A loud "meeeeeeeee" rings out over the shark pond. "OK, then, everyone find their buddy. We are going to walk down this ramp, and then we're going to walk straight ahead. Here we go," I say, as everyone scurries to find their buddies.

We all make it to the starfish pond without incident, the girl with the thick glasses heedlessly abandoning her buddy so she can walk up front with me. "All right," I shout over the din; they're all hanging into the starfish pond, a few of the intrepid ones reaching in and prodding some of the starfish with delight. "Cut that out! You wouldn't like it if someone poked you when you were sitting and hanging out in your house, would you?" I joke, and a few dutifully say, "Noooooo."

"Anyone who wants to hold a starfish, you pick it up like this," I say, gingerly placing my palm under the slimy thing and holding my hand out. The creature begins moving slightly, eliciting an "eewwww" from a trio of blondes near the front of the group. "Be gentle," I warn. "No pulling on it, and absolutely no throwing. When you're ready to put it back in the water, let it down slowly. Then, when everyone's done, we'll talk a little bit about starfish and how their bodies are different from most other kinds of fish," I finish. The words are barely out of my mouth before the poor starfish are under siege, as dozens of small hands reach into the pond.

It's only my second day, but if I do say so myself, I feel like I'm doing a pretty good job as the in-house educator for the Fins & Claws program here at the New England Aquarium. This is the job that wasn't, then was, then wasn't, then was again. In the spring, when Sue initially suggested I take the part-time, low-paying job and I brushed her off, the desperately needed funding for the position was unexpectedly cut, and the job requisition was closed. A few months later it was

—296—

reopened, and several candidates were interviewed, but according to Sue, none were suitable. But once summer camp and its requisite day trips swung into high gear, and it was clear that Fins & Claws needed an educator sooner rather than later, the aquarium honed in on an applicant who was not their ideal candidate but was as close as they hoped to get. Until I called Sue at the aquarium a week ago, curious about the position and whether it was still open after all this time. She nearly screamed and apparently hung up the phone and begged her friend to interview me immediately. It was a good fit: I was ripe for a part-time gig, they were looking for someone who was excited about fish and teaching and children. They ran a background check on me, and two days later I was offered the job.

"Aaaaaaaaaah!" a dark-haired girl in a Hello Kitty T-shirt yelps as she pulls her hand out of the pond. She's unwittingly chosen a starfish that is missing one of its arms, and her face is a mask of fear and guilt. "I hurt it!"

"No, it's OK," I say in a soothing tone, one that would probably be too cloying and motherly for pre-teens but hopefully is just right for a group of third- and fourth-graders, the groups that make up the bulk of the summer camp outings to the aquarium. I don't know for sure; I'm still trying to find my voice with this age group, but so far, everyone seems pretty happy. "Sometimes they are missing one or more of their arms," I assure her. "You didn't do anything." She heaves a sigh of relief, gently places it back in the pond, and searches for a more complete starfish to pick up.

"Hey," an adult voice says behind me. "Nice shirt." I turn to see Sue, who is holding the logo side of her New England Aquarium shirt away from her body and pointing it toward mine.

"Yeah, I like it," I say happily, peering at the nose-picker, who is now in up to his second knuckle and seemingly unconcerned with picking up a starfish. Which is probably just as well for the starfish.

"How're you feeling?" she asks, her eyebrows knitted together as she studies me.

"I feel OK," I answer truthfully. "Not perfect, but not nearly as bad as before, thank God."

"I was reading about it on the Internet. You gotta go for tests all the time and stuff like that?" she asks, screwing up her face.

"Yup, I do. But things are a little better every day," I say, taking notice of some preliminary splashing that seems to be going on between the same two boys who were shoving by the shark tank. I turn to Sue. "Thank you again for helping me get this amazing job, I still can't believe I work here," I gush.

She waves my thanks away and puts her hands on her hips. "I only wish the pay weren't so shi . . . so bad," she says, correcting herself when she realizes she's about to swear in front of children.

I shrug. "What can you do? It's part-time. That's perfect for me right now. I just want you to let me know if there's ever anything I can do for you," I say, walking over to the two boys, who are now involved in an all-out water war.

Sue follows me and puts her hand on her chin as she thinks. "I don't think there's anything you can do, really. Hey, maybe when you get done, we can go to an early dinner?" she asks. I nod and am about to rebuke the boys when she says in a loud voice, "Moxie, I forgot to tell you—I'm bringing in my daughter later this week and she's dying to meet you. You're her hero ever since you punched that guy in the face." As if by magic, the splashing stops immediately and order is restored to the starfish pond.

I stop back at my apartment first to change out of my New England Aquarium shirt. I only get one and it's a tiny bit sweaty, but I need to wear it again the day after tomorrow, and I don't feel like laundering it before then. Then I walk downstairs and give a quick little rap on Steven Tyler's apartment door. I'm pretty excited to see him, as I now understand just how important he has been in helping me choose my life's new course.

When I went, alone and sweaty and knock-kneed, to the offices of Finkel, Finkel, and Shapiro after receiving their imposing letter, I finally got to see the letter I wrote at the hospital. In it, I said I had lupus and called Dr. Luttman incompetent and imperceptive and a ninny. I wrote that a casual acquaintance of mine with no medical training could tell that there was something wrong with me; and that as someone with medical training, Dr. Luttman should be ashamed. I wrote that he wrecked a chunk of my kidneys and could have wrecked my life. I used the words "unfit to practice medicine," and "malpractice," and the most dreaded of all dreaded words, "sue." I slung that one three times. I wrote that I had half a mind to sue him, and that I probably *would* sue him upon my release. Which was pretty accurate, since I was operating on about half my mind then.

Luttman evidently took this letter very, very seriously, forwarding it to Finkel, Finkel, and Shapiro, who sat before me with tented fingers and explained that Luttman would like to put this whole thing behind us. Putting the whole thing behind us, according to Finkel, Finkel, and Shapiro, involved my signing a statement absolving Luttman of any responsibility, either now or in the future, and my receiving a sum of money. When they told me the amount of this sum, I was agape. It wasn't so large that I could retire to a tropical island, but it wasn't so small that I would need to continue shilling satin and rayon if I didn't want to. It was enough to, say, buy a nice, entry-level BMW, but an entry-level BMW isn't something I wanted. What I wanted was a way out, a way to pursue another kind of life, at least temporarily, and I said yes.

After getting home from Finkel, Finkel, and Shapiro, I had an ethical crisis of tremendous proportions. I hadn't really planned to actually sue Luttman; Dr. Buchman had said lupus was a wily illness, sneaky and hard to catch. Who was I to take his money? So Steven Tyler and I talked about it, almost nonstop, for two days. He told me about how weird he felt when the dog attacked him and his parents subsequently won him a gigantic cash settlement, without even asking him how he felt about the whole thing. It was a *dog*, he said, grinning and eating one of my powdered Dunkin' Donuts Munchkins. Dogs don't really have free will, do they? But in the end, Steven Tyler was glad he had the money. Upon turning twenty-one, he was relieved to know that he could try something a little bit unusual, take a different path. He asked me what I would do if I had that money, regardless of where it came from, and I replied without a second's hesitation that I would work at the New England Aquarium. When I tentatively called Sue and found out about the position, I almost cried with delight. And then when I opened my apartment door to Steven's paintings that morning, I knew just what to do.

Steven Tyler opens the door and smiles broadly. He's got a small, flat-bristled paintbrush in one hand, and he beckons me into the room. The apartment is much smaller than mine: a studio setup, with two easels and a heaping pile of tidy, crisply crimped paint tubes and other accoutrements in one corner, a hastily made bed with a lumpy black comforter pushed up against a far wall, and a small hallway that I assume leads to a tiny kitchen and bathroom. There are also cardboard boxes and bubble wrap everywhere—detritus from all the fan mail he receives, I assume. I notice with some satisfaction that he's got the Steven Tyler bust on display, as well as the "Sweet Emotion" lamp, and many of the other odd gifts I've seen him open or helped him carry up the stairs. It speaks to a sweet sense of sentimentality, the way I used to save presents from my students, cheap soap sets and chunky coffee mugs at Christmastime. We walk over to a painting in a nascent stage; right now it's just pencil lines on the tiny canvas and a few specks of crimson red paint that match the one on the brush. I stand next to him, and he moves very close to me, smelling of turpentine and something spicy and a bit sweet.

"How was it?"

"What?" I ask, nervous to be this close to him. I can count the freckles on the right side of his nose. Eight.

"The aquarium," he says, smiling.

"Oh!" I say, blushing. "It was great. Today we did the starfish pond." I finish and look at the floor, my toes pointing inward. Just then a buzzer goes off.

"Pizza," he says, walking away from me and toward the tiny hallway. "Be right back."

"I can come back if . . ." I start to say, but then something catches my eye under a tall pile of newspapers. It looks like the ugly mint green and lavender color scheme of the cover design of *The Women's Guide to Lupus*. What the hell? I move a tiny corner of the newspaper, and sure enough, that's what it is. I drop the edge of the paper in a hurry as I hear him walking back. He resumes his spot next to me in front of the canvas, even closer this time. My heart is beating so fast I'm sure he can hear it in the quiet apartment, and as I turn a bit to face him, he does the same. We both laugh a little and speak each other's names at the same time.

"You go first," he says.

"Oh, well, I just . . . I wanted to thank you again for helping me these last few weeks. It's really been . . . well, it's been awesome," I say earnestly.

"Yeah, I was going to say something like that," he says a little nervously before pulling me toward him and kissing me square on the mouth. I kiss back as though my life depends on it, pressing my body hard into his. He is an exquisite kisser, just the right amount of pressure—not so little that it feels as though he's fallen asleep while on my mouth, and not so much that my teeth will smart afterward. He puts the paintbrush down and reaches around to put his hand in my hair, and when I realize I'm afraid that it might fall out in his hand, I pull away.

"Wait, wait," I say, breathing hard. "I'm sorry. I just . . . I feel like, I'm sort of damaged goods or something," I say sadly. So this is what the book meant when it said it can be stressful when the realities of the disease start to sink in, I think as I look hard at the canvas and try not to cry. It said in the beginning, you look at everything through the lens of having lupus. And it's not a pretty lens.

"What?" he asks. "No, that's not true, not true at all. I bought this same book you have," he says, rustling around in the pile of newspapers until he finds it. It takes him a while, and I want to say, "It's right here!" but of course I don't. He removes it from the pile and shows me the cover, then puts it back down. "I don't mean to make light of it; it sounds like it can be kinda bad sometimes. But it's not enough to deter me, if that's what you mean."

"Oh," I say softly. "OK," I decide, won over by his infinite sweetness, and we go back to kissing, this time more passionately. I defy all laws of physics as I push up against his body and simultaneously take one, two, three, four steps backward until we reach the edge of his bed. We flop down, I roll on top of him, and all hell breaks loose—I'd come to think of my body as something to be despised and feared when I was sick, then something to be medicated and coddled when I was diagnosed, and it's been so long since I've thought of it in a sensual or feminine way. Now that everything on my body feels warm and open, I'm consumed by an uncontrollable lust. Steven Tyler is taking my frenzied lead, and in no time at all, all the buttons on my blouse are undone, and I'm pulling at the zipper on his black denim shorts when he's the one to put on the brakes.

"Hold on," he pants, looking at me. "My turn to stop." He takes a deep breath, and I let go of his crotch and think, *oh no. Maybe the dog bit other things besides his neck and his ear.* Although it certainly didn't feel that way when I was pushed up against him. I decide to prepare for the worst anyway, and he says, "The book—the book I read, over there"—he gestures to the pile of newspapers—"it said that sometimes, you know, if you have pain in your joints or whatever, it might hurt, so, you know, I'll have to count on you to tell me if you aren't liking it."

I nod OK before he's even got the last word out of his mouth, he unhooks my bra with one deft move, and I get back to yanking his shorts off. He needn't worry about me not liking it, because I do. I like it two more times before midnight, in fact.

I'm in one of the fitting rooms at the store today, bras and camisoles and babydolls swirling all around me on the floor. After a quiet day working on the Resource Room, where I decided on a crab and clam theme for the far wall and spent the day in the marine biology staff's small but well-stocked library reading about crustaceans, I didn't feel like going home right away, and, as if by force of habit, my footsteps led me here. Mary Alice greeted me warmly and asked me if I was shopping, to which I replied in a somewhat surprised voice, "Well, I guess I could."

And as I try on the fourth bra in my pile of items, a striped number from the summer line, something strikes me. This is *fun.* It's fun to try on this stuff, see what flatters, and see what looks ridiculous. Even with my new fuller figure, it's fun. Even knowing that this stuff is made of cheap, crappy materials, it's fun. It's fun to hear the two women in the next fitting rooms giggling to one another about the merry widows they've decided to try on. It's fun to think about which item you might wear when you're with your boyfriend next and imagine his eyes growing wider and wider as you expose more and more of your lingerie-enhanced self. And now I understand why this chain makes $4 billion a year selling what essentially amounts to tiny bits of fabric and elastic. I just never saw it from the other side of the fitting room curtain.

I emerge with four pieces: the striped bra, a pretty, pale blue, stretchy lace bra with a front-hook closure and matching bikini briefs, and a utilitarian, black, Lycra bra with a load-bearing underwire. I head up to the counter where I get in line and chuckle when I think about the irony of never once having used my employee discount on anything foxy, and not having it anymore, now that I could really use it. I reach the front of the line and Mary Alice says with mock solicitousness, "Did you find everything you need today?"

"Oh, yes, thank you. This is a well-run store," I say back in the same genial tone. Then we both laugh.

"You look good, Moxie," she says, zapping the SKU numbers into the register and quickly hitting the keypad with fluttering fingers. "That will be $42, all together," she says evenly, pulling out a shopping bag.

I do some quick math in my head; this isn't right, not by a long shot. I know the prices of these items like the back of my hand, and this is way off. It's thirty-five percent off, to be exact. The same as our employee discount. I reach for my wallet and say carefully, "Well, that is quite a value. Thank you *very* much." Mary Alice unfurls a piece of tissue paper and holds it up in front of her face, but I can still see her pointy chin sticking out of the bottom and can tell she is grinning.

23

Pinkberry Nail Polish
with Clear Topcoat

"So I'm afraid that the tour ends here today," I say with my back to the Penguin Pond, beaming with pride when a few disappointed "awwwws" come from the crowd. "But maybe I'll see you soon, now that the school year is about to begin. In the meantime, all the penguins and I thank you for coming to the New England Aquarium." As if on cue, Chaka Khan noisily honks from the giant rock in the center of the pond, flapping his wings and making all the kids twitter. I knew that penguin and I would make a good team.

I'm exhausted today, and sore all over. No, no; that's not right. I'm exhausted, yes, but only sore from my upper hips to my lower thighs. That's because Steven Tyler and I went on a date last night—an actual date, prompted by the shared fear that we might end up as one of those weirdo couples that never does anything outside of their apartment, or in our case, apartment building. We went to the Museum of Fine Arts, where each and every one of the Wednesday-night guards recognized Steven Tyler and greeted him with hand-shakes and smiles. He took me to the large rotunda on the first floor, which houses modern art paintings that made him swoon. After walking around the entire rotunda twice, I decided that Stuart Davis' *Hot Still-Scape for Six Colors—7th Avenue Style* was my favorite, with its broad fields of eye-popping color and chunky squiggles. This sat very well with Steven Tyler, who emphatically stated that he thinks Stuart Davis is underrated. Then we tried to find a print of the image in the museum gift shop, which was bursting with Georgia O'Keefe flower postcards, but no Stuart Davis. Steven Tyler just shook his head and said he'd just have to paint me a reproduction of it himself.

We took the T back to our apartment building, making out like all the drunken teenagers you see heading back to the sub-urbs after having come into the big city for a baseball game, and made it to the front foyer, where my pale blue, front-closure bra induced the kind of hysteria I thought it might when I tried it on in the fitting room. I stood against the wall with the mailboxes, my foot resting on a package addressed to Steven Tyler in big, swirly handwriting, burying my face in his neck and trying not to kick the box in my excitement. Even though the box wasn't very large, he opted to let it stay there on the floor as we made our way up the stairs, thus leaving his hand free to slip inside my matching lacy briefs when we reached the first-floor landing. It was very lucky that his apart-ment is only on the second floor, because I am quite certain that if it were any further away, I would have ended up naked and astride him right there on the scuffed, metal-tipped stairs.

I leave the aquarium and get on the T, where I close my eyes, and before I know it, I'm at the Copley stop. I walk to the mall and into the Neiman Marcus, where Gerard is busily stocking the new Issey Miyake fragrance, his back to me.

"Hi," I say, tapping him on the shoulder. He jumps, sending three glossy boxes to the marble floor with a clatter.

"Moxie!" he exclaims, then takes a step back and studies me as two heavily made-up, overly tanned women rudely reach past him for the Chanel tester. "You look awfully tired. Are you all right?" Steven Tyler said the same thing to me this morning, and begged me to go in late or leave work early. The lupus books all talk about this—everyone who cares for you will try to protect you, even question your judgment, to try and keep you well. But the books also stress that the people only do it out of love for you. The taller of the two shoppers elbows past Gerard with a little entitled sniff, and I decide to give these bitches a show.

"I was up late having sex with Steven Tyler," I say loudly, enunciating every syllable as though I'm in a spelling bee.

"Ohhhhh," says Gerard, playing along as the two women snap their heads up and look at me. "That must have been hot."

"You bet," I say, winking at him. "But you're right, I am pretty worn out," I add, putting my hand to my mouth to keep from bursting out laughing. The women fix me with one more confounded stare before wandering away. "Actually, I was hoping maybe you could get me a little drink of water, because I should take some medicine," I say sweetly. The lupus books warn about this, too—you should never use your illness as a crutch or as something to manipulate others. But the writers of the lupus books have probably never dealt with a giant piece of plastic dog shit and the gleeful revenge inherent in practical jokes. I had forgotten all about the old boy until I waved hello to Joe the other day, and now I'm dying for it to see some action. Gerard ambles to the back room, and I quickly reach over the giant, dark wood counter and place it in the tissue paper slot, which is quite a bit wider and deeper than the one at my old store.

"Here you go," Gerard says, handing me a tiny, blue paper cup filled to the brim with ice-cold water. As I take my first bracing sip, I realize that I don't actually have to take any medicine right now and wonder how I'm going to get out of this. Fortunately, Gerard's manager sticks his head out of the back room and tells Gerard to finish the Issey Miyake display. I decide to cool my heels for a minute in the men's clothing section, which surrounds the fragrance area on all sides, featuring racks and racks of stylish garments in lush colors and touchable fabrics. I'm admiring a Dolce & Gabanna T-shirt that would look splendid on Steven Tyler—until I realize that it's $160—and as I drop the price tag with a little snort, I look up and see a tall, very handsome, sandy-haired man wandering into the fragrance area. He is wearing a black T-shirt and well-fitting jeans, and he's got an equally sandy-haired boy with him. I'm thinking gosh, he looks *awfully* familiar, and with one deep gasp, I know who it is.

He walks slowly past Gerard, who is oblivious, busily pulling boxes of fragrance and deodorant and shave balm from a larger cardboard box, and almost brushes against him by accident but swerves just in time. I tiptoe over to a foppish hat display on the perimeter of the fragrance area and almost scream as James Spader slowly opens his full lips and nearly taps Gerard on the back, but then changes his mind, choosing to help himself instead. He pulls down a tester bottle of Jil Sander for Men, a stout glass container with a chunky, oval cap, and gives it a sniff. He walks over to the counter with a boxed version, where he whistles through his teeth for a few seconds, looking around the store and gesturing to the sandy-haired boy to stop fooling around with the giant, revolving Gucci "G" display. Realizing that there is a customer at the counter, Gerard's head snaps up and he walks over, whereupon he nearly faints.

"Oh my God!" he gasps, his mouth making a perfect O as he takes his spot behind the counter. "*James Spader!*" James

Spader nods a few times, smiling with his mouth closed in that fake way where his lips seem happy but his eyes aren't. Still, he's a good sport, and he reaches across the counter to shake Gerard's hand, which makes Gerard nearly hyperventilate.

"Moxie!" he screams. "I'm on *The New Candid Camera*, right? I knew it!" he shrieks, and James Spader takes one slow step back from the counter. "Come on, let's bring in Peter Funt! Aha-ha-ha-ha-ha-ha!" he laughs maniacally, banging the counter. "This is great!"

"Gerard," I say from over by the hat rack, making James Spader whip his neck around to see who might be throwing her voice from a stack of fedoras. "This isn't *The New Candid Camera*. I didn't do this, I promise." I give him a pleading look, but there's no stopping him now.

"Wow! I can't *believe* they got you to do this!" he exclaims to James Spader, who looks him square in the eye and would probably grab him by both shoulders if necessary.

"Son," he begins deliberately, in that smooth, resonant voice. He licks his lips and looks at the ceiling for a few seconds. "I'm not sure what's going on here, but I just want to buy this cologne. OK?"

"OK, all right, but don't think I'm going to look surprised when Peter Funt comes out here. Where is he?" he asks excitedly, leaning out over the counter and craning his neck around. James Spader is starting to get impatient; the child, who must be his son, with that hair and those pretty hazel eyes, is tugging on his hand.

"Look, I'm sorry if this isn't what you thought it was," James Spader says exasperated, with his eyebrows furrowed, as though he can't quite believe how he got into this situation. "But if you could just ring this up, I'll sign an autograph for you or whatever you want."

"Sure thing!" Gerard says jauntily, mooning for TV cameras that aren't there. And with that, he rings up the cologne, reaches for a piece of tissue paper with a dramatic flourish, and sends what looks like a giant piece of dog shit flying into the air. Gerard screams and jumps back as he tries to catch it in mid-air, and, off-balance, his weak leg comes down first and he falls to the floor.

"Daddy, is that doody?" asks James Spader's son.

"I'm not sure," he replies evenly. He peers over the counter, raises his eyebrows, and says, "Uh, don't get up; really, it's OK. Maybe you could just get your manager. All right?" Gerard slowly stands, red-faced and even more disheveled than usual, and slumps to the back room with whatever is left of his pride.

———

Ten minutes later, we are sitting on the benches outside of Neiman Marcus—the very same benches where I was to begin my date with Allan—because Gerard has been forced to take an unscheduled break, probably the first ever in the history of retail. His manager, after apologizing profusely to James Spader and offering the bottle of cologne for free (which James Spader didn't take him up on, I was pleased to see), ordered Gerard out of the store for five minutes, where he was told to pull himself together. But I don't see how that's possible, since we are both berserk with laughter. Now not only am I sore in my "sexy parts" (as one of my students shyly used to call them during the sex education unit at school), my sides are splitting as well.

"James Spader thinks I'm a freak!" Gerard gasps, laughing so hard he can barely force his lips to form the "f" in "freak."

"He thinks you're a freak!" I repeat, doubled over and crying from laughing so hard.

"James Spader thinks I keep dog shit at work with me!" he howls.

"He thinks you keep dog shit at work with you!" I cry.

"He hates me!"

"He *loathes* you," I say.

Gerard stops to take a deep breath and wipe his face, then our eyes meet and we dissolve into hysterics all over again. "OK, I've got to get it together here," he says, closing his mouth but letting the laughter force its way out his nose with loud sniffs. He straightens his tie, and I reach over and tidy the lapels of his jacket.

"You all right?" I ask, my face smarting from laughing so much.

"Moxie?" he says, turning to me with a suddenly serious expression that catches me off guard. "You know what the weirdest thing is?"

I shake my head no.

"I didn't even think he looked that handsome in real life. I'm actually . . . after meeting him in person, I don't think he's the guy for me, after all," he says, his voice a mixture a mystification and relief.

"Really?" I ask. "I actually thought he looked better in real life than he does on screen. But I'm not the expert," I concede.

"Yes. Yes," he says resolutely, ignoring me. "I was wrong. Everything I thought was wrong." He shakes his head as though waking after a long sleep and smiles. "I should probably go back to work now," he decides, the corners of his lips turning up a little as he watches me start to giggle. "Don't laugh, because I'll start again and never stop," he warns. "Are you going to be all right?"

"Oh, yeah," I assure him.

I watch him walk back into the store and decide that he's absolutely right. Everything we thought was wrong. I wasn't the girl who was unable and unwilling to handle the pressures of teaching; I had undiagnosed lupus. Mary Alice isn't a blind, little sheep, obeying the store's rules and regulations every waking minute of her workday. Allan wasn't madly in love with me; he is a dashing guy who is divorced and confused but worried about my well-being. Steven Tyler isn't a slacker who sells drugs; he's a talented, aspiring painter who wraps himself around me in the night and assures me that my puffy face looks even cuter than it did before. A café near the Fleet Center isn't a terrible idea—it's a great idea, and I've got the kayak to prove that, with a winning name, it can be a total success. And James Spader—well, he's charming and stunning, but I guess he's not the guy for Gerard, after all.

But there is one thing I was right about. Just one. And as I congratulate myself on my one accomplishment, I realize that despite the fact that I'm tired, there is one more place I need to go today.

The TV is blaring so loudly with the news of a corporate merger between two giant biotech firms that for a few seconds, no one even takes notice of me. I stand awkwardly in the doorway, wondering whether or not I should stay, when Trang takes notice of me and says something in rapid Vietnamese to one of the younger girls, who is rolling a bottle of buff-colored nail polish between her hands and watching the TV with interest. There is a little hush and then some excited talk between several of the women, and Trang walks slowly over to me, the hem of her blousy housecoat fluttering from the large fan in the corner. I smile at her and she barks, "Pick your polish!" Then she sits down at a small table and begins busying herself, preparing a bowl of soapy water and metal tools.

I look over at the plastic, wall-mounted display with the misspelled script "Nails Polish Center" emblazoned across the top and become a bit overwhelmed by the sheer number of bottles. There are so many reds, pinks, burgundies, peaches, creams, purples, lavenders, and browns that I start to panic, and when I glance at another patron for inspiration, I catch Trang's eye, and she gestures for me to sit down. I impulsively choose a deep pink, pluck it from the Nails Polish Center, and timidly sit at the Formica table beneath a garish poster of an impossibly long-nailed, French manicured hand stroking a Persian cat. My New England Aquarium ID badge, which I wear on a twill, fish-patterned necklace that came with the ID, clicks as it hits the front of the table. Trang grabs my hands and studies them as the TV blares overhead; evidently the merger will have a ripple effect on all biotech stocks, and this makes two of the girls, both dressed in baby tees, Spandex shorts, and pink flip-flops, crow with unfettered delight.

Trang scratches her head, tugging on her bun. She picks up one of my hands again and looks at me. "The nails, they show the health of the person," she says in heavily accented English. "You been sick, things not good for you." She peers closely at my fingernails again. "But things, your life, they get better now."

I look from her to my hands, and I think about how I'll have to take pills every day for the rest of my life. I'll have to have blood tests and urine tests forever, and I fervently hope that I can learn how to manage this disease. I'll have to see how well I do working at the aquarium and not push myself too hard, even when I want to, when school's back in session and the tours are coming thick and fast. Then my eyes travel to the photo on my New England Aquarium ID badge, where I'm smiling broadly and there's unmistakable energy in my eyes. I think of Steven Tyler, who is eagerly awaiting me right now in his small apartment, who was waiting for me much longer than I ever knew. And I think of Gerard and Sue and Mary Alice and all the people who went out of their way to help me get my moxie back.

"Yes," I say as she dunks my left hand in the bowl and begins scrubbing my cuticles with a soft brush. "That sounds right."

0000840023
BRECKER, REBECCA
DOB 09/09/74
BUCHMAN M.D., EDWARD L.
12209788

07/08/02 F

Want More?

Turn the page to enter
Avon's Little Black Book —

the dish, the scoop and the
cherry on top from
EUGÉNIE SEIFER OLSON

Gerard Oliver's Ten Rules
for Stylish Living

1. Never stand when you can sit.

2. Never sit when you can lie down.

3. Although some things can be used in place of cologne in a pinch, you should never spray anything on your body that comes from Home Depot.

4. Or Staples.

5. Even if you think you can use your Handy Stitch to repair clothing you are currently wearing, it's best not to try.

6. Do not date guys who think it's funny to call you "Geraldo."

7. When in doubt, wear it again.

8. Never eat at a hospital cafeteria. If you're hungry while visiting a patient, wait until she falls asleep and eat her food.

9. While it is true that a cute dog might get you some action, a pathetic cat will always get you sympathy.

10. A bad episode of *The New Candid Camera* is better than a good episode of almost anything else on TV today.

A Neighbor by Any Other Name . . .

So what's the deal with a character named Steven Tyler? The truth is that the idea came directly from something in real life. Back in the early nineties, I was working at my first job out of college, at a museum in Boston. One of my co-workers was a twenty-something guy with the same name as one of the members of the band Boston. He lived with one of the girls in my department, and I ended up becoming friendly with both of them, which gave me a window into his everyday life as a dude with the same name as a beloved Boston-area rock icon. It was both a blessing and a curse for him, much as it is for Steven Tyler in *The Pajama Game*: it netted him lots of fun fan mail and gifts but could also be a pain sometimes. Because it was so long ago, I had a hard time remembering the specific offerings Tom got from ardent fans, so most of the items Steven Tyler received were from my own imagination. The lamp fashioned from an old-time gas station pump was real, though.

Incidentally, Steven Tyler's looks, style, and the basis for his character were inspired by a guy I've met only one time, a New Yorker who was the best man in my friend's wedding. He had fiery red hair, a million freckles, wore all-black clothing on a warm May day, and looked rough and wild. But he was the height of kindness and consideration. I remarked to my friend that his best man reminded me of a sweet pirate— that he'd rape and pillage but then probably tidy up afterward and make sandwiches for everyone. I jotted this thought down, and the character of Steven Tyler grew entirely out of this one sentence.

Contents of Mary Alice's Purse

1–package birth control pills in yellow plastic case

1–set of keys on oversized, ancient key ring featuring vinyl figurine of Pat Patriot, the New England Patriots' retired mascot

1–frayed, red coaster from downtown pub

2–wadded-up tissues (unused)

3–rectangular Lego bricks left by four-year-old cousin at church

6–squashed pieces of gum

1–folded photocopy of new mall security rules

1–navy blue leather wallet with embroidered floral pattern

1–T pass

1–cell phone with Pink's "Get the Party Started" ring tone

2–thongs (on clearance and with discount, 99¢ each)

Moxie Brecker's Block

When I was thinking about where Moxie should live, I knew I wanted her to rent a crummy apartment downtown, a sad and sagging setting that reflected her low-energy life. I knew someone who lived in a similar linoleum-floored hovel on Tremont Street in Boston many years ago, and before starting the book, I walked there and scouted out the area. The joke shop is real (albeit with a slightly different name), as is the 7-Eleven, but I wanted more elements of a real neighborhood, where Moxie could interact with different kinds of people in her community. So I drew from the neighborhood in which I live now, where there's a $10 nail salon with blaring TVs and a women's health clinic that draws protesters two mornings a week and most of the day on Saturdays. Like Moxie, I often have to walk by there en route to other places, but unlike Moxie, I avoid confronting anyone! As an aside, I created a nail salon character very early on, an annoying patron who conducted loud-mouthed cell phone conversations and drove Moxie crazy while she was getting her weekly manicures. But as Moxie's character began to emerge, I realized that she was not the kind of girl who would be going for manicures, so I had to scrap that character and storyline.

Feng Shui Fun with Gerard

- Empty corners in a bedroom can look so stark and un-welcoming. Warm them up with gently sloping piles of dirty clothing.

- One word about litter boxes in direct sunlight: don't.

- Hanging pots and pans on kitchen walls is said to clutter the mind and deflect wealth. Put them in a low cabinet for safekeeping and order out for the rest of the year.

- Scented candles are an easy way to bring warmth, beauty, and the power of aromatherapy into your home. For an optimal experience, be sure to remember to re-move plastic shrink-wrapping first.

- Dark-colored walls make inhabitants prone to self-reflection and introspection. Avoid at all costs!

Paging Author Olson...

Did you know that I began my writing career working in hospitals as a medical writer? I bet not. My first writing gig was at a consumer health Web site run by a pediatric hospital, where I wrote articles about diseases and conditions for parents, kids, and teens. After that, I moved on to writing and editing for a communications group at a Boston cancer hospital. In this type of writing, the challenge comes from taking something complicated and making it clear and simple but still compelling. My hope is that this helps me in my fiction writing, that the distilling of information and detail allows me to paint an interesting but always clear picture in the reader's mind.

When I was working on my first novel, *Babe in Toyland*, I got on this major nonfiction kick and was devouring books about health and medicine in particular. My favorite was Ben Watt's miraculous and beautifully written *Patient: The True Story of a Rare Illness*. When I finished reading Watt's book about his experience with a very rare illness called Churg-Strauss syndrome, I thought to myself, *That's so great he can use the fact that people already know who he is* (he's a musician, producer, DJ, club owner, and half of the fabulous English duo Everything But the Girl, for the uninitiated) *as a way to give a voice to people with this disease, or people who have other diseases that are rare or misunderstood.*

And then I thought, *Duh, you could do the same thing.* I have lupus—and although I'm not as well known as Ben Watt and my disease isn't nearly as rare, I mulled it over and decided, *maybe that's a good idea.* When writing *The Pajama*

Game, I tried to capture that same feeling he conveyed so well in *Patient*, where something is very wrong and it's really frightening, and the whole situation is made so much worse by the fact that no one can determine what the problem is, or that people are unbelieving or indifferent. The circumstances surrounding Moxie's actual diagnosis were much more dramatic than my own, but the rest of the details are all a painfully accurate retelling of my own experience.

Most people don't know what lupus is. If they do, then their knowledge tends to be pretty hazy, even if they know a lot about other diseases. (Incidentally, this is why I made Moxie a bit of a know-it-all science girl, to illustrate how easy it is to not know a blessed thing about lupus. I was a health writer and didn't even consider it as a possibility when I was so mysteriously sick for so long.) So if I've given people with lupus a voice and helped others understand it a little better, then I'm happy.

Play Moxie for Me

For me, music is so entwined with the creative process that I can't even think about characters or plots without it. The funny thing is that I can't actually listen to music when I write—it's too distracting. But I listen to it nonstop when thinking about what I plan to write and where the story will go next, as well as when I'm editing, after the first draft's been written. While working on *The Pajama Game,* some songs in heavy rotation on my iTunes playlist included:

"Race For the Prize" by The Flaming Lips
"Sound and Vision" by David Bowie
"Maps" by the Yeah Yeah Yeahs
"Rainshine" by Bran Van 3000
"Does this Bus Stop at 82nd Street?" by Bruce Springsteen
"Imitation of Life" by REM
"Jóga" by Björk
"Lost in the Supermarket" by The Clash
"Walk on Water" by Aerosmith
"Cannonball" by The Breeders
"A Kiss at the End of the Rainbow" by Mitch & Mickey
"Down Together" by The Refreshments
"5.15" by The Who
"Green-Eyed Stars" by Varnaline
"My Fault" by Faces
"Bring on the Dancing Horses" by Echo and the Bunnymen
"Bennie and the Jets" by Elton John
"Call that Gone?" by Paul Westerberg
"El Sol" by Zwan

"New England" by Jonathan Richman and The Modern
    Lovers
"Survival Car" by Fountains of Wayne
"Comfort Eagle" by Cake
"The Land of Chocolate" by Homer Simpson
"So it Goes" by Nick Lowe
"The Ballad of El Goodo" by Big Star

My Mercedes Was Robbed (or, How *America's Next Top Model* Brought Me to My Knees)

At first she was just Lupus Girl, because there were so damn many of them that we couldn't remember their names. Plus, you hate to invest too much energy in any one girl so early on, since she could get the ax at any time from smiley Eric Nicholson, sensible Nigel Barker, or fiberglass-faced Janice Dickinson. But once the group was whittled down to six or so, we began calling her Mercedes. Oh, we didn't love her just because she has lupus, of course. We loved her for her wide, guileless grin, her pluck and determination in the face of repeatedly being told that she was too commercial, and her unfaltering ability to get along with every willowy creature she was forced to live with and compete against. The lupus only sealed the deal, and anyone who has lupus or knows someone who has it could look at Mercedes and know that she was doing something remarkable.

When she made it to episode ten, it was a nervous group that gathered at my apartment. We weren't too concerned about Shandi—blond and impossibly lanky, she initially had us worried when she was propelled to the front of the pack courtesy of her versatile looks and preternatural ability to pose. But when she helped herself to an Italian delicacy in the form of a raven-haired hottie, we rightfully suspected that it would be curtains for her. Then there was Yoanna. Yoanna, with her piercing gaze and enviable sense of style. Yoanna, with that sharp, stunning jawbone that no girl taking steroids could ever hope to have in a million years. But she's *awkward,* we assured one another during commercial breaks. Her graceful presence is a trick, we decided; she tries to carry herself like Jackie Kennedy, but she shambles and takes falls more like Teddy Kennedy. She's not bubbly or engaging or warm. She's no competition for our Mercedes, in other words.

You can imagine our elation when Mercedes received her photo and Shandi was sent packing, only to be followed by the shattering disappointment when Tyra announced the winner and embraced Yoanna with her toned, tanned arms. I actually cried, not as forcefully as Mercedes did, but we did have to turn off the TV. I've seen photos of Yoanna in magazines since, beautifully dressed and neatly coiffed, smiling with an unnatural, too-wide grin, the kind that Mercedes could easily best in her sleep. I sometimes think about what could have been and have decided that whatever Mercedes does, it will be great. Rock on, Lupus Girl.

To: joan.tyler@cksinsurance.com
Subject: birthday

Hi Mom, how're things today in Hartford? You asked me what
I want for my birthday and as always it's paint . . . I know you
hate to get me this because you think it's a boring present. But
it's what I want. Thanks and say hello to dad and Danielle for
me.

Winsor and Newton Oils, 120 ml tubes: cadmium red, cadmium orange, burnt sienna, cerulean blue, phthalo blue, alizarin
crimson, raw umber, yellow ochre, viridian green, cadmium
yellow.

Love, Steven
(Also, Moxie says hiya!)

Boston Brewin'
For when you've got game and
need the latte to go with it

By Julie Obst, Staff Reviewer
Filed May 9

I've reviewed dozens of Boston cafés and coffee shops in the last few years, and was—how should I say it?—filled with dread when I was told to head to Causeway Street and check out yet another one in an already glutted market. But not just another one—Boston Brewin' caters to visitors to the Fleet Center, making it at once too frightening to contemplate and much too intriguing to ignore. Yet a few hours later, there I was, bellying up to the counter with jubilant Celtics fans, ordering my own frothy mocha drink and very much enjoying myself. With understated décor, jovial sales help, and the ever-present chatter of sports fans, Boston Brewin' thankfully lacks the pretension of so many coffee bars. But don't be fooled—it more than holds its own in the food and beverage categories, offering bold and delicious coffees, excellent blended juices, and an assortment of fresh muffins and pastries. Some of the names were a bit much for this reviewer (the Cam Neely croissant and Larry Bird latte, in particular), but if you don't mind this kind of lyrical nomenclature, a visit to Boston Brewin' should be in your future, whether you're en route to cheer on your team or not. Oh, and that clever moniker? Dave Chapman, the shop's owner, tells me that it was the winning entry in a naming contest. Boston Brewin', (888) 4-BREWIN, 12 Causeway Street, Boston. Open daily, 7:00 A.M. to 2:00 A.M. AE, Di, MC, Vi. No liquor, wheelchair accessible.

JOE'S JOKE SHOP
226 TREMONT STREET, STE. 1
BOSTON, MA 02115
ATTN: JOE WEINBERG

BILL OF LADING

Please see attached invoice and remit payment within 30 days to FunTime Novelty Company.

Item	Quantity
Rubber Pencil	25
Farting Key Chain	25
Garlic Bubble Gum	50
Dribble Glass	10
Latex Lips	50
Blue Mouth Candy	25
Magic Ink	50
Squirt Flower	10
Instant Worms—FREE SAMPLE	1

WE HAVE HUNDREDS OF ITEMS ON SALE—BLOOD CAPSULES, FOAMING SUGAR, PENIS NIGHTLIGHTS, AND MORE, ALL AT LOW, LOW PRICES. ASK ABOUT OUR NEW KITTY KRAP.

EUGÉNIE SEIFER OLSON

EUGÉNIE SEIFER OLSON was raised i a northern New Jersey town known for man years for its outsized White Castle. She went t Boston University and has lived in Bostor Philadelphia, and Milan, Italy. Likes: Clark Teaberry Gum, *Pootie Tang*, baseball, animal with big noses/beaks/snouts. Dislikes: sur the dirty-sounding phrase "wet Swiffer," olive putting cover sheets on her TPS report When not writing, Eugénie can be found eithe in Sephora, on her couch waiting for a rerun c *Futurama*, or at Charlie's Kitchen in Harvar Square. She lives in Brookline, Massachusett with her rockin' husband, David, and their spec tacularly strange cats, Loki and Kiddun. Dro Eugénie a line at *eugenie@readeugenie.con*